P9-DUY-450

THE DEVERAUX LEGACY LIVES ON!

"Am I getting to you?" Daisy asked.

Jack's eyes narrowed. Perspiration beaded his temple. "This won't help your situation."

Daisy laughed softly. When he didn't move—didn't react in any way—she recklessly reached behind her and released the zipper on her sundress.

Jack's expression grew even grimmer, more forbidding. Although she could tell he wanted her, he was not in the least bit amused by her antics. "Don't do this," Jack whispered. His fingers gently encircled her wrist, forcing her hand down. "It wouldn't help either of us," he said sternly.

More tired than she could ever say of being told what to do, think, even feel, Daisy replied, "We'll just see about that." And before Jack Granger could respond, she stood on tiptoe, wrapped her free hand around the back of his neck, tilted his head down and pressed her lips to his....

Dear Reader,

Have you ever felt that you just didn't belong somewhere? Or that everyone knew what was really going on behind the scenes but you? Heiress Daisy Templeton has felt that way her entire life. Her intuition tells her there are secrets that have something to do with her adoption into the blue-blooded Templeton clan, and she is determined to discover the truth about her heritage. When she does, it rocks her world. She is a true heir to the Deveraux legacy. Her real mother and real father have been in her life all along!

Jack Granger, on the other hand, knows more than he cares to about his sordid past and wishes fervently he were a member of a family like the Deveraux. That isn't possible, until he's given the assignment by his boss Tom Deveraux to keep the beautiful and spirited Daisy safe. A job that soon becomes a lot more personal for Jack.

Daisy doesn't want Jack around or cleaning up Tom's mess. But soon their lives are entangled more deeply and irrevocably than they ever could have imagined.

I hope you enjoy this book and the rest of THE DEVERAUX LEGACY as much as I have enjoyed writing all six books. And don't forget to look for *Taking Over the Tycoon*, coming in June 2003 from Harlequin American Romance.

Happy reading!

CATHY GILLEN THACKER

THE HEIRESS

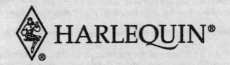

HARLEQUIN®

TORONTO • NEW YORK • LONDON
AMSTERDAM • PARIS • SYDNEY • HAMBURG
STOCKHOLM • ATHENS • TOKYO • MILAN • MADRID
PRAGUE • WARSAW • BUDAPEST • AUCKLAND

ISBN 0-373-83572-8

THE HEIRESS

This edition published by arrangement with Harlequin Books S.A.

® and TM are trademarks of the publisher. Trademarks indicated with
® are registered in the United States Patent and Trademark Office, the
Canadian Trade Marks Office and in other countries.

Visit us at www.eHarlequin.com

Printed in U.S.A.

ABOUT THE AUTHOR

Cathy Gillen Thacker has published over sixty books, more than fifty with Harlequin American Romance. And with good reason! The family dramas and romantic comedies are very close to her heart. Her books have made numerous appearances on bestseller lists and are published in seventeen languages and thirty-five countries around the world. She lives in North Carolina with her family.

To my darling daughter Sarah—
who understands the "creative process"/art of
storytelling like only another former English lit
major/Web site designer/law student can. Thanks for
listening, kiddo. (A lot!) This one is for you.

CHAPTER ONE

WE HAVE TO STOP MEETING *like this,* Daisy Templeton thought.

Not that she and Jack Granger were really socializing. Just that, for the last month or so, the two of them had been showing up at the same locations in Charleston, South Carolina, at the same time with disturbing regularity. Sometimes, the handsome attorney said hello and engaged her in the kind of brief chitchat one had with an acquaintance. On other occasions—like tonight—the sexy bachelor kept his distance, remaining clear on the other side of the airport baggage claim.

Daisy knew Jack Granger hadn't been on her return flight from Switzerland in any case. The tall sandy-haired southerner with the nicely chiseled jaw would have been impossible to miss. But, as company counsel, he certainly could have been somewhere for Deveraux-Heyward Shipping. He was dressed in a dark-blue pinstriped business suit, white shirt, tie. As always, his clothes were sharp, if a little worn.

He had been standing there, arms crossed, leaning up against the far wall, when Daisy walked through the security gate that separated arrivals and departures from the rest of the Charleston, South Carolina, airport. Dark aviator sunglasses on, a cell phone pressed to his ear, he appeared to be waiting for someone or something. But unlike everyone else—Daisy included—who was gathered around the motionless baggage claim, waiting impatiently for their luggage, Jack Granger didn't seem to care whether the ear-splitting warning buzzer ever sounded. He appeared more interested in whatever was being said to him on the other end of the line.

Not that it should matter to her what Jack Granger was doing, Daisy reminded herself as the red light flashed and the conveyer belt finally began to move. Others crowded in. She wedged her way in once she saw her case, grabbed it by the handle, lifted it off the conveyor belt, pulled up the handle, then wheeled it toward the automatic doors.

The August heat was intense, the South Carolina air was warm, moist and scented with saltwater. Grateful to be back home, even if she wasn't happy about what she had to do next, Daisy headed quickly for the long-term parking lot, and the car she had purchased six weeks ago after she had been disinherited. Her adopted parents hated the beat-up red sedan with the dented fender, yellowing hood and two pine-green doors, but for Daisy, the reconditioned, decade-old vehicle was a crowning symbol of her achievement. She had paid for the car in cash, using money she had earned as a professional photographer. And it had facilitated her during her search for the truth about her heritage. Now that she was back in the States again, she was going to take herself to confront her biological mother and father.

Eight o'clock, the traffic was light as she headed for the downtown Historic District of elegant homes, to the Hayes residence, where Daisy's older sister, Iris, resided. The stately lemon-colored three-story home, with the black shutters, double wraparound verandas and mansard roof, was one of the larger homes on Concord Street, opposite Waterfront Park.

Her heart pounding with a mixture of anger and anticipation of the blowup to come, Daisy slammed out of her car, the red accordion file filled with proof in one hand, her fringed buckskin carryall slung over her shoulder, and marched up the steps. Iris's maid, Consuela, answered the door, and ushered Daisy to the antique-filled morning room, where her much older "sister" was seated.

Iris had on a sleeveless pale-blue summer sweater and slim white skirt, high-heeled shoes that made the most of her slender, elegant, forty-seven-year-old form. A cardigan had been tied neatly across her shoulders. A strand of pearls and matching earrings were the only accessories aside from the heavy diamond wedding and engagement rings Iris still wore, a year after she had been widowed by one of the city's wealthiest—and in Daisy's opinion, most repulsive—men. Copies of *Vogue* and *Town and Country* magazine were spread across her lap. Mozart was playing on the stereo.

Iris took one look at the expression on Daisy's face and dismissed her maid with a silken-voiced "That will be all, Consuela. And please, shut the doors behind you."

Consuela nodded and disappeared as silently as she had come in.

Daisy's heartbeat kicked up another notch as she regarded the woman who had secretly given birth to her, and then, just as heartlessly, abandoned her child. "Hello, Mother."

For the first time, Iris's poise faltered. She put aside her magazines. "Daisy. I didn't know you were back."

You mean you were praying I would never come back. "Just got in."

Iris wet her lips nervously, swallowed hard enough

for Daisy to see it. "I don't know what you found out over there—"

Aware her legs were beginning to tremble with a combination of exhaustion and nerves, Daisy eased into a tapered-back Hepplewhite chair, circa 1790. Unable to help herself—hadn't she promised herself on the plane she would give Iris a chance to explain, before she tore into her?—Daisy countered ever so quietly, "How about the truth?" *How about the end of all my childish dreams?* She was only twenty-three, but she felt so much older, now that she knew about all the lies.

"But it's not anything like what it must seem," Iris continued.

"Really," Daisy replied. She studied the mixture of guilt and regret on the older woman's face, and knew that her long-held hope of finding out to whom she really belonged was not going to bring her the peace of mind, the love and acceptance she had sought. "Then suppose you explain all the documents I have in this file." Daisy patted the pleated red folder clenched between her fingers on her right hand. "The birth records that say I was born in Switzerland to American citizen Iris Templeton, and not to two tragically killed parents in Norway—as I was always told. Or the travel visa to Norway and then the United States with my name on it, issued to Charlotte and Richard, by the U.S. embassy. Or the story of the scandalous predicament that got you in trouble and landed you in the convent, recounted to me by the long-retired and still very remorseful Sister Agatha." *Suppose you tell me about all the lies. About your affair with a very married man.*

Silence fell as the color drained from Iris's beautiful face. Tears glimmered in her eyes as Iris pressed a hand to her pearls and spoke with difficulty. "I was very young when it happened."

Not that young. "You were twenty-three—the same age I am now, college-educated and wealthy to boot. I think you could have handled having me if you had wanted to," Daisy concluded resentfully.

New color dotted Iris's flawless cheeks. Iris looked Daisy square in the eye. "It wasn't that simple, Daisy."

"Right," Daisy agreed bitterly, tears sparkling in her own eyes, too. She wondered why she had ever hoped, even for one overly idealistic second, that the always contained Iris would tell Daisy what was in her heart, then or now. "You had a fortune to amass, a gross old man to marry."

Pique simmered in Iris's pale-green eyes. "I tried to do right by you."

Daisy blinked, the self-serving audacity of those closest to her as astounding as ever. "How?" she demanded incredulously. "By lying to me? Having everyone else lie to me?" Iris had known how important it had been to Daisy to discover the true circumstances of her birth, that Daisy had been looking, off and on, for the past five years. And never once lifted a hand to help her, or even act as if she understood Daisy's quest to discover just what it was about her that made her so secretly loathsome in Daisy's "parents'" eyes. Now, of course, it all made sense. Richard and Charlotte Templeton had seen Daisy as the living proof of their only real daughter's scandalous indiscretion, and probably worried Daisy would "go wrong," too. Whereas Iris had been protecting herself and her reputation. What Daisy had needed or wanted or felt hadn't mattered, still wouldn't, she admitted miserably. No, when it came to protecting the family's good name, Daisy and other individual members were completely dispensable.

Iris turned her glance away. "Your adoption was for the best," Iris stated stiffly.

"For you, maybe," Daisy replied, her heart aching all the more as she looked around, observing what Iris's bargain with the devil had earned her. A hefty bank account, all the clothes and cars and jewelry she could ever want and one of the most luxurious mansions in Charleston's nationally recognized Historic District. "Not for me. Never for me." But, Daisy realized, Iris was not going to apologize for that, any more than Iris would apologize for pretending to be nothing more than Daisy's older sister all these years.

Deciding she'd learned as much as she was liable to learn at that juncture, Daisy stood and headed for the door. Iris followed her as far as the front door, before stopping and drawing her folded cardigan closely to her bare shoulders. "Daisy, for pity's sake. Think of the family's standing in the community and don't do anything to create a scandal."

Daisy shot the woman who had given birth to and then promptly disclaimed her a hard look over her shoulder. "A little too late for that, don't you think?" As far as she was concerned, the damage—and to be honest there had been a hell of a lot of it—had already been done.

JACK GRANGER HAD BEEN hoping and praying Daisy Templeton wouldn't show up at Tom Deveraux's mansion that evening. He didn't want the impossible task of trying to control the wayward heiress. But it appeared it had fallen to him, nevertheless. Trying to ignore how attractive she looked in the short, pink-floral

sundress, fringed suede knee-high boots and dangly turquoise bead earrings, he blocked her path. She was a
good bit shorter than he, slender and fit, with sexy legs.
Her eyes were blue like a stormy ocean and her sun-
kissed blond hair tumbled down around her fair freckled
shoulders in loose waves. Her profile was flawless, her
chin hitched in determination. She was also eight years
younger than he was, in actual years—probably a lot
more than that when it came to life experience. And
that, plus a lot of other things, made the capricious
beauty clearly off-limits to him, Jack reminded himself
sternly as he tore his eyes from her soft naturally pink
lips. Bracing himself for the emotional argument likely
to come, he inclined his head in the direction of Tom
Deveraux's Historic District home and told her flatly,
"You can't go in there."

Daisy's eyes gleamed with audacity as she stomped
even nearer. "Oh, really." She propped her hands on
her hips. "Says who?"

Jack was close enough to inhale her orange-blossom
fragrance. "Says me," he told her firmly.

"Funny." Daisy's soft, kissable lips curved into a
taunting smile as she swept around him and headed for
the front door. "The last I heard, Jack Granger, you
were legal counsel to Deveraux-Heyward Shipping not
the bouncer."

Jack caught up with her before she had a chance to
ring the doorbell and again blocked her way. "I still
am."

"Uh-huh." Daisy looked him up and down in a way
that stirred his blood. "Then why are you here tonight,
screening guests? Do you provide the same service to
the airport?"

She was looking at him with a mixture of suspicion

and disdain. So she remembered seeing him at the baggage claim. What she didn't know was that he had been at the airport only to see if she had made it safely back to the States, and what—if anything—she planned to do upon her return from Switzerland. When she had gone straight to see her sister, Iris, he had hoped—unrealistically, he now saw—that she would leave any confrontations with Tom Deveraux until tomorrow.

"Why aren't you inside with the others?" Daisy continued. "Why were you sitting out here in your SUV watching that mansion and that party—" Daisy pointed to the Deveraux clan, visible through the windows, milling about in the formal front rooms "—like some little match boy looking in?"

Because that's exactly what I am, Jack thought. A kid from the docks, who just works for these people. Aware he'd get nowhere if he let his emotions get the best of him, Jack did his best to contain a weary sigh. He faced Daisy stoically. "Because Tom asked me to try and talk to you if you showed up here tonight." *Looking for trouble.*

Bitterness clouded Daisy's Deveraux-blue eyes. "And why did he think I might do that?" she asked in a dangerously soft, sexy voice. She regarded Jack carefully, as if trying to gauge how much he knew. And whether or not it might be possible to get him on her side, instead of his boss's.

As the seconds—and silence—drew out, Jack ignored the vulnerability suddenly emanating from Daisy. He had a job to do here—it was Tom he was protecting, not her. Jack shrugged and continued to keep his own emotions out of it. "Tom knew you were headed back from Switzerland. That you'd be tired—" *and perhaps overwrought* "—when you got here." *Not to mention confused, angry, hurt.*

Jack had been instructed to provide the strong shoulder to cry on and the voice of reason until Tom could get to Daisy and deal with her tomorrow once she settled down.

"Then he also knows what I found out while I was over there." Daisy's vulnerability disappeared as suddenly as it had bloomed. "Perfect."

Jack ignored the reproach in her tone. "It's not what it seems, Daisy."

"Of course not." Daisy shook her head in mute disapproval. "Which is why Tom Deveraux is suddenly so desperate to keep me away from him and his family." Daisy reached around Jack and punched the doorbell. Seconds later, Theresa Owens, Tom's housekeeper answered the door. She was wearing a navy-blue uniform-dress with a white collar. Her auburn hair was drawn into a knot on the top of her head. "I need to see Tom," Daisy said without preamble.

Theresa hesitated. "This really isn't a good time, Ms. Templeton. The family is having a private dinner this evening."

Daisy smiled in a way Jack didn't begin to trust. "You mean they're all here," she said.

"Yes."

"Even the former Mrs. Deveraux?"

"Yes."

"Splendid." Head held high, Daisy pushed past Theresa and advanced through the foyer.

Jack swore silently to himself. Short of dashing after Daisy, tossing her over his shoulder and carrying her out to the curb, there was no way to stop her from making a scene. All he could do now was try to limit the damage. "I'll handle this," Jack promised Theresa as he strode after Daisy, who was already following the laughter and marching into the double drawing room, where, from the looks and sound of it, a wonderful, warm and intimate family party was going on.

Tom's oldest son, Chase, was the first Deveraux to spot Daisy. Champagne in hand, the magazine editor made his way toward her. "Hey, Daisy," Chase greeted her cheerfully with a kiss on the cheek. "You're just in time to toast the newest members of the Deveraux clan. Amy and Gabe's wife, Maggy, are both pregnant. And the entire family is, as you can imagine, thrilled to be expanding."

Jack noted that news only made Daisy's expression turn more turbulent. "Too bad that hasn't always been the case."

Chase's forehead creased. As did Amy's, Gabe's and Mitch's, all of whom were standing within earshot. Watching, it was all Jack could do not to groan out loud. There was no telling how Tom's children with Grace were going to react to the news of their father's digression years ago. Chase was probably the best bet for understanding. The oldest son, and publisher of the popular *Modern Man* magazine, had sowed a few wild oats of his own before he married his childhood sweetheart and settled down. Mitch was a possibility, too. The most like his dad, he was a pragmatic businessman, who could always be counted on to see through the murkiness of any situation, get to the bottom line and do whatever was necessary to correct the situation. Third-oldest son Gabe was known for his compassion, and as a critical-care physician, he was no stranger to people's most private problems. Amy, the baby of the family and the owner of her own redecorating business, was always pulling for a reunification of her divorced parents, despite past hurts. Might not want to start with her, Jack thought.

Unfortunately, even if Tom and Grace's children eventually understood and accepted what had happened years ago, Tom's ex-wife, recently unemployed network television mornings-news show host, Grace Deveraux, probably would not. All of which, of course, Jack's boss, Tom Deveraux, realized. Which was why Tom was glaring at Jack, as if he couldn't believe the way Jack had let him down, now, of all times.

Desperate to control the damage, Jack grabbed Daisy's arm and pulled her against him, so her slender back was pressed against his chest. Bad enough, Jack figured, that Daisy had barged in here, uninvited, despite Theresa Owens warning this was not an appropriate time to be a drop-in guest. Tom didn't need all four of his children, their spouses and his ex-wife, witnessing this confrontation, too. "You don't want to do this," Jack murmured persuasively in Daisy's ear. "Not now. Not this way."

"The hell I don't!" Daisy jerked free of Jack's staying grip and whirled to face him. Temper shimmered in her eyes. "I've been hidden in the shadows long enough!"

"Daisy—what are you talking about?" Amy asked, aghast. "What's wrong?"

Tom threaded his way through the group, while Grace hung back looking, if possible, even more distressed.

Jack wrapped his arm around Daisy's shoulders companionably and leaned down to whisper in her ear. "I think you've made your point, now let's go," Jack said firmly. "I'll make sure you get to talk to Tom alone first thing tomorrow morning."

"Thanks, but I'd rather make a scene." Daisy broke loose and strode forward, heading straight for Tom. "No more pretending, Daddy. The secret's out."

DAISY'S TEMPER skyrocketed as Amy regarded her father in confusion. "What secret?" Amy demanded, upset. "And why is Daisy so mad at you?"

Even more color drained from Grace's face. A mixture of guilt and culpability shimmered in her eyes. Which meant, Daisy thought, even more hurt, that Grace had known, too. And had helped—maybe even encouraged—Daisy's birth father to walk away…and pretend that Daisy had never existed. Or was she the reason Tom and Grace had eventually divorced? Daisy wondered. Or had there been other, even more devastating problems, too?

"Daisy and I need to talk privately," Tom told everyone in the room sternly.

Deep in her heart, Daisy had hoped that there was a highly romantic and even laudable reason Tom Deveraux had never lifted a finger to rescue her from her unhappy childhood. In the wake of the cold disapproval emanating from him, however, the guilt and the grim resignation, her misguided hopes fled. Like it or not, she had to face it. She had been willfully and wrongly abandoned—by both her birth mother and birth father. Even worse, to this day, neither of her real parents wanted her in their lives. She was to Tom and Grace and Iris, and God only knew who else, exactly what she was to Richard and Charlotte Templeton—a sordid, unwanted reminder of a time best forgotten. Well, no more. She was tired of feeling ashamed, of being blamed for something that was definitely not her doing! "Don't look to me to perpetuate any more dirty little secrets," Daisy warned the man who, more than anyone, was responsible for her lifelong unhappiness. Because she wasn't going to do it!

Mitch frowned as he struggled to make sense of what was going on. "Have you been drinking?" he demanded of Daisy, striding closer.

"Not yet. But as they say, the evening is young," Daisy continued sarcastically, picking up the bottle of champagne and waving it in front of her like a red flag in front of a bull. "And we have much to celebrate."

Gabe moved forward and just as promptly removed the heavy dark-green bottle from her hand. "Look, Daisy," Gabe said, setting the magnum aside, "I don't know what's going on here, but you're obviously upset, and—"

Daisy gritted her teeth, her anger and disillusionment building to an untenable degree. There were times when she welcomed Gabe's inherently good nature—this wasn't one of them. "That a medical opinion, brother Gabe, or just a personal observation?" she asked with a saccharine smile.

Trembling visibly, Grace murmured, "God help us," and sank into a chair, covering her face with her hands.

Tom gave Jack another look, even sterner and more commanding than before. No words were necessary between the two men. Daisy knew what the orders were— Jack was to get her out of the house, pronto. Ever the faithful, loyal Deveraux-Heyward Shipping Company employee, Jack slid an arm around Daisy's waist and held her tight. "Obviously, Daisy is in no condition to be talking to anyone here tonight. So Daisy and I are going to be leaving now,'' Jack announced firmly but pleasantly.

"Not before I tell everyone what I came to tell them,'' Daisy said, looking around at the tense, wary expressions on her half siblings' faces. "That I'm Tom Deveraux's love child.''

AMY GASPED, Jack grimaced, Grace moaned. All three of Tom's sons were shocked, silent. "It wasn't love,'' Tom corrected Daisy impatiently.

Yet another illusion down the drain. "A mistake,'' Daisy guessed.

"And there's no proof you're even my child,'' Tom continued, even more defensively.

Daisy reeled at his unwillingness to claim her as his, even now. She knew what a loving father Tom was to his other children, that being a father was one of the primary joys of his life, aside from his work at Deveraux-Heyward Shipping. It was evident in everything he did and said. Hell, he'd even been a surrogate father to his housekeeper, Theresa Owen's illegitimate child, Bridgett, over the years, out of nothing more than the goodness of his heart. Which made his refusal to claim her, Daisy thought, all the more stinging. Shoulders stiffening, Daisy regarded Tom resentfully. "You're denying you slept with my birth mother?''

Tom's jaw clenched. "It was a one-night fling.''

Like that excused and explained everything, Daisy thought even more furiously.

"Daddy! You cheated on Mom?'' Amy said.

Tom shook his head and released a short, aggravated breath. "It was one night,'' he defended himself impatiently.

"But once, as they say, is enough," Grace added in a low voice thick with tears.

"Man, Dad." Chase shook his head.

"I don't believe this!" Gabe murmured in horror.

Mitch was silent, tense as he struggled to make sense of it, too.

"But you knew you made Iris pregnant," Daisy continued probing.

Amy blinked and whirled to face Daisy. "Iris...?" she echoed.

"Templeton-Hayes," Daisy supplied the rest. "My *sister*. At least the woman I always thought was my adopted sister. Turns out she was really my birth mother and my adopted parents—Charlotte and Richard Templeton—are really my biological grandparents. And Connor is my uncle not my adopted brother. Funny, huh?" Not waiting for a response from the shocked half siblings around her, Daisy turned back to Tom, still struggling to find a way to obtain her own peace of mind. "Which brings us back to you. Why did you turn your back on me?" *And please,* Daisy prayed silently, *let it be good.*

Tom uttered another long, tortured sigh. "Because I never knew for certain that you were mine."

"You never asked?" Daisy regarded him incredulously. How was that possible? A wealthy, self-assured, successful CEO, he wasn't afraid of anything. And he certainly wasn't shy about going after what he wanted! Tom ran his hands through his short, gray-brown hair and began to pace. "Iris went to Europe to learn the antique business, after our interlude. It seemed like a good move, a way to get both our lives back on track, and I wished her well." Tom paused and frowned. "It wasn't until Richard and Charlotte unexpectedly and suddenly adopted a baby some nine months later that I realized it was possible she'd become pregnant during the encounter and you were mine. So I confronted Iris.''

"And…?" Daisy questioned impatiently.

Tom shrugged his broad shoulders restively. "She denied ever having a child. I asked for a blood test anyway." Tom scowled, recalling, "She said I would have to sue her publicly to get it, and if I did, she would not only refuse to take the test but countersue me for slander." He looked at the assembled group, pleading for understanding. "I was trying to put my marriage to Grace back together, Iris was engaged to be married to Randolph Hayes IV in what was shaping up to be the wedding of the year. You were well taken care of, Daisy, with people who loved you and wanted the best for you. It just seemed right to let the matter drop." Tom paused again, looking even more conflicted. "Even now, I don't know that you're actually my child, Daisy. Just that you could be.''

"Well, I *am* your child," Daisy countered hotly, incensed that Tom Deveraux could be trying to duck his responsibility, even now, when she had a red accordion file full of proof sitting on the front seat of her car. "At least according to the nuns at the convent in Switzerland, where my mother stayed when she was pregnant." At Tom's blank look, Daisy continued explaining, "Iris confided in one of them. Sister Agatha knew all about you. How you led her on, flirted with her for weeks and weeks, and then—one night—took her to bed, and then afterward, after you got caught by your wife, told her to pretend it had never happened.''

The skin across Tom's cheekbones stretched taut as he glared at Daisy. "You're making it simple. It wasn't."

"Oh, I think it was," Grace interjected bitterly, standing and addressing everyone in the room for the first time. "Your father screwed around. He got caught. It happens all the time, especially to men of his ilk."

Chase looked at his mother, surmising humorlessly, "Dad's infidelity is why you two divorced, isn't it?"

Tears gleaming in her eyes, Grace nodded and continued matter-of-factly, "Lord knows I tried to put it behind me. I really did. But after that, after I walked in on him and Iris, I could never trust him again."

Silence fell as everyone contemplated what an ugly scene that must have been, both during and after the philandering.

Mitch looked at Daisy curiously. "What does your birth mother, er, uh, Iris, and the rest of your family— the Templetons—have to say about this?"

"I haven't talked to Charlotte, Richard or Connor yet," Daisy said quietly.

"Why not?" Gabe asked gently.

Daisy threw her hands up in mute frustration. "Because they lied to me for years. All of them." She looked at Tom again, aware there was a part of her, regardless of how angry, that already thought of him as her father. Just as Richard and Charlotte, who had adopted and reluctantly reared her and guided her through childhood, would always remain Mother and Father to her, too. Daisy sighed, and aware Tom was still waiting, still struggling to understand her motivation as desperately as she was trying to comprehend his, continued with a weariness that came straight from her soul, "And I wanted to hear your side of the story first. Now that I have—" Unable to go on, Daisy shook her

head at Tom. Her throat aching unbearably, she turned
and headed blindly for the door. "I've got to get out
of here," she mumbled. And she fled.

TOM FOLLOWED THEM BOTH and stopped Jack in the
front hall. Knowing he could trust the Deveraux-
Heyward Shipping attorney to do whatever needed to
be done, he looked Jack in the eye and told him
brusquely, "Go after her. Do whatever you have to do,
but stay with her and make sure she doesn't do anything
even more foolish or self-destructive than what she did
here tonight." Tom inclined his head toward the elegant
front room where the rest of the family was still gathered. "I'll take care of things here, and then catch up
with both of you later."

Jack nodded his understanding and headed out after
Daisy.

Relieved that was going to be taken care of, Tom
strode back into the double drawing room. One mistake.
Who the hell would have known one slip could have
blown his entire life to smithereens? But it had, and
now, judging from the looks on the faces of his kids
and their spouses, and his ex-wife, it was about to get
much worse. Grace was seated on the antique sofa, her
features tight with resentment. Their children were
gathered around her, while their spouses mingled uncertainly in the background, not sure whether to stay or
leave, only knowing—like Tom and Grace—that this
was one hell of a mess the Deveraux were in.

"I'm sorry about that," Tom said.

"You should be!" Amy cried, as always, the most
emotional of the group. She dabbed furiously at the
tears on her cheeks. "I can't believe you would do
something like that!" she fumed resentfully. Beside
her, Grace seemed to concur.

"Was there just the one indiscretion?" Gabe asked warily, struggling to understand.

Chase regarded Tom with his customary cheekiness. "Or should we brace ourselves for other illegitimate heirs, to liven up our family gatherings?"

Tom glared at his sons. Gabe's lack of faith and Chase's sarcasm weren't helping. Before Tom could censure them, however, his second-oldest son Mitch put in his two cents'. "Chase and Gabe have legitimate questions," Mitch pointed out, taking his usual businesslike approach. "News like this could affect our reputation in the community. There are some who might not want to do business with Deveraux-Heyward Shipping if we're embroiled in one scandal after another."

"There won't be any more scandals," Tom said, disappointed in his family's seemingly united stand against him. "Nor will there be any more illegitimate children showing up on our doorstep. Now, if you kids will excuse us, your mother and I have a lot to talk about."

As soon as everyone left, Tom closed the doors to the double drawing room, and turned to Grace. "I'm sorry," he said softly. It was lame, but he didn't know what else to say.

Grace glared at him with years of pent-up resentment, the look in her eyes making him feel about two inches tall. "You should be, you son of a bitch," she retorted just as quietly.

Tom wished she would just haul off and slug him and get it over with, instead of continuing to punish him, day after day, year after year. "Don't hold anything back," he advised just as sarcastically, wondering how much longer Grace was going to continue to make him pay for this.

Since the divorce, they'd been civil to one another

at family functions, for the sake of the kids. Every time they had tried to do more than that, either be friends or something more, the issue of his infidelity would come up and they'd end up fighting again. Tom was tired of the discord. He sensed Grace was, too. But as for how to move on, move past this…

Grace stood and went over to the table where she had left her handbag. Her cheeks pink with distress, she picked it up and head bent, began to rummage through it. Tom studied her, thinking how pretty his former wife looked in the silky turquoise pantsuit. Her blond hair was much shorter these days—worn in attractive layers that framed her face and the nape of her neck—but her figure was still trim, her beautifully girl-next-door face unlined. As always, when he was near her, he found himself wanting to nurture and care for and protect her. Not that she would allow it. Not after what he had done.

"I always knew this was going to happen someday," Grace said.

Grace glared at him. "I hoped it never would." She fished out her keys and held them in the palm of her hand. "What are you going to do about Daisy?"

Tom shrugged. Now that he knew what Daisy thought was the truth, he hadn't a clue. Daisy was one troubled young woman. Tempestuous, wild and unpredictable, and already the talk of Charleston, even without this revelation. The Templetons had spent years trying to control her. To no avail. Tom wondered if what Daisy had been told by Sister Agatha was true. Was Daisy his child? Or had Iris been with someone else in that time frame? And even if he was Daisy's father, Tom admitted to himself, would he have any better luck, trying to parent Daisy, than Richard and Charlotte Templeton had had, during their tenure, as Daisy's adopted mom and dad? Aware Grace was still waiting for his answer, Tom said bluntly, "I don't know. I'll give her until morning to simmer down, and then see if I can reason with her. And go from there."

Grace arched her elegant eyebrows in skeptical fashion. "Good luck with that."

He would need it, Tom admitted. And even then it might not be enough. Just as his apologies over the years hadn't been enough. "Grace…"

She paused en route to the foyer. Wheeling halfway to face him, she said, "What?"

"You can't leave." Tom held out a beseeching hand. "Not like this."

Grace shook her head, refusing his plea to stay, and at least try to work things out. She regarded him with a mixture of contempt and displeasure. "Daisy isn't the only one who needs time to cool off."

GRACE KNEW she shouldn't have walked out on Tom like that. She should have stayed and tried to work out a way to deal with this very explosive situation. Publicly, it could be disastrous, if word got out right now. She had a new TV show in the works. She didn't need this kind of bad publicity in the wake of her firing from *Rise and Shine, America!*

It had been bad enough going from one of the most watched women on morning television, from the coveted cohost position she had held for fifteen years, to being unemployed. But now this…

Grace didn't know if she could handle living in the same city with Tom again, if she had to confront his illegitimate child—and therefore his infidelity—day after day after day.

It wasn't that she didn't want to forget and forgive.

But that she couldn't.

Lord knew she had tried. But every time he had touched her or tried to kiss her or hold her, she'd ended up flashing back to the day she had found him making love with Iris. Every time she had run into Daisy, or Iris, or any member of the Templeton family, she had experienced the same sick feeling inside her. Along with the feeling that she would never be smart or sophisticated or sexy enough to hold Tom. Not in any real or lasting way. Because if Tom could cheat on her once, the practical side of Grace knew, he could cheat on her again. And eventually, after nearly nine years of trying to work things out, and failing, she had known their marriage had to end. So she'd told him she wanted a divorce. And, in the end, he'd had no choice but to give her what she wanted, because she wasn't coming back, not to him, and not to his bed.

Lately, of course, that had begun to change. In the wake of her job loss and public humiliation, she had flirted with the idea of trying again. Seeing if maybe she and Tom couldn't find a way to work things out, to resurrect the love they had once shared. But now, with the resurgence of Daisy in their lives—as his illegitimate daughter no less—she knew she had just been fooling herself. She had to move on. Put him out of her heart and mind forever. And there was only one way, Grace knew, that she would ever be able to do that.

CHAPTER TWO

DAISY COULDN'T BELIEVE Jack Granger was still following her. It had been nearly two hours, and he was still on her tail. She'd been all over Charleston, out to Sullivan's Island, Kiawah and back to Folly Beach and he was still right behind her in his black SUV, trailing her around the countryside. Not that she cared much one way or another, Daisy told herself as she drove past several rural churches, which were dark and silent that time of night, and into the marshland that comprised much of the island. Ignoring the turnoff for a summer camp, she drove past several large farms and a tomato-packing shed, thought briefly about stopping in at a down and dirty-looking honky-tonk just to see what Tom Deveraux's "henchman," Jack Granger, might do about that, and then continued cruising toward the center of the island.

Sooner or later, Daisy told herself as the warm ocean air blew in through her open driver-side window, caressing her body and ruffling her hair, Jack Granger had to get bored or give up and go home. Go back to her uncaring and irresponsible birth father. Something. Anything. So she could go unencumbered where she was really headed for that night. Because right now all she wanted was to be alone. To try and deal. Not that that was going to be easy, either, she acknowledged with a beleaguered sigh. And that was when it happened. The bad day to end all days became even worse as her car began to sputter and shake.

"I don't believe it." Daisy swore as her car came to a trembling halt on the side of the two-lane road. She looked at her dashboard, and saw the red light flashing the words *Service Engine.* Swearing even more passionately, Daisy tried to restart the car. There had to be a gas station around here somewhere. Otherwise she'd have to get a tow truck and another ride.

Jack Granger pulled up behind her. He left his engine and lights on as he stepped out of the car and walked up to her window. He leaned down, like a policeman giving a ticket and rapped on the glass, his jacket off, tie loosened and shirtsleeves rolled up. "Problem?"

She stared straight ahead. "Nothing I can't handle. Now go away."

"Sorry." He remained beside her, hands braced on his hips. "I can't do that."

"Suit yourself." Daisy tried once more to start her car, and then gave up. She took her keys out of the ignition, grabbed her purse, and deciding he could be responsible for getting himself out of her way, bolted out of the car.

"I'll give you a ride," Jack said.

"No." Daisy tucked her purse under her arm and started walking in the direction she'd been headed.

Jack caught her arm and swung her around to face him, his big strong body dwarfing her petite frame. His touch gentling ever so slightly, he regarded her impatiently. "Look, I know you're a strong, independent woman and all that, but you can't gallivant around here alone this late at night. It's not safe."

Daisy surveyed the rumpled state of his sandy-blond hair, the evening beard lining his face, and knew he had to feel every bit in need of a long hot shower and a good night's sleep as she did at that moment. Refusing to let him tell her what to do, or when to do it, she merely drawled, "Is that so."

Half his lips curved upward in a coaxing smile. He held his ground just as resolutely, promising kindly, "I'll take you where you want to go."

Daisy sighed. The truth was, she was exhausted from the long flight home, the confrontations with Iris and Tom and the driving around aimlessly. Right now she wanted a safe, quiet place, and a bed to call her own. She didn't want Jack Granger—or anyone else—knowing where she was, but she supposed at the moment anyway that couldn't be helped. "Fine," she said tersely. "Take me to Folly Beach and I'll direct you from there."

"THERE" turned out to be a run-down lodge and a dozen or so private cottages in equally miserable shape. Jack knew Folly Beach had been devastated during a particularly bad hurricane some years back, and for a while few had vacationed there because of the huge amount of devastation, but that was once again changing. Expensive vacation homes were cropping up amidst the various businesses and year-round residences.

Jack looked at the weathered buildings, with the unkempt grounds and peeling paint. "If it's a hotel room you're needing, we can do a lot better than this," he said, surveying the faded sign that proclaimed it Paradise Resort. "Let me take you to one of the premium resorts or hotels."

Predictably, Daisy ignored his attempt to help her. "This'll do just fine," she said, her soft lips tightening mutinously as she disregarded his offer and slid out of the car. She slung her purse and camera around her neck, and picked up her red accordion file while Jack reluctantly got her wheeled suitcase out of the rear of his SUV. Taking it from him, she headed for the lodge, leaving Jack no choice but to follow. By the time Jack got inside the lobby, Daisy was already being greeted by a thirtyish woman in cutoffs and a T-shirt. Slender and dark-haired, with lively dark-brown eyes, she had a paint roller in her hand and pale-green paint streaked across one golden-skinned cheek. "Hey, Daisy. I didn't expect you back so soon!" She paused to rip off a plastic painting glove and extend her hand to Jack. "I'm Kristy Neumeyer—I own this place."

"Jack Granger." Jack took her hand and shook it warmly, his regard for the establishment being renovated becoming abruptly more positive. A little elbow grease and some tender loving care would go a long way to making Paradise Resort a top-notch vacation hideaway.

Kristy turned back to Daisy, her pretty smile widening even more. "I thought you were staying in Europe indefinitely." Kristy easily picked up her conversation with Daisy.

"I'm back." Daisy said, her weariness abruptly beginning to show. "And I need a place to stay tonight." Daisy looked at Kristy, as if knowing what a big favor she was asking, under the circumstances. "Can you rent me one of the cottages?"

Kristy regarded Jack curiously, then turned back to Daisy. "Uh… Listen…I…none of the cottages are ready yet. In fact, they're all in pretty dismal shape. As you can see, I haven't even gotten the lobby painted."

"But you and your twins are living here," Daisy protested.

Kristy held up her hands with a helpless shrug. "Susie and Sally are eight. They just like being close to the beach, and being able to build sand castles and collect seashells every single day."

"Where are they now?" Jack asked.

"Asleep for the night. Which leaves me free to resume my efforts to spruce up this place enough to get it open for business again. Hopefully, by October fifteenth. Meanwhile, I'm closed to guests."

"I just need a place to lay my head," Daisy told Kristy persuasively. "If there's a pillow and a mattress or even a floor, that's really all I need."

Kristy studied Daisy. Understanding passed between them as Kristy realized how badly Daisy needed refuge. "Well, in that case..." Kristy stepped around the paint pan and roller and slipped behind the desk. She lifted a drop cloth, then came up with a key. "You can take cabin six. It's at the other end."

"Thanks," Daisy said gratefully.

"Need help with your luggage?" Kristy asked.

Daisy shook her head. She turned to Jack and offered him a tight you-can-get-lost-now-that-you're-no-longer-useful smile. "See you around," she said, grabbing the handle of her wheeled suitcase once again. And then she was gone.

"So Daisy confronted her biological father tonight, too," Richard Templeton said shortly after midnight.

Iris looked at her parents grimly, nodding. Richard and Charlotte had been at a charity function and were still in their evening clothes. As always they made a very striking couple. Both were slim and fit, blessed with elegant, aristocratic looks and an inordinate sense of style, but Iris couldn't help but note, only her mother looked her age. Mostly because Charlotte refused to take advantage of the latest plastic surgery techniques or dye her chin-length silver hair. Richard, however, had no such compunction. He'd had not one—but two—face-lifts over the years and had been "keeping" his dark-brown hair that hue with regular visits to the salon. All Richard's efforts to retain his youthful visage had paid off. Although Richard and Charlotte were both sixty-seven, Richard looked a good ten years younger than his wife. Iris knew that bothered her father, but her mother didn't seem to care.

Aware they were still waiting for her answer, Iris said, "Tom Deveraux called me half an hour ago and told me about the scene Daisy created at his home this evening." Briefly, Iris explained about the family party Daisy had disrupted.

Charlotte Templeton removed her diamond and sapphire necklace and earrings, and put them back in the case. "And you say Grace Deveraux was there, also?"

"Yes." Iris watched her father open the safe in the library and put the jewelry case carefully inside, with the others. "Apparently, Grace and the rest of the family were very upset."

Charlotte frowned, her resentment of the man who had turned her eldest child's life upside down, evident. "I imagine they would be."

"Are the children going to tell anyone about this?" Richard demanded.

"Tom made them swear to keep it quiet. Apparently, they all agreed. None of them want to endure the public humiliation of a scandal."

"That was decent of Grace," Charlotte said.

Because she was among family, Iris made no effort to hide her dislike of the woman the media had once dubbed America's Sweetheart. "There was nothing noble about what she did. Grace Deveraux was protecting herself, as much as Daisy and Tom and the rest of their kids," Iris countered. After all, it was Grace's fault Iris and Tom had never married. If Grace hadn't been determined to save her marriage—a marriage that had ultimately failed anyway—Iris could have told Tom about the pregnancy and gotten him to marry her. She would never have had to marry Randolph Hayes IV to get the cash to fill the Templeton-family coffers and save her family from public disgrace. She wouldn't have had to pretend all these years that she was Daisy's adopted sister instead of her mother. And best of all, Daisy would've been brought up by her real parents.

"In any case, we need to talk to Daisy and make her see reason," Richard said.

"I agree. And as soon as we find her, I plan to do just that," Iris said, hoping that by then Daisy would be more willing to listen to their side of things, and continue to keep quiet about what had happened in the past.

"And you're sure Daisy isn't at your home?" Charlotte said, looking increasingly worried.

"Consuela has instructions to keep her there, and call me on my cell, if she does show up. So far, nothing." Iris hadn't heard from her housekeeper. Which meant Daisy could be anywhere, doing anything.

"What about Connor—has he seen her?" Richard asked, looking equally worried about what the unpredictable Daisy might do. They all knew Daisy was never more prone to act out than when hurting emotionally.

"Not yet. But I called him and told him to be on the alert." Iris paused. "We're going to have to tell him what we've done, too."

"We'll get to that," Richard promised. "Not that we have anything to worry about when it comes to your brother. He knows how to see both sides of every issue, no matter how complex."

That was true, Iris knew. Connor was the peacemaker in the family. But even he would probably have trouble dealing with this. Not to mention the fact that he, too, had been lied to many times over the years.

"We can't let Daisy's parentage become public knowledge," Charlotte said. "It would ruin us socially, if people were to know just how we covered up your mistake."

Which was, Iris thought, part of the problem. Even after all these years, of loving and caring for her, her parents couldn't quite forget how Daisy had come to be.

Richard looked at Iris in disapproval. "This is your fault, you know. If you had let me instill more discipline in Daisy the way I did in you, Daisy would be following our orders without question instead of causing one episode after another."

Iris's insides twisted as she recalled the unrelenting pressure she had received from her father when she was growing up. Richard felt then—as now—he had been helping her to be a better person. And to an extent he was right. His continual upbraiding had made her stronger. Strong enough to save her family by marrying a man years older than herself whom she had never loved or even liked, and still present a happy face to the world. Strong enough to take the family antiques business that Richard had nearly ruined with mismanagement and neglect and turn it into a profitable operation once again. Strong enough to find a way to be happy and content in her life despite all of that.

But Daisy hadn't needed to go through the same social and emotional regimentation she had. Iris had known that and taken steps to protect her, before giving her baby over to her parents to adopt and rear as their own. "That would have only made things worse," Iris stated, knowing if she had done one good thing in her life, it had been to protect Daisy from being forced to select a mate and marry for money and social position rather than love. She hadn't been able to keep her parents from cutting off all Daisy's funds several weeks ago, but she still hoped—over time—to remedy that, too, and return Daisy to a position filled with choices, rather than one directed by an absence of funds.

"So you've said," Richard returned coolly. He walked to the bar and poured a healthy splash of bourbon into his glass. His expression grim, he regarded her steadily over the rim of his glass. "We'll see if you still feel that way if that bastard child of yours ruins your reputation—and ours—in the community."

KRISTY HADN'T BEEN kidding when she said the place still needed an awful lot of work, Daisy thought as she let herself into cottage six and deposited the stack of threadbare linens and hotel-size bar of soap on the water-marked table. The paint was peeling off the walls, rust stains coated the sink and the shower, and the bed—well, lumpy didn't begin to describe it, Daisy thought, sitting down on the edge of the mattress to test it out. But it was a place to sleep that she could afford. It faced the ocean. Daisy didn't know why, but sitting and watching the timeless motion of waves rolling onto sand always soothed her. And after the past couple of days, she needed soothing more than she could say. Sighing wearily, Daisy removed her fringed suede boots and socks, grabbed enough change for the soda machine located between the lodge and the cottages, and headed back outside. And that was when she saw Jack Granger checking in to the cottage beside hers.

"What the hell are you doing?" She walked barefoot through the grass to confront him.

"Same as you. Bunking down here for the night." Jack took the hotel-size bar of soap and stack of thread-bare linens Kristy had given him and put them inside cabin five.

"Why?" Suddenly, Daisy was angry. Angrier than she had been the whole night.

Jack removed a cheaply made Paradise Resort tooth-brush and tiny bottle of shampoo from his shirt pocket and tossed them onto the stack. "I want to be nearby in case you need anything."

"Like what?" Daisy retorted, aware that the emotions she had successfully kept under control all evening were beginning to spiral out of control. Way out of control. "The truth?" Her pulse pounding harder with every second that passed, Daisy lingered in the open doorway of his cottage. She glared at Jack resentfully. She didn't understand why she felt so betrayed by him. She just knew that she did. "You weren't exactly instrumental in helping me get that in the weeks before I went to Switzerland." Instead, he'd kept bumping into her, in a way that she now saw was anything but accidental. Kept striking up idle conversation, surreptitiously trying to get closer to her. Not because he was interested in her as a person, or her plight to uncover the mystery of her birth. But because he had been trying to subtly stay one step ahead of her while simultaneously running interference for his boss.

"You never asked me to do that."

Daisy slanted a glance at the private home some one hundred yards down the beach. Unlike the resort, it looked expensive and brand new. And there was some-one—a man maybe—seated on his deck, looking their way.

Annoyed at being observed without her consent yet again, Daisy turned back to Jack. "And if I had asked?" she wondered out loud.

Jack shrugged his broad shoulders and came back outside to stand in the warm, salt-scented breeze. "I couldn't have helped you because I didn't know until tonight exactly what the connection between you and Tom was."

Daisy listened to the waves crashing into shore, on the other side of the sand dune. "But you knew there was a connection," she said as the sea oats waved in the wind.

A guilty silence fell between them. Eventually, Jack looked back at her and said very carefully, "I knew for a fact that Tom was worried about you, that he'd heard from his daughter, Amy, that you had hired Harlan Decker to help find your birth parents. Tom knew those things sometimes went badly or turned out in ways people didn't expect. Because of that, he felt you might need some help, and that if that was the case, he was prepared to give it."

"Why?" Daisy asked doubtfully.

"Because he's, by nature, a generous, compassionate man. Because you were friends with his children, moved in the same social circles, worked as a photographer for the entire Deveraux family and their various businesses. Maybe it was just due to the fact that he had watched you get into one scrape after another as you grew up and just didn't want to see you get in any more! Who cares what precisely the connection might be or why he would want to help you get your life under control again? He just did."

Daisy studied him skeptically. "And I'm supposed to believe that?"

"Believe what you want," Jack advised her roughly. "It's the truth. Tom never told me you were—or might be—his biological daughter."

But had Jack guessed as much on his own? Daisy wondered. And if Jack had, how did that figure into his feelings about her? Was he, like everyone else who knew the truth, seeing her as Tom's bastard child— somehow less acceptable than Tom's other kids? Was she a problem to be solved? A liability to be handled? Lawyer style, of course.

Daisy continued to study Jack, certain he was still withholding every bit as much as he was telling her. "And yet you were all too willing to stand guard in front of his mansion tonight," she probed, wanting desperately to hear the rest of it, whatever it was. "Why?" Had Tom warned Jack there might be trouble? And left it at that?

Jack sighed, his exasperation with her obvious. He gave her a censuring look. "I work for him, Daisy."

Once again, Daisy decided, that was only half the truth. The half Jack wanted her to know. "As Dever-aux-Heyward Shipping's legal counsel, but my parent-age doesn't have anything to do with that." Daisy paused warily. "Or does it?" Her mouth dropped into a round "oh" of surprise as the next thought occurred.

"Don't tell me Tom thinks I'm going to come after a piece of his family company!"

Jack shrugged and stepped closer, his nearness setting off all her internal alarm bells. "As a potential heir, I suppose you could try."

"But you wouldn't let me succeed," Daisy guessed unhappily.

His intent, golden-brown eyes narrowed. "I'll do whatever Tom tells me to do."

Despite her determination not to show him any emotion whatsoever, she found herself backing away as she asked sweetly, "Even mix business with personal and spend the entire evening coming after me?"

Jack didn't say anything, but then he didn't have to. Daisy had only to look into his eyes to know that he was still following orders from her birth father, and probably withholding information from her, too. "Never mind," Daisy muttered in disgust. She was not sure why it mattered to her at all, but she had not wanted Jack to be there for any reason other than genuine concern for her, and what she was going through. Realizing that wasn't the case, or anywhere near it, she strode past him, her temper climbing with every second that passed, and headed for the refreshment cove, located on the outside of the main lodge. The covered, concrete-floored portico had an ice dispenser and vending machines containing snacks and beverages. She put in her change, pushed one button. Nothing happened. She punched her fist against the next and the next. Finally, on the fourth try, a can of root beer—which she detested—tumbled through the machine and out of the slot. Daisy picked it up and popped open the top. Aware of Jack loitering just behind her, she held it to her lips and drank a big gulp of the sweet icy-cold liquid.

She wiped the excess moisture off her lips with the back of her hand, and slowly turned around to face him. Wordlessly, he moved by her, and put some change into the machine, too. He also got a can of root beer. Looking content to be there all night, if need be, he popped the top and took a sip.

Daisy didn't know why Jack was getting to her—maybe it was the way he kept watching over her in that infuriatingly calm and deliberate manner—but she was determined to get a rise out of him. It was the only way, she calculated with a certain weary reluctance, she would ever get rid of him. And that was what she wanted most of all, because she didn't like seeing herself and her inability to control her feelings reflected in his eyes. "It's not going to work, you know," she told him sassily as she leaned against the weather-beaten wooden post.

"What?" Jack asked, taking up a position opposite her.

Her throat unaccountably dry, Daisy watched him take another lazy drink of root beer. "You're not going to win Tom Deveraux's approval this way." She looked him over from head to toe before returning her taunting gaze, ever so vampishly, to his eyes. "That is what this is about, isn't it?" she queried softly, refusing to accept defeat, knowing this was one—maybe the only—battle she would win. "Your running interference with me for Tom, is simply a way to get in his good graces, to make him think of you as something more than an employee."

Jack's broad shoulders expanded against the starched cotton fabric of his white shirt. "Why would you think I would be interested in that?" he asked gruffly.

Knowing she had hit a nerve, Daisy rolled her eyes

and continued goading him relentlessly. "Come on. It was all over your face tonight when we were at the Deveraux mansion." The look in Jack's eyes, as they had stood outside, had matched what Daisy had been feeling, not just at that moment, but all her life—like she was the little match girl, looking in. Wishing she could join the party. And feel loved and wanted. Like she belonged in such a warm and wonderful place. Only it couldn't have been that wonderful after all, she reminded herself firmly, or Tom wouldn't have stepped out on Grace. He wouldn't have slept with Iris and, in the process, both made a baby and destroyed the happiness of his family.

"What was on my face?" Jack shifted his weight restlessly, abruptly looking as on edge and ready to do combat as she.

Raw emotion. The kind of vulnerability that was missing now that he had his guard up once again. Determined to pierce his armor the way he so easily seemed able to get through hers, Daisy taunted him softly, "You were mortified that you weren't able to keep me from crashing that Deveraux family party tonight. You were afraid that Tom was going to be ticked off at you—which he clearly was. So now you're trying to make it up to him by keeping me in your line of vision."

To her disappointment, Jack didn't even try to deny it. "You could have tried harder to lose me," he said, as if he could have cared less how the evening turned out.

"Maybe I didn't want to," Daisy baited Jack lazily. "Maybe I was curious."

The muscles in his shoulders and chest becoming more pronounced, Jack drained his root beer and tossed the can into the trash barrel next to the soda machine. He turned back to her, his expression grim. "About what?" he demanded curtly.

Daisy rubbed her bare toes against the cool concrete. She knew sparring with Jack this way was dangerous. But she couldn't help it. She needed an outlet for her anger and frustration. Like it or not, this was it. "How far you'd go—or not go, as the case might be—to please Daddy Dearest. For instance—" Able to see she was getting to Jack at long last, Daisy let her lips curve in a soft, goading smile and tossed her soda can, too. "Would you deny yourself a chance to sleep with me?" Ignoring the racing of her heart and the weak funny feeling in her knees, Daisy held Jack's eyes and undid the string tie at the back of her neck. When he didn't move—didn't react in any way—she reached behind her recklessly and released the zipper on her sundress.

Jack's expression grew even grimmer, more forbidding. Although obviously aroused, he was not in the least bit amused by her antics. "Don't do this," Jack said.

"Why not?" Wanting to annoy him the way he had her, Daisy pushed the fabric past her hips, and stepped out of it. Her heart was pounding so hard she could hear it in her ears. "Am I getting to you?"

His eyes narrowed. "Put your dress back on," he ordered roughly.

"I don't think so." Daisy reached for the clasp on her strapless bra.

He caught her hand before she could undo it. Perspiration beaded on his temple. "This won't help your situation."

Daisy laughed, softly and bitterly. "You mean it

won't help you to be caught sleeping with the boss's other daughter.''

His fingers gently encircling her wrist, he forced her hand down between them. "It wouldn't help *either* of us," he said sternly.

More tired than she could ever say, of being told what to do, think, even feel, Daisy replied back, "We'll just see about that." And before Jack Granger could respond, she stood on tiptoe, wrapped her free hand around the back of his neck, tilted his head down and pressed her lips to his.

CHAPTER THREE

JACK KNEW he could get fired for this, but he couldn't seem to stop himself from responding to the fervor of her soft lips, any more than Daisy seemed able to put an end to what she was doing. Not that Jack hadn't known going into this assignment that Daisy Templeton was wild and reckless to a fault. But this was something different, Jack realized as Daisy flattened the softness of her breasts against his chest as she kissed him. Even through the starched cotton of his shirt, and the transparent lace of her bra, he could feel her nipples budding, her skin heating.

"No," he said, tearing his mouth from hers. Afraid of what might happen if he didn't call a halt to this, and soon, he took her abruptly by the shoulders. Doing his best to keep his eyes from straying lower, to the tempting curves spilling out of her next-to-nothing underclothes, he forced her inside, to the safety of her cabin. "No."

The misery pouring out of her faded, ending the possibility that she might just burst into tears and get rid of her pent-up emotions that way. As Daisy locked glances with Jack, hurt flashed in her eyes, then defiance. And unbelievably, Jack knew he was in an even worse quandary than before. He was the protector here, the defender. Not the man who took advantage...of any woman in turmoil.

"Okay." Daisy smiled fiendishly and stepped back, reached behind her once again, and successfully unfastened her bra. She whisked it off and let it drop to the floor.

Jack immediately grew hard as a rock—like never before. He swallowed again, his whole body aching, and pretended he didn't want to give Daisy what she was asking—no, begging—for. "Cut it out," he told her grimly.

"Nope." Daisy continued to hold his gaze as she tucked her thumbs into the edges of her thong panties, and slid them down, to reveal her downy soft curls.

Jack tried to appear unaffected by Daisy's striptease, but it was impossible. She was without a doubt the most beautiful woman he had ever seen. Her skin glowed with vitality, her breasts high and full and round. Her nipples were as rosy and tempting as ripe raspberries. Her stomach flat and sexy, her mound covered with curls a shade darker than her wavy blond hair.

Delighting in his perusal, she lifted her arms above her head and stretched. Slowly, deliberately, she pirouetted, giving him ample time to study her tiny waist and curving buttocks, the long slender thighs, firm calves, trim ankles and dimpled knees. Turning all the way back to face him, she smiled again, and reached for a towel on the rack. "I think I'll go for a swim."

Not naked, she wasn't. The last thing he needed was to have her either arrested—or assaulted—on the beach. And given that even the private beaches such as this were patrolled periodically during the evenings by local law enforcement, Jack moved to block her way. "You can't do that," he told her firmly. "Not without a swimsuit."

"Sure I can. You can, too." She sashayed forward,

tucked her fingertips in the front of his trousers.
"Haven't you ever skinny-dipped?"

"Put your clothes on, Daisy. Now," he ordered
gruffly and succinctly.

"Why?" She batted her eyelashes at him flirtatiously
and continued to play the vamp. "Am I bothering
you?"

More than you could ever know.

"Just go to bed," Jack continued to suggest with
deceptive casualness. *And sleep off your hurt and your
fury.*

"Sure thing." Daisy sashayed closer in a drift of
orange-blossom perfume. "But only if you join me."

His heart thudding at the seductiveness of her smile,
Jack asked in a taut, strangled voice, "Why are you
doing this?" And why was he even considering giving
in to temptation and making her his? Especially when
he could see she was nearly as apprehensive as she was
eager.

"I think the real question is, why are you resisting?"
Daisy went up on tiptoe, linked both hands around his
neck, and like a daring kid playing a game of Truth or
Dare, pressed her nude body against the clothed length
of his.

The heat of his desire burned through Jack's skin.
And it was all he could do not to tumble her back on
the bed and see how silky wet and sweetly accommo-
dating he could make her. "You know the answer to
that." As much as he wanted to make love to her—
here, now—using her that way would hurt her, and Jack
did not want her to suffer any more pain. She'd borne
enough at the hands of her family.

Daisy's Deveraux-blue eyes glimmered with a mixture of relief and wounded pride. "What I know," she

stated in a low tone, "is that you're afraid and I'm bored. And I hate to be bored."

Her chin set stubbornly, she moved past him toward the door. Jack caught her by the arm before she could step outside the cabin. He could see that she had been torn apart inside by the lies and the betrayal. But making love out of spite was no way to fix the mess she was in. All that would do, Jack knew, besides potentially cause *him* to lose the job he had worked long and hard for, was increase her emotional devastation. Maybe not now, while blindly reaching out for any comfort or distraction she could find, but when her frustration with the situation, with those close to her, subsided, Daisy would regret her rash behavior here tonight. Of that, he was very sure. Just as he was certain he would not be able to just talk her down. "You're hell-bent on stirring up even more trouble tonight, aren't you?"

Daisy shrugged her slender shoulders, attempting unsuccessfully to break free of him once again. "I have to give them something to talk about. The way I see it—" the corners of her lips turned down mutinously "—I have just enough time to get arrested and make the morning papers."

Not on his watch, she wasn't, Jack thought. Not after what she had already pulled earlier, when she had gotten past him and crashed the Deveraux-family gathering. Using his firm but gentle grip on her wrist, he reeled her in, not stopping until she was positioned close against him once again. With his free hand, he smoothed the silky blond hair from her cheek and tilted her face up to his. They weren't even kissing yet, and he was already throbbing. "This is really what you

want?'' he said, making sure they were clear. ''To go
to bed with me?''

"Yes," Daisy said even more stubbornly. "It is. But
if you're not going to play—"

"Oh, I'll play all right," Jack said. If it was the only
way to keep her out of jail and out of the papers. "I'll
play," he repeated softly. And then he did what he had
been wanting to do for what seemed like forever. He
traced the sexy bow-shaped outline of her lips with the
pad of his thumb and slowly, deliberately, lowered his
mouth to hers.

IN THE PAST, the only thing Daisy had changed more
than her colleges or her clothes was the men in her life.
With the exception of one disastrous roll in the hay,
which was over almost before it began, she had no sexual experience with guys, save the occasional boring
kiss—and with good reason. She got rid of her dates
before they could make demands or try to get close to
her, place demands on her.

Now, as Jack Granger wrapped her in his arms and
folded her against the warm, strong length of him, kissing her hotly and thrillingly all the while, she wondered
what she had been saving herself for. It wasn't as if she
believed in marriage. Or even, at this point, love. On
the other hand, sex was supposed to be great. And Jack
Granger was the kind of man who knew what he was
doing in the sack, she reasoned securely, the kind of
man who could and would give a woman pleasure. And
right now Daisy was desperate for even a smidgen of
happiness in her life, no matter how fleeting. She
wanted that and she wanted revenge on all those who
had hurt her. Jack Granger was perfect for both. And
they both knew it.

Moaning softly, she let him guide her over to the bed. He let her go long enough to throw a sheet over the bare mattress, and while she watched, dry-mouthed and trembling, shuck his clothes. The next thing she knew, that Adonis-beautiful body was next to her again, and the two of them were tumbling down onto the bed. It had felt lumpy earlier. Now, with Jack draped overtop her, kissing her, touching her, their berth felt like sweetest heaven. She had never experienced desire like this, and an overwhelming flood of emotion swept through her, as timeless, as unstoppable as the tides, as he stroked her, gently and ephemerally, until something wonderful was happening to her, something beyond her control. And yet, even as he spread her thighs and prepared to enter her, she wasn't afraid. She could feel his iron control as he entered her with aching slowness, kissing her all the while, letting her body adjust to the size and pulsing heat of him.

He took his time possessing her, lifting her hips in his hands, adjusting the angle of penetration until it was just so, until she was kissing him back madly and rocking urgently in rhythm with him. Until he was reaching that sought-after inner place, the one guaranteed to send a woman over the edge. And he did, Daisy thought as she moaned softly and shattered and fell apart in his ever-so-capable hands.

Seconds later, Jack followed in a blissful, overpowering rush of sensation and the two of them collapsed together, breath still coming rapidly. Unhappily, though, the physical release did little to ease the deeply lonely and conflicted way Daisy was feeling inside. Too late, she realized, even having a fling with an accomplished lover would do nothing to make her forget or feel better. Oh, Jack knew the moves, all right. He could even make her come, without half trying, which was something no one else had ever even come close to doing, but he couldn't touch her heart or her soul. And without that, Daisy realized sadly, there really was no connection. Not one that meant a damn anyway. Once again, Daisy mused as she extricated her body from Jack's and curled onto her side, facing away from him, she was adrift and alone. She knew who she was now, where she'd come from. She'd even made love with a man successfully. But sadly, nothing of importance in her life had changed.

TOM SLEPT very little during the night. At 6:00 a.m., he finally got up and shaved, showered and dressed. Going down to the kitchen, he found Theresa getting a tray of lemon-blueberry muffins out of the oven. He nodded at the sugary confection. "Pack a half dozen or so of those in a paper bag for me, please."

Theresa did as he asked and handed it to him wordlessly. Relieved his longtime housekeeper was sensitive enough to appear not to recall what had happened the night before, Tom murmured his thanks and walked out to his Jaguar.

Banking on the fact that Grace had been no more able to rest than he, given the tumultuous turn their lives had taken, Tom drove the short distance through the downtown Historic District of residential homes to the single house Grace had leased from their daughter-in-law, Lauren. As usual, parking in the area was limited. It took him a while to find a space. When he did, he doubled back to her place, saw a light on upstairs and what looked to be movement behind the lacy white curtains. Feeling more confident now—that his ex-wife was not only awake but up, he took his cell phone out of his pocket and dialed. Grace picked up on the second ring. Working to conceal his uneasiness, he said, "It's me. I'm on the front stoop."

He stepped back so she could see him. Saw the curtains part. He lifted the bag of muffins and continued speaking quietly into the phone. "I brought breakfast. We need to talk, Grace."

"Tom..." Just one word. Her reluctance was evident.

Refusing to take no for an answer, Tom said, "Come to the door, Grace," and severed the connection before she could argue further.

Seconds later, he saw a slender silhouette coming down the stairs through the frosted glass on either side of the portal. The lock turned and the door opened. Grace was in a satin robe and, it appeared, to Tom's discomfort, little else. Her cheeks were flushed, her lips unusually red, almost chapped. "This isn't a good time."

It was a perfect time, Tom disagreed silently, aware all over again how sexy Grace was when she had just tumbled out of bed, with her hair mussed and her eyes still soft with slumber. Their divorce had done nothing to limit his desire for her. Tom knew he would always want her. Even if she never again wanted him. That was just the way it was.

Grace continued to regard Tom resentfully.

Which wasn't a surprise to Tom, either.

For years, he and Grace had had this secret hanging over them, curtailing their closeness. Now that Daisy's parentage was out in the open, at least as far as the family went, anyway, the two of them could finally begin dealing with his infidelity and Daisy's presence in their lives. Tom knew there was anger and disappointment in him among Grace and their kids, but even that was probably less than the disappointment he felt in himself. Even now, years later, he found it difficult to believe he had been foolish enough to throw it all away for one clandestine tumble in the sack. But he had, and like it or not, they all had to deal with that, and hopefully, at long last, just move on.

"I still want to come in," Tom repeated flatly. Not waiting for an invitation that was unlikely to come anyway, he brushed past her.

"I don't think that's a good idea," a low male voice said.

Tom stopped, shocked, and looked up. A buff, long-haired man the same age as their sons stood at the top of the stairs. He was naked except for the towel around his waist as he came down the stairs, acting more like the man of the house than Grace's yoga instructor.

The color in Grace's cheeks went from pink to white. She held out an imploring hand. "Paulo, please."

Jealousy ripping through his gut, a muscle working in his cheek, Tom swung back around to his ex-wife. "A little early for a naked yoga lesson, isn't it?" he asked sarcastically before he could stop himself.

"She asked you to go," Paulo said as he joined them at the foot of the stairs.

"Gladly," Tom said. Feeling as if he'd been kicked in the gut by a mule, Tom thrust the bag of baked goods at Grace and said sourly, "Enjoy your breakfast."

Pushing Paulo aside with one hand, Grace followed Tom out onto the stoop. "Tom…"

When he kept going, her delicate hand curved around his arm, tightening until she stopped his flight. Tom tensed. Whatever she was going to say, he didn't want to hear it. He continued looking out at the street. "We're even, right?"

Grace moved around, so Tom had no choice but to look into her face. "What do you mean?" she asked, clearly upset.

Tom pried her fingers from his bicep. He stepped back a pace. "You paid me back. In spades."

Hurt flashed in her eyes at his low, brutal tone. Her lower lip trembled with resentment. "I don't know what you're talking about."

Didn't she? Tom wondered. "You caught me with Iris. Now I've caught you screwing Paulo. We're even, okay?"

"You don't have to be crude," she admonished coldly.

Tom lowered his face to hers, his mood more dangerous than it had been in years. "And what should I be, Grace?" he retorted caustically, wanting to wound her the way she had just hurt him. "Understanding? You sure as hell weren't!"

Grace compressed her lips together tightly. "We were married then," she reminded Tom angrily.

And we should still be married now, Tom thought bitterly. If she hadn't been so damn stubborn and unforgiving. The cell phone in his pocket began to ring. Tom looked at the caller ID screen, saw it was Jack Granger. Probably with news about Daisy. "I have to get this," he said.

"Of course." Grace abruptly turned on her heel and headed back toward Paulo, who was lounging in the portal.

Good thing, too, Tom noted, because other residents on the street were beginning to stir. Interior lights going on, exterior lights going off. Others stepping out to get their morning paper and head to work or out for a jog. Turning his back to Grace and Paulo, Tom answered the call and demanded, "Yeah, what do you have?"

"Daisy spent the night or most of it at the Paradise Resort on Folly Island," Jack replied, sounding no less stressed and out of sorts than Tom felt.

Tom frowned. "I thought they closed that eyesore last year, when the owner died."

"They did. The new owner is fixing it up. She's a friend of Daisy's and she let us both stay here, although the accommodations are less than stellar."

"Are you still there?"

A brief hesitation on the other end. "Yes."

"I'll be there in fifteen minutes." Tom ended the call, then turned back to his ex-wife, who was scowling at him as resentfully as ever.

"Just go," Grace said, indicating with a lift of her hand she didn't want to hear it. Figuring he'd had enough turmoil for one morning, Tom did as she asked and headed back for the Jaguar. What the hell had he been thinking? Tom berated himself grumpily as he drove away. Hoping Grace might finally be willing to work through this problem if not actually forgive him for a misjudgment? Nearly twenty-four years had passed since he'd been with Iris and his ex was still out to punish him, as readily as if it had happened the day before. His involvement with Iris Templeton would never be forgiven. Not ever.

JACK GRANGER WAS WAITING for Tom outside cabin five. He was unshaven, bleary-eyed and wearing the same clothes he'd had on the night before. Not, Tom thought, necessarily a good sign. "Where is she?" Tom demanded, anxious to talk to Daisy. Alone this time. Father to daughter.

"I don't know," Jack admitted reluctantly, his low voice as grim as Tom's mood. "She took off with my SUV, one of my credit cards and all my cash sometime during the night."

In all the years Jack had worked for Tom, Tom had never known Jack to be foolish or careless. "How the hell did she manage that?" he demanded.

"I don't know," Jack said, sounding even more uncomfortable as he tugged at the knot of his tie. "I was asleep when it happened."

Tom blinked. "With the door unlocked?"

Jack flushed with embarrassment and looked all the more chastened as he admitted reluctantly, "We were…uh, in the same cabin."

The bad mood Tom had put on hold reared up again. Hands knotted in fists at his sides, he glared at Jack. "You spent the night in the same cabin with my daughter?"

Jack shrugged, the guilty look in his eyes increasing. "That wreck of a car she's been driving lately broke down. She wanted to come here. I gave her a lift. She checked into cabin six. I checked into cabin five. She was upset and about to do something really reckless and crazy."

"And you stopped her," Tom guessed.

Jack looked away before admitting, "Yeah."

"How?" Tom asked, not liking the sound of this, not one bit.

Silence.

"Don't tell me you slept with her."

What the hell was Jack supposed to say to that? He wanted to protect Daisy and keep what had happened between them strictly between the two of them. But he couldn't lie to the man who he had looked up to as a trusted mentor. Especially when he knew, given her impetuous nature, that Daisy would probably announce the tryst to her biological father anyway.

Figuring it would be best coming from him, Jack reluctantly owned up to his mistake. "I—we—didn't mean for it to happen," Jack said, knowing all the while that even if the impulsive one-night stand had meant something to him, it had been nothing more than yet another form of payback for Daisy.

"The hell you didn't," Tom exploded as his fist came flying toward Jack.

Too stunned and disbelieving to duck, Jack took a right cross on the jaw. The impact knocked him off his feet and sent him flying into the exterior cabin wall. The next thing Jack knew, he was lying on the ground. Tom was standing over him, fists clenched, more angry and disapproving than Jack had ever seen him. Chest heaving, Tom instructed fiercely, "I don't care what you have to do, but you find her, goddamn it. And when you do—" Tom paused, to let his words sink in "—you bring her to see me."

BUCKY JEROME'S FATHER was waiting for him when he arrived at the *Charleston Herald* newspaper offices at five minutes after eight that morning.

With a pointed look at the clock to let his son know he was late and a jerk of his severely balding head, Adlai Jerome motioned Bucky into his office. Adlai gave Bucky another long assessing look, focusing on Bucky's spiked black hair, rumpled khaki's and trendy shirt, letting Bucky know he didn't approve of his son's "look" any more than he liked Bucky's writing. Which was no surprise, Bucky thought, sighing inwardly. He and his "button-up-shirt-and-tie" father had been at odds as long as he could remember. "I'm putting you on the society beat," Adlai said.

The society beat! His entire 5'8" frame stiffening with tension, Bucky plopped down on the leather sofa in the publisher's office and stared at his father, knowing Adlai too well to think this was a joke. His dad was one of the original hard-asses, loaded with money in his own right but determined to own and manage the paper that had been in their family for generations, instead of selling out—for millions—to one of the big chains. Bucky respected his father's determination to make it on his own regardless of their family's personal wealth. He didn't like Adlai's theory that everyone—whatever their pedigree—must begin their work career at the very bottom.

Adlai shrugged and gave Bucky a look, like, What did you expect? "You said you wanted off the obits," Adlai explained, "so I'm moving you to the society page. Specifically, the 'Around the City' column."

He'd gone to Duke and worked his ass off for four years for this? "Shirley Rossey already writes that," Bucky argued, not about to take what he considered a demotion lying down.

"Not anymore." Adlai took a sip of inky-black coffee, poured from the pot in the newsroom that was, Bucky knew, almost never washed. Just filled and refilled and refilled again. Which, of course, made any coffee brewed in it taste like something from the bottom of a trash barrel.

"She's being bumped up to lifestyles editor," Adlai continued explaining in the don't-give-me-any-crap tone he always used with Bucky. "I'm promoting from within instead of hiring from the outside. So you're it, Bucky." Adlai looked at Bucky over the rim of his *Charleston Herald* mug, which was washed almost as much as the pot. "I want you covering every event. And be sure you take lots of photos. The folks in Charleston like to see their pictures in the paper, especially when they are all gussied up."

Bucky scowled at his father and gripped the double latte he'd gotten at Starbucks on his way over. "This isn't fair," he told Adlai grimly. "I want to do something important."

Adlai dropped into his swivel chair and turned his attention back to the stack of papers on his desk. "You want to run this paper someday, you've got to learn it from the ground up, just like I did. And that means working every single department, Bucky."

When Adlai had first laid out the deal to his son, Bucky hadn't taken his father literally on that particular point. He'd figured after his initial mind-numbing stint in the classifieds sales office last summer that he'd work as a reporter for like a year, and then move into the editorial offices alongside his father. Too late, he was beginning to see that might never happen. That he should have tried harder to find a job on one of the big city papers when he had graduated from Duke instead of returning to Charleston.

Desperately, Bucky tried to change his father's mind. "You promised me the police beat."

"And you'll get it," Adlai agreed smoothly, taking another sip of coffee, "just as soon as you learn how to make even the most mundane interesting."

Bucky scowled, knowing it would be futile to argue further. Once his father had made up his mind, that was that.

"And concentrate on getting as many under forty mentions as those forty and above," Adlai cautioned as Bucky pushed to his feet. "We've had complaints recently that section of the paper is getting too stodgy."

No kidding, Bucky thought, trying hard to think how to turn this situation around. The assignment might not be what he wanted, but he was certain if he was smart, he could make it work to their mutual advantage just the same. After all, where there was smoke there was fire and where there was a lot of money there was usually scandal. It was just up to him to uncover it. "Assuming I take this position," *rather than quit,* "you'll give me free rein? I can write it like the gossip columnists in the New York City newspapers?"

Already losing interest in the conversation, Adlai began booting up his computer. "You have to concentrate on the people who actually live here or are visiting the Charleston area. But yes, as long as it's not actionable, or too editorialish, you can do what you want. Your goal should be to get people so excited about reading 'Around the City' that they'll turn to that section of the newspaper the moment they pick up their papers."

Bucky knew that was the same stock advice his father gave to all the journalists on his paper, with the exception of the obits. There, Adlai just cautioned that the items should be the best obits—the most concise, loving and compassionate—anyone had ever read. But Bucky was going to take Adlai's advice to heart anyway, and use the column to make a name for himself.

"Who knows," Adlai continued in an obvious effort to motivate Bucky to do his best, "if it's good enough, snippets of your column could even get picked up and run in other papers, too."

He was right about that, Bucky mused. They did have

at least one national celebrity in their midst. Grace Deveraux. Who, rumor had it, was currently seeing some model-type half her age. If he could get something on that, something factual and not actionable, proving the relationship wasn't just a platonic one, maybe it would get picked up by other newspapers. Or get him noticed by one of the big outfits in New York City.

Adlai handed Bucky a typewritten sheet of paper. "Here's a list of society parties and other gala events this week. Make sure you put in an appearance at all of them."

"No problem," Bucky said, his spirits already lifting as he savored the excitement and notoriety ahead. Adlai might think he'd just given Bucky a low-level assignment, but nothing could have been further from the truth.

CHAPTER FOUR

"So, SHE GOT YOUR SUV, your AMEX card and three hundred in cash from your wallet," Harlan Decker stated as he sat back in his swivel chair and lit a cigar.

Jack nodded and looked over at the casually dressed private investigator, feeling damn embarrassed. As always, the burly ex-cop was dressed like a tourist, in a loud shirt, knee-length plaid shorts, wide-brimmed straw hat, knee-high crew socks and well-worn running shoes. He had a camera slung around his neck and a street map sticking out of his shirt pocket. His face and neck were sunburned, his gray hair damp with perspiration from the heat and humidity outside. Jack knew Harlan's disguise worked like a charm—Harlan could wander in practically anywhere, look a little lost and distracted, and not be paid any mind. He was also an ace at both uncovering and keeping secrets.

Too tense to stay seated for any length of time, Jack got up to pace the P.I.'s office. Knowing he could trust Harlan to guard the Deveraux family and shipping company's reputation the way he always had, Jack warned, "Tom doesn't want any publicity. This is a private family matter. He wants it to stay that way."

Harlan's glance cut to the bruise on Jack's face. Too discreet to inquire how *that* might have occurred, Harlan picked up his pen and asked, "How much money did Miss Templeton have on her own, do you know?"

"Probably not much," Jack predicted, worrying a little about that. The lack of ready cash, combined with her need to stay hidden, could lead Daisy to some dives that were not necessarily safe. Jack didn't want to think about anything happening to her, especially when he was the one who had prompted her to take off the way she had. If only he had been able to walk away from temptation and contain his lust for her.... The situation might be very different now. Jack let out a long, self-effacing breath, aware Harlan was waiting for him to continue. "As you probably already know, since you just got finished doing a job for Daisy yourself, the Templetons cut Daisy off weeks ago and she just returned from several weeks in Switzerland that, according to Amy, had Daisy down to her last couple of bucks."

Harlan made a note on the pad in front of him. "I'll start checking the airports and train stations, but my guess is she's still driving your SUV."

That was Jack's theory, too.

"Less chance of her movements being traced."

And more of a chance of being arrested and creating a situation embarrassing to both families. If there was one thing Daisy Templeton was interested in, it was payback. And Jack had the feeling she wouldn't rest until she'd gotten it. Knowing how upset she still was and, Jack admitted reluctantly, probably had every right to be, he slid his hands in his pockets and looked out the window at the parking lot below. In retrospect, he knew he should have expected Daisy would pull something after they made love. He should have talked to her, tried to work things out verbally. Or at least try to discuss what had just happened between them. But like an infatuated fool, he had figured conversation could wait until morning and wrapped her in his arms and held her until she—they both—fell asleep.

Now, thanks to his lack of foresight, Daisy was out there somewhere, feeling the way he had for as long as he could remember—like no one had ever really loved her, or ever would. Like she was a source of shame, existing only to sully the family honor. And that was a miserable way to live, Jack knew.

"Eventually, though," Harlan continued pragmatically, "she'll start working somewhere and have to use her social security number, or she'll have to start charging on your credit card."

And that was how they would locate her. "I'll check my American Express account daily for any transactions," Jack promised, his customary confidence beginning to return.

"And I'll start looking for her right away," Harlan retorted with a narrow glance. "How fast I find her will depend on just how badly she doesn't want to be found."

PAULO LIFTED HIS LIPS from Grace's breast, the frustration he felt evident on his face. "Why are you pretending?"

Grace's skin warmed self-consciously. She shifted away from Paulo and tugged the sheet upward to cover her nakedness. "I don't know what you mean," she said in the cool polite voice she used to keep people at bay.

"Last night. This morning." Like a scientist in the midst of a perplexing experiment, Paulo stroked his hand across her belly. "You merely pretended to feel pleasure. Why?"

A shiver of revulsion ghosted over her insides.

"What makes you think that's the case?" Grace tried hard to keep the defensiveness out of her voice. And how was it this man knew what Tom had never once guessed in all their years of marriage?

"You moan, you sigh, you go through the motions, but you're not wet here unless I wet you with my tongue." Paulo gently caressed her between the thighs, and Grace felt…nothing. Except the wish he would stop touching her. "Your nipples bead when I touch them but you don't tremble with arousal. Instead, you fake it. And I want to know why," Paulo insisted. "I want to know if it's me, if it's something I'm not doing or should be doing to excite you, or if it's just that you can't relax the way you want to right now."

Her body taut with equal parts frustration and embarrassment, she sat up and swung her legs over the side of the bed. "I think you should leave." She didn't talk about this. Never had. Never would. Her mother had been right. Sex was dirty. Meant for bringing children into the world and little else, except maybe a man's gratification.

"Grace—"

"I mean it, Paulo." Grace reached for her satin robe and shrugged the sensual fabric over her shoulders, loving the way it felt, the way she had never loved a man's touch. Feeling more humiliated than she had when she'd been fired, she continued in a low, flat tone, "Being with you was a mistake. I was just too caught up with emotion to tell you, and that was wrong on my part." Despite their failure to bring each other genuine pleasure, she was grateful to the sensual young man for trying, for being so patient with her, even when it didn't work. She swallowed around the lump of emotion in her throat. "I'm sorry." She didn't know why she had even tried this, after years of abstinence, after being with no one but Tom. She looked her yoga instructor in the eye, knowing after what had just happened those lessons were going to have to end, too, because she would never be able to have his hands on her again without thinking about this. And she didn't want to think about this, any more than she wanted to think about all the times she had put aside her dislike of sex and feigned enjoyment with Tom.

She swallowed hard around the tight knot of emotion in her throat, even as she yearned for a long hot cleansing shower, the kind that had relaxed her so much in the past. "If you think I led you on—"

Paulo shook his head. He stood and, taking her cue, began to dress, as well. "I knew when Tom showed up this morning what the problem was." Paulo looked sad but not surprised. "You're still in love with him, aren't you?"

Grace didn't respond. But then, she thought sadly as she put on her slippers and exited the bedroom, she didn't have to. Everyone knew the answer to that, just as they knew their marriage never had, and never would, work. The problems she and Tom had had in the bedroom—with her not wanting him, and him eventually not wanting her, either—had only been the half of it. She had two things she could count on to make her happy—her kids and her work. And that was it.

GRACE SPENT the next week and a half immersing herself in her work. At the soundstage, she was overseeing the construction of the kitchen, bedroom and livingroom sets for her new television show, when Amy came to see her. Grace knew immediately there was trouble—

she could tell by the pinched look on her only daughter's face.

"Mom, I'm worried about Dad."

Grace did not want to talk about Tom, and especially not at the soundstage, with various grips, cameramen and set designers around. Grace put the fabric swatches for the sofas aside and regarded her daughter stoically. "Amy, I'm trying to work here," Grace murmured with as much patience as she could muster, and it wasn't a lot.

Amy took her mother by the elbow and led Grace over to a deserted corner of the warehouselike building, where *At Home with Grace* was going to be taped. Ignoring Grace's wish they save this for later, Amy continued anxiously, "He hasn't gone to the office for ten days."

Grace smiled at Amy as if they were discussing something as mundane and happy as Amy's imminent need of a shopping expedition for maternity clothes. "I suspect he's probably long overdue for a vacation."

Amy clamped her arms over her gently rounded belly and regarded Grace mutinously. "He isn't taking a vacation."

Grace put up a hand to ward off the approach of a staff member and continued talking to Amy. "Then what is he doing?"

Amy sighed, her blue eyes abruptly filling with unshed tears. "Not much of anything from what any of us can tell," she said in a low, quavering voice.

Grace knew Amy was more emotional now—the hormones of pregnancy ensured that—but that didn't mean Grace would change her feelings when it came to her ex. "Honey," Grace said as gently as possible, "this isn't my concern." And she didn't want it to be, ever again.

"Then who else is going to get Daddy off the yacht?"

Grace blinked. Amy had lost her. "What are you talking about?"

Amy drew a tremulous breath. "Apparently, after the party, Daddy didn't leave the house for about three days. He didn't shave or shower, he just sat in the library brooding and drinking. Theresa was concerned— she wanted to call a doctor. Daddy wouldn't let her, so she called Mitch and he went over and found Dad. Not drunk but not exactly sober, either. Dad wouldn't talk to him. So Mitch called Gabe and Gabe went over."

"And?" Grace prodded anxiously. If anyone would be able to tell if there was something medically wrong, causing Tom—the epitome of tranquillity under stress—to behave that way, Grace knew it would have been Gabe.

Amy shrugged. "Gabe said that medically there was nothing wrong with Daddy—he wasn't clinically depressed—he was just totally devastated."

"Well, he's allowed to take a break," Grace said, telling herself Tom's emotional state had nothing to do with finding Paulo at her place, and everything to do with being identified as a philanderer to his grown children.

Amy laid a hand over her heart. "That's what we all thought initially. But now that it's been going on for nearly two weeks, we're beginning to get scared."

Grace had to agree, that didn't sound like Tom. Not at all. Even in the midst of the divorce and their darkest days together, he had never taken off work. But instead had sought solace and refuge in his work, just as Grace was doing now.

Grace paused, still trying to make sense of Tom's actions. "Is he taking the yacht out?" Tom did love to go boating, always had. And it was an affection he had passed on to all their children.

"Occasionally." Amy stuck her hands in the front of her overalls, which were emblazoned with the name of her redecorating business. "Mostly he just sits on the yacht and broods."

That didn't sound good, but it didn't sound lethal, either. Grace sighed and for the benefit of staff around them kept the carefully composed smile on her face. "Have you talked to your father about this?"

Amy hesitated. She ducked her head, studying the toe of her sneaker. "I haven't seen him."

Grace wasn't surprised. In the past, when she and Tom had been quarreling, their children had pretty much run for the hills and tried to stay as far away from any familial turmoil as they could. None of them had wanted to take sides in Grace and Tom's marital problems, and Grace couldn't blame them. Their mutual anger and resentment had been hard enough for her and Tom to deal with. Neither of them had wished it on their children. Besides, their four kids—five if you counted Daisy now for Tom—had their own problems, careers and lives to attend to, and each other to go to for comfort and counsel. But, Grace determined that didn't mean Amy could identify a problem, dump it on Grace's doorstep and then run away. "If you're so concerned—and I can see that you are—why haven't you seen your dad?" Grace asked quietly.

Amy's chin took on a petulant tilt and her eyes glowed with blue fire. "Because I'm still mad at him,

and I don't want to make things worse, and anyway—
Nick said I should wait until I cool off and can listen
objectively to what Daddy has to say about what happened.''

That sounded like Amy's husband, Grace thought,
realizing all over again how glad she was that Nick was
now a member of the Deveraux clan. Nick had not only
helped Grace find a new career path to take in the wake
of her firing from *Rise and Shine, America!* by signing
her to do a television show for his production company,
he had given Amy the tenderness, stability and practical
guidance Grace's ever-so-romantic daughter needed to
remain grounded and optimistic.

"But honestly, I don't know when that will be.
Chase, Mitch, Gabe and I have had several discussions
about this, and we are all still very mad at him—even
Mitch—who is Dad's lieutenant in just about everything. I mean, all these years we thought you were responsible for the divorce, that you going to New York
City to take the job when you knew Dad's work and
all our lives were here in Charleston, was what caused
the breakup. But now we know the truth.'' Amy's voice
dropped to an anguished murmur as the production staff
and construction workers continued to give Grace and
Amy wide berth. "We know what Daddy did to you.
And we still can't believe that he slept with Iris Templeton! My God!'' Amy's eyes welled with tears once
again.

Grace saw the disillusionment in her daughter's eyes,
remembered full well how that felt, and her heart went
out to her. "Oh, Amy, honey—'' Grace put her arm
around Amy's shoulders.

"And poor Daisy,'' Amy interrupted before Grace

could comfort her further. "She's apparently disap-peared, too."

Grace paused as that news sank in. "What do you mean, disappeared?" Grace demanded uneasily.

Amy drew a deep, quavering breath. "She took off with Jack Granger's SUV and his credit card, and she even stole some cash out of his wallet. They've got that P.I. Dad likes—Harlan Decker—looking for her, but there's no telling how long it will be before they find her."

As always, the mention of Tom's illegitimate child, and the problems Daisy perpetually seemed to cause, ignited a core of resentment within Grace. Try as she might, she couldn't see the young woman as anything but proof of Tom's betrayal. But figuring Amy didn't need to know that, Grace turned the conversation back to Tom once again. "I'm the last person your father would want to see right now."

Amy shrugged. "That may be true, Mom." Her voice dropped beseechingly. "But you're probably also the only person who can help."

TOM HAD FIGURED Grace would show up sooner or later—he figured the kids would send her. So it was no surprise when she walked across the gangplank onto his yacht at 5:00 p.m. Thursday evening. Unlike Tom, who was wearing only a pair of navy-blue swim trunks and a pair of sunglasses, she looked pretty and professional in a white silk pantsuit. She also looked irked, and she didn't waste any time starting in on him, either. "What do you think you're doing?" she demanded, propping her hands on her hips.

Tom continued disassembling the reel he'd been working on. "Exactly what it looks like, I'm repairing my fishing rod." It had taken a heck of a beating the last ten days or so, given the way he'd been using it.

Grace strode closer, her high heels clicking across the deck. She held a hand above her eyes to protect them from the glare of the sun. "People are going to start to talk."

Tom shrugged. Like he gave a damn about that.

When he made no move to defend or explain himself, Grace released a short, aggravated breath, dragged a deck chair over and sat down beside him. She leaned forward. "Do you really want to disillusion our children any more than you already have with this extended vacation of yours?"

If Tom didn't know better, he would've thought she cared about him, given the way she was acting. "Is that what I'm doing?" he asked dryly. He reached down into the toolbox beside him for a pair of pliers.

Grace huffed and spoke between tightly gritted teeth. "If you stay out here on the boat much longer, people will realize you're not just taking a much-deserved few days off from work."

Reassuring his ex would have been easy, but Tom decided not to tell Grace he had already determined he would return to work the following day, the Deveraux mansion that very night. After all, it wasn't her business what he did, just as it wasn't his business what she did.

Grimacing as the reel refused to cooperate with him, he decided to remind her she was hardly one to talk. "I'm surprised you were able to tear yourself away from your young lover."

Pink color that had nothing to do with the summer heat and humidity flooded Grace's cheeks. "I won't discuss Paulo with you."

Tom nodded gravely. "And no wonder," he returned

sarcastically, "since being with *him* makes *you* a hypocrite."

Grace's eyes flashed with anger. "Me?"

Tom dropped both the reel and the pliers into the toolbox and reached into the cooler beside him for a beer. Eyes on Grace, he shook the excess water off the bottle and twisted open the top. "Weren't you the one who always said that sex was something sacred, only to be embarked upon within the love and sanctity of marriage?"

Since their divorce, Tom noted, that view obviously hadn't lasted. Not that Tom had been a saint, either, in the fifteen years he and Grace had been apart. He had made love to a dozen women over the years, enduring everything from a single one-night stand to a relationship that had lasted almost four months. But none of the entanglements had been satisfying, because he hadn't loved any of the women, not the way he had once loved Grace.

Grace stood, her slender shoulders stiffening. "This isn't helping."

You're telling me. It had been days now and all he could think of was Grace naked beneath that robe, her young gigolo standing there in a towel. Had Paulo discovered how spectacular her body was? Had she kissed him back like she meant it, or had she simply endured her young lover's caresses, the way she had often tolerated his?

Grace clamped her lips together. "You have no right to comment on my actions." She glared at Tom resentfully. "We're not married anymore."

Tom stared right back at her. "But you felt compelled to flaunt your affair with that guy in my face anyway," Tom noted bitterly as he ran his hand across his jaw, which was scraggly with a beard. His gut twisting with jealousy, Tom took another sip then set his bottle down beside him and turned his attention back to his reel.

"I didn't ask you to show up at my place at the crack of dawn," Grace continued, defending herself.

Not buying her excuse, Tom stopped rethreading the reel and regarded Grace steadily. "After what had happened the night before, you knew I would come to see you as soon as I could, to talk about Daisy and our four kids. Not that the other morning was the first time. You've been with that overrated, overpriced gigolo for weeks now!" And it killed Tom because he had thought—hoped—the relationship was just a flirtation, that at heart it was platonic. How foolish had that fantasy been?

Grace turned her face to the breeze.

Tom watched the soft blond layers of Grace's hair get whipped around sexily by the salt-scented wind. "Being with him that way is wrong," he snapped grimly. *And you know it.*

A mixture of shock and fury widened her eyes as she turned back to him. "Says who?" Grace advanced on him emotionally, looking as though she was tempted to haul off and hit him. "You?" She poked her index finger against his bare chest. "The arbiter of extramarital sex? Please." Grace threw up both hands in aggravation. "You've squired your share of young and beautiful women around since we split. And for all I know, even before we separated."

That was unfair but typical, Tom thought. He stood, and really pissed off now, squared off with her. "I was only unfaithful to you once," he said.

"And since?" Grace queried, arching her delicate blond eyebrows at him.

It was Tom's turn to move his glance away. A muscle working convulsively in his jaw, he shifted to the harbor beyond. "You left me, remember?"

"For good reason, if you recall," she reminded him.

Tom shook his head in exasperation. "Yeah, because you put a wall between us."

"We had children, a home together…" She spoke as if she didn't believe he was turning the tables on her.

But Tom knew it was the truth. And he knew, whether she liked it or not, it was past time his wife faced just how cold and unaffectionate she had been prior to his interlude with Iris. "Yes, Grace, you distanced yourself from me."

"I was depressed! Finding out I was sterile was a devastating blow."

Or an excuse. Tom tread nearer, trying not to recall how much he had wanted to make love to her then, how much—despite everything—he still did. "We already had four children, Grace."

"Five," Grace countered miserably, "if you count the baby we lost when I miscarried, the year after Amy was born."

"But you wanted more, didn't you?" Tom remembered bleakly. And when she couldn't have them, she had completely turned away from him, in her heart and in their marriage.

"We both wanted more kids. Half a dozen, remember?" Grace's voice became a strangled sob as she forged on. "Only I couldn't because of the complications I had after the miscarriage. But that didn't stop you, did it?" Her eyes gleamed with hurt as she reminded, "Because you went right on to have another child without me—you had Daisy."

Tom saw it all—the jealousy, envy, resentment—that another woman had given him what Grace no longer could. "That was never meant to be more than one night," he told her with gut-wrenching honesty.

Grace stared at him and slowly shook her head, appearing as if she could hardly believe his naiveté. "That night created a child, Tom. It destroyed our family." Tears flooded her eyes and rolled down her cheeks. "But you can't admit that to yourself even now, can you? You persist in saying and feeling I should just get over it."

Tom swallowed hard. "Why can't you?" he demanded, feeling more frustrated than ever.

Grace threw her hands up. "You know why I can't! Because you betrayed me."

Tom clamped down on his own hurt. Jaw set, he said, "I made a mistake." It had been a bad one, yes. But it should not have ended their marriage.

"You ripped my heart in two," Grace accused with insurmountable bitterness.

And, Tom thought sadly, she had never allowed him to put it back together again.

Grace turned away from him and walked over to the edge of the deck. Her back to the marina, she stared out at the harbor, and the coming together of the Ashley and Cooper Rivers. "It doesn't matter anyway," she said in a low, defeated voice.

Tom crossed to her side. Hands on her shoulders, he turned her resisting body to face him. "How can you say that?" he asked hoarsely. Didn't she understand—would she never understand—his heart had been ripped into pieces, too?

"Because—" Grace turned her sad eyes up to his and continued dejectedly "—it would've happened eventually anyway." She paused, shook her head in silent remonstration. "My grief and depression were just an excuse to do what you already wanted to do in your heart, Tom, what you had probably always wanted to do, which was forget the wife you had at home and bed down with some young, rich and sexy society girl."

"That's not true. It was *you*, Grace, who didn't want *me*."

Anger flared at the corners of her mouth. "Will you stop blaming me for what you did that night?" She balled her hands into fists. "You walked out on me, Tom. You answered Iris's distress call and went to her apartment. You unzipped your pants, took off your trousers, and you were with her. And you probably would've kept right on seeing her if I hadn't found you two."

Tom knew it had been an ugly time. All because he'd had too much pride to go to Grace and tell her how lonely—how bereft and shut out—he felt. He should have gotten down on his knees and begged her to love him again. Instead, he had allowed himself to become angry, vengeful. And looked to another woman, who was just as needy and unhappy in her own way, for comfort. And for that, Tom would always blame himself. Just as virulently as Grace blamed him.

Mustering what little patience he had left, Tom explained, "You know I regret what happened that night with all my heart and soul. As for the rest…I stayed with you because I wanted to work it out."

"No," Grace corrected. "You stayed with me because you didn't want to lose custody of your kids or hurt your business or let your infidelity become public knowledge!''

What could Tom say to that? It was true. He hadn't wanted any of those things to happen. He hadn't wanted their life to fall apart, any more than it already had. And a divorce would have ensured even more misery than they had already suffered.

''So now you're blaming me for wanting to stay married to you, is that it?''

''I am blaming you for destroying our family!'' She advanced on him, voice breaking, looking if possible even more dejected and disillusioned with the situation they had found themselves in years ago. ''You never should have cheated on me—on us—no matter how rejected you felt or what the situation was with us at the time. You should have done whatever we had to do to work it out and make our marriage strong and enduring instead of turning to someone else to warm your bed. And most of all—'' she began to cry ''—you should have *honored* the vows that we took, the promises we made to love each other and only each other for as long as we both live. Because if you had—if you had acted less selfishly—we would still be together now. And somewhere deep inside, Tom, you have to know that.''

Tom's heart exploded with anger. He was tired of being painted the only wrong-doer here, tired of making apologies that fell on deaf ears. Tired of not being given the opportunity to make it up to her. ''You know I'd do anything if I could take back what happened,'' he said huskily, near breaking down himself. ''But I can't.''

Grace withdrew into herself, into the place where he had no hope of reaching her. ''No,'' she said before assuming her on-air television personality, "you can't."

"And that pleases you," Tom accused.

Grace stared at him as if she couldn't possibly have heard right. "What?"

"Let's be honest here, Grace." Tom decided to cut the courtesy and lay all their cards on the table. "This wasn't all bad news to you. You *wanted* an excuse to lock me out of your heart and keep me out of your bed. Because all you ever wanted me for was the big house and the cushy lifestyle and the kids."

Grace gasped in indignation. "That's not true!"

"Isn't it?" Tom lifted his eyebrow. As much as he loathed to admit it, he knew the truth. "You were never happy being my wife, Grace, even *before* Iris."

Grace looked at him then as if she had never known him at all. "Maybe because back then that's all I was. I needed a career. I needed—"

"Self-esteem?"

Grace reeled backward, as if he had slapped her. "You knew a career was important to me when you married me!"

"And I also knew it shouldn't have mattered that you grew up in a small town, the daughter of parents who owned and ran a dry-cleaning store," Tom said bitterly. He looked at his ex-wife, his heart aching. "You were everything to me, Grace. Everything. But you never let yourself believe it."

"WELL?" Chase said when Grace met her son and his new wife for dinner at a popular downtown-Charleston restaurant.

Chase had come straight from the offices of *Modern Man* magazine, and was dressed, as usual, in pleated khaki trousers and a short-sleeve linen shirt perfect for the balmy September weather. Bridgett, a financial advisor, and noted author in her own right, was wearing a trim black skirt and silky black-and-white cardigan set. Grace smiled. The two of them looked so strikingly handsome together. Chase, with his wavy dark-brown hair, lively slate-blue eyes and tanned athletic presence. Bridgett, with her auburn hair, deep chocolate eyes and slender feminine frame. And more important, Grace thought, they were happy. And so much in love with each other, it filled her heart with joy.

Grace sat down and spread her napkin across her lap. "I didn't get anywhere with him, either."

"So he's still on the yacht." Chase returned to his own seat after helping Grace with her chair.

Grace nodded at both Bridgett and Chase, marveling again at how happy—how very much in love—they looked. "Yes," she said quietly. "But you'll be relieved to know that your father's not drinking so much as brooding." Feeling sorry for himself, angry at the world, at her.

Chase scowled as he opened the menu. "I'd go try and talk to him myself but I want to slug him."

Having already decided what she wanted—the crab soup and a salad—Grace closed her menu wearily. Chase was her strongest defender, as well as her firstborn and oldest son, but in this case he was also dead wrong. She regarded her son steadily and said, "This isn't your fight, Chase. It's mine."

Chase clenched his jaw, at that moment looking very much like his incredibly strong-willed and stubborn father. "Wrong, Mom." Fierce resentment gleamed in Chase's slate-blue eyes. "When Dad betrayed you, he betrayed the whole family."

Grace sighed and shook her head. "You still have to forgive him," she advised calmly.

"Why?" Chase challenged. "You obviously haven't, and it's been what—more than twenty years now?"

What could Grace say to that? It was true. All these years and she hadn't been able to put it out of her mind, hadn't been able to believe Tom's stepping out on her was merely a cry for help. But what if she'd been wrong? What if Tom's lovemaking with Iris was as emotionally unsatisfying as her tryst with Paulo had been? Had she thrown it all away, refused to ever trust Tom again, for nothing?

CHARLOTTE WAS in the library, updating her social calendar on the computer Iris had given her and taught her how to use, when Richard walked in. He'd spent the afternoon playing tennis at the club, but was now dressed in his customary suit and tie. Knowing now was as good a time as any, Charlotte broached the subject that had been on her mind constantly for days, before he could leave for that evening's dinner-meeting with their accountant.

"I want to hire a private detective to locate Daisy."

The look in his eyes becoming pure resentment, Richard's jaw clenched. "It's out of the question."

"Why?" Gearing up for battle, Charlotte saved the data she had just entered and watched as Richard opened the wall safe in the library. "We can afford it." The growing success of the family antiques business, and their financial stake in it, had seen to that.

Richard released a long breath and turned to Charlotte in exasperation, "Daisy will come home when she's ready."

Would she? Charlotte wondered. "She's been gone for days now," Charlotte pointed out, unwilling and unable to suppress her worry. "We haven't heard a word from her."

"Which, given her likely mood, is probably just as well." Richard moved the handgun and box of ammunition he insisted they keep for their personal safety to one side and withdrew a fat envelope of cash. He took out a number of bills and returned the envelope to the safe, setting it on top of Charlotte's jewelry case and copies of their insurance papers, wills and real estate deeds. "Right now, Daisy is behaving like a temperamental child." Richard shut the door to the safe, covered it with the painting and slid the money into his wallet before looking at Charlotte once again. "And I for one am glad Daisy is not here misbehaving for all our friends to see."

"I still want to find her," Charlotte retorted steadily.

"And I still say no."

Richard gave Charlotte a look to let her know the conversation was closed, then exited the room. Seconds later, the front door shut behind him. The big house was cloaked in silence.

Charlotte stared at the photos of family that decorated the shelves to the right of the heavy antique desk. She didn't know when or why or even how it happened, but the truth was indisputable now. Somewhere along the way, she had failed both her daughters. Perhaps even their son, Connor, too. During the crisis of Iris's pregnancy, Charlotte had been so certain she and Richard were doing the right thing, keeping the affair and pregnancy from ten-year-old Connor, and sending Iris to that austere convent in Switzerland to have her baby in secret. Iris hadn't wanted to go, hadn't wanted to give

Daisy up, but Charlotte and Richard had worked together to convince Iris that her life—indeed, all their
lives—would be ruined if she didn't do as they said.

In return, Charlotte had promised Iris that she and
Richard would love Daisy and bring her up as their
own. Iris would never have to worry or wonder what
had happened to her baby—she would be able to see
Daisy every day because they would grow up as sisters.
And Charlotte had kept her promise. She had loved
Daisy every bit as much as she had loved her own two
children, if not more. But she had also known in her
heart of hearts that Daisy was her first—maybe her
only—grandchild. And consequently, she had tended to
be too lenient with Daisy, as grandparents were wont
to do. Whereas Richard had gone the other way and
been too strict. Poor Daisy had been caught in the middle from day one, as their adopted daughter. No wonder
she'd floundered around and felt there was something
amiss. Because, Charlotte thought fiercely, there had
been.

Now, Daisy knew the truth.

She knew they had all lied to her.

And she couldn't forget and she couldn't forgive.

Was Daisy ever going to come home? Charlotte wondered.

And what would she do when she did?

CHAPTER FIVE

IT TOOK JACK ONE MONTH, two days and sixteen hours to find out where Daisy had run off to, and another half day to travel to Nevada. When he finally made it to the crummy studio apartment she had rented at the edge of town, he was mad as hell, and exhausted to boot. And she didn't look much better when she opened her door to him. Her fair skin held the golden glow of desert sun and she was dressed as sexily as ever, in snug, worn, navel-baring jeans, tangerine tank top and western boots. Her wavy hair was as clean and silky-looking as always and caught up in a clasp on the back of her head. But there were shadows beneath her eyes and a weariness in her body language that hadn't been there before.

Not that she was about to let him know that, however, Jack noted as their eyes clashed. "I was wondering when you would show up."

Jack took the open door for invitation and followed her inside. The place was a mess. Although it was nearly noon, what looked like a breakfast of a glass of milk and a sweet roll sat on the table. The sofa bed was still pulled out and unmade. There were clothes, shoes and toiletry items scattered all over the place. He shut the door behind them, noting the laptop computer, printer and digital camera that were hooked up together. Even as they spoke, what looked like color tourist photos were spitting out of the printer one after another. Which explained how she had been getting by once her cash ran out. "It would have been sooner if you'd let me know where you were," he said.

"What? And take all the fun out of it?" Daisy plucked her glass off the table and took a sip of milk. Expression sobering slightly, she continued, "I was going to contact you soon anyway."

Jack had expected as much—when Daisy was ready. She was too confrontational to let what had happened between them that night go by without being addressed. Not that he was taking the blame for everything. She was at fault here, too. Figuring she would want him to give as good as he got, he said back, just as dryly, "To return my car, repay the cash you stole and reimburse me for the $2358.29 in credit card charges you racked up the last two days?"

Daisy shook her head, took another sip of milk, and still holding his gaze, said, "To tell you I'm pregnant."

Her matter-of-fact tone hit him like a sucker punch to the gut. Jack tensed, attempting to frame a retort, only nothing came out. Finally, he said, "That's not funny, Daisy."

An emotion he couldn't quite identify glimmered in her eyes. "Oh, I don't know." She waved her hand through the air, some of her customary rebelliousness coming back to her stance. "There's a certain irony to it, don't you think? I mean, the bastard of Tom Deveraux having the love child of his most trusted employee slash henchman. If you ask me—" her lips curved with mocking pleasure "—it's like something straight out of a trashy novel."

He was beginning to realize she wasn't kidding. "Except this is real life, Daisy."

Daisy sighed and put down her milk. "Ain't that the sad truth," she agreed.

Jack came closer. Unable to help himself, he looked at her stomach—it seemed as flat as always, but then if the baby was his, and his gut was telling him that it was, she was only four and a half weeks or so along. He swallowed around the unaccustomed tightness in his throat and returned his gaze to her face. "You're sure about this?"

Daisy wiped her hands on a napkin and walked down to the other end of the narrow kitchen countertop. She plucked a piece of paper out from beneath a little sample bottle of what appeared to be vitamins and handed it to him. "I went to the Lake Tahoe clinic two days ago."

He noted that the receipt said the clinic had billed her for a pregnancy test, new patient exam and consultation.

In a bored tone, Daisy continued, "You can go check out the test results for yourself if you want. I told them you were the father and you might be coming by."

Still struggling to absorb the fact that he was going to be a father—that he was going to have a baby with Daisy—never mind figure out what this was going to mean to him, his life and everyone around them, Jack handed back the receipt. "That's not necessary," he said stiffly, guilt—and his own sense of failed responsibility—along with the news of his impending fatherhood, combining to hit him with the force of a sledgehammer. He forced the words through numb lips. "I believe you." Just as he now believed they were in one hell of a mess, that was likely only going to get worse as time went on.

Daisy tilted her head as she studied him with narrowed eyes. After a moment, she noted softly, "You haven't asked if the baby is yours."

No. He hadn't. And why hadn't he? Jack couldn't say why he was so sure. He only knew his gut was saying it was his kid. And his street smarts about people, whether they were good, bad or somewhere in between, were never wrong. Daisy might act out wildly, but she would never lie to him about something like this, especially given the way she had grown up, not knowing to whom she had been born. "I'm sure because I know you," he stated firmly, more sure of that with every second that passed.

For reasons Jack couldn't understand, his faith in Daisy's honor upset rather than reassured her. "And how do you know?" she retorted, the deeply cynical look returning to her face. "Oh!" She snapped her fingers as if something just hit her with amazing insight. "I forgot. You and my biological father have been tracing my movements ever since I decided to try and find my real parents a few months ago." She trod closer, bristling with a mixture of indignation and contempt. "That's kind of ironic, too, don't you think? That I hired the same private investigator my biological father hired to keep me from finding out what the Templeton and Deveraux families would've preferred I not ever know?"

Yeah, it had been a sticky situation, all right. Hardest on the top-notch P.I. who had unexpectedly found himself at the center of the quandary, being asked to represent both sides. But that was neither here nor there now, Jack thought. He shrugged. "It's not surprising you both hired Harlan. He's the best private investigator in the city."

"I'm surprised he didn't refuse to help me, given the fact that Tom had signed him first," Daisy said sulkily.

"Harlan did go to Tom. Told Tom that you wanted to hire him and why and wanted to know what Tom wanted him to do. Harlan said he could refer you elsewhere or help you himself, but he wouldn't lie to you or take your money or try and stonewall you—do anything else unethical or underhanded."

"Good for Harlan. If it weren't for him finding out I had been born in a little convent in the Swiss Alps, instead of Norway as I had always been told, I still wouldn't know the truth."

Jack nodded, glad they agreed on this much. "Harlan Decker's a good guy, all right. Although for the record—" Jack gave Daisy a stern look, letting her know she wasn't completely off the hook for her actions, either "—Harlan thought I should've turned you in for stealing."

Daisy shrugged. "What can you expect from a former cop?" she volleyed back. Silence fell between them, less tense this time.

Jack studied Daisy knowing he already had his own thoughts on the matter, but wondering where she wanted to go from here. "So what now?" he asked her casually.

Daisy bit her lower lip and regarded Jack uncertainly as her printer finally sputtered to a halt. "You're really going to take me at my word on this pregnancy?" Clearly, Jack thought, she wasn't used to being trusted.

Jack watched as Daisy went over, picked up the stack of finished photos from the tray and began thumbing through them. "I don't have any reason not to believe you."

Daisy went back to her computer and typed in another series of commands. "Nevertheless," she said as calmly as if they were discussing the terms of a new photo shoot instead of the permanent interlinking of their lives, "I'd feel better if we went over to the clinic and let you see the results, and maybe have you take a paternity test or whatever it is they do these days to establish paternity."

Jack pulled up a chair next to her and sat down. "I'd feel better if we just got married and got it over with," he stated, wondering how long Daisy was going to be able to keep her cool, act as if this hardly mattered, when in reality it was the most earth-shattering revelation of both their lives.

Daisy continued typing in commands until her printer started going again. She turned to him, as yet another series of tourist pictures began spitting out into the tray, the only indication of her heightening emotions the tensing of her jaw. "And why would we want to do that?" she asked steadily.

That, Jack thought, was easy. Letting her know with a look that she and their baby would be able to count on him the way she had apparently never been able to count on anyone else in her life, he said, "So the baby you're carrying will be born legitimate, and have a mother and a father."

Once again, Daisy's teeth raked across her soft, bare lower lip. "This wouldn't have anything to do with Tom Deveraux, would it? Because I don't have to tell him we slept together. At least not yet," Daisy amended hastily before Jack could get a word in edgewise. "When my baby is born, of course I'll make his or her paternity a matter of public record—there's no way I'll ever lie to my child the way my parents lied to me all these years. But until then—I mean, no one has to know. We don't have to put ourselves in a position where we're both going to be getting a lot of grief.''

Jack supposed that was true, but he saw no reason in putting off the inevitable, either. "The worst thing we could do is let our kid think we're ashamed of him or her,'' Jack said. He had grown up that way, feeling the slings and arrows surrounding the scandal of his birth. There was no way he was doing it to his own child. Frowning, Jack continued humorlessly, "Tom already knows we slept together.''

Daisy did a double take. "You told him?''

"Not exactly." Because it was clear she wasn't going to just let this go, Jack continued reluctantly, "He figured it out when you disappeared the way you did.''

"Because you were acting so guilty, I bet.''

Knowing where she was going with this, Jack pushed the words through his teeth. "I'm not sorry we made love." Especially now that they had a baby on the way because of it. He gave her a level look. "I'm just sorry about how and why and when it happened.''

The wall around Daisy's feelings only became stronger and more inaccessible as Daisy scoffed in a cynical tone. "You would have preferred recreational sex, is that it?''

"It was more than that, and you know it." Jack knew Daisy was trying to shock and turn him off. He wasn't going to allow her to do it. Especially not now, when they had a child they were going to be responsible for.

"Exercise?''

"It was raw emotion and need—and you know it.''

"I don't need anyone.''

Yes, Jack thought. *You do.* They all did. Maybe what he and Daisy had shared wasn't love. Maybe it would never be love. But they could be there for each other and their child in other equally important ways. And whether she wanted that or not, he was going to see that it happened, because the two of them had more than just themselves to think about now. They had a baby to consider. A baby who would need the love and care and cooperation of both parents.

"But back to Tom Deveraux." Daisy changed the subject to something safer. She studied Jack curiously. "What did he say when you told him about us?"

Jack recalled the punch that had landed him in the dirt and left his jaw aching for days, and decided Daisy didn't need to know that Tom was still so angry he was barely speaking to Jack. "Nothing that bears repeating," Jack finally said.

She rolled her eyes. "I'll bet."

"Look, Daisy, let's get out of here," Jack said, ready to go back East and reclaim his job and whatever was left of any respect Tom Deveraux might still have for him. Hopefully what he was doing now to make an honest woman of Daisy and set things to rights would go a long way in repairing the damage that had been done. And if not, he hoped he would at least continue to have his job with the Deveraux-Heyward Shipping Company. "We'll get married and hop a plane back to Charleston."

Daisy took the rest of the printed photos out of the tray and stuck them in an envelope emblazoned with the name Tahoe Mountain Tours. Apparently finished with the work she had to do, she shut off her printer and computer and closed the lid on her laptop. "I'll marry you for the sake of the baby, Jack, but I'm not going back to Charleston."

Jack had expected some resistance on that score after

the way she had run away, and had prepared for it. "Afraid, are you?"

Daisy shot to her feet and squared off with him. "I'm no coward," Daisy lashed back.

"Hey." Jack flattened his hands on his chest and gave her a look of mock innocence. "That's what a person is who refuses to face the consequences of their actions."

Daisy thrust her chin out as she slapped both hands on her hips and stomped nearer. "I've never been afraid of anything or anyone in my life," she swore, glaring up at him.

"Then prove it," Jack threw down the gauntlet, knowing damn well a woman like Daisy would pick it right up and brandish him with it in return. "Marry me. Come home with me. Help me show everyone that we know that we don't care what they think."

"There'd have to be a few conditions," Daisy warned after a moment.

At last, a chink in her emotional armor, Jack noted solemnly. He couldn't wait to hear those.

The taunting look was back in her Deveraux-blue eyes. "You'll give my baby a name and we'll have a physical relationship—that's it!"

Jack didn't mind the prospect of hitting the sheets again with Daisy, he also knew they had some very important boundaries to set. "Fine. I also don't want to be jerked around."

"Fine." Daisy glared right back at him.

They seemed to be circling each other like two wary animals—neither willing to make the first move. Maybe the thing to do was to make it real and go from there. They could worry about the details later.

He regarded her sternly, chastening, "And one more thing. No one's bed but mine, got it?"

A slow, sexy, victor's grin spread across her face. Looking as if she was the one in the driver's seat, Daisy shrugged and said, "Whatever."

DAISY HAD TO ADMIT that like Jack, she didn't appreciate being manipulated, either. To the point she tended to behave perversely and illogically if she felt she was being used. Nevertheless, Daisy thought as she rummaged through the clothes in her closet, looking for something to don for a quickie wedding, she was very relieved Jack had not only shown up so swiftly, but offered to help her muddle her way through this dilemma she found herself in. Because she had the feeling that the next eight months or so were going to be rough in a lot of ways. And she and the baby needed a man like Jack, who was known for his steady presence and selflessness to help her through all the life changes she was going to have to make if she wanted to be a good mother, and she did.

"How soon can you be ready to go?" Jack asked.

Daisy shrugged as she took several things on hangers into the bathroom and hung them over the shower rod for trying on. "I don't know. Ten or fifteen minutes."

It ended up taking her thirty, but that was okay, Daisy thought as she examined herself in the mirror, because with her hair put up in a neat twist on the back of her head and some makeup and dangly earrings on, she looked pretty darn good. Smiling, she spritzed herself with perfume and walked out into the studio in her stocking feet.

Jack had changed clothes too in her absence. The sport shirt he had been wearing when he arrived was now in a carry-on garment bag. He was wearing a navy blazer with his khaki slacks, white shirt and dark-olive tie.

Jack finished zipping up his garment bag and turned to face her. "That's what you're going to wear?" His eyebrow lifted in surprise.

Unable to help but note how good Jack looked, not to mention to feel a little hurt he disapproved of her choice, when she had so little to choose from, Daisy shrugged. "What's wrong with it?"

Jack made a face. "It's black, for starters."

Daisy looked down at her long sleeveless dress. It was woven out of a linen-cotton blend that fell just above her ankles. It was cool and summery and yes— with its sensual drape and cutaway armholes, sexy as all get-out. But if he didn't like it... "I've got some pink capri pants," she said, deliberately suggesting something even more outrageous. "Or a yellow floral mini."

"Never mind." Jack picked up Daisy's computer, printer and camera—which had all been put in their cases while she was changing—and set them in a pile next to the door. "Let's just load this stuff in my SUV and get going."

Knowing he had also been on the phone making arrangements while she got ready for the momentous event, Daisy threw the rest of her belongings into a suitcase as quickly as she could. "Which wedding chapel did you pick?"

Jack helped her get the rest of her things together, which admittedly weren't much, as he told her matter-of-factly, "We're getting married on the upper deck of a paddlewheel boat on Lake Tahoe."

Daisy's eyes widened with surprise. "That's a little extravagant, isn't it?"

Jack gave her a look that indicated he didn't think so. "We're only going to do this once. It might as well be memorable."

Daisy wondered if he would have the same view of the wedding night then quickly pushed the thought from her mind. She couldn't risk making this a romantic occasion, even in her mind, because it simply wasn't. Methodically, she collected the tourist photos she had to deliver to Tahoe Mountain Tours en route to the ceremony. "What about rings and a license and blood tests?" she asked, mentally making a note to give her notice while she was there so they could find another photographer to take her place.

Jack picked up several of the heavier items, then held the door. "They'll have everything we need there, including the paddleboat captain who is going to marry us, the marriage certificate, license and two plain solid-gold wedding rings. There's no waiting period. And no blood tests are required. All we have to do is show up."

Somehow, Daisy didn't find that at all encouraging. But refusing to be the first to back out, Daisy merely smiled and said, "Right." As they loaded Jack's truck with all her gear and his small travel bag, Daisy kept expecting Jack to renege, demand to go over to the clinic, wait until paternity tests could be completed, and otherwise put off such a risky, impulsive decision. But he didn't. Instead, she was the one with cold feet about joining their lives on any level—and they both knew it. But every time she faltered, he was right there, giving her that goading look that sent her temper flaming and made her feel all the more reckless and determined not to bow out or back down.

Not that she was going to allow Jack to have the upper hand with her. No one got that. She wasn't like her older sister slash birth mother Iris, who had married a man twice her age to please her parents. Or her brother, Connor, who prided himself on being able to mediate his way out of every and any situation. She was strong and independent and she did whatever she needed to do to ignore the constant criticism and disapproval coming her way. She knew how to look out for herself because she had learned very early that no one else, either within or outside the family, was going to do it for her.

Jack, of course, didn't know how impossible Richard and Charlotte Templeton could be, or how much they could—and often did—upset her. But soon he would be subject to the same kind of familial pressure. And would be right there beside her to either deflect it or help her deal with it, Daisy reassured herself seriously as she was handed a bouquet of flowers and she and Jack climbed the metal stairs to the upper deck of the boat. And perhaps in that sense, because she would no longer have to fight every battle alone, Daisy thought as Jack took her hand in his, her life would get better.

Daisy and Jack said their vows at sunset, as the wedding package touted, with the granite mountains towering in the background, above the beautiful blue surface of the mountain lake, and two marina employees serving as their witnesses. To the two of them, it was a solemn, not romantic, occasion, and Daisy couldn't help but wonder, even as she said their highly personalized vows, how—and if—they could ever be true.

Would she be able to respect, honor and cherish Jack for as long as they both shall live? Or even the rest of the month, once they got back to Charleston and the complications they faced there?

And what about Jack? Would he be able to care for her, in sickness and in health, for richer for poorer, for the rest of their married lives? Or would this, too, end in disaster?

Daisy had no answer. And given the conflicted look in Jack's eyes as he bent to chastely kiss her lips at the conclusion of the ceremony, he didn't know, either. But he was determined to do the right thing by her and their baby. That was something, she supposed.

"WE'RE NOT DRIVING HOME?" Daisy asked in disappointment as Jack turned the SUV away from Lake Tahoe and onto the highway that would lead them to the Reno airport.

"No." Jack set the trip computer on his dash. "That would take several days. I need to get back to Charleston."

"So I'll drive."

He slanted her a look and said dryly, "We've done that already. You took off without me."

Daisy gave him a smile of exaggerated enthusiasm. "Great," she said, settling deeper into her comfy leather seat. "So how long is this all going to take?" she asked wearily, wishing she had a bed she could just curl up in.

"It's around four hours from Reno to Dallas–Fort Worth, where we change planes, and another four or so to Charleston. Our flight leaves at midnight. We'll fly all night and be home by morning."

Daisy didn't particularly enjoy sleeping on airplanes, but she reluctantly conceded that was probably better than staying in a hotel and trying to play it cool on what was, technically speaking anyway, their wedding night. So maybe, she decided as Jack busied himself switching on the radio, flying home tonight wasn't such a bad idea after all...

Jack had booked them into first-class, so they had comfortable seats and plenty of legroom. Daisy was so exhausted she slept on both flights and so did he. When she was awake, she kept herself busy reading, as did he, which meant conversation was at a minimum, and suited Daisy just fine. However, once they landed in Charleston that changed. "How do you want to do this?" Jack asked as they strode through the airport terminal toward the baggage claim.

"Do what?" Daisy asked as she struggled to keep up with his longer strides.

Jack gave her a sidelong glance, and noticing she was struggling, shortened his steps to a slower pace. He took her camera bag and put it over his shoulder, gallantly relieving her of that weight, which left her with just her purse. "I promised Tom I would take you to see him as soon as you got back."

That might have been Jack's priority—it wasn't hers. Especially given the way she still felt about her biological father. Sighing, Daisy consulted her watch. With the three-hour time difference, and the additional time they had spent in the DFW airport changing planes, it was nearly noon, eastern time. Daisy felt grimy and exhausted and nowhere up to another confrontation with Tom Deveraux. "I really want a shower," Daisy said as they grabbed their luggage off the carousel and headed for the exit.

"Then we'll go to my—our—place," Jack said. "We can both get cleaned up and then call Tom and see where he wants to meet—the office or home."

Daisy tried not to think how intimate "our place" sounded. Never mind how close and cozy their life ahead might be. Daisy studied Jack's face, realizing she wasn't about to get out of this meeting with her new husband's "boss." "I want to meet at Tom Deveraux's office," Daisy stated stubbornly. "It'll be shorter, less personal, that way."

Jack lifted a curious eyebrow. "I thought you wanted to get to know him, that's what your search for your real parents was all about."

Daisy's heart hardened a little more as she followed Jack's lead across the hot pavement to the short-term parking lot. "I probably would want to get to know them if they were strangers. But given the way both Iris and Tom abandoned me, and lied both to and about me, even and especially when both knew how very much I wanted to find my real parents and was looking for them, I really don't have any interest." Her feelings had been crushed enough already by the fact Iris hadn't wanted her, and Tom Deveraux hadn't even cared enough to find out if she was his child. But instead had been content to let Daisy grow up without so much as ever guessing at her and Tom's connection. Never mind being as loved as his legitimate children, or made to feel a part of his family, or told she had four half siblings, who as it turned out, she had gotten to know and befriend anyway. Instead of making her feel wanted and loved for the first time in her life, Tom and Iris had left her feeling even more rejected and forsaken. Listening to their excuses, or worse—realizing neither of them felt they really owed her an apology—just made her feel worse. Which was why, of course, Daisy had run away. So she wouldn't have to help Iris and Tom feel better while she was made to feel even worse than she already did.

His expression unsympathetic, Jack walked to the end of the row and stopped in front of a decade-old red sedan. The vehicle looked familiar to Daisy, with a few exceptions. The hood and door were now painted the same fire-engine red as the rest of the car. In fact, the whole vehicle looked as if it had had a paint job. The dent was gone from the fender. Even the upholstery had had a good cleaning.

Jack shrugged at her stunned look. "You've been driving my car, I've been driving yours," he explained.

Daisy could see that. And even as she admired the way he had given as good as he got in assuming the use of her vehicle without her okay, she did not like his presumptuousness in messing with a good thing without her blessing. Daisy scowled at Jack. "I didn't give you permission to fix it up." She had liked her secondhand car the way it was. The vehicle's noticeable disrepair had gotten under countless skins. It's new spiffed-up appearance would not.

Jack merely quirked an eyebrow and looked at her without an ounce of regret. "You should have thought about that before you left it with me," he said.

MAYBE IT WAS BECAUSE she had been raised in such a big, cold, forbidding house, but Daisy had always liked small, cozy places. Jack's home on the beach, a mile or so down from Chase and Bridgett's and Maggie and Gabe's, was just what she would have ordered, if she could have afforded to buy a home for herself at that point. The one-story beach cottage was one hundred and fifty yards away from the ocean and built in typical Low Country fashion, with a high, deeply pitched roof and gabled front door. It was small—Daisy guessed no more than twelve hundred square feet, if that. But pretty and very well maintained. Obviously built before it became fashionable to have the parking area beneath the house, the building had dark-gray siding, snowy-white trim, shutters and door and a light-gray roof. Palmetto trees shaded the front of the house, which faced the street. Hedges of tall, neatly trimmed flowering bushes insured maximum privacy from the neighbors on either side, despite the relatively small lot sizes.

"Do you rent this or is it yours?" Daisy asked as they parked in the small gravel driveway and got out.

"It's mine," Jack declared with no small amount of pride as he unlocked the door and led the way in. "I'll show you around and then go back and get the luggage."

Curious to see how he lived, Daisy followed. The first thing she noticed was that there appeared to be nothing antique or exceedingly valuable in the home—the furnishings were all sturdy, attractive, department-store stock. There were miniblinds, not heavy velvet draperies, on the windows, and practical off-white ceramic tile on the floor.

To the left of the foyer was a living room with a white stone fireplace, to the right a masculinely appointed study complete with a large desk and leather chair, computer, printer, fax and copier, a wall of built-in bookshelves and several black-metal vertical files. The living room had a sectional sofa in the same slate-gray hue as the exterior of the house, an impressively outfitted entertainment center, upholstered reading chair and matching ottoman and not much else. Behind that was a surprisingly well-equipped kitchen and dining area at the rear of the house. A laundry room was located in the middle, just off the covered back porch.

Farther down the hallway that ran the width of the home, was a single bathroom with a tub and shower combination, commode and sink all located in a very tiny space, and what appeared to be not just the master bedroom but the only bedroom, Daisy noted.

Daisy studied the king-size bed, with the brown, burgundy and taupe paisley sheets and coverlet. It looked comfortable and seemed to dominate the room. How comfortable it would be if the two of them were in it together, she did not know.

His hand just above her elbow, Jack directed her back to the hall. "The clean linens, towels and washcloths are in here. If you want to go first—" He tilted his head at the shower.

Daisy did.

"I'll bring in your things."

DAISY WASTED NO TIME getting into the shower, taking advantage of the time alone no doubt. Jack went to his study at the front of the house to the vertical files. He made sure they were locked then sat down to try to figure out what he was going to do with all the information locked inside. He couldn't take it to the Deveraux-Heyward Shipping offices, his or Tom's. There was too much of a chance of it being spotted by someone else. He didn't want to leave it in a storage facility, where anyone could break in and or come across it and wonder just what the hell Jack had been doing the past ten years at Tom Deveraux's behest. And he didn't want to destroy the information, either. Some of it meant too much to him.

One thing was for certain, though, he didn't want Daisy laying eyes on it. Not yet. Maybe not ever.

GINGER ZARING WAS STARING at the balance in her bank account, wondering how she could magically conjure up the sum she needed, when her daughter, Alyssa, walked into the kitchen, a stack of mail in her hands. She set the envelopes on the counter then went straight to the refrigerator and pulled out a tube of chocolate chip cookie dough. Ignoring Ginger's frown—Ginger preferred they eat their cookies *baked*—Alyssa chopped off a liberal chunk and set it on a plate.

"Anything interesting in the mail?" Ginger asked her daughter.

"Yeah." Alyssa tugged off the butter-stained polo she had to wear for her movie-theater concessions job and, still clad in a black T-shirt and black cotton slacks, collapsed wearily onto one of the breakfast-bar stools. She paused to pop a chunk of dough into her mouth. "I got another reminder from Yale. The rest of my tuition is due in two weeks, and they want my room and board to be paid in full, too."

Ginger nodded, as if it were no big deal, but inside, her heart was sinking. She had fully expected to have all the money she needed by now, to pay those bills. But she didn't, and now, as the time approached for her only child to leave for college, the clock was ticking ominously.

Alyssa studied her mother, at eighteen seeing a lot more than Ginger cared to admit. "Maybe it's not too late for me to go to USC with the rest of my friends," Alyssa said quietly.

Ginger shook her head, vetoing that. Alyssa had opportunities here that most of her high-school graduating class could only dream about. "Honey, we've been through this. I told you if you got accepted to Yale, you'd go." And Ginger had promised her daughter that, knowing full well that expenses for the year would exceed her thirty-five-thousand-dollar salary. But she'd been determined to provide for her only child, and provide she would.

"But…" Alyssa's lower lip trembled; her hazel eyes suddenly filled with tears. "We don't have the money yet. Do we?"

Ginger refused to make this her daughter's problem—hadn't she already hurt Alyssa enough by marrying and divorcing such a loser? She explained patiently, "I told you. I don't want you worrying about this."

"How can I not worry," Alyssa demanded plaintively, "when we're not poor enough to be eligible for any of the need-based scholarships or financial aid, and not rich enough to qualify for the private loans?"

Exactly the problem, Ginger thought. Fortunately for the two of them, where there was a will there was always a way. "Look, I know this is tricky, but I have arranged to get the funds for you."

"From that private funding source," Alyssa ascertained uneasily.

"Right," Ginger said.

"And you're sure the money has been guaranteed to us?"

"Absolutely." Ginger smiled.

Alyssa continued to regard her mother suspiciously. "It's not a loan shark or anything, is it?"

"No. Of course not," Ginger said firmly. She might be willing to take a little risk, but not that much! "Just a wealthy friend of a friend with a philanthropic streak."

"Then what's taking so long?" Alyssa demanded petulantly.

Exactly what I'd like to know, Ginger thought, secretly feeling more than a little irked herself. She'd been working darn hard to hold up her end of that particular bargain for months now. But thus far, despite the generous promises made to her, she had actually garnered only nine thousand in cash from Alyssa and Ginger's secret benefactor. Not that she was about to let him fail to pony up! Twice last week, he'd told Ginger he was going to bring her the balance of the money when they met. Twice, he had forgotten. Ginger wasn't about to let him do so again.

"Maybe we could ask Daddy to help us," Alyssa said hesitantly.

Ginger would have given anything if that were possible. But she knew she couldn't count on Mack Zaring for anything, and the sad truth was she never had been able to. During the ten years they'd been married he had spent every dime they both brought in, and then some, leaving the three of them deeper and deeper in debt with every year that passed. The final straw, however, had come when Mack turned thirty and decided he hated his life. Telling Ginger privately that the mundaneness of their life together was suffocating him, he walked out on Ginger and eight-year-old Alyssa. Quit his job as an electrical engineer, moved to a shack in the Blue Ridge Mountains and began working on and off as a fishing guide. Since then, he'd been chronically late with child support payments, criminally unenthusiastic about their daughter's many stellar achievements and completely unsupportive of Alyssa's goals and ambitions for the future. Personally, Ginger didn't care if she never saw Mack again, but for Alyssa's sake, she knew she had to keep some connection going. It was important, Ginger knew, that Alyssa think her father loved her every bit as much as Mack should have loved her. "Honey, I'm sure he would help us if he could," Ginger fibbed gently. "But your daddy doesn't have that kind of money. You know that."

Alyssa ducked her head, discouraged, and Ginger understood full well how dejected Alyssa felt. Her own parents' lack of money and ingenuity had kept her from going to a great private university. No way was the same thing happening to her daughter. Alyssa, Ginger determined resolutely, was going to have the opportunities in life that Ginger had never had. Alyssa was going to get the Ivy League education, and the prestige and hefty salary that went along with a degree. Even if it meant Ginger had to forfeit her pride and keep moonlighting at her second "job" in addition to her work as an airlines reservation agent. Deciding it was best to simply change the subject to something more hopeful, Ginger asked, "Do you still have that list of things you're going to need for your dorm room—like extralong twin sheets—for your bed?"

Alyssa nodded. "It's on my desk."

"Well, why don't you go get it?" Ginger suggested cheerfully. "And we'll go to the outlet mall and get what you need as soon as I finish up here."

Alyssa's face broke out into a relieved smile, sure now that everything was going to be all right. "You mean that?" she asked excitedly.

"Absolutely." Ginger hugged her daughter warmly. "Just give me a few minutes."

As soon as Alyssa dashed upstairs to her room, Ginger picked up her cell phone. Knowing this was a good time of day to get him, she walked outside onto the patio, where she couldn't be overheard, and grimly dialed the number she knew by heart. That man had made her a promise. And by God, whether he wanted to or not, he was going to keep it.

CHAPTER SIX

DAISY CAUGHT JACK'S ARM before they could enter the Deveraux-Heyward Shipping Company executive office building. As Jack looked down at her, he couldn't help but note how beautiful and fragile she looked in the snug-fitting capri pants and white sleeveless tank top, with a sweater knotted casually around her neck. Her hair fell loose to her bare, freckled shoulders. She abruptly tightened her grip on his bicep and confided in a low, compelling tone, "Before we go in, Jack, we need to make a deal."

"Okay." Jack paused in the shadows of the building. The protective way he was feeling right now, she could have whatever she wanted.

She turned to face him and took a bolstering breath. "I don't want to tell anyone about the pregnancy just yet."

His wife's request was surprisingly inconsistent with the rest of her behavior, especially when all along she had been the one demanding the entire truth be brought into the open. Unable to recall ever meeting a woman so full of contradictions, Jack countered just as firmly, "Secrets are trouble, Daisy. You should know that better than anyone."

"Maybe." Daisy's pretty chin took on that familiar stubborn tilt. "But I'm not up to hearing that I shouldn't do this because I'm not at a point where my life is settled and orderly.''

"And deadly dull?" Jack joked, seeing where this was going.

"You know what I mean." Daisy's lower lip shot out petulantly as she dropped her hold on him and stepped back a pace, wedging a little more distance between them. "I wasn't married yet when it happened, to someone I loved more than life itself. I didn't have a prosperous career and a house, two cars and a dog— or, as Charlotte and Richard would have wanted, a suitably blue-blooded husband with a bank account to match.''

Ouch! That certainly got him where he lived. But there was nothing Jack could do about growing up on the wrong side of the docks, or being the offspring of a long line of brawny, uneducated dockworkers.

"Sorry," Daisy amended quickly, realizing she had both insulted him and hurt his feelings. "But that's how my adopted parents, Charlotte and Richard, are going to feel about my hooking up with you. I guarantee you, the confrontation with them won't be pleasant.''

Jack had already figured as much, and braced himself for the familial maelstrom to come. "It likely won't be pleasant with Tom, either," Jack added with a warning glance.

Daisy looked down at her toes. "In any case—" Daisy's voice became not just petulant but overly emotional "—I don't want anyone ruining this pregnancy for either of us with predictions of doom and gloom about what kind of parents we're going to make." She looked up at him earnestly. "It's too special, too new.''

Jack nodded, in that respect knowing exactly how his wife felt. "For me, too," he said quietly. Because although Daisy's pregnancy had been unexpected and un-planned, it had also brought joy to Jack's life, and, as he adjusted to the idea of becoming a father, under these less-than-ideal circumstances, hope for the future unlike anything he had ever experienced. "All right, we won't tell anyone until we both feel the time is right," Jack promised.

"Thanks." Relief shining on her face, Daisy stood on tiptoe and pressed a quick, casual kiss to his cheek. Together, they headed up to the executive suites.

Tom was waiting for them in his office. To Jack's relief, Tom seemed genuinely happy and relieved to see them both. "I'm glad you're back, Daisy," he told her in a cordial tone as he ushered Daisy to one of the two armchairs flanking the sofa in the corner. Tom took a place on the sofa closest to Daisy, leaving Jack to the chair at the far end of the coffee table. "I was really worried about you."

"Yeah." Daisy sighed, morphing into the smart-ass she became whenever she felt threatened. And Tom, and his ability to hurt her, threatened her, Jack noted as the hair on the back of his neck prickled, the way it always did before a business meeting totally broke down.

"Nothing like having a wild cannon on the loose," Daisy continued, giving Tom a vaguely reassuring wink, "but you don't need to worry. Because I am not going to tell anyone outside the family that you're my father."

That was news to Jack. Daisy hadn't said anything of the kind to him! Furthermore, he was surprised she would agree to that, given all she had gone through these past five years to uncover the truth about her real identity.

Oblivious of the impending danger, Tom shot Jack a grateful look, giving Jack credit where none was due. "I think that's wise," Tom said, pleased.

Daisy's smile broadened as she bounced to her feet and circled the coffee table to where Jack was seated. She eased behind Jack and put her hands on his shoulders. "I am however going to tell everyone under the sun that I'm now married to Jack here."

Tom stared at them in stunned amazement. He looked at Jack and demanded grimly, "Is this a joke?"

Jack swore virulently to himself and wished once again he hadn't gotten himself into such a mess. Wondering if Tom was going to haul off and punch him out again, and how Daisy would react if Tom did, Jack said calmly, "It's not a joke."

"Why?" Tom narrowed his eyes. "Is she—"

Daisy came out from behind Jack's chair and did a princesslike pirouette and curtsy for both men. "You'll be relieved to know I am as wild and reckless as ever, but otherwise, as you can see, quite fine."

A muscle working in his cheek, Jack's mentor glared at him. "Damn it, Jack! I told you to find her, not—"

"Make an honest woman of me?" Daisy interjected when Tom had sense enough to censor himself.

Daisy shrugged and continued to pace as dramatically as if she were onstage in a Broadway play. "I know what you mean." She flattened a hand across her breasts and uttered a divalike sigh. "I tried to convince Jack it wasn't necessary to put a ring on my finger, that I had no reputation to speak of, save that of being very wild, reckless and unpredictable. And that just because he's slept with me didn't mean he had to marry me for heaven's sake! But in some ways—" Daisy paused to pat Jack's cheek and give him an exaggeratedly affectionate look, before continuing her soliloquy "—Jack here is very old-fashioned. And he assured me this was for the best, so I said okay, I'd give the holy state of matrimony a shot. I mean, what else am I going to do besides take pictures of stuff? Which is, by the way, contrary to popular opinion, something I never plan to give up. What else would I do, anyway? Go back and enroll in an eighth college to try and get an undergraduate degree in something I'll never use anyway?"

Jack was relieved to note the more Daisy acted out, the more Tom, an experienced father, calmed down. Tom shot Jack a thoughtful look. "It's not like you, Jack, to be so impulsive," he said.

Looking frustrated that her attempt to drive Tom to losing his temper completely wasn't working, Daisy dropped into Jack's lap. "Guess I inspire him," she said in a low, vampy voice. "Or maybe—" Daisy ran a caressing hand across Jack's chest in an attempt to further aggravate her biological father "—my little hubby is just a wild and crazy kind of guy and never knew it until now."

Tom sighed, clearly perplexed. Meanwhile, in an attempt to limit the damage before this situation completely disintegrated, Jack discreetly tried to lift Daisy off his lap, and found, to his increasing consternation, she would not budge. And instead settled her bottom even more cozily into his lap, which in turn created another problem. The kind that necessitated she stay on his lap rather than get up and reveal the tightness at the front of Jack's slacks.

Tom looked at Jack, blissfully unaware of Jack's helpless arousal. "You're sure," Tom said heavily, "there isn't anything else that I should know about this?"

Promising himself that Daisy was going to pay for her antics later, Jack kept his promise to Daisy and said nothing about her pregnancy. Although, he had to admit to himself pragmatically, it probably would have made him look better in his boss's eyes if he had confessed the pregnancy. At least then, Daisy and Jack's impetuous actions would have made some sense.

"Well," Tom continued reluctantly, looking from one to another and back to Jack again, "if you're not going to have the marriage annulled—"

Jack said firmly, sure of this much, "We're not."

Tom looked at both of them. Speaking more to Daisy than to Jack, Tom continued in a lecturing, paternal tone, "Then I expect you to make a concerted effort to stay married."

Well, that was something the Deveraux and Templeton families agreed upon, Jack noted. That marriage should be for life.

Daisy, however, clearly could not have agreed less as she rolled her eyes and vaulted off Jack's lap once again. "Spoken like a true father." Daisy glared at Tom and began to pace the CEO's office once again. "The only thing is, you have, by your own volition, never been a father to me, Mr. Deveraux."

Despite Daisy's angry reaction, Tom kept his cool. "Which brings me to the next very important point," he said, standing and crossing to where his biological daughter stood. "I want to remedy that, Daisy. Which is why I called Gabe a few minutes ago and asked him to arrange for you to have a DNA test at Charleston General Hospital this afternoon. I had one weeks ago, and my results are already back. All you have to do is go to the lab at the hospital—they're expecting you. They'll draw some blood, and we should know defi-

nitely if you are my child in a matter of weeks." Tom
paused, reading the wariness and uncertainty on Daisy's
face as easily as Jack did. "This is just a formality,
Daisy," Tom explained gently, looking at that point
very much like a father to Daisy, "but a very necessary
one. After all the lies, well…" Tom paused and compressed his lips together. "You understand why I want
us both to be sure you are indeed my child."

Jack was fairly certain he saw tears glimmering in
Daisy's eyes before she determinedly blinked them
away. "And then what?" Daisy asked contentiously,
moving away from Tom yet again.

"For starters," Tom said, resisting what Jack could
see was the natural urge to take Daisy in his arms and
comfort her as a father would. Instead, he leaned
against the front of the desk. "I think we should get to
know each other," Tom continued optimistically. "And
you should become a member of our family."

Jack wondered if Daisy knew how lucky she was to
be getting the offer of entry into the Deveraux world.
Because, despite the problems Tom and Grace had suffered over the years, due to his infidelity and their eventual divorce, the Deveraux were a warm and loving and
genuinely caring family. One of the most grounded and
truly compassionate and mutually supportive that Jack
knew. He would have given anything to have an offer
like that. And it had nothing to do with the money and
privilege they enjoyed. But rather the love and acceptance they offered each other, the knowledge that if you
were a Deveraux you were never alone.

Daisy raked her teeth across her lower lip as she
continued to study the man who, under different circumstances, would have been the father who'd loved
and reared her. "You really want that?"

Tom's eyes shone with a mixture of regret and hope. "Yes—at least privately, I think that's the right thing for us to do. Don't you?"

"Right now I'm really not sure what I want," Daisy said quietly, looking—to Jack's mind, anyway—dangerously subdued. "But I will have that DNA test. Just to put your mind at ease."

"And maybe later this evening the three of us could have dinner," Tom said pleasantly.

Abruptly, Daisy's expression became closed and unreadable once again. "I don't think so," she said, her voice more chilly than polite. "I have to get my stuff out of my brother Connor's place." She threw Tom a look meant to provoke. "Now that I'm married to your company counsel, I'm going to be moving in with him."

"YOU WERE KIND OF ROUGH on him, weren't you?" Jack said as soon as the elevator doors closed and the two of them were alone.

Daisy swallowed and tried not to think how handsome and relaxed Jack looked in his cream-colored knit shirt and tan slacks. Or that he was not just the father of the baby she was going to have, but her husband. Suddenly, everything was moving way too fast for her and she leaned against the opposite wall as the elevator continued its short ride to the lobby.

For years, she'd dreamed about finding her real parents.

But the prospect of being a Deveraux.... And yet not really being a Deveraux—at least not to the public at large—was depressing.

She had known going into this that she might experience a less-than-warm welcome from the two parents who had given her over to others to raise, but it still hurt, feeling as if she was once again being rejected and abandoned, albeit all so carefully and nicely this time.

"Would it have hurt you to have dinner with Tom tonight?" Jack continued, playing the role of Tom Deveraux's trusted legal counsel and all-around henchman yet again.

Daisy wasn't going to let herself feel guilty about that, even if Jack was looking at her as if she should. Her biological father had pushed her away yet again, after first beckoning her near. Now it was her turn to do the same to Tom. "What I said was the truth," Daisy said stoically as the elevator stopped at the ground floor and the doors slid open. She preceded Jack through the exit. "I do need to get my stuff out of Connor's. And if we hurry—" Daisy checked her watch "—we can do it before he gets home for the evening."

Jack hurried to get there first and hold the door for her. "What about telling your family?" he asked as she breezed past.

Daisy dug for her sunglasses in the bottom of her purse, and slid them over her eyes. "That can wait."

His sandy hair gleaming gold in the afternoon sunlight, Jack followed Daisy across the parking lot to her spiffed-up sedan. "You're sure?"

Daisy waited while Jack unlocked the passenger side. "Of that? Very."

As Jack opened the door, a blast of heat came out at them. They stood back, waiting for the temperature inside the car to subside a little before getting in.

Deciding the car was cool enough to get into, Daisy tossed her purse onto the middle of the front seat and climbed in. "Do you think he's going to forgive you?"

Jack climbed in behind the wheel. "Who?" he asked as he fit the key into the ignition.

"Tom," Daisy replied as she tried to get her lap belt on without burning her hand on the hot metal. As Jack started the car, hot air streamed out of the AC vents and they both lowered their windows. "I saw the way he looked at you when we told him about us," Daisy continued as Jack began to back out of the space. "He was really disappointed in both of us for getting married, but especially you. Although I suppose marrying me has to be better on some level than just using me and walking away."

Jack hit the brakes so hard, she bounced against the seat. He turned to face her, expression grim. "I didn't just screw you, Daisy. We made love."

Daisy understood why Jack wanted to make it seem romantic, in retrospect—she did, too. What they had done was a lot easier to accept that way. But she knew how sordidly the encounter had begun, she knew how angry and disillusioned and in need of some comfort she had been. She knew their baby hadn't been created out of love. Which she supposed was another great irony, since their baby's mother hadn't been conceived in love, either.

"Call it what you want." Daisy sighed. "The end result is the same." Because of their mutual impetuousness, in nine months they were going to have a baby. And they had to deal with that, openly and honestly, as they tried to figure out their future and the finances involved in having and supporting a child. "Tom's initial reaction to our elopement was fury."

"So?" Jack appeared to be concentrating on the downtown-Charleston traffic.

"So is he going to fire you?"

Jack gripped the steering wheel with both hands. "I don't know."

Even though Jack was doing his best to act as if it didn't matter to him either way, Daisy could tell how much Jack's job—and Tom's approval—meant to him. She knew from things that Amy and her brothers had said that Jack really liked working for Tom and Deveraux-Heyward Shipping. And as much as Daisy would've liked to get under Tom Deveraux's skin and pay him back for the way he had hurt her in the past, she didn't want to hurt Jack, who had obviously been dragged into this by way of his employment. Which meant she was going to have to create some sort of firewall between the men that separated their business and personal lives.

She looked at Jack, wondering if Jack, who usually seemed to be at least two steps ahead of her in this situation, had already been thinking that way.

Before she could stop herself, Daisy turned to Jack with cheerful abandon. "In that sense, I suppose marrying me was a good insurance policy on your part." She spoke as if she fully applauded his highly political maneuvering behind the scenes. "Tom can't fire you now that you're my husband. That'd be akin to throwing us both out on the street. Although—" Daisy stopped, bit her lip, as the next even more disturbing thought occurred to her.

"What?" Jack turned into the outpatient services lot and parked in the first available space.

Daisy whipped off her seat belt and pushed open the passenger door. "If Tom gives me a significant trust, under the community property laws, as my husband you'd be entitled to a chunk of it, too."

Jack met up with her at the rear of the car and took

her hand in his. "That's assuming we divorced and Tom was foolish enough to have the family's trust attorneys set the fund up so I could have access to the money in the event of a dissolution of our marriage." Jack leaned down so he was speaking directly in her ear, carefully emphasizing every word. "I assure you, Daisy, Tom would never be that shortsighted." Jack leaned back so she could see into his eyes. His hand tightening on hers, he continued tranquilly, "Even as your husband, I will never be able to touch anything he gives you."

And Jack looked as if he were not only very much okay with that, but wanted it that way, Daisy noted with relief. But wary of being too quick to trust and getting burned again, Daisy countered just as knowledgeably, "That's probably true—his attorneys would protect both me and Tom on that score. But they can't control everything. For instance, if we stayed married after the baby was born, you could certainly enjoy the benefits of all that money."

"I didn't marry you because you were once an heiress and could conceivably be so again, if Tom decides to settle some money on you, or Richard and Charlotte reverse their decision to disinherit you and give you renewed access to Templeton-family funds," Jack said hotly. "And what do you mean *if* we stayed married after the baby's born? I thought that was a given. I thought we agreed how important it is for us not to desert our baby."

Being so close to him was suddenly overwhelming. Daisy withdrew her hand from his and edged away from him so she was walking even closer to the cars. "We can be good parents to our child without remaining yoked to each other for the rest of our lives." Daisy couldn't think that far ahead! She just wanted a husband for the transition, while she gave birth and got used to being a parent and settled in. She just wanted her baby to have a name, to be legitimate, with no question about where or from whom he or she came.

"Ask any kid of divorced parents if that's true. Ask Amy, Chase, Gabe and Mitch. They know what it's like to have their parents split."

Daisy slanted Jack a curious look. Taken aback by the unaccustomed emotion in his voice, she slowed her steps to his, wanting to hear what he had to say about this. "I'm gathering by the way you're speaking you were witness to that?"

Jack nodded. "I had a summer job in the mailroom at Deveraux Shipping during the first days of Tom's divorce from Grace, thirteen years ago. I know how miserable everyone in that family was back then. And in some ways, still is. Divorce hurts, Daisy—maybe even worse than being abandoned at the outset, because at least then you're not really aware of what is going on."

Daisy had to admit Jack made sense, but only to a point. She squared her shoulders and continued to the outpatient services entrance. "If we divorce when the baby is an infant, the baby won't know any better."

Jack followed Daisy through the automatic glass doors. He put his arm around her shoulders and guided her into a deserted alcove near the coffee shop. "You were abandoned when you were too little to know what was going on with your real parents. Does it hurt any less?"

Bull's-eye. Daisy ignored the sudden ache in her heart as she looked up at him and said quietly, "You are one difficult man. You know that?"

Jack cupped a hand beneath her chin and gently tilted her face up to his. "I am a man who will always tell you the truth," he said. "Even when that truth is uncomfortable for you to hear."

Daisy's heart pounded as his lips lowered. She wanted very much to kiss him. But wary of where it would lead, Daisy pulled away, took a deep breath, then looked at the watch on her wrist. "We better hurry if we want to get up to the lab before it closes for the day," she stated crisply.

Jack acceded to her wishes promptly, but only, Daisy feared, because theirs was a discussion that could be continued later.

THE BLOOD TEST WAS DONE quickly. Scant minutes later, they were back in the overheated red sedan. "So where does Connor live and just how much stuff do you have over at his place?" Jack asked casually.

"Not that much," Daisy said as she directed Jack to turn right out of the lot. "I like to travel light. And his loft is in a converted warehouse on Chalmers Street." Daisy directed while Jack drove.

"Interesting," Jack said a short while later when Daisy had used her key and let them in. Connor's loft was one of three in the building. His was on the third floor. The large space had distressed-brick walls and concrete floors, and had only one walled-off area—the bathroom. Everything else—bedroom, living, kitchen and dining areas—was completely open. There were no blinds on the plentiful multipaned windows, and the area was flooded with golden light. Daisy's stuff—two suitcases and several boxes of clothes, shoes, books and portable stereo—were heaped in an untidy mess in the corner. "Just as I left it." Daisy grinned, glad she could count on her older brother not to disturb her stuff.

Jack braced his hands on his waist and considered the disorder with an amused shake of his head. "You're messy, aren't you?"

"About some things." Daisy couldn't resist teasing him a little. "And you're neat, obviously."

Jack nodded, eyes sparkling. "I'll see what I can do about training you," he promised as he lifted the first load of stuff. Daisy started to help, but he held her off. "Maybe you shouldn't, you being pregnant and all."

"I won't carry too much at once, okay? And nothing heavy. But there's nothing wrong with me riding up and down in the freight elevator and walking across the parking lot. Besides, it'll go faster if I help."

Jack conceded reluctantly. Together, they each took a load and headed back down. Just as they had finished putting her belongings in the trunk, Daisy's luck ran out. She smiled at her brother, who had parked his Mercedes next to their sedan, and was walking across the parking lot toward them. "Connor."

"Hey Daisy." Looking, as always, very handsome and self-assured in a classic Brooks Brothers suit and tie, the dark-haired Connor leaned forward to kiss Daisy on the cheek. "I didn't know you were back from wherever you were."

"Well," Daisy said brightly, hoping they could leave it at that, "I am."

Connor looked at Jack curiously. "Aren't you going to introduce me to your friend?"

Daisy waved at the two men hastily. "Jack, Connor. Connor, Jack."

"Connor Templeton." Connor extended his hand.

Jack shook it warmly. "Jack Granger."

Connor's eyebrows knit together. "I don't believe we've ever met."

"I'm company counsel for the Deveraux-Heyward Shipping Company," Jack said.

Connor shot another inquisitive look at Daisy.

"Also, Daisy's new husband," Jack continued before Daisy could prevent him. Daisy swore beneath her breath. Too late, she realized she should have asked Jack to let her tell her family about the marriage. But now the cat was out of the bag.

"Connor's in commercial real estate," Daisy said, hoping to change the subject. "And he's quite successful, too."

"That's terrific," Jack said.

Connor nodded absently. "Thanks." Connor's glance fell to their wedding rings. Whatever he was thinking about the nuptials, Daisy noted, Connor was keeping it to himself. Which was typical, Daisy thought, as her brother tried never to take sides on any issue when he could mediate it instead. "Do Mother and Father know?" he asked politely.

"Not yet," Daisy said. "And I would appreciate it if you didn't tell them, at least not this evening, because it's already been a very long day. And I don't want to have to deal with them, too."

Connor frowned, his affection for their parents evident. "You should really cut them some slack, Daisy," he said.

Daisy scowled. "Somehow I knew you would defend them, Connor." Then again, Richard and Charlotte had never criticized him. They had saved all that for their "daughters."

"I'm not defending them—lying to you and trying to pass you off as an adopted child was wrong," Connor retorted compassionately as he wrapped a brotherly arm around Daisy's slender shoulders. "But I do understand they were trying to protect you."

Daisy shrugged off his grip and turned to confront him. "You knew all along, didn't you?" she asked angrily.

Connor shrugged, not about to lie to her. "I suspected something was wrong, I just didn't know what exactly."

"And didn't ask?" Daisy countered incredulously.

Connor's dark eyebrows knit together. "I was ten years old when they brought you home, Daisy. All I knew was that Iris was still in Europe, and that there had been a lot of fighting, a lot of tears before she left." He ran a hand through the layers of his neatly shorn brown hair. "When she came back, she was engaged to be married to Randolph Hayes IV, and she was, if not exactly happy, relieved or content or something. And I was delighted to have you in my life. You were a real ray of sunshine, Daisy, and you still are."

Daisy didn't doubt her older brother felt that way about her. Connor was a good guy who had more or less always gone his own way, popping up now and then to play peacemaker within the family, but he wasn't like anyone in the family. Wasn't stuffy and overbearing like Richard or a follower and worrier like Charlotte, or into the family antiques business and the old-money lifestyle Iris was, nor wild and reckless like herself. Connor, Daisy thought, was more of a regular guy, who appreciated the finer things in life but didn't absolutely have to have them like the rest of the Templetons, save Daisy. What Connor did need was peace and tranquillity amidst those around him. Hence, his habitual absence from the Templeton mansion.

"I love you, too," Daisy said quietly. He was kind and gentle, and although he didn't always or even often approve of what she did, he was a steady presence in her life, offering unconditional familial ties instead of trying to control her by cutting her off, emotionally and financially.

Connor looked at her beseechingly. "Mother and Father should not have to hear about your marriage from someone outside the family, Daisy."

Daisy sighed. She knew a losing battle when she saw one. "Do whatever you think best, then, Connor. I know you will anyway." Daisy gave him her permission to break the news for her and kissed his cheek. "But I'd appreciate it if you would wait until morning."

They all said goodbye and Jack helped Daisy into the car. "Maybe your brother's right," he said as he started to drive away. "Maybe we should tell Charlotte and Richard now."

Daisy disagreed. "I really think it would be best if the initial information came from Connor."

Jack continued to look skeptical. "You don't know them like I do. They're going to be very demeaning when they find out I've married someone without an ounce of blue blood flowing through his veins. Not that I mean to insult you," Daisy added hastily.

"You didn't." Jack fit the key in the ignition and started the engine. Frowning at the music coming from the CD player, Jack reached behind him, in the back seat, and brought forward a canvas case. He popped it open and began sorting through it, even as he continued in a low distracted voice, "It's the truth. I'm the illegitimate grandson of a dockworker for the Deveraux-Heyward Shipping Company." He gave her a look beneath the shadow of his eyebrows. "Technically speaking, anyway, there probably is no good reason you should be with someone like me."

Except for the fact that he was kind and strong and smart and decent, and not afraid to either go head to head with her or stand by her in the midst of a storm. How many men could she say that about? Daisy wondered. Not many. Aware he had mentioned his grandfather but no one else, Daisy said, "What about your parents?" Who had they been?

Jack pushed a button and ejected the CD. "My father was a merchant marine who didn't want any part of me or my mother. He split before I was born and my mom took off when I was three."

So, Daisy thought, making note of the veiled pain in his eyes, she and Jack had more in common than she knew. She watched as Jack shrugged and flipped open another CD case. He put the disk in the player and adjusted the volume.

"Do you have any memories of her?" Daisy asked.

"Any memories I have as a little kid start at some point after that." Jack turned his attention to his safety belt. His manner abrupt as his mood, Jack demanded, "So where to next?"

Wondering how much more there was to Jack that she didn't know, would never guess, Daisy lifted both hands, palm up. "I guess we should go home so I can get moved in, and get back to work tomorrow."

JACK COULD SEE Daisy was nervous about the prospect of living with him. It was apparent from the way she dallied, requesting they stop at a popular fish shack for fried clams and coleslaw on the way home, the video store and grocery. Jack didn't mind the errands, or even her nonstop chatter about nothing in particular, but he did worry about her increasing emotional distance. It was as if she was ill at ease about how much she had revealed of herself to him and needed to wall herself off, keep him not just from getting too close, but from getting close at all.

Jack had lived his entire life like that, with people setting out conditions, letting Jack know exactly how close he could get and no closer. And Jack had put up with it because in most situations he had no choice. But Jack was damned if he was going to begin the only marriage he would ever have that way. For the sake of their baby, he and Daisy had to do their best to make this union a real one in every way. Starting tonight.

IT WAS NEARLY FIVE O'CLOCK when Charlotte stopped her longtime housekeeper, Maisie, in the upstairs hall. "Did Mr. Templeton leave his tuxedo out for dry cleaning this morning?" she asked.

Maisie stopped dusting the furniture in Daisy's old room. "No, ma'am. Do you want me to get it?"

"No, Maisie, you go ahead with this room," Charlotte said. "I want to get several of his other suits out, anyway." Charlotte didn't know what was going on with her husband. Usually, Richard was meticulous about leaving his suits out for the twice-weekly 6:00 p.m. pickup by their dry cleaner. But lately, ever since Daisy had gone off to Switzerland, he had been careless in the extreme, with all sorts of things. Charlotte knew Richard was upset by the recent turn of events. They both were. But that was no excuse for him to be so wrapped up in his own activities, whatever they were, that he might as well have been on another continent himself, for all the time he spent with her.

However, there were worse things than an emotionally distant husband, Charlotte thought as she stepped into Richard's closet, removed several suits from hangers and began routinely going through the pockets, pulling out business cards, spare cash, an *I'm a Grandpa* cigar, and a... Thong? What in heaven's name! Charlotte stared at the scanty silver lamé undergarment. Where would Richard have gotten this? And why was it in the inner pocket of his favorite glen plaid suit?

Blood draining from her face, Charlotte dropped the crumpled material into the trash, then immediately thought better of it. She didn't want Maisie seeing such an item. Who knew what conclusion the housekeeper might leap to? She could think Richard had been to one of the strip clubs in the seamy part of town. Or worse, had a trampy mistress.

Charlotte knew better, of course. Richard was not only quite impotent, he did not approve of extramarital affairs. And he loathed slutty women. Why, even in the early days of their marriage, he had forbidden Charlotte to wear anything with even a hint of décolletage. When other women were raising their hemlines to a disreputable degree, Richard had made sure Charlotte's remained at the knee. She hadn't minded, she'd liked the fact that Richard hadn't wanted other men ogling her.

Which was why, Charlotte thought firmly as she wrapped the offending garment in tissue and took it back to her room, to hide for later disposal, she knew not to worry.

A number of their friends had had grandsons getting married. Most had had bachelor parties of some sort or another, a few of which Richard had actually attended. No doubt this, Charlotte thought grimly, was simply a remnant of one of those tawdry, gentlemen-only affairs.

CHAPTER SEVEN

AT 10:00 P.M., Daisy was sitting in an Adirondack chair on Jack's deck, looking out at the ocean. It was a beautiful star-filled summer night and the air was warm and scented with the tang of saltwater. Sitting there, watching the tide roll in and listening to the sound of the waves crash against the beach, Daisy felt more content and relaxed than she had in a very long time. Until she heard the sound of the sliding door open, and soft male footsteps coming up behind her. Then it all came rushing back, the marriage she had embarked upon yesterday and the wedding night they had spent sleeping on the plane.

Jack came to a stop beside her. Daisy was still wearing the clothes she'd had on earlier in the day, but he was wearing a pair of boxers and nothing else. The shadow of evening beard on his face, he smelled like mint-flavored toothpaste and cologne. "What are you thinking about?" he asked softly.

That was easy. Refusing to look at his impossibly broad shoulders or the bare sculpted muscles of his chest, or remember how strong and warm his body had felt when he had held her in his arms, Daisy turned her gaze to the crescent moon in the sky above. "How funny it is that I'm married."

Jack sifted his hand through her hair, let his palm come to rest against the curve of her cheek, then hunkered down beside her so he could look into her face. He traced the bow-shaped line of her lower lip with the pad of his thumb in a deliberately sensual manner that made her shiver in the balmy evening breeze. "Come to bed, Daisy."

Four little words, and yet they held so much promise. Too much maybe. Daisy swallowed around the sudden tightness of her throat, and avoiding the sensual expectation in his eyes, the tingling of her body, she turned her glance back to the waves rolling onto shore. "I'm not sleepy," she told him stubbornly.

Jack dropped his hand from her face, closed his callused palm around hers and got to his feet once again. "You don't have to be sleepy."

The breath hitched in her throat as she continued to play it cool. All sorts of erotic images filled her head, all of them of Jack and the one night they had spent together. A night that was already beginning to mean far too much. "Jack..." Daisy cautioned on a quiet sigh. How was she going to keep her heart intact if he insisted on behaving in such a sincere manner? She didn't want to fall in love with him. Didn't want to feel anything, except maybe friendship. And even that...

Suddenly he caught her wrist and tugged her to her feet. Thrown off balance by the unexpectedness of his actions, Daisy stumbled into him. "What are you doing?"

Jack's smile spread even more enticingly as he rubbed his nose with hers. "Just living up to my end of the bargain, sweetheart." Sliding one arm beneath her knees, the other behind her back, he lifted her up in his arms and carried her toward the open sliding glass door off the deck. "And giving us that wedding night we both so deserve."

Doing her best to hang on to her composure as her husband carried her into the house, Daisy looped both arms around Jack's neck. Looking into his eyes, she murmured softly, "I thought we had a deal."

"You're right." Jack closed the door with his elbow and then continued through the informal living area, down the hall, to the only bedroom in the house. "We did." Jack lowered her gently onto the turned-down covers of the king-size bed. Grinning, he summed up the gist of Daisy's prewedding demands. "As I recall, I was to marry you and give our baby a name."

"And you've done that."

She watched, mouth dry, as Jack stepped out of his boxers and joined her, completely naked, on the bed, his body already in a state of obvious arousal. Jack undid the button at her waist. "So?"

Daisy caught his hand before he could draw the zipper down. "So you don't need to pretend this is anything more than a marriage of convenience," Daisy stated breathlessly, aware he hadn't even kissed her yet and already her heart was pounding, her skin covered with goose bumps.

Turning his attention to her throat, he lifted her hair and traced a wickedly arousing pattern, from the U of her collarbone to just behind her ear, with lips and teeth and tongue. "Tell me that again in five minutes, Daze, and I'll believe you."

Daisy hitched in another breath as one thrill after another swept through her, leaving her shaking, confused. And traitorously—despite her decision to take this marriage her way, on her terms—wanting so much more. "Jack..." she murmured again, even more plaintively.

"Five minutes," Jack repeated, and then both hands

were tunneling through her hair and his lips fastened over hers. Daisy meant to fight the need to be with him again, the truth was she didn't want to need anyone, but when their mouths fused in an explosion of wet, soft heat, she could no more deny the conquering pressure of teeth and tongue than she could forget to breathe. He tasted exactly the way she remembered him, dangerous, dark, male. He commanded, he conquered, he took what they both needed, wanted. And she melted into him helplessly, into the kiss, letting the longing and the pleasure and the overwhelmingly sensual sensations overwhelm her. It felt good. It felt right. And, given the unattractively plump shape her body was about to take, she didn't want it to stop. Still, she knew they were setting a precedent here for how things would be in this marriage of theirs. And she didn't want him thinking he had the upper hand or could boss her around. So, reluctantly, decisively, she tore her lips from his, stared up at him, her chest heaving as she worked to catch her breath.

Jack smiled at her. "It's going to take more than five minutes, isn't it?" He didn't seem to mind at all.

Daisy flattened a hand against his chest. "It's not going to happen," she told him sternly. Not like this. Not with him calling all the shots, setting the agenda.

"Oh, I don't know about that, Daze." Jack dropped his head to kiss the back of her wrist, the inside of her forearm, the heart of her palm. He smiled as Daisy, unable to help herself, felt her senses quicken. "I haven't forgotten how beautiful you are." He cupped her breast through the layers of cotton knit and lace bra, and ran his thumb over the crest. Smiling, he dropped his head. His lips following the path of his thumb, he suckled her through the cloth until Daisy's thighs parted of their own volition, and she arched against the unyielding hardness of his chest and thigh. "Or how much you enjoy being touched here," Jack whispered, managing that zipper at long last and sliding his hand beneath her panties, settling it at the damp juncture of her legs. "And here," he swept it through the petal-soft gateway, with such tender finesse she nearly came undone, "and here—" he slipped his fingers inside her as she opened herself to him.

Daisy caught her breath as a tiny explosion went off inside her body, shooting heat through all her limbs. Jack smiled and aligned his lips with hers. Still caressing her gently, moving his fingertips from delicate nub to deep inside and back again, he kissed her deeply, resolutely, as if branding her as his. And oh, Daisy thought, how she wanted to be his, how she wanted to take him deep inside her once again.

His golden-brown eyes glimmering with a mixture of anticipation and need, Jack gently caressed the sides of her face with his palms and feathered soft kisses along her hairline, then sat up just long enough to strip off her top and undo the front clasp of her bra. Her response every bit as elemental and inevitable as his, Daisy moaned softly as Jack bared her to the waist. His eyes raked her breasts, making her feel more beautiful and womanly than she had in her entire life. He was making her feel reckless and impetuous again, and those two things always got her in over her head.

"You're not playing fair," Daisy whispered, her heart beating even harder as her body continued to ache and burn with everything that had been missing from her life. Stronger still was her desire not to let something this wonderful go by unexperienced and unexplored. Maybe this wasn't love. Maybe it would never be. But it felt so good, so right, Daisy thought as Jack continued to kiss her.

His body pulsing with the need to take her and make her his, Jack bent and kissed the soft, freckled valley between her breasts, her nipples, every inch of the sweet plump mounds. "That's one thing you should realize about me, Daze." Knowing marriage had sealed their fate, he slid his hands under her, cupping her bottom possessively, holding her close, rubbing himself against her until he was certain she wanted him the way he wanted her, with every fiber of her being.

"And what's that?" Daisy teased back between sweet, arousing kisses.

He tried—and failed—to keep the smile from his voice. "When it comes to getting what I want when I want, I don't feel honor-bound to be anything but driven and unstoppable."

"Well, I guess we have that in common, then." Her deep-blue eyes gleamed with a mischievous light as she laced her hands around his neck. "Because I want what I want when I want it, too."

A woman after his own heart, Jack thought. The difference being he was steady and reliable. And Daisy was, well…Daisy. Reckless and headstrong, daring and passionate, and yet still secretly the innocent in so many ways. And for that he had to be careful, Jack knew. Not to push her too hard or too fast. Or scare her with talk that was too serious. No, Jack thought as he brought her back into his arms and kissed her soundly. That would come later, after their baby was born, when they would be able to hold their child in their arms and realize what a lifelong commitment this was. Then she would know in her heart what he already did, that their feelings, their happiness, didn't matter so much as their child's. And that they could and would make any and all sacrifices necessary to ensure the security and happiness of the baby they shared.

In the meantime, Jack thought, reveling in the hunger of her kisses and the more urgent demand in him, they had this to forge new bonds and bring them together. Determined to make the most of the chemistry flowing between them, he hooked his hands inside the elastic of her panties and pushed them down, along with her capri pants. She stirred as he kissed his way down her body then kissed her way down his. Savoring the sweetness of her unexpected acquiescence to him, he turned her so she was beneath him and wrapped his arms around her, groaning at the softness of her body, the sense of rightness, the instinctive knowledge he belonged inside her. Sliding a pillow beneath her, he parted her thighs, kissing the hollow of her stomach, stroking the soft insides of her thighs. Then dropped lower still to deliver the most intimate of kisses, until her body took on a primitive rhythm all its own, until there was no doubting how much she needed him. Jack parted her gently and eased into her. Deepening his penetration even more, he kissed her slowly and thoroughly. Until she groaned, soft and low in the back of her throat and looked up at him with eyes that were glazed with need.

"Like this?" Jack asked softly, his body trembling with the effort it took to contain his own pressing desire.

"Yes," Daisy whispered, meeting him with abandonment. "Oh yes."

He couldn't get enough of her as she rose to meet him, and wanting to draw out every ounce of pleasure for both of them, he filled her with slow, sensual strokes. Going deeper, then easier, hotter, wilder until they were clinging together, overwhelmed, in a fierce storm of passion, tenderness and need. For a long blissful moment they hung there, shuddering and reaching for the inevitable in that perfect weightless world. And then it was nothing but a blazing explosion of heat. Free fall. And down-soft contentment.

A few moments afterward, Daisy moved to the edge of the mattress, but Jack caught her by the waist and pulled her back into his arms. Daisy scowled at him. "I'm not going to be a conventional wife, Jack. So I don't want you acting all territorial."

Jack gave her the grin of a very sexually satisfied male. "I don't want us to act the way everyone else thinks we should act, either, just because that's what is expected," he said, the sense of purpose back in his eyes as he tangled his legs intimately with hers.

"Then what do you want?" Daisy asked breathlessly. *Aside from the baby I'm carrying, and maybe just maybe, my birth father's approval, entrée into the Deveraux family and family holdings I might someday inherit.*

But to her surprise, he didn't seem interested in any of that. "I want us to be lovers," Jack replied, looking down at her as if all of this that was happening was somehow ordained. He paused to kiss her again, greedily, insatiably, then smiled even more broadly. "Think you can handle that?"

TOM HAD JUST SAT DOWN to breakfast in the dining room, when the doorbell rang. Seconds later, Theresa appeared in the portal. Her expression tentative but hopeful, she said, "Grace is here. Shall I show her in?"

His attitude as cautious as his longtime housekeeper's, Tom nodded. Wondering what would prompt his ex to come by at this early hour—they hadn't exactly parted on friendly terms the last time they had seen each other—he pushed his chair back. After a few moments, Grace breezed in looking fresh and lovely, every bit the career woman, in a deep-rose silk shantung pantsuit. She waved off his attempt to help her with her chair. "I only have a few minutes," she said briskly as she took the chair closest to him. "I have to be at the studio to begin taping a show at ten."

"May I get you some breakfast?" Theresa asked from the doorway.

Grace shook her head. "Just coffee will be fine, thank you, Theresa."

Theresa poured, then said, "If it's all right with you, I'll be heading on over to the market to do my shopping for the day before it gets any warmer."

"That's fine," Tom said. He welcomed the privacy. As soon as they were alone, Grace removed a folded section of newspaper from her purse and put it in front of him. "I'm guessing by your perplexed look, you haven't seen this."

Tom focused on the section of Bucky Jerome's "Around the City" column circled in red marker and began to read:

Parting Such Sweet Sorrow?

Back-again celeb-resident Grace Deveraux is no longer studying yoga with the acclaimed Paulo. Whispers had them dating for at least a month, but now, according to sources in the know, the May-December relationship is kaput. Will her ex, shipping magnate Tom Deveraux, be waiting in the wings? Only time, and this column, will tell.

Grace released an annoyed breath. "I've already had a call from a New York City gossip columnist and *Personalities* magazine, wanting to know if it's true."

Tom ignored the hope rising inside him and focused on her face. "What did you say?" he asked with deceptive casualness.

Grace made a so-so motion with her hands. "That I returned to Charleston after my stint at *Rise and Shine, America!* because my family is here and you're part of that family, even though we're still divorced."

Tom knew the media well enough to realize the scandal-hungry press would not have been satisfied with just that. "What did you say about the Paulo part of it?" *Was it over? And why did he care so much if it was?*

"That there's nothing to report," Grace replied, the look in her eyes turning both steely and defensive.

"Which is true as far as it goes," Tom guessed warily, pushing the lingering image of his ex and her lover from his mind.

"Which is true, period," Grace corrected, candidly meeting his glance.

Was that regret Tom saw shimmering in her eyes?

"I'm not seeing him anymore in any capacity."

Tom should have felt happy about that, maybe even relieved, given that a guy like Paulo was all wrong for Grace. But he felt angry and resentful instead. Hating that he was reacting like a jealous husband, when he and Grace were way past that, and had been for years, until he had foolishly got his hopes up about a reconciliation once again, Tom turned away from her, pushed back his chair and stood.

Striding out of the dining room, he dismissed her

with a curt "Thanks for coming by to alert me, but this is really none of my business, Grace." And in future, he amended silently to himself, he'd rather not hear about it or know who she was or was not sleeping with. It hurt too much going back down that road.

Grace followed him down the hall and into the portal of his study. "I know, but I just thought you should know the truth and be prepared for anything, if reporters start calling your office."

Tom grabbed the files off his desk and slid them into his briefcase. "I appreciate the heads-up," he said brusquely.

Grace lingered in the doorway, her cheeks unusually pink. The morning sunlight pouring in through the windows sparkled in her casually coiffed hair, making it look even blonder. "How are you doing?" she asked with more than the usual interest.

Tom shut his briefcase with a snap, aware this whole encounter had turned way too intimate and personal for his comfort, under the circumstances of their latest estrangement. "All right."

She straightened and glided closer, in a drift of Chanel N°5 perfume. "What about Daisy and that whole situation?"

Despite his aggravation with her, Tom could see Grace really wanted to know. Because what happened with Daisy would in turn affect the four children he and Grace shared, Tom had no choice but to inform her. He grabbed his cell phone out of the charger and slipped it into the leather holder on his belt. "Daisy agreed to a DNA test yesterday. We should have the results back in a couple of weeks."

To Tom's surprise, Grace looked accepting of that.

If not necessarily happy about it. "And in the meantime?"

Tom tensed as he thought about all the things that could still go wrong as they attempted to sort out this very difficult and delicate situation. "Daisy and I have agreed to say nothing publicly about what we know."

"You think she will hold to that?" Grace asked sympathetically.

Tom shrugged, feeling as uneasy about the possibility of this scandal exploding in their faces as Grace was. "I don't know," Tom told his ex-wife honestly. "As you know, Daisy is unpredictable, to say the least." Tom paused, and seeing no way to preface it, finally said bluntly, "For example, she married Jack Granger two days ago."

Grace blinked. Her mouth opened into a round "oh" of shock. "What?"

Tom knew just how Grace felt. He was still reeling from the news, too. Grimacing, he continued, "Apparently, they slept together the night she came back from Switzerland, when she left the party. I sent Jack after her." Jack, Tom realized in retrospect, had been following the Daisy trail for too long. Enough to become fundamentally attracted to her on some level, Tom guessed. He shook his head in silent regret, reflecting. "I suppose, knowing Daisy, how wild and reckless she can be, that what happened next was as much my fault as anything."

Grace tilted her head at Tom and gave him a familiar glance. "You don't look as if you really believe that."

Tom shrugged. He should have known Grace would have picked up on that—her parental instincts were unmatched. "You're right... I think Jack could have—should have—restrained himself. It would have been a lot better for all of us if he hadn't slept with Daisy that night. But the bottom line is he didn't use good judgment, nor did she. And Daisy did what she always seems to do when she is hurt or upset or frightened, she took off on another wild jaunt."

Grace regarded Tom with a mixture of shock and sympathy. "Jack told you this?" She seemed unable to imagine this, and again, Tom knew exactly how she felt.

"Reluctantly, the very next morning," Tom replied, remembering that emotional confrontation and the resulting scene, when everything became clear to Tom. He shook his head, continuing, "He had no choice. He's too honest and straightforward. I'm sure he knew it would be a mistake for me to hear the news from anyone else first or find out what had happened any other way—say, from Daisy herself."

"But you didn't fire him."

Tom shook his head. He had been sorely tempted, and was, in fact, still so disappointed in his employee for what he had done that he could barely talk to the man in a civil manner. But Tom had also known this was more and more a situation of his own making. Jack hadn't offered to get involved in this whole Daisy mess. Tom had drafted him into it and kept him involved, even during the times when he knew Jack did not want to be dealing with whatever it was that was going on. And Tom had done so because Jack was the kind of man who could be trusted to be completely discreet, which he had been. Jack didn't ask questions of Tom that he did not want to answer. Instead, Jack simply did what his employer wanted him to do. Until now. And as much as a part of Tom wanted to, he could not discount everything Jack had done for him over the years.

"It wouldn't have been appropriate for me to fire him," Tom explained eventually. "Not from Deveraux-Heyward Shipping."

Grace looked even more distressed. She flattened a hand over her chest. "Did you at least tell him to stay away from her—I mean a month ago, when all this was first going on?"

No, he hadn't. And that had been another mistake, Tom reflected. A big one. Again, he shook his head, and briefly explained about the stolen SUV, credit card and cash, the decision by Jack, Harlan Decker and Tom not to go to the police but merely to wait until Daisy surfaced, as they knew she eventually would. "When she turned up in Lake Tahoe a few days ago, Jack came to me and asked me what I wanted him to do. I told Jack to go and get her, and do whatever he had to do to straighten things out between the two of them, and then bring her back to Charleston ASAP."

"And did he?"

"Yes." Tom grit his teeth. "But as his wife." And Tom was still trying to figure that one out. Had Jack really felt Tom expected him to make an honest woman of Daisy and marry her? Was Jack going the extra mile to impress Tom, the way he had on so many other Deveraux-Heyward Shipping–related tasks in the past? Or had Jack eloped with Daisy simply because Jack wanted to, for reasons of his own? Either way, Tom concluded angrily, Jack and Daisy did not behave as if they were in love. Lust maybe, but not love. And lust was capricious at best, Tom knew.

"Thereby, adding one mistake to another," Grace added softly.

Tom nodded, agreeing with his ex-wife's assessment. Except he didn't know who to blame for this latest foolhardiness. Daisy, Jack or even himself for allowing any further contact between Jack and Daisy, period. The only thing Tom knew for sure was that none of what had happened was like Granger. Jack simply did not behave in an impetuous, irresponsible manner. Daisy, however, excelled in such reckless and inappropriate behavior. There had been dozens of stories about her antics over the years, starting when she was a little girl. Some had made the newspaper, many had not. But all were reported and savored—sometimes viciously—in Charleston society. Tom sighed, for the first time having an inkling of what Richard and Charlotte Templeton had been dealing with all these years. He didn't envy them the task of trying to rein Daisy in. Or himself, for having to possibly try and parent such an accomplished hellion at such a late stage. "I don't know what either Jack or Daisy was thinking," Tom stated finally.

Grace leaned toward Tom confidentially. "You don't think she's pregnant, do you?"

Daisy and Jack's actions would make sense if Daisy was carrying Jack's baby. But Jack hadn't said so and Tom would have expected Jack to have come right out and done that if that was indeed the case. Tom shrugged in open frustration. "If she is, they're keeping mum. Although, I wouldn't put it past Daisy to have forced or talked Jack into this marriage simply to get under the Templeton family's skin. Jack Granger is an excellent attorney, and aside from this mess-up, a fine man." One Tom respected. "But Jack Granger isn't what Charlotte and Richard would have wanted for Daisy, that's for certain."

"LOOKS LIKE WE'VE GOT company," Jack said as he and Daisy drank coffee together the next morning. Her

whole body still tingling and alive from the night of
nonstop lovemaking, Daisy glanced out the living-room
window and swore like a longshoreman. Oh, no, she
thought, vaulting up off the sectional sofa. No…

Jack, who was just about ready to leave for work,
anyway, arched a teasing eyebrow her way. "Not very
ladylike, Daze."

Daisy smiled at the endearment he'd adopted for her,
even as she sighed in unmitigated dread. "You want
ladylike, you've got the right person coming up the
front walk." Ducking beneath the view of the picture
window, she grabbed Jack and pushed him toward the
visual cover of the foyer. "Let's just pretend we're not
here," she hissed, even as the doorbell rang. "Or we're
still in bed or something."

Already tying the tie he had carelessly looped around
his neck, Jack headed for the door. "No sense putting
off for tomorrow what can be done today."

Jack opened the door, and Daisy looked at the
woman she had called "Mother" for as long as she
could remember. Only, Charlotte Templeton wasn't just
her adoptive mother, Daisy reminded herself firmly.
The silver-haired, beautifully put-together Charlotte
was also her biological grandmother.

Daisy could tell by the way she was dressed, in a
lovely lavender suit and matching low-heeled shoes,
that Charlotte was on her way to a steering committee
breakfast meeting or one of the many charities she sup-
ported. No one worked harder to raise funds for the less
fortunate, and Daisy couldn't help but respect Charlotte
immensely for that, even as she braced herself for the
inevitable confrontation that always came when Daisy
did something Charlotte and Richard had not preap-
proved.

Deciding it was better to be the aggressor than the victim, Daisy demanded brusquely as Jack ushered her mother inside, "What are you doing here?" Daisy knew she had every right to refuse to see Charlotte at all. After all, Charlotte and Richard had not only lied to Daisy for years about her parentage, they had disinherited her to try and manipulate her behavior. So Daisy knew she didn't owe them anything. But the need to be unconditionally loved and accepted by the family who had reared her, made her want to at least listen to what Charlotte had to say, in the vain hope that something—anything—would have changed for the better, in light of her discovery. Because she didn't enjoy fighting with her family or feeling so chronically misunderstood.

Charlotte stepped over the portal and took a brief unhappy glance around before returning her attention to Daisy. "Connor came over to see us last evening and told your father and I about your elopement." The gently disapproving look Daisy knew so well was back in Charlotte's pewter-gray eyes. "Your father asked me to come and talk to you this morning about your actions."

Which meant, Daisy thought, she was about to get blasted with Richard's words coming out of Charlotte's mouth. "Don't you mean grandfather?" Daisy asked sweetly. "Grandmother?"

Charlotte didn't blanch at her rudeness, merely said in the same cordial tone, "Darling, don't be difficult. It isn't becoming."

"Would you like to come in and have a cup of coffee with us, Mrs. Templeton?" Jack asked.

"Yes, I would. Very much." Charlotte smiled at Jack in the way people smiled at each other as they moved down a receiving line of relative strangers. Daisy reluctantly introduced the two. Then, while her limousine and her driver, Nigel, sat at the curb, Charlotte followed Jack down the hall to the breakfast nook. Jack helped Charlotte with her chair while Daisy dutifully found a mug, paper napkin and spoon, and put them in front of her. Sitting ramrod straight in the sling-back chair, Charlotte continued in a pleasant but serious tone. "Daisy, your father wants you to annul this marriage."

No surprise there, Daisy thought, although she was willing to bet those were not the words Richard Templeton had used. "And what about you?" Daisy asked casually as she poured and Jack brought out the sugar and cream. "Are you in agreement with Richard on this?"

Charlotte sighed audibly as she stirred in a tiny amount of cream and set her spoon on the paper napkin beside her plate. "If you want an annulment, if you've made a mistake, we can make this all go away. But you need to understand, Daisy darling, that if you decide to stay married to Jack, you will be married to him *for life*." Charlotte paused to look solemnly at them both. "There are no divorces in this family."

"I don't want a divorce," Jack said as he refreshed his own coffee then pulled out a chair for Daisy and autocratically motioned her into it.

Jack sounded so sure, Daisy thought, sliding reluctantly into the seat next to her mother. Too sure for Daisy's comfort, when her feelings were so confused. Yes, she wanted their baby to be born legitimate and have both a father and a mother in his or her life. But did she really want a husband? Or just a lover and a friend?

"What about you?" Charlotte asked Daisy steadily.

"Are you ready and willing to let Jack be the head of your household? Are you willing to gear your life to what he wants and says?"

Daisy would have laughed out loud at the outrageousness of the idea had her mother not been so serious. "Marriage doesn't have to be a dictatorship," Daisy countered stubbornly. In fact, that was one of her major frustrations, that Charlotte always deferred to Richard's wishes, even when Daisy could see Charlotte not only disagreed but was in the right.

Charlotte took a delicate sip from the faded Vanderbilt Law School mug. "Your father and I expect you and Jack to either come to your senses immediately and annul this quickly and quietly—"

"Or what?" Daisy asked, knowing full well there was more. Lots more to the ultimatum being delivered to her.

Charlotte set her mug back on the table and regarded Daisy evenly. "Or act like rational adults and show the world this is indeed the real deal."

Daisy didn't even have to ask what Richard and Charlotte wanted. Her "father" wanted her to wed only on his timetable, to whatever moneybags he personally selected for her, and the disappointed look in Charlotte's eyes gave her mother's feelings away. "You want me to end it, too, don't you?" Daisy guessed quietly.

Charlotte hesitated and glanced at Jack as if not wanting to offend him, when he at least had been so cordial to her. Turning back to Daisy, Charlotte said gently but bluntly, "Honey, a life without the kind of money you are used to is no life at all."

Meaning, Daisy thought, as long as she was married to Jack, her parents would not reinstate her trust fund, or give her access to her multimillion dollar inheritance. She'd have to live off what she and Jack earned, and while that was certainly more than adequate, it wasn't the same as being an heiress.

Daisy glanced heavenward, almost too exasperated to speak. "And what would you know about that, Mother?" Daisy baited emotionally, annoyed to find herself having to defend her actions to her exceedingly uptight adoptive parents yet again. "You and Father were both born with silver spoons in your mouths. You both come from very old money."

"Well, I suppose technically that's so, but—"

"But what?" Daisy asked when her mother stopped in midsentence.

Charlotte glanced at Jack cautiously.

"You can trust him, Mother," Daisy said impatiently. "He's not just my husband, and as such the newest member of the Templeton family, he's a company counsel for the Deveraux-Heyward Shipping Company. He knows how to keep a secret."

Jack nodded, letting Charlotte Templeton know this was so. "Nothing said here today will leave this room."

Charlotte took a deep breath and pushed on reluctantly, wringing her hands all the while. "I've never told you this, Daisy. I've never told anyone, but our life was not always luxurious."

"Meaning what exactly?" Daisy said in mounting frustration.

"Meaning," Charlotte continued in a strangled voice, "unbeknownst to Richard and I, both your father's family and mine were slowly going broke when they arranged for us to marry. Our mutual near poverty was a cruel irony we discovered only after we had married, in one of the biggest and most lavish weddings Charleston had ever seen.''

Daisy recalled seeing the photos. Both Charlotte and Richard had looked ecstatic at the time, so different than they looked today.

Appearing determined to bring Daisy around to her way of thinking, Charlotte continued her recitation sadly, ''For years we struggled, amassing more and more debt as we tried to keep up appearances and hold on to both Rosewood, your father's family estate, and our home in the city, which was my family's residence. It was such a relief when we finally got things turned around.'' Charlotte paused, biting her lip emotionally. ''I never wanted you to have to suffer that way, darling.''

Daisy could tell by the look on Charlotte's face that it had indeed been difficult for a woman accustomed to having only the very best, but that didn't mean that Daisy agreed with Charlotte. In fact, Daisy thought her mother was dead wrong. ''We'll be fine,'' Daisy returned.

Again, Charlotte shook her head. She looked even more distressed. ''Daisy, you're used to fine things, designer clothes. The money to travel and do whatever you like. Whether you realize it or not right now, those things are the key to your happiness.''

Wrong, Daisy thought. She would have traded it all when she was growing up—the money, the social position, the entrée to all the best schools and parties—to live in a house filled with love and laughter with parents who were warm and loving and understanding. Where what mattered was sticking up for each other through thick and thin instead of worrying about what the others in blue-blooded Charleston society would think. Without trying to have the most luxuriously decorated houses, the most exclusive parties, the best lifestyle, the most lavish vacations. But that would never be the case in Charlotte and Richard's home, where separate bedrooms for the mistress and master of the house were the norm, and Charlotte filled her emotional needs by doing good deeds for others.

Charlotte leaned forward earnestly and caught Daisy's hand. "It's still not too late, Daisy. Your father and I can make a good match for you, just like we made a good match for your sister, Iris."

Daisy just bet they could. She wasn't, however, about to let them. She pulled her hand away from her mother's and bolted from her chair. "Randolph Hayes IV was an old goat," she declared flatly.

Charlotte looked as horrified as always by Daisy's outspokenness. "Daisy, I won't have you talking that way about such a fine man."

Daisy made a face as she continued to pace the breakfast room. "That man was thirty years older than Iris, Mother! He spent the last fifteen years of their life together in a wheelchair, surrounded by a bevy of male nurses." What kind of marriage was that for someone as young and vital as Iris? Daisy wondered, upset. Especially when there was no love, no companionship or true friendship whatsoever involved, at least not that she could see.

Charlotte glared at Daisy. "Randolph was also very very good to Iris financially. And unlike many lusty young husbands, he didn't run around on her."

With good reason, Daisy thought. There was no way Randolph Hayes had been capable of the sex act in his frail condition. Absolutely no friggin' way. Not that sex seemed to matter at all to Iris after what Daisy now knew was Iris's failed love affair with Tom. No, Iris had seemed content to live the life of a dedicated career woman, albeit a very rich and privately lonely one. Just as Daisy probably would have done if she hadn't met Jack and learned just how great lovemaking with a handsome, virile, kind man could be.

Not that she should let herself get used to such incredible pleasure, in any case, Daisy reminded herself wearily. Not when she and Jack were together because of a night of reckless passion, and the baby who'd resulted, and that was all. Not when—like everything else important or valuable in her life—it could all be taken away from her at any moment. Leaving her bereft and alone.

"What are you thinking, dear?" Charlotte asked while Jack looked at Daisy as if wondering the very same thing.

That I could tell you about the pregnancy, and the cries for an immediate end to my marriage to Jack would probably stop. But Daisy didn't want to make things even worse than what they were, because contrary to popular opinion, she did not enjoy fighting with Richard and Charlotte, or bringing their considerable disapproval down on her shoulders. Not at all.

Aware Charlotte and Jack were both still waiting for her answer, Daisy drew a deep, bolstering breath and looked her mother straight in the eye. "I'm not going to get an annulment, Mother. I made the decision to marry Jack and I'm sticking to it."

Charlotte took a moment to absorb that. She handled the news with amazing tranquillity. "Well, then—" Charlotte gave them both a bracing smile "—I guess we move forward with the official announcement of your marriage."

Daisy held up a hand, stop-sign fashion. "There's no need for that, Mother. Word will get around."

As always when she disagreed, Charlotte simply ignored Daisy's protests and charged on. "Your father and I were already planning a soiree tonight with one hundred of our dearest friends. We will simply use that party to honor you and your new husband," Charlotte said calmly. Charlotte looked at Jack. "The dress is formal. I assume you have a tuxedo?"

Jack nodded, suddenly looking, Daisy thought, every bit as tense and wary as she felt.

"Please be sure you wear it, then." Charlotte smiled at Jack, then turned to Daisy as she rose with quiet dignity and prepared to take her leave. "Cocktails will be served at eight. We would like you both there then."

"THAT WAS IT?" Jack said moments later, as soon as Charlotte had left. "Your parents are going to accept our marriage just like that?" He seemed stunned by Charlotte's about-face.

Well used to her parents' defensive actions by now, Daisy shrugged and leaned back against the kitchen counter. She folded her arms in front of her. "They don't want a scandal. They'll do anything they can to avoid that, even if it means sweeping their true feelings about what we've gone and done under the rug. They are both ever so efficient at that."

Jack studied her with a half smile. Finally, he shrugged. "Do you want to even go to the party then, knowing they aren't sincere?"

As if it were that simple, Daisy thought with no small trace of irony. Doing her best to keep the bitterness out of her voice, she said, "I have to."

"Why?" Jack cupped gentle hands around her shoulders. "If it's going to stress you out and make you unhappy?"

Oh, she liked how this man thought, how he constantly wanted to protect her, even if his approach was wrong, wrong, wrong. Aware he was waiting for an answer, as well as an explanation, Daisy released a beleaguered sigh and let him take her all the way into his arms. "Because they won't give up on the idea until they do publicly honor us in some way. They have their reputations to maintain, you see, and if we don't show up, it will only make gossip worse. Which in turn will cause Charlotte to hound me, and sic both Connor and Iris on me, as well. And, as if all that were not enough, I would then be called in to receive some stern lecture from my adoptive fath—from Richard." Daisy let her head fall forward to rest on the solidness of Jack's chest. "It's easier to just go tonight and get it over with, and be done with it."

"Is that the only reason?" Jack asked, rubbing his hands soothingly up and down her back.

Daisy cuddled closer to Jack's warmth. "It's not like they could disinherit me," she murmured against his chest. "They've already done that. They cut off my access to my trust fund months ago when I refused to call off my search for my birth parents."

Jack tucked a hand beneath her chin and tilted her head up to his. "You know what I mean," he said softly.

When they were close like this, Daisy found it hard not to smile. "Actually, I'm not sure I do."

Jack inclined his head slightly to the side. "Maybe now that you do know the truth about yourself, and why they did what they did, even if it was misguided," he suggested softly and compassionately, "you'd secretly like to make up with them. Let bygones be bygones. They are your family, after all.''

How had he known? Daisy wondered. And why did it bother her so much that he did see that vulnerability in her, the need to be liked and loved and accepted by Richard and Charlotte, the way she had always longed to be, and had never been in the past. Even when she was seven and too young and too sweet and too innocent to cause much trouble at all. Even then, her family had—with the exception of her decade-older brother Connor—looked at her as if there was something wrong with her that only they could see, something not quite acceptable. And Daisy had felt their mute disaffection to her bones.

Eventually figuring if she wasn't going to be liked for herself anyway, she might as well do something to make herself unlovable in their eyes, she had begun acting out. That way, she had reasoned subconsciously as a very young child and a teenager, at least her world sort of made sense. Then she had known precisely why they were unhappy with her—she hadn't used proper table manners, she had sworn in front of the ladies at tea, she had tracked mud on the one-hundred-year-old Aubusson rug in the grand foyer. It had been, while she was growing up, a lot easier to simply misbehave and take her punishment than go on wondering if they were looking at her funny or distastefully because they just didn't like her nose. Or more likely still, knew something shameful or awful about her mysterious beginnings they just didn't want *her* to ever know.

''That's not gonna happen,'' Daisy said. As much as she might want it to… Daisy sighed, shook her head. ''I gave up wishing for the impossible years ago. But

as for the party tonight—that might not be so bad."
And, in fact, Daisy thought with her customary per-
verseness kicking in, it might be fun to watch them
squirm.

CHAPTER EIGHT

THAT EVENING, Daisy insisted Jack dress and shower first, then shooed him out of the master bedroom and bath. An hour later, he decided it had been worth the wait. Daisy was absolutely gorgeous, and she smelled every bit as glamorous and sexy as she looked as she swirled around, giving him the full view of her evening attire.

As Daisy ended her pirouette, she paused. Some of the pleasure left her eyes. "You don't like it. Do you?"

On the contrary, he thought, sorry he had inadvertently hurt her feelings. He liked the way she looked, maybe too much. "Don't get me wrong," he said, studying the silky white stretch tank top that cupped her small high breasts like a lover's hands, and ankle-length pale blue chiffon skirt with the uneven ruffle at the hem. "You look absolutely stunning." And more like the incredibly wealthy heiress she had grown up to be. The one that was way, way out of his league.

"Thank you." Daisy beamed, pleased. "It's something I've had for a while and it's Armani."

"But—"

Daisy grinned mischievously, knowing full well what he was about to say as she went up on tiptoe to lightly, teasingly brush his lips with hers. "My navel is showing?"

Fighting the urge to say the hell with the damn party

and appeasing the Templetons, and take her right back to bed, where the two of them communicated best anyway, Jack caught her against him, so the softness of her breasts were pressed against his chest. He wanted to kiss her until she couldn't so much as catch her breath, but he couldn't do that when they would be attending a very proper party announcing their marriage. So Jack told himself reluctantly, the lovemaking would have to wait for a more appropriate time, while the two of them dealt with the dilemma at hand.

He looked down at her sternly. "Somehow, I doubt this—" enjoying the silky feel of her fair freckled flesh, Jack dragged his palm lightly across the exposed skin of her still-flat abdomen and felt her quiver in response "—is what your mother had in mind, Daisy." In fact, Jack was certain that Charlotte and Richard both would expect Daisy to show up tonight in something a lot more conservative than what she had on now. But that was apparently tough, as far as his new wife was concerned. If Daisy was going to do this, she was apparently going to do it the way she did everything else—on her terms.

Jack tried not to think how this latest rebellion of Daisy's might complicate things as Daisy shrugged. "I've got to be me," she announced as if that were that. "You look nice." She turned her attention to straightening his bow tie.

Her expression admiring, Daisy ran her hands over the expensive black fabric, caressing his shoulders and chest. "It looks new."

It was his turn to shrug as he said gruffly, "I didn't want to embarrass you—or your folks. And I figured, given the way we got married…" He left the thought hanging.

Daisy's eyes sparkled as she fervently leaped to his defense. "You wouldn't embarrass me if you went to the party in beach shorts."

Jack grinned at the hilarious image that conjured up. He had a feeling that was about what the Templetons expected, given the fact he had more or less grown up on the docks. And if not for Tom Deveraux's mentorship and steady belief in him, might still be there, too. But that was neither here nor there. Knowing they were already late, and this would probably be frowned on, too, Jack offered Daisy his arm. "I can see where you'd get a charge out of that," he commented dryly. Jack had been trailing Daisy long enough to know there was nothing she'd liked better than to create a stir when things got too oppressive. One thing was certain, Jack thought. Life would never be dull as her husband.

Jack could tell by the way Daisy babbled nonstop during the drive to the Templetons' residence that she was nervous. As he listened to her cheerful monologue, he laughed occasionally, smiled often and silently promised to make the evening as easy as he could on her. Lord knew, her adoptive parents wouldn't. And that was a feeling confirmed the moment Jack was taken through the crowd of guests into an alcove beneath the stairs and introduced to Richard Templeton. "So, you're the upstart who eloped with my Daisy," Richard said. His tone and cordial smile said he was teasing, his eyes did not. They were cold, assessing and hard as flint.

Daisy looked uneasy. She might not care so much about herself, but it was clear she didn't want Jack taking any slings and arrows from Richard. Tensing visibly, she asked Richard with remarkable poise under the circumstances, "Have you made an announcement?"

"I'm about to." Ignoring the hurt radiating from Daisy's eyes, Richard stepped up onto the grand staircase that divided the formal rooms at the front of the mansion where a hundred or so guests were all circulating, champagne glasses in hand. With a nod, he indicated Daisy and Jack should both join him then gestured broadly and waited until he had everyone's attention.

"You all know our beloved Daisy," Richard said as a white-coated waiter handed Daisy and Jack each a crystal flute of champagne. "What you may not know is that her last name is no longer Templeton. It's now Templeton-Granger." Richard smiled as if genuinely happy as a murmur of surprise swept through the formally dressed crowd. "Daisy and Jack eloped in Tahoe a few days ago. She didn't give us a chance to give her a proper wedding, but Charlotte and I are determined to make up for that, and plan to give Daisy and her new husband something very special from our private stock of antiques at Rosewood—"

An envious murmur swept through the crowd.

Doing an excellent job of feigning both warmth and delight, Richard turned to Jack and Daisy. "So let's lift our glasses to them in toast. Daisy, Jack…we all wish you the very best."

Richard's words were seconded by the crowd as glasses clinked all around and everyone smiled and sipped champagne. Richard Templeton put a proprietary arm around Daisy's shoulders, and, leaving Jack to follow in their wake, proceeded to take Daisy through the crowd so their guests could congratulate them one by one. On the surface, Jack noted, Daisy appeared to handle it well. But he could tell by the tense set of her shoulders and the slight brittleness of her smile that she was just going through the motions for her family's sake. And that she resented the absence of her older sister Iris.

After about fifteen minutes of playing the doting father, Richard left Jack and Daisy to circulate on their own. They had just made their way back to the front hall, when the fifty-something Winnifred Deveraux-Smith, the social doyenne of Charleston, and her long-lost great-aunt Eleanor Deveraux, about whom all of Charleston was still buzzing, entered.

Jack wasn't surprised to see both women there. A party wasn't truly considered on the A-list unless Winnifred showed up. And since Winnifred and Charlotte Templeton both chaired steering committees on all the most important charitable organizations in the city, it made sense Tom's sister had been invited. Winnifred and the eighty-year-old Eleanor made a beeline for Daisy. Looking as stunning as usual in a shimmering red evening gown, the dark-haired Winnifred made introductions briefly then said cheerfully, "What have we missed? Anything?"

Daisy looked at one of the true beauties of that generation and said quickly, as if wanting to get it over with, "Jack and I got married."

Given the compassionate understanding way Winnifred was looking at them, Jack guessed Tom had finally confided the situation with him and Daisy and Iris and Grace to his only sister, something he had apparently been reluctant to do until now. However, the rest of the Deveraux family seemed suspiciously absent from the gala.

But Tom hadn't yet told Winnifred about the marriage. And about *that* Winnifred Deveraux was very surprised.

"When?" Winnifred gasped, still looking a little stunned. Beside her, the frail but energetic-looking Eleanor simply looked pleased.

Daisy's cheeks flushed slightly at the romantic expression on Winnifred's face. Jack knew how Daisy felt. He kept wanting to correct people, too, so it wouldn't feel so much like they were simply lovers, living a lie. "A few days ago in Tahoe," she said.

Winnifred turned back to Jack, politely doing her best to hide her concern. "How does my brother feel about the nuptials?" she asked.

Good question. The cynical part of Jack was still waiting for another punch to the jaw, while the naive kid in him—the kid who had looked up to Tom for what seemed like forever—kept hoping it would all work out for the best in the end. And that he and his boss could put all the disillusionment and disappointment behind them. Not quite sure how to answer the woman, Jack said finally, "I think he's still getting used to the idea."

Ever the romantic at heart, Winnifred smiled. "Well, you two will simply have to come by for dinner some evening and tell Eleanor and me all about it."

Jack smiled back, knowing the invitation was a genuine one. "What have you two grand ladies been up to?"

"Well, this afternoon, Eleanor and I were over at 10 Gathering Street. Lauren and Mitch were showing us their plans for the secret room."

Jack knew, as did Daisy, they were referring to Tom and Grace's son Mitch and his wife, Lauren. Lauren had received the historic twenty-four-room mansion as a gift from her father, Peyton Heyward, in exchange for dating Mitch for one week. Lauren and Mitch had initially resisted the plan—which had smacked of an arranged marriage from days of old—but eventually they agreed to Peyton Heyward's terms when Peyton also promised a business merger of the Heyward and Deveraux shipping firms, which Mitch had wanted for some time. Neither Mitch nor Lauren had expected to fall in love with each other during their week of prearranged marathon dating, but they had, and now were married and living happily ever after in the gifted mansion.

"What secret room?" Daisy interrupted curiously.

"The one behind the library, where I used to tryst with Captain Douglas Nyquist," Eleanor said, a mischievous sparkle in her eyes that oddly enough reminded Jack very much of Daisy. Yet another indication, he supposed, of the Deveraux blood coursing through her veins.

"I visited there undetected for years," Eleanor said as she used her silver-handled walking cane to ease into a chair, "because no one knew about the room or the secret passageway leading to it from the garden. But when Lauren received the house from her father last spring, she found both. As well as all the mementos of my love affair that I had hidden there. Of course, it caused quite a stir in the family, because at that time they didn't know I was still around." Eleanor smiled, reminding Jack and Daisy how she had faked her own death years before to escape the terrible scandal and resulting curse surrounding her ill-fated love affair. "But now they do, and they've welcomed me with open arms."

Jack knew that to be true. The delightful Eleanor had quickly become a treasured member of the Deveraux clan once again. And the legacy of failed love that had followed the Deveraux for years had also been broken, as all four of Tom and Grace's legitimate offspring were now very much in love and happily married.

"How wonderful that you've become a part of the family again," Daisy said sincerely as she pulled up a chair to sit beside Eleanor. "And how romantic to actually have rendezvoused in a secret room!"

Jack could see where the clandestine nature of such an affair would appeal to his adventure-loving wife. Happy to talk about something other than her elopement for a change, Daisy continued chatting with Eleanor. "I used to look for secret passageways in this house when I was a kid," Daisy said, "but I could never find any."

"Neither could I," Connor said, coming up to join them. He gave Daisy a hug. "Hey, sis."

"Hey yourself, Connor."

"Jack." Connor shook Jack's hand.

"Do you have any secret places in your house?" Daisy asked Winnifred.

"No secret rooms, but we do have a passageway from the attic that leads to the outside." Winnifred smiled. "When you and Jack drop by, I'll show it to you."

"If memory serves, there was one at Rosewood, too," Eleanor said.

"You're kidding!" Daisy turned to Richard, who had noticed Winnifred and Eleanor's arrival and come over to welcome them. Daisy looked at Richard, her eyes shining with excitement. "Eleanor says that there's a secret room at Rosewood."

Richard cut off Daisy's enthusiasm with a genial shake of his head and discounting smile. "That rumor has been around for years, but there is absolutely no truth to it. I know that mansion inside out. There are no secret rooms or passageways, or if there were, they were uncovered and opened up years ago. I've had it checked out by an architect and a structural engineer.''

Before he could go on, a guy with a camera slung around his neck and a notepad in his hand, pushed his way forward. Daisy turned to get a look at the tuxedo-clad interloper. And all the color drained from her face.

FOR A LOT OF REASONS, Bucky Jerome was the last person Daisy wanted to see tonight.

"And here I thought tonight was going to be just another party," Bucky remarked with a cheerful smile that didn't fool Daisy in the least. He lifted his camera and snapped what had to be a particularly unflattering picture of her and Jack standing side by side. "Just so you'll all know to look for it—" Bucky let the camera fall back against his chest "—that will be in tomorrow's newspaper."

"Great," Daisy said. That was just what she needed. Another item about herself on the society page.

Bucky picked up his pad and pen. He looked Daisy over from head to toe in a way that was not only bound to irk Jack but reminded her of things she would much rather forget. "So how long have the two of you been seeing each other?" he asked in a bored, disrespectful tone.

"Long enough," Daisy said tensely, wishing Bucky Jerome would just go away. And stay away. Before the conversation turned any more personal.

Bucky turned to Jack. Waited for what seemed an interminable length of time before Jack deigned to answer.

"Daisy and I like our private life to stay private,"

Jack replied politely. "So just report the facts—that we eloped in Tahoe—and leave it at that."

"Hmm." Bucky knew Daisy well enough not to believe a word of that.

And of course, Daisy thought uncomfortably, Bucky was right. Her relationship with Jack wasn't anywhere near that routine. Her relationship with Jack was as unexpected and complicated as it was possible to be.

"If that's the way you want it," Bucky said with an offhand shrug, turning his full attention to whatever it was he was writing.

"It is," Jack said firmly.

Not bothering to look up again, Bucky scribbled something else on his pad and moved off.

"Thanks for helping me with that." Daisy breathed a sigh of relief the moment she and Jack were alone.

Jack gave Bucky—who was already busy taking photos of Eleanor Deveraux and Winnifred Deveraux-Smith, with Charlotte and Richard Templeton—another long thoughtful glance, then turned back to Daisy. "There's some sort of angst between the two of you, isn't there?"

Daisy really did not want to get into this—particularly with Jack. "We went to school together, from kindergarten on up." She'd prefer to just leave it at that. "And?"

Daisy pretended to study the array of appetizers laid out on the buffet. "I dated him a long time ago, okay?"

To Daisy's dismay, Jack wasn't buying her he's-just-an-old-boyfriend-and-now-it's-awkward-between-us excuse. He watched her pick up a plate and load it down with hot crab dip and crackers. "Why did it end?"

Leave it to Jack to cut straight to the chase, Daisy thought. Knowing the lawyerly inquisition wasn't going to stop until Jack found out the reason for the peculiar vibes between her and Bucky and that it was probably best if he heard it from her—and not Bucky—Daisy scooped some dip onto the end of a cracker and said, "Because we did not have a good time together at our senior prom."

His expression more gallantly protective than ever, Jack helped himself to a plate of stuffed mushrooms and appetizer meatballs. Grabbing a fork and napkins for them both, he steered her out onto the portico and quietly shut the door behind them. He looked around to make certain they were alone on the shadowy veranda, then sat down on the low wrought-iron bench next to the side of the house and continued prodding. "Why do I think there's more to this story?"

Because there is. Figuring he might as well hear the basics from her instead of someone else, Daisy finished chewing her cracker. "I was pretty wild back then."

Jack shrugged and looked at her expectantly. "An understatement, if there ever was one, and not completely untrue today, either."

Daisy grinned at the gentle hint of teasing in his voice. She'd finally found a man who could appreciate her love of excitement. Although now that she was pregnant and married, to boot, she found her outlook on life—and perhaps her actions, too—becoming a lot more serious. Because it wasn't just herself she had to think about now. She had the baby. And Jack, too.

"So what did he do?" Jack continued as Daisy took a seat next to him on the bench. At that moment, he looked all of his thirty-two years. "Get drunk and throw up all over your prom dress?"

Daisy wished that was all that had happened that

night, five years ago. "He rented a hotel room, and he—we—it was my first time and it was awful. So we broke up."

"And Bucky Jerome was pissed," Jack guessed.

"Oh yeah." Daisy drew a breath, recalling Bucky's emotional reaction to her leave-taking. "He, uh…"

"Wanted to continue being your lover."

Daisy nodded, glad the shadows of the porch were hiding the hot embarrassment she felt. She looked Jack square in the eye, figuring she might as well tell him the rest. "He said I hadn't given him a fair chance and he wanted another go at it."

"But you weren't interested?"

"I realized it was a big mistake because…"

"What?" Jack asked when she didn't immediately go on.

Because I didn't like it, Daisy thought, blushing all the more. But knowing she couldn't say that—it would sound too hokey and she wasn't a hokey kind of girl, she said only, "Because he wasn't special to me, so—" Daisy paused and shrugged her shoulders. "I got out of it. Anyway, my parents sent me to Europe with Iris that summer to try and get me interested in the family antiques business, which of course didn't work, and then Bucky and I both went off to college, so our paths have rarely crossed since. I knew he was back and that he was working at the newspaper for his dad because he's set to inherit it someday—the Jeromes have owned the *Charleston Herald* forever."

"But for now, he's writing the society column 'Around the City.'"

Daisy's eyes widened in surprise. "You know about that?" She wouldn't have figured Jack was the type to read the society page. Any society page.

Jack nodded, his expression turning even more grim. "He put a mention of Grace and Paulo in the column. No one in the Deveraux family was happy about it."

So Jack had learned about Bucky's superambitious style through the Deveraux clan, Daisy thought. That made sense. "That doesn't surprise me." From what Daisy had been able to figure thus far, Bucky was copying the supersalacious style of some of the big-city gossip columns. It was a way to get famous fast, if you didn't get sued, beaten up, fired or slandered yourself first.

"Do you want me to talk to him?" Jack asked, looking protective again.

Daisy frowned impatiently as she put her half-eaten appetizers aside. "And tell him what? He can't print news of our marriage in the paper?"

Jack shrugged. "We could refuse to let him run our photo tomorrow, for starters."

"No. The last thing we want to do is make him more curious than he already is about our elopement. Bucky curious is a very bad thing." He was almost nosier than Daisy was. In fact, it had been Bucky who had encouraged her nonstop her senior year to try and find out who her real parents were the moment she turned eighteen. At the time, Daisy had been grateful for Bucky's support in that regard—he was one of the few people who had understood, never mind applauded, her need to know where she came from. But as for the rest of it, Bucky was self-centered to a fault, and as reckless and relentless as she was. Worse, he was determined to make a name for himself in journalism circles, and he didn't care who he had to step on, or over, to do so.

"All right." Jack set his plate aside and stood. "But if he gives you any trouble, if he even looks at you funny from now on, I want to know."

"You're not going all protective on me, are you?" Daisy asked as Jack pulled her to her feet.

He wrapped his arms about her waist. "Would it really be such a bad thing if I was?" Not giving her a chance to answer, he leaned down and gently kissed her lips.

JACK HAD TO GIVE Daisy credit—she was everything Richard and Charlotte could have wanted in a daughter that evening. She was cordial to everyone, not leaving until the last guests were out the door. But, Jack noted immediately, that was absolutely as long as Daisy was going to stay.

She paused to kiss her mother's cheek as they were headed out, and merely nodded at her father. "Thank you for the party."

"I meant what I said about the wedding gift," Richard stated as he walked them to the door. He looked directly at Daisy. "Meet me at Rosewood tomorrow afternoon at two and we'll pick something out."

Daisy edged closer to Jack. "You have to work tomorrow afternoon, don't you?"

Jack could tell Daisy was looking for a way out of the meeting. Fortunately, Daisy was correct in her assessment and he didn't have to fib. Jack flashed Richard and Charlotte an apologetic smile. "I'm tied up all afternoon with Tom and Mitch—we're working to resolve a dispute with one of the Deveraux-Heyward Shipping Company customers. But if we could do it later in the week, or perhaps early next week," Jack said.

"I'm afraid that is impossible for me," Richard Templeton said coolly. "But that's all right. It's not necessary for you to be there anyway, Jack. I'm sure Daisy can pick something out for the two of you, can't you, dear?''

For a moment, Jack thought Daisy was going to rebel at her father's pushiness. "Sure," Daisy said after a moment, the spirit seeming to drain out of her as quickly as it had appeared.

"Do you always do that?" Jack asked as he and Daisy got in the car.

"What?" Daisy busied herself putting on her safety belt.

"Bend to your father's will."

"Obviously not." Daisy rolled her eyes at him and continued dryly, "Or I wouldn't have earned a rep as the wild child of Charleston society."

"Then why are you doing it now, first with Charlotte and then Richard?"

"Isn't it obvious?" Daisy wrapped her arms around her middle, as if trying to give herself a comforting hug, and seemed to shrink into herself. "I'm trying to save *you* some grief."

If Jack weren't in the midst of traffic, he would have taken her in his arms again and kissed her until she saw things his way. As it was, all he could do was lift his right hand from the steering wheel and reach over and gently cup her knee through the silky fabric of her skirt. "You don't have to protect me, Daze," he said softly, appreciating her efforts nevertheless.

"When it comes to my family, someone should." The stubborn note was back in her voice.

As traffic cleared, Jack sped up. "Maybe I can re-schedule that meeting tomorrow." There had to be some way he could help her.

"You don't have to. I'll be okay. I promise." Arms still clasped in front of her, Daisy stared straight ahead.

"He probably just wants a chance to lecture me on how I've dishonored the Templeton name and reputation once more with my recklessness. Believe me," Daisy sighed heavily, "it's not anything I haven't heard before."

CHAPTER NINE

BUCKY JEROME'S NOSE for news told him there was a lot more going on with Daisy and Jack Granger than she or her family wanted to let on. So first thing the next morning, he headed over to the family business to see what he could weasel out of Daisy's uptight older sister, Iris, who was also the only member of the family who hadn't been at Richard and Charlotte's party the night before.

"Hello, Bucky. You're here bright and early," Iris Templeton said pleasantly as she unlocked the door of Templeton's Fine Antiques and ushered him inside. Although Bucky felt a little bad about forcing himself on Daisy and her new husband the night before, he had no such compunction about Daisy's snotty older sister. Iris had never been nice to him—except in the most insincere socially adept way—and he sensed she never would. And the same went for Charlotte and Richard Templeton. They had never for one second approved of Daisy's association with him, Bucky knew. Not even five years before when he and Daisy had been boyfriend and girlfriend.

"I brought you a copy of the newspaper." Bucky handed it over helpfully. "Thought you might like to see the mention of your younger sister and her new hubby."

To Bucky's disappointment, Iris's face registered no

emotion about the nuptials, either way. How was he going to get a gossipy behind-the-scenes story about the Templeton clan if she didn't reveal more?

"Thank you. I read it over breakfast. And the mention was nice. Although—" Iris looked down her elegantly chiseled nose at him "—the accompanying picture of them could have used some work."

That was an understatement and then some, Bucky knew, doing his best not to grin. Jack's face was half turned away, and Daisy was grimacing at the camera. Which just went to show, Bucky thought, even two people as good-looking as those two, could take a bad picture. "Yeah, well..." Aware Iris was waiting for an explanation or an apology or both, Bucky shrugged. "You'll need to talk to my dad about that. He won't assign me a photographer to go to these events, and I don't know a lot about taking pictures."

Iris walked from window to window, efficiently raising the blinds. "I haven't noticed you having a problem taking a decent photo of anyone else."

Bucky followed her. "You think I did that on purpose?"

Iris shot him a censuring look. "Didn't you?"

"Maybe. Could be I'm a little jealous," Bucky fibbed, knowing the truth was he had stopped thinking he and Daisy would ever get back together a long time ago. What he wanted now—besides maybe a little revenge for the way Daisy had so unceremoniously dumped him—was fame. If there was even half the story behind Daisy's sudden elopement that Bucky sensed there was, he would have a very juicy story to write. "Which is why I wanted to talk to you. I thought you might be able to give me the lowdown on what's really going on there."

Iris walked through the shop, her high heels clicking on the wide-planked wooden floor. "You're a reporter, Bucky. I don't discuss private family business with the press."

"So then the family has nothing to say about the match?"

Iris plucked a feather duster from behind the sales counter at the rear of the shop. "Whether or not the family approved would be a moot point, since Daisy and Jack are already married."

Bucky watched Iris dispense with little spots of dust here and there. "You could pressure her to have the marriage annulled," he said, still trailing along behind her. "It's not as if that hasn't been done before. An heiress runs off with someone clearly not of her ilk—the parents intervene and call in a few markers—presto, change-o." Bucky snapped his fingers. "It's like it never happened."

Iris gave him a condescending look and countered sweetly, "You have an active imagination. Has anyone ever told you that?"

All the time. Bucky whipped a pad and pen from his pocket. "How long has she been dating him?"

Iris put the feather duster away and ignored him.

Able to see the professional approach was not going to work, Bucky put his notepad and pen back in his pocket. "By the way, I was sorry to hear about your husband passing last year."

"Thank you."

"You'd been married for a long time, hadn't you?"

"Almost twenty-two years." Iris walked over and turned on the store's interior lights.

"Wow. Think Daisy and Jack will make it that long?"

Iris smiled at him again, lethally this time. "Bucky...?"

Wondering if he should duck and cover before answering, Bucky responded, "Yes?"

"This is getting tiresome. So if it's the only reason you're here—"

"Actually, it's not," Bucky interrupted before Iris could throw him out of her prestigious shop. "I need to buy a present for my dad's birthday, and I was thinking something for his office at work might be nice." Where Adlai could see it every day and hopefully be reminded that Bucky was, if nothing else, the dutiful son. "I was hoping you could help me pick it out."

Iris studied him. "I'd need to know a lot more about your father's taste. I don't think he has shopped here much in the past."

"Actually, he's not ever really been into antiques, not the way some of the other residents of Charleston are, but I was thinking that could change if I bought him something really special. You know, a conversation piece. So what do you say? Can you help me?" And in the meantime, Bucky hoped, maybe Iris would relax a little and inadvertently let something slip. Or he'd be able to find out something salacious that could end up in print just by nosing around.

"How much would you like to spend?"

Bucky thought about what his father was paying him at the *Herald*. "Low end," Bucky said. "Definitely low end." There was a limit, after all, as to how much he was willing to put himself out for a ploy that might or might not work, on either level.

The door clanged. A looker in high heels and an airline uniform with a photo-identification badge dangling on a chain between ample breasts walked in. She was in her late thirties, early forties, and had shoulder-length red hair, savvy green eyes. As a rule, Bucky wasn't into older women, but if he was, he would definitely be into...Ginger Zaring, Reservations Agent.

Iris shot Bucky a look that instructed him to control his gawking, then turned to Ginger Zaring. "May I help you with something?" Iris asked kindly.

"Yes," Ginger said, her expression sober. She looked at Iris meaningfully. "I'd like to speak to you privately, if I may."

For a second, Iris looked taken aback by the unmistakably intimate plea in Ginger Zaring's eyes. Then she tensed. "Certainly," Iris said in the too-cheerful tone of an experienced businesswoman bracing for trouble. Iris looked at Bucky. "Why don't you have a look at the mantel clocks, and also the lamps and the crystal figurines at the front of the store."

Bucky couldn't imagine his father with a figurine, but what the heck.

"Sure thing," Bucky said as Iris led the looker back to the rear of the store and into her office for a tête-à-tête behind the closed glass door.

THE WOMAN STARTED the confession that Iris absolutely did not want to hear the moment her office door was shut.

Her lower lip trembling as if she was about to cry, Ginger Zaring lowered her eyes and said, "I'd give anything if the situation were different, but...I know you saw us yesterday afternoon and are very aware of what is going on."

Iris stared at Ginger Zaring in frustration. Didn't this naive woman understand that if they just pretended nothing had happened they could make it all go away, at least as far as the two of them were concerned, anyway? "I don't know what you're talking about, and I don't know you," Iris lied tersely.

Ginger gave Iris a weary look that seemed to come straight from her soul. "It was during the open house for the Greenville Garden Society. The upstairs loft in one of the antique barns at Rosewood. Does any of *that* jar your memory?"

Iris squirmed at the ribald image that popped into her head. She hadn't gotten a really good look at the time, for one simple reason, she hadn't wanted to know.

"Look," Ginger said even more unhappily, "I don't have the time or the energy to play games with you."

Iris swallowed the revulsion gathering in her throat. She couldn't believe this was happening to her again. "It wouldn't be wise of you to try. Therefore—"

"I want you to talk to him," Ginger continued.

Iris drew a stabilizing breath and continued to play the innocent she wished like hell she still was. "Who?"

"You know who—your father."

Iris looked down at the stack of receipts on her desk, garnered from yesterday afternoon's sale. "Isn't this your business?" she queried coolly.

Ginger paused, then continued in a low, stumbling voice, "The thing is, I thought I could handle this. I *was* handling it, even though it's not really my thing. But lately he's been really pushing the envelope." Ginger looked up at Iris, a frightened, pleading look in her eyes. Her lower lip started trembling again. "I don't think I have to tell you that this is the kind of foolishness that gets people killed."

No kidding, Iris thought.

Her face a map of emotions, Ginger rushed on, "I've got a kid who means the world to me and I don't want what I've been doing with him to become public knowledge.''

So stop it instead of whining to me, Iris thought.

"And I sure as hell don't want to *die* getting caught doing it,'' Ginger continued in a low, choked-up voice.

Aware Bucky was just on the other side of the door, and this could well become a very ugly scene if she didn't get it in hand, Iris worked to put her own revulsion aside, and said with as much empathy as she could muster, "I'm sorry you're having difficulty, miss.''

Ginger breathed a sigh of relief and dabbed at the tears welling in her eyes. "I was hoping you'd understand.''

"But this isn't the kind of thing I can discuss with him or you,'' Iris continued stoically.

Ginger blinked, her heartbreak beginning to fade and be replaced by anger. "You can't want this to come out any more than I do!''

Iris straightened the receipts on her desk. "No, of course not.''

"Then what do you expect me to do?'' Ginger demanded, looking completely forlorn.

Iris shrugged and gave the best advice she could. "Take it up with him.''

"I've tried,'' Ginger said emotionally. "He's not answering his cell phone and short of calling the house—''

Oh God, Iris thought, please don't do that. Please don't involve anyone else in this mess. "I don't know what to tell you except maybe you shouldn't have gotten yourself into this in the first place.'' It wasn't as if he would listen to her anyway.

Ginger started to leave in frustration, then came back.

Looking as if she, too, were at wit's end, she snapped at Iris, "He owes me money, you know. Lots of it."

"Ms. Zaring," Iris said icily, refusing once more to get involved in something beyond her control, no matter how desperate the woman was, "that is not my concern. It's yours. And his."

Ginger Zaring regarded Iris threateningly. "I am *not* going to let him stiff me. Bad enough, the stuff he's had me doing lately. One way or another, I'm getting paid what I am due. And soon. The only question is—" she looked at Iris in grim contemplation "—exactly how ugly is it going to get?"

BUCKY WAITED until Iris had her back turned to him then edged as near as he dared. Without being too obvious about what he was doing, he tried to listen in as best he could. To his frustration, all he had heard was mumbling. Until...

"Damn it, I told you, just leave me out of it," Iris all but shouted.

"I wish I could," Ginger Zaring replied louder, "but you're family and you know what's going on, not to mention how wrong and how nuts it all is! And I'm desperate, truly desperate. You have to know that. Otherwise, I wouldn't be here, like this, talking to you and opening myself up to God only knows what other kind of risk..."

So, Bucky thought, Iris—or the Templetons—were being blackmailed by Ginger Zaring, airlines reservation agent. Was Jack Granger somehow in on the extortion, too? Was that why Daisy had suddenly married him, when as far as Bucky had been able to find out thus far, from phone calls to their mutual friends, Daisy and Jack hadn't even dated? Or was Jack—an attorney—working to protect the Templetons? Or perhaps just Daisy? Or was Jack completely and naively in the dark about what was going on in the family he had just married into? On the surface, of course, Daisy's new husband seemed like such a straight arrow, a fact that should have made him fit right in with the exacting and controlling Richard and Charlotte Templeton. But Bucky had been around long enough to know that the uptight, ultra-do-gooding politicians, star athletes and pillars of the community were often the ones with secret mistresses, illegal business deals and gambling habits on the side. It was always a shock when whatever was going on was uncovered. People just couldn't fathom it.

Revelations like that sold newspapers and made careers. Bucky grinned. Was it possible he had just hit on his entrée to the big time? The only thing he knew for certain was that he had to find out more. Even if, Bucky thought, a tad guiltily, he ended up hurting or embarrassing Daisy a little in the process.

The front door opened and the bell above it jingled, letting Iris know there was someone else in the shop. A group of six very well heeled ladies strolled in, looking ready to spend. Out of the corner of his eye, Bucky saw Iris look toward the front of the store, grimace and reach into her desk. Pulling out some sort of invitation, she put it in Ginger Zaring's hand and then said something low that Bucky couldn't catch at all.

The office door swung open.

Iris practically pushed Ginger out the back entrance into the alley before the other customers could get a good look at her. She locked the door after Ginger, then strode forward, rubbing her hands together. "Bucky— did you find what you needed?"

Not nearly. "I think I'm going to need more time," Bucky said honestly, glancing at his watch. "Unfortunately, I've got this chamber of commerce breakfast I'm supposed to be taking photographs at right now—"

Iris looked at the customer studying the tag on the Hepplewhite china cabinet. "You go ahead, and come back later, then. Ladies!" She lifted her hand in a cheery hello. "I'm Iris Templeton, the shop proprietress. May I help you?"

Bucky waited until Iris had started helping the customers, then surreptitiously reached into his camera bag and the small container he carried with him for just such emergencies. He smeared a streak of black axle grease on the inside of his left palm, then went back up to Iris with a puzzled look on his face. "I just noticed I've got what looks like grease or something on my hand. Is there a place where I could wash up?"

Iris looked both irritated by his interruption and eager to get rid of him before he did any damage to her valuable merchandise. "Yes, Bucky, there's a bathroom in the back, at the end of the hall. Now—" Iris turned back to the group of ladies assembled around the china cabinet "—as I was saying. About this piece—"

With everyone else thoroughly occupied, it took no time at all to wash his hands and even less to slip into her office, pluck an invitation from the stack in her desk and slide it into his camera bag. Finished, Bucky rushed back to the front of the store. "Thanks, Iris." He flashed her an appreciative grin as he let himself out the shop door, onto King Street. *I'm all set.*

DAISY WASN'T SURE why she disliked going out to Rosewood so much. The family's country estate wasn't a far drive—it was only a half an hour west of Charleston, forty-five minutes from the beach. The rambling two-hundred-acre grounds were beautifully landscaped and maintained. The breathtaking pink brick Georgian mansion had three floors and some twenty-four rooms, all beautifully furnished with priceless antiques in mint condition. Behind that were three temperature-controlled barns that used to house even more antiques. Those pieces were so expensive that they were shown only to prescreened private collectors, repeat customers and interior decorators, and small, socially prominent groups or clubs.

She supposed it was the fact that except for a few rare events—a Halloween party when she was a child that had ended disastrously, the occasional wedding anniversary, the estate had never been used for family gatherings—only Templeton's Fine Antiques business—and parties relating to that. There were no pets or horses, or places to have fun. Not even a TV or stereo. What little music was provided was done so by members of the Charleston symphony or various string quartets. Thinking about the few galas she had been forced to attend here while growing up, which she could count on one hand, it was all Daisy could do not to yawn.

Even now, knowing why she was here—to pick out a gift—Daisy couldn't help but feel a little bit resentful and a lot on edge. She had tried to cover it up, to not be too out of sorts about having to come all the way out here simply to appease Richard and Charlotte and get them off her back yet again, but she hadn't been entirely successful. Jack had asked her twice before she had dropped him at the Deveraux-Heyward Shipping Company offices if she wanted him to try and get away and come with her. But she figured one of them listening to her father's opinion of her hasty marriage was quite enough.

Hopefully, Daisy thought as she turned her red car into the long red driveway and drove up to the guard-house in front of the closed black wrought-iron gates and electric fence, it wouldn't take too long.

"Daisy Templeton…er, Granger, here to see my father," Daisy said to the uniformed guard on duty. She flipped open her wallet, showing her ID, which had not yet been changed to reflect her married name, but the guard waved her off.

"That's okay, Miz Templeton. Your father told me you'd be here this afternoon."

"Is my father here yet?"

"He should be along shortly. But you can go on in the house and wait for him." The guard smiled at her reassuringly. "I can turn off the alarm from here." He pointed to the computer panel behind him.

"So I can just open the front door?"

"And go on in. Yes, ma'am. The locks are all electronic now. Your father and sister have access to remote controls, and of course we do here at the guardhouse, but that's it. The regular household staff has to be let in by me."

Daisy nodded, taking it all in. She knew the precautions might have sounded excessive to some, but given the value of the antiques on the property, which generally speaking totaled millions of dollars, it made sense. The guard opened the gates, Daisy drove through and on up the lane.

As she got out of the car, she felt a little weird—sort of nervous, but she told herself it was probably her pregnancy. It had nothing to do with the trauma she had once suffered here, years past, or the nightmares she sometimes still had about that awful Halloween party. She was an adult now. She was fine. Pregnant maybe, but fine.

Doing her best to shake off her lingering uneasiness, she let herself inside and walked through the front hall. "Hello?" she called, wondering if there were any staff within earshot, but no one seemed to be here.

Daisy walked through the downstairs rooms, trying to recall exactly where the kitchen was. Eventually, she found it at the center of the first floor, tucked into a large windowless room. Designed like a hotel kitchen, it was all fluorescent lights, stainless-steel counters and huge commercial appliances. Daisy found a few bottles of soda and orange juice in the subzero refrigerator and poured herself a glass of juice, hoping it would normalize her blood sugar and make her feel a little better. And it did help a little. But not enough.

She still felt creeped out for some reason. Maybe because the house was so huge and she was so completely alone. "What I need to do is occupy my mind," Daisy instructed herself firmly, her voice echoing in the cavernous rooms of the mansion. "Find something to do to pass the time." But what? There were no magazines. No TV or radio. She hadn't brought a book with her or her camera.

Instead, she just wandered the massive building trying to occupy herself. Heading back to the front of the house, she walked through the front hall and then through the parlors on either side. She was in the library, examining bookcases and tapping on walls, when someone suddenly loomed behind her. Daisy jumped as a man's shadow fell over her. She'd been so busy distracting herself, she hadn't heard anyone come inside the house.

"What are you doing?" Richard demanded as he stepped closer. He, too, was perspiring from the oppressive heat and humidity outside, his dark-brown hair clinging damply to his forehead and the back of his neck. At sixty-seven, he still looked fit and virile. Partly because he always made sure he got enough sleep, ate right and worked out regularly under the guidance of his personal trainer. But also because he took care to dress elegantly every day, dyed his hair and made use of the latest plastic surgery techniques.

"Just looking around," Daisy said. Why did she know he would be annoyed? Even if she had just been standing there, he would have been annoyed. Daisy sighed inwardly. It was just like old times: him prickling with resentment and her feeling awful about herself.

Daisy continued to stand there, wondering if she was ever going to stop wanting the two people she had grown up thinking were her adoptive parents—instead of her biological grandparents—to love and accept her for who and what she was. Sometimes Daisy felt close with her mother, but to Richard, Daisy feared, she was simply the Templeton black sheep who would never, because of her illegitimate beginnings, quite be up to the family's blue-blooded standards.

Richard took a handkerchief out of his pocket and blotted the back of his neck, his face. "Let's go upstairs to the third floor," he said.

Her spirits sinking ever lower—Daisy knew that more stinging criticism was yet to come—Daisy swallowed her resentment and followed along. Too late, she wished she had let—no, insisted—that Jack come out here with her, even if he had to leave work.

"I have to tell you, Daisy, your mother and I were

very upset about your elopement," Richard said as he led the way up the stairs.

"Who are you talking about?" Daisy asked, doing her best to look innocently confused. She couldn't help it—she had to break the flow of his prepared speech, and throw him off his rhythm, and there was no quicker way to do that than by asking a stupid question. "Iris or Charlotte?"

Richard grimaced as he tackled the third flight. "Charlotte is your mother."

"By adoption." Daisy followed along dutifully, aware she was beginning to feel just a tiny bit nauseated. "Iris—"

"Daisy," Richard interrupted in a loud, intimidating voice, "I am not going to discuss this with you." He paused on the steps, towering over her. "Iris made a mistake that has long since been remedied. I will not have you bringing it up again, with me or anyone else."

Of course not, Daisy thought, quaking a little at the repressed anger she saw on her father's face. *Because then we Templetons might actually begin to deal with our problems.*

"But, since you are married," Richard continued in a kinder though no less patronizing manner, "perhaps I can help you to succeed in your new endeavor."

Daisy didn't like the direction this lecture was going. Or the increasingly icky feeling in her stomach. "What do you mean?"

"A wife, even one as young and untutored in the ways of matrimony as yourself, has certain duties and responsibilities to her husband."

Daisy couldn't wait to hear what those were in Richard's view. "Such as…?"

"If she is wise, she will be sure she does everything

she can to make certain she is a good wife to her husband.''

"I don't get it," Daisy said blankly.

"Then I'll spell it out for you." Richard's eyebrows arched autocratically. "There's a difference between being a proper, upstanding wife and a floozy!''

Daisy stared at him in disbelief. She couldn't believe her father had just said that. She turned away, her face flaming. "I resent that," she countered angrily as bile climbed from the center of her chest into the base of her throat. Although she doubted she would be able to convince him of that once he and her mother learned of her pregnancy.

"Maybe," Richard stated in cool disapproval, "but you certainly dress like one. Which is why I am asking Charlotte to take you shopping for some proper clothes, more suitable to your new role in Charleston society, and why I want her to sponsor you as a new member in all her charitable activities and clubs.''

At that, it was all Daisy could do not to moan. "You have got to be kidding," she retorted, taking a deep breath.

"I most certainly am not." Richard turned to her as he led the way into one of the antique-furnished bedroom suites. "The busier you are, the better. Furthermore," he lectured her sternly, wagging a finger in front of her face, "you're a wife now. No more wild behavior. We expect you to act like the young lady we reared you to be. Not some wild party girl.''

Daisy swallowed in an effort to hold back the bile. She couldn't believe the baby had chosen now to give her her very first episode of morning sickness. Not that it was unusual for her to be feeling a little sick when her father criticized her like this, the force of his disapproval had always had the power to twist her stomach into knots. "And if I say no?" Daisy asked, wondering if her face was as green as it felt.

"Then you'll have no hope of ever regaining access to the annual allowance from your trust fund."

Daisy shrugged and wondered if some fresh air would help. "Maybe I don't want it," she said, praying she wouldn't throw up all over her father's shoes.

"You'll change your mind." Richard snorted in disgust. "When it comes to money, women always do."

Daisy wasn't surprised by her father's attitude. Richard was a chauvinist and then some. But there was no use arguing about his antiquated sexist views. He wasn't going to change his mind. She drew another deep breath and perched on the edge of an authentic Chinese silk–covered chaise, hoping the lack of motion might help. "I thought I was here to pick out a wedding gift."

"You are looking at it." Richard turned and gestured to the magnificent carved cherry-wood bed with the half-tester. Daisy didn't need to know anything about antiques to know the piece was worth tens of thousands. "Of course, we would send the bureau, the washstand and writing table along with it. Even the chaise if you want it."

"That's very generous of you." Daisy said politely, counting the seconds until she could leave. "But it would never fit in Jack's beach house. The tester alone is taller than the ceiling in his bedroom."

"Then we'll find something else," Richard said as footsteps sounded in the hall, and seconds later, Iris walked in. "Here you are," Iris said pleasantly, giving Richard a look heavy with a meaning Daisy couldn't begin to read. "I need to talk to you, Father."

Richard looked immensely irritated again. "It can wait until Daisy and I finish," he said stonily.

"No. It can't," Iris disagreed with surprising force. "Daisy, please excuse us and go downstairs and wait there. Father and I have some very confidential things to say to one another."

Daisy wondered what was going on. Iris, usually so cool and collected, looked rattled. Deciding she needed some air if she was going to keep from puking, Daisy stood and said, "Sure thing." Turning on her heel, she left the room and walked shakily down the stairs, feeling increasingly less able to breathe and more nauseous with every step she took.

Thinking if she could just get to her car and sit there for a while, with the air-conditioner vents blowing in her face, might help her to feel better, Daisy walked out the front door.

To her dismay, the shimmering summer heat and humidity hit her like a blast furnace in the face. The precarious hold she'd had on herself slipped. The taste of bile moved up her throat. Daisy swore and lurched toward the edge of the porch.

JACK SAW DAISY COME OUT the front door of the mansion. She was moving slowly and seemed to be having some sort of difficulty as she lifted a hand to her face. Wondering what the heck was wrong, he parked in front of the house just as she staggered over to the edge of the porch, grabbed on to one of the tall white columns with one hand and leaned forward into the bushes. By the time he got out of the car, she was already losing her lunch, and from the sounds of it, breakfast, as well.

He hurried over to her side and wrapped a stabilizing

arm around her waist. "Charming, huh?" she joked weakly as she took the handkerchief to wipe her mouth.

"Oh, very." He helped her to the closest vehicle, which happened to be his, and opened the passenger door. "Here." He helped her into the truck then handed her the bottle of water he had been drinking en route to Rosewood.

"Hey, you got your SUV back," Daisy noted as she took a sip of water.

Jack smiled, glad to see a little color coming back into her cheeks. "Yep. It was delivered to me about an hour ago at the office. I took it as a sign I was meant to be out here with you, so I told Tom and Mitch that I had to go and came on out."

Tears of distress sparkled in Daisy's eyes. "Just in time to see me—" Her voice broke. She ducked her head, embarrassed, and couldn't go on.

"Hey," Jack said, gently touching the side of her face. "It's okay. I'm a guy, remember? I spent my entire college career watching guys toss their cookies. Okay, not my entire college career, but a good part of every weekend." At Vanderbilt, there had been no shortage of fraternity boys with too much money to spend and too little ambition. As a work-study student assigned to a housekeeping crew for the dorms, Jack had cleaned up more than one mess. But this was different. This was his wife. Carrying his child. "You think you're going to be okay?" Jack stroked her hair.

"What's going on here? What's wrong?" Iris and Richard rushed across the marble porch.

"It's all right." Daisy held up both hands to ward them off. "I just—food poisoning, I think. I knew I shouldn't have had that chicken salad at lunch," Daisy explained miserably as fresh tears appeared in her eyes.

Richard backed up a step, not willing to get too close under the circumstances. Iris looked even more distressed. "You're sure that's all it is?" she asked Daisy, concerned and ready to help in any way she could.

Bypassing the opportunity to tell her family of her pregnancy, Daisy nodded. "I don't know if I can drive, though."

"You could go inside and lie down," Richard suggested reluctantly after a moment. "I've got an appointment with someone, but I'm sure Iris could help the two of you."

"No," Iris quickly overrode her father's offer. Ignoring the resentment-filled way Daisy was looking at her, Iris glanced at Jack sternly and spoke as if underlining every word. "Daisy needs to go home if she's not feeling well."

"Don't trust me around all those antiques, huh?" Daisy mugged weakly.

"We're having a party here tonight," Iris explained to Jack and Daisy. "The caterers and staff will be arriving any minute to start setting up."

"Well, we certainly don't want me tossing my cookies again and killing that party mood," Daisy concurred dryly.

Iris gave Daisy a look that was more mother in that instant than older sister. Daisy didn't appear to see it, nor did Richard, but Jack did. The mixture of vulnerability and concern in Iris's eyes made him realize just how hard it had been for Iris to give Daisy over to her parents to bring up. Clearly, Jack thought, Iris loved Daisy as a daughter, even if Iris didn't quite know what to do with those feelings except hide them. Oblivious to the direction of Jack's thoughts, Iris looked at him.

"Can you drive her and make sure she's taken care of?" she asked.

Jack nodded. "Sure."

"And I'll have one of the staff here drive your car back," Iris reassured Daisy gently. "Just give me the keys and the address." Iris held out her hand. Daisy reached into her purse, and handed them over. Jack gave her the address. Richard remained impatiently in the foreground, glancing at his watch and the driveway beyond.

Concerned with only one thing—his wife—Jack helped Daisy with her seat belt. "Do you need a few more minutes to just sit here?"

Daisy closed her eyes and relaxed against the back of her seat. "Let's just go." She opened her eyes and gripped his hand tightly. "Now, Jack."

CHAPTER TEN

"YOU'RE SURE IT'S NOT food poisoning?" Jack asked again as they neared Charleston.

"Positive," Daisy said as she stretched out in the passenger seat beside him, still feeling a little embarrassed about the way she had lost the contents of her stomach back at Rosewood. "For one thing, if it were, I'd probably still be retching." Since Jack had come to the rescue, she had felt a lot better. "So it's got to be a bout of morning—or in this case," she amended, "afternoon sickness." Brought on by stress, heat, travel and her father's critical, overbearing attitude.

Jack slanted her a concerned glance. "Have you been throwing up before today?"

"No. It's my first time for that, and hopefully the last," Daisy said, speaking with genuine feeling about this much. "Because I gotta tell you, Granger, this part of pregnancy sucks rocks."

Jack grinned at the drama—and truth—in her low tone. "Speaking of pregnancy," he said, reaching over to rub a knuckle gently over her stomach, "don't you need to be going to a doctor here in Charleston?"

Daisy tensed until he put both hands back on the steering wheel. Swallowing hard and telling herself she did not want to be foolish enough to fall in love with a man who had only married her out of a sense of duty, she pressed her lips together and said, "I called my doctor when I got back. My first appointment with an obstetrician is next week.''

Jack's eyes lit up with enthusiasm. ''Is it okay if I go with you?''

Daisy put her hand on her tummy—unconsciously protecting the baby inside? She studied Jack's face, unable to help feeling pleased about his excitement. ''You're really getting into this.''

''Hey—'' Jack slanted a glance at her, ''—it's my kid, too.''

A fact he was taking on faith. How odd was that, Daisy mused, that a man she had slept with but barely knew would trust her about something that important, when her own family had never really trusted her at all. At least not enough to tell her the truth about her parentage.

Silence fell between them as they drove the causeway that crossed the marshland between Charleston and the beach where Jack lived. Daisy stared down at the intermittent pools of deep blue-gray water and tall marsh grass waving in the wind, beneath the sunny Carolina-blue sky. It was so beautiful here, but also so dangerous beneath the murky depths. She couldn't help but make the parallel to her life.

She turned to Jack, aware of a deep sense of foreboding within her. ''We're going to be okay parents, aren't we?''

Jack nodded. ''The best.''

''I hope so.'' Daisy sighed and bit her lip as she thought about everything that could—maybe even would—go wrong, before everything was said and done. ''I don't want...''

''What?'' Jack pressed when Daisy didn't go on.

Daisy shook off her feeling of unease. ''I was just

going to say I hope I am not as spineless as Charlotte or critical as Richard were when I was growing up. I don't want our baby to ever feel that he or she isn't pretty or smart or well behaved enough. Or that he or she doesn't have parents who will stand up for him or her.''

"I'm sure our kid will be perfect.'' Jack tossed her a confident smile, amending teasingly, "In our eyes anyway.''

Recognizing the truth of that, Daisy chuckled softly as Jack parked the SUV beneath the carport of his beach cottage. As gallant as always, he circled around to help her with her door and slid a steadying hand beneath her elbow as she got down from the passenger seat. Daisy looked at him in a way that let him know he did not have to handle her with kid gloves. "I'm not an invalid.''

He slid his arm around her waist. "Just want to make sure you're okay.''

"I am. Although I think I need a nap.'' The drive out to Rosewood and back, combined with being sick, had left her feeling drained and weary to her bones.

"Good idea,'' Jack said.

Daisy went straight to the bedroom, kicked off her sandals and curled up on the king-size bed. Jack brought her a blanket from the linen closet and draped it over her. He lingered at the bedside, watching over her tenderly. "Can I get you anything else—some tea maybe?''

"Soda would be good,'' Daisy murmured, snuggling farther into the pillow and closing her eyes. She didn't know what it was about Jack, but whenever she was with him she felt so safe.

THE INVITATION BUCKY had filched from Iris Templeton's office said the preferred customer party at Rosewood began at eight o'clock, but just to be on the safe side, Bucky Jerome waited until eight-thirty before he drove up to the gatehouse and handed his official invitation to the uniformed security guard on duty. The guard looked closely at the invitation, then waved Bucky on through the electric gates. Roughly one hundred luxury cars and limousines were parked on both sides of the tree-lined lane leading up to the mansion. In the parking area behind the house were the catering trucks and less expensive vehicles. Bucky found a space in the latter group, for his Volkswagen Jetta. He straightened his tie, got out of the car and headed toward the brightly lit house. He had a digital camera small enough to fit in the palm of his hand tucked into his pocket. And enough questions to fill two books.

Parties at Rosewood were common—it was a well-known fact that Templeton's Fine Antiques sold run-of-the-mill antiques to tourists and modestly wealthy clients out of their King Street shop, but hosted galas for their very best clients and catered to the elite at their private country estate, where the most expensive pieces were kept. It was the way they kept their customers happy and managed to keep moving the high-end pieces no matter the state of the economy. So it was no surprise to Bucky to see that the place was packed.

What was unusual was for a mere airlines reservation agent to go to Iris, behave with demonstrated unhappiness and then get an invitation to the party. Bucky had grown up in Charleston. He knew everyone on the social register, all the prettiest girls at the prep schools and around town. Some of whom were prone—like Daisy Templeton—to rebel against their uptight, blue-blooded parents by dressing and acting like anything but well-bred young heiresses. Ginger Zaring was not one of that group. And he sincerely doubted she could afford even the least expensive of the very fine antiques housed at the Templetons' Rosewood estate.

Which made Bucky wonder what Ginger would be doing at Rosewood tonight. As Bucky neared the front door of the house, he got his invitation out again. Showed it to the butler answering the door. The butler gave Bucky a deferential look and ushered Bucky inside.

It took Bucky less than five minutes to make his way through the throngs of wealthy patrons populating the downstairs rooms. The auburn-haired Ginger Zaring was stationed near the bar. Unlike many of the other stodgily dressed females there, Ginger was wearing a low-cut scarlet dress that ended several inches above her knees, and what Bucky liked to think of as hooker heels. She looked uncomfortable. Nervous even, as she fended off the passes of one wealthy man after another.

More curious than ever, Bucky plucked a flute of champagne off a passing tray and started toward Ginger. Before he could get to her, she glanced at her watch, put her glass aside and began making her way through the guests, toward the rear of the mansion. Curious, because she seemed so deliberate now, when she had been so uncertain just moments earlier, Bucky followed her. When she reached the kitchen, she picked up her pace, as did Bucky, moving through the uniformed caterers toward what looked like a large butler's pantry on the far wall. Wondering what the heck the woman would be doing in there, Bucky hastened to catch up with her. And that was when Iris Templeton caught his arm from behind then stepped around in front of him. "Bucky," Iris exclaimed, smiling broadly. "I'm surprised to see you here this evening." Her eyes narrowed. "I wasn't aware we had given you an invitation."

Bucky shrugged as casually as if he had actually been invited. "I heard about the party and thought I'd drop by." At Iris's penetrating stare, he continued, fibbing easily. "I'm still looking for that gift for my dad, and I thought maybe you might have something out here."

Iris smiled even more. "What a wonderful idea. And you're right. We probably do have something exactly right."

The butler appeared at Iris's side, said, "Several guests are asking for your father."

"He's out in the barns, doing a last-minute check of our inventory," Iris said. "I'm going to take Bucky out there, so I'll give my father the message and have him come back inside."

Shoot, Bucky thought. He had wanted to follow the woman, see what she was up to in the butler's pantry. Now he wasn't going to have the chance.

Iris gripped Bucky's arm just above the elbow. "Shall we...?"

Figuring he could catch up with the auburn-haired Ginger later, Bucky nodded. Making small talk all the while about what might be an appropriate gift for Bucky's father, Iris led him outside via the back entrance, through the impeccably manicured gardens and across the lawns, toward the barns. "I assume you want to spend between three and five thousand dollars," Iris said.

Bucky winced. This was getting to be an expensive investigation. "More like five hundred," he specified.

Iris's lips tightened into a perplexed frown. "Well, that does limit things quite a bit," she said.

Bucky had figured as much.

"But I'm sure we can find something."

Something turned out to be a cuckoo clock, circa 1812.

Trying not to appear as impatient as he felt, Bucky handed over a bad check that he fortunately had in his wallet. Two minutes later, Iris in tow, he was carrying his find toward his car. And that was when he saw Ginger emerging alone from the rear of the mansion. She looked as if she'd had a tumble. There was a run in one stocking. Her hair was mussed, lipstick off. Seeing her hasten toward a small economy car and climb in, Iris frowned.

Bucky looked at Iris. "I wonder if she found what she wanted tonight," he said.

"WE HAD A DEAL," Iris told her father furiously as she climbed into the limo that would take them back to Charleston, shortly after midnight. "I run the business. You don't get in my way. Tonight—" she regarded him steadily, thinking about what sordidness Bucky Jerome had almost stumbled onto "—you got in my way."

Richard regarded her with the same disrespect he had always shown her, when not under the watchful eyes of others. "Nonsense. I sold fifty thousand dollars' of antiques tonight."

Iris's voice shook with emotion. "I told you. I won't stand to be used like I was in the past, as a cover for your peccadilloes. And I won't let our business fill that role, either."

Richard gave Iris an impassive look that said he didn't care what they had agreed, then or now. "I'll live my life any way I please. You worry about yourself and getting Daisy and her latest scandal off the society page.''

Iris glared at her father in frustration. ''Daisy has never listened to me, you know that, and now she resents me more than ever.'' And for that, Iris couldn't blame her. If only she had been stronger when she was pregnant with Daisy, she could have stood up to her parents and found a way to keep her baby. Either alone, or with her new husband. Instead, she had been talked into giving Daisy over to them and pushed into a marriage with a man who had never wanted or would have accepted children. That union had given her a life of luxury and enabled her to save the family business, but had never made her happy. All the while, watching helplessly, as her child was brought up by her parents.

She had thought—hoped—Charlotte's love, and the stipulations Iris had put on Richard and his philandering, would be enough to ensure Daisy a happier childhood than Iris had been blessed with. But she'd been wrong. In the end, Richard had done to Daisy what he had done to Iris. He'd made her feel insecure and reluctant to trust men. And for that, Iris was having a hard time forgiving him.

His expression one of pure aggravation, Richard helped himself to a shot of whiskey from the bar in the back of the limo. ''What was Bucky Jerome doing at the party tonight?''

Iris shrugged, and passed on her father's wordless offer of something alcoholic. ''Nosing around, obviously.''

Richard put the bottle back in its holder. He took a sip and regarded Iris over the rim of the glass. ''For what?''

Iris rubbed at the knotted muscles at the back of her neck. "He saw Ginger Zaring at my shop today."

Her father's eyes narrowed as he demanded, "Did he overhear anything?"

Iris hesitated. "I don't think so. I took her back to my private office to have our discussion."

"Then why was he at Rosewood tonight?" Richard insisted.

Iris glared at Richard, resenting her father's third degree almost as much as his careless actions. "Because obviously he knew something was up and your girl-friend was going to be there." At Richard's warning look, Iris lowered her tone with effort. "Bucky must have seen me give Ginger Zaring an invitation and then helped himself to one also when I wasn't looking. Because that's the only way he could have gotten into the party tonight."

Richard took a moment to mull that over, then asked, "Why was he at the store?"

Iris shrugged, and thought, dumb luck. "He's been interested in Daisy's elopement," Iris said finally. "I think he senses something more going on with her than what anyone is saying."

Richard leaned forward urgently. "Tell me there's no way he could find out what you did."

Iris flushed. Why was she still guilty over that? Her unexpected pregnancy was ancient history. "He'll never hear it from me," she retorted stonily. And she hoped like heck that Bucky wouldn't ever hear it from Daisy, either. Iris couldn't imagine trying to explain to their friends and customers why she had allowed herself to be bullied into giving up the one thing, besides the family antiques business, she had ever really truly loved.

"He'd better not find out about Daisy's parentage. The family reputation is at stake."

Unable to help herself, Iris scoffed. "It seems to me if you were really concerned about that, you would have used more discretion this evening, Father."

Richard gave Iris a quelling look. "You worry about Daisy and destroying any physical proof of her origins she dug up in Switzerland. I'll worry about me."

Iris's heart pounded. "And how am I supposed to do that?" It wasn't as if Daisy would simply hand the documents and private investigator reports over to her!

Richard shrugged, as uncaring as always. "You figure it out. Just make sure it's done."

IRIS TELEPHONED DAISY three times the next day. Each time, she left a message on Daisy's voice mail, asking Daisy to please call her as soon as possible so the two of them might get together.

Daisy ignored the request and instead spent her morning making phone calls to drum up work for herself, and her afternoon trying to clear a little space in Jack's closet and dresser for her own things. And she was still at it when he came home from Deveraux-Heyward Shipping around five-thirty.

"I hope you don't mind—" Daisy indicated the quarter of his closet she had filled with her things.

"Take all the room you need," Jack invited as he walked into the master bedroom. He hung up his suit jacket, stripped off his tie and wrapped that around the hanger, too. While unbuttoning his shirt, he told her casually, "Mitch and Lauren Deveraux have invited us over to their place this evening."

"Yeah?" Daisy stopped folding her pajamas and looked up at Jack. This was certainly unexpected. The last time she had seen Tom's kids, they had all looked at her as if her mere presence was at least partly responsible for their parents' divorce. And they had been right. If not for Daisy, Tom and Grace might not ever have divorced, Tom's infidelity or no.

Jack tossed his dress shirt into the wicker hamper in the corner and took a short-sleeve polo shirt off a hanger. "It sounds like fun."

Daisy watched him pull the shirt on over his white T-shirt. "It sounds," she corrected, "like a setup."

"You're right." Jack dispensed with his socks then suit pants and hung those up, too. "I guess in a way it is."

Daisy tore her eyes from his long, muscled legs. "And...?"

Jack pulled on a pair of old, faded jeans almost as threadbare and disreputable as the ones she was currently wearing, the difference being his did not have a frayed rip in one knee. He gave Daisy a bluntly assessing look, taking in her upswept blond hair and tummy-baring cap-sleeved black T-shirt, before returning to her face. "They all want to talk to you—Gabe, Amy, Chase and Mitch—and their spouses. Now that they know you are their sister."

Aware she wouldn't be able to wear clothes like this much longer—already her navel-baring jeans were feeling pretty snug around the hips—Daisy slid her pajamas into the dresser drawer and shut it. "Aren't they jumping the gun a little bit?" she asked. "My paternity isn't official yet." And because it wasn't, she hadn't heard from Tom since the afternoon of the blood test.

"Your half siblings seem to think it may as well be. Anyway, you know Lauren has been renovating 10 Gathering Street. And she's having a wallpaper-stripping party, and wants us to come." Jack grabbed sneakers from the bottom of his closet and put those on, too.

Daisy could tell Jack wanted to go.

His expression fell just a little. "But if you don't feel up to it—"

Actually, she'd been feeling a little strange all day. Nothing specific. Just not quite right. Taking it fairly easy all day hadn't really helped her malaise. Maybe getting out and seeing people would. "Well, I have been wanting to talk to all of them. Lauren, Chase and Amy were among the first to hire me when I started freelancing. I could sure use some more photography jobs from them." Not knowing how they would react hearing from her, she hadn't called any of them today. And instead, had waited for them to make the first move. Now, Daisy noted, it seemed they had.

"Mitch said they'd provide dinner if we provided the labor."

"How come Lauren doesn't just hire someone to do the work?" Daisy asked as she found a pair of sandals and began to get ready to go. "She and Mitch surely have the money between them." Both were trust-fund babies and successful professionals.

Jack leaned against the wall, watching as Daisy restored order to her wavy blond hair. His attentiveness sent shivers of awareness down her spine.

Shrugging, Jack answered Daisy's question, "Lauren says she'd rather do this to stay in shape than do three miles on her treadmill at the gym, at least part of the time. Mitch will do whatever it takes to make Lauren happy. The rest will be there just to party and hang out together, as well as lend a helping hand."

JACK WASN'T KIDDING about lending the helping-hand bit, Daisy noted forty-five minutes later. When Daisy and Jack arrived, all eight of them were hard at work on the two foremost downstairs rooms. "Hey, Daisy." Chase Deveraux was the first to put down his steamer and make his way over to her. "I'm glad you could come."

Chase was nine years older than she, but he was the most visibly unjudgmental about her antics—maybe because he had, in the past, possessed a penchant for wild and reckless behavior himself. Now that he was happily married to Bridgett Owens, he had calmed down considerably, but was no less understanding when it came to her. Daisy looked at him uncertainly. She needed to be clear. "Are we going to be okay?"

Chase nodded and wrapped an arm around her shoulder. "You know it."

The next thing Daisy knew, she was surrounded by everyone there, accepting hugs and warm welcomes and congratulations from them on her marriage to Jack. For the first time in her life, Daisy had an inkling of what it must be like to be a member of a big and loving family. And she noted, Jack, an only child and outsider himself, seemed to be enjoying the novelty as much as she was. "I'm sorry about the scene I caused when I first found out," Daisy apologized to one and all, knowing that much was past due.

"Don't blame you one bit," Gabe Deveraux said sympathetically, wrapping his arm around his pregnant wife, Maggie.

Amy Deveraux nodded and added sympathetically, "You had every right to feel betrayed."

Mitch Deveraux stepped forward to agree, and looked at Amy earnestly. "But we're all hoping we can put the past behind us and move forward. We don't

care how you and Dad decide to handle this, Daisy—
whether you want to go public with your paternity or
keep it quiet—we just want you to know that we all
consider you part of our family now. And we plan to
treat you accordingly."

Daisy hesitated. Except for her brother, Connor, she
hadn't been close to anyone, growing up. Never mind
been part of a big, boisterous group like the Deveraux
family. A family that had now been ripped down the
center because of her. "To be honest," Daisy said
eventually, swallowing hard around the growing lump
in her throat, "I don't know what I'm going to do."
She wanted this, but not at their expense. And unless
Grace Deveraux changed her feelings about Daisy,
there would be no room for both Daisy and Grace in
the Deveraux-family gatherings, no matter what Tom
wanted.

"That's okay, too," Amy said with a frankness and
gut-level honesty Daisy appreciated. "Just know we all
plan to stand by you. That we're not going to punish
you for something that was completely beyond your
control."

Daisy could see all four Deveraux siblings and their
spouses, were in total agreement on that. And although
she was relieved about that—she would have hated to
lose her friendship, not to mention the work she got
from the four Deveraux siblings—she knew that was
only part of the havoc within the Deveraux clan. So,
much as she was loath to do so, she had to ask, "What
about your father?" She got the words out with difficulty. "How do you all feel about him now?" The last
time she had seen them, they had all been furious
with Tom.

Uneasy glances were exchanged all around. "We're working on that," Gabe said eventually.

"To be honest, we're all finding it a lot harder to come to terms with Dad's actions, the way he simply turned his back on you as if you didn't even exist when he had to know—at least suspect. But even assuming we buy that," Chase said in a low, clipped tone before going on protectively, "we still have to deal with his infidelity and what that did to Mom, as well as our entire family, and that's even harder to forgive."

"Although we are trying," Mitch put in. He gave Chase a reproving look before turning back to Daisy and explaining, "Because we know that the family is not going to be able to come together again, the way it should, unless we can all stop placing guilt on each other and just move on."

It was a good plan, albeit not a very practical one, Daisy thought. Because feelings and emotions, as she well knew, were not so easily manipulated. You couldn't just decide to be happy if your whole world was falling apart around you. Not for any length of time, anyway, because sooner or later the circumstances around you would get to you again. Just like her circumstances were getting to her now.

"How do *you* feel about...Dad?" Amy asked curiously, studying Daisy. "Are you going to be able to forgive him for abandoning you so completely?"

Ah yes, the ten-million-dollar question. "I don't know," Daisy said quietly. Afraid she was going to be overcome with emotion if this discussion went on any longer, and start sobbing her heart out, she turned her attention to the walls, which were in dire need of work.

"So." Daisy smiled a lot more energetically than she felt as she planted both hands on her hips. "Where should Jack and I start?"

"I DON'T THINK you should try and handle one of the steamers," Jack told Daisy a few minutes later as they all got to work.

Daisy frowned at Jack. "It's fine."

"It's too heavy."

"Not that heavy," Chase disagreed. "These machines weigh only ten pounds. I think Daisy can handle one. The only reason we don't want Amy and Maggie using them is because they're pregnant."

Exactly Jack's point about her, Daisy thought, turning back to Jack. Daring him to try and announce her condition to the group, to use that to slow her down, she waited to see what he would do.

He merely smiled and continued stubbornly, "I still prefer to use the steamer. You scrape." He handed her the appropriate tool.

Deciding to let her husband win—for now, and enjoying the camaraderie of the group—Daisy went back to the wall. Aware she was beginning to feel a little funny—or maybe just *pregnant,* again—Daisy concentrated on making conversation. "So how is Grace's new TV show coming?" Daisy asked Nick Everton, the producer of the show, who'd just showed up. And was Grace still as mad at Tom as she had been five weeks ago, when Daisy had barged in and made her announcement to the family? Daisy knew she had no reason to feel responsible for any of their unhappiness, but somehow she did just the same. They were good people and she wanted them all to put this terrible situation behind them.

"Very well," Nick replied as a tiny spasm rippled through Daisy's lower back on the right side.

Oblivious to the discomfort Daisy was beginning to feel, Amy broke in cheerfully, "They're going to be interviewing for a show photographer pretty soon."

That was nice, Daisy thought as another spasm rippled through her, this time in the vicinity of where her appendix was supposed to be.

Lights flashed behind Daisy's eyes. There was a peculiar weakness in her knees.

"Are you interested? Daisy?" Amy's glance narrowed as she took in the perspiration beading Daisy's face. Amy leaned closer, touched Daisy's arm as Daisy put her scraper down. "What's wrong?"

"I don't know," Daisy said, leaning back against the wall and bending over from the waist as a piercing pain ripped through her abdomen. She felt really dizzy and strange again. Not quite nauseous. But there was no reason for it, Daisy told herself sternly. She hadn't eaten anything weird. She hadn't strained her body in any way. Yet there it was again. Pain so sharp and debilitating it seemed to consume her entire being.

Suddenly, Jack was there beside her, too, pulling her away from the wall and wrapping his strong arms around her. "Daisy?" His voice came at her, as if far away.

Daisy turned to him, sweat breaking out on her face and chest as another shudder ripped through her body. Then without warning, Daisy felt the stabbing pain a third time, and this time the ferocity of it nearly ripped her in two as she gasped, closed her eyes and everything mercifully faded to black.

DAISY KNEW it was bad the moment she awakened and found herself in what appeared to be a hospital bed.

Jack was sitting in a straight-backed vinyl chair beside her. His jaw was lined with a beard. His eyes were red-rimmed and bloodshot. He looked as if he hadn't slept all night. Daisy wet her lips. She felt groggy and out of sorts. Funny, but in a different way than before. Sort of drugged, maybe. "What happened?" She had to force the words through her dry, parched throat.

"You collapsed," Jack said quietly, leaning forward and taking her hand in both of his. "Do you remember that—or the ambulance?"

Daisy struggled to find the memory and finally shook her head.

She waited, knowing instinctively it was bad.

The silence drew out between them. Jack swallowed hard and his eyes glistened. He opened his mouth as if to speak, stopped, and had to start again. "You had an ectopic pregnancy, Daisy," he told her thickly. His golden-brown eyes shimmered all the more. "The embryo was implanted in your right fallopian tube instead of your uterus. That's what caused the pain."

Daisy struggled to absorb what he was telling her, as panic swept through her in great numbing waves. "So...what do we do?" Daisy asked desperately. *What marvel of medical science did they need to fix this?*

Unbearable sadness filled his eyes as he gripped her hand all the harder and continued in a low, miserable tone, "Mother Nature already took care of it, Daisy." He hesitated, lip quavering. "That's why you had the pain."

A sob rose in Daisy's throat, even as she struggled to deny everything he was saying, to somehow make it not true.

The tears overflowed, dripped down his face and his voice broke. "Daze—you lost the baby."

CHAPTER ELEVEN

JACK DIDN'T WANT to tell Daisy the rest, but he figured she should hear it from him before anyone else let it slip. "There's more," Jack said reluctantly. "Your admission to the hospital last night made this morning's newspaper."

Tears still flowing freely, Daisy stared at him in disbelief.

"It's in Bucky Jerome's 'Around the City' column," Jack said. He plucked the newspaper off the tray table next to the wall and handed the society page over for Daisy to read.

One of our own, the beautiful Daisy Templeton-Granger, was taken to Charleston Hospital via ambulance early last evening. No reason for the admission or emergency surgery was given by her husband of one week Jack Granger, high counsel to the Deveraux empire, but I'm sure you all can join me in wishing the newlyweds well.

"Damn Bucky," Daisy said bitterly.

Jack seconded the feeling. As far as he was concerned, he would like to see Bucky Jerome damned all the way to hell. Daisy's only blessing, Jack figured, was that there was no photo of her being rushed in on a gurney to go with it. That image was something he—

and the rest of Daisy's half siblings—were never going to be able to forget. But at least Daisy couldn't recall any of it, and wouldn't have to see a photo record of that terrifying time, either.

"I figured you'd be calling my name." Bucky Jerome strolled in as if he owned the place. Black hair spiked in a fashionable style, he was wearing a pair of khakis and a loud shirt. He had a camera around his neck, sunglasses resting on the top of his head. "How are you, Daisy?"

Jack had never been prone to violence, but there was something about the nosy reporter that made him want to smash his face. Given that Jack had half a foot and a lot more muscle on the stocky reporter, he'd probably be able to take him in one or two punches, too.

Deciding, however, that a brawl wouldn't help things, Jack put the lid on his more violent urges and contented himself with a threatening step toward the obnoxious newspaperman. "How'd you get in here?" Jack demanded.

Bucky gave Jack a look that reeked of both the arrogance and smugness that was as common to those with old money as syrup was to pancakes.

As Jack's temper flared, Bucky grinned. "It's a public hospital, or didn't you know?"

"Get out." For Daisy's sake, and the sake of the other patients on the floor, Jack held himself back with effort.

Ignoring the warning in Jack's eyes and the grim forbidding set of his jaw, Bucky pushed past Jack to get directly in Daisy's face. "Would you like to make a statement, Mrs. Granger?" Bucky flipped open his notepad and pushed out the writing end of his pen. "I notice you're on the floor with all the OB-GYN patients.''

Daisy gasped. A combination of shock and hurt radiated in her eyes.

"That does it," Jack growled. Not about to let Daisy endure any more than she already had, he grabbed Bucky by the back of his shirt and the belt of his pants and half shoved, half carried him out the door.

"You can let go of me now," Bucky said as they reached the elevator, looking annoyed, but too arrogant and indifferent to struggle.

"I don't think so." Jack rode with him down to the lobby, then walked Bucky over to the security guard. Seeing the potential for trouble, another guard quickly appeared to assist. A short explanation later, Bucky was being issued a warning and escorted out the lobby doors.

Relieved to be rid of the pesky reporter/newspaper heir, Jack took the elevator back up and strode down the hall to Daisy's hospital room. She was sitting up in bed, staring sightlessly at her untouched breakfast tray. "He won't be back."

Daisy folded her arms in front of her, looking as if she might burst into tears at any second. "Sure he will," she said in a low, dispirited tone.

"Not while you're here," Jack reiterated. Thinking it might help Daisy to have something to eat or drink, he ripped the foil cover off her plastic container of orange juice and stuck a straw in it. "If he sets foot in the hospital or approaches you again in any way, he's going to be arrested."

Bucky was tenacious, Jack knew. But he wasn't stupid. Getting arrested would be stupid.

Daisy was about to say something else, when the

doctor came in. The young, plain-faced obstetrician was rail thin and dressed in loose-fitting blue scrubs. She had a gauzy white cap over her dark hair. Jack had had several occasions to talk to Dr. Rametti through the night—she had been nothing but kind and first-rate.

"How are you feeling?" Dr. Rametti asked Daisy gently.

Daisy's fingers clenched the tissue in her hand as she looked at the sheet across her lap. "Okay, I guess," she answered weakly.

"I talked to you and your husband both last night, when you were coming out of recovery," Dr. Rametti continued as she sat down next to Daisy on the bed and took Daisy's hand in hers, "but I'm guessing you don't remember much of it."

Jack leaned back against the wall, while Daisy nodded in response, acknowledging this was so.

Briefly, Dr. Rametti explained the simultaneous loss of the fetus and the rupture of Daisy's fallopian tube, and the resulting laparoscopic surgery to remove both. "The good news is there is nothing to prevent you and your husband from having another baby, Daisy, as you still have one working fallopian tube. I'm going to ask you to wait on that until you heal fully from this, and to hold off on intercourse until after I see you again in two weeks," she continued as Daisy flushed a bright, embarrassed pink. "Once I check you out and make sure everything is okay, you two can go back to acting like newlyweds again."

Except, Jack thought, he and Daisy never had been newlyweds. They'd been adversaries who'd been brought into marriage by the baby she was carrying.

"Additionally," Dr. Rametti continued talking to Daisy, "you're going to be feeling some discomfort for a few days, so I've prescribed some pain medication for you. In the meantime, you're going to need a lot of rest, and I'd like someone to be with you at home while you're recuperating. You shouldn't be alone for the next few days," Dr. Rametti stressed soberly before turning to look at Jack. "Can you handle that, or do we need to arrange for another family member or private nurse?"

Jack didn't even want to imagine how Daisy would react if one of the Templetons was called over to care for her. Besides, it was his responsibility, as her husband. "I'll handle it."

Daisy gave Jack a look that her obstetrician didn't see, that said this was not what she wanted.

That was too bad.

Jack wasn't bowing out on his responsibilities now.

Dr. Rametti picked up the chart on her lap and stood. "Daisy, you or your husband can go ahead and call my office later today and make a follow-up appointment. But right now, the discharge nurse will give you a list of post-op instructions to follow." Dr. Rametti turned to Jack with an empathetic look. "And see that she does, okay?"

Jack nodded.

The doctor looked back at Daisy. "Call me if you have any concerns."

Daisy promised she would.

Dr. Rametti patted Daisy's arm, the sympathy in her eyes speaking volumes. "You're going to be weepy. You and your husband have suffered a tremendous loss."

At the compassion in Dr. Rametti's voice, Daisy's eyes welled with tears.

"It's okay to cry. In fact, it will probably help you

both." The doctor looked at Jack, too, as he steeled himself to show no emotion and be as strong as Daisy needed him to be.

"Plus, your body's been through a lot. You were pregnant, now you're not. Your hormones are going to be in an uproar until your body gets itself back to normal. So you may be moody and that's okay, too. Just give it time. And you—" Dr. Rametti pointed at Jack "—be patient with her, okay?"

Jack nodded again. He could do that. Hell, he could do a lot more than that if Daisy would only let him. Right now, he wasn't sure that was the case. Already he could see the walls around her heart going up. Feel her pulling away from him. From what had happened, not just to her, but to both of them.

"YOU DON'T HAVE to do this, you know," Daisy said as soon as Dr. Rametti had exited the room.

Jack knew what she was going to say—that he didn't have to take care of her, but he didn't want to hear it. Not yet. Maybe not ever. He knew they had come together for reasons other than love alone, but he wasn't ready for any of that to end. And especially not now, when she still needed him in her life.

"We'll talk about this later, Daisy," Jack told her sternly as he moved to help her get dressed in the same clothes she had come in to the emergency room the night before.

Daisy shot him a contentious look, a hint of her old spirit showing through her grief. "I think we should."

"Nope. And it would help me out immensely," Jack continued as he knelt next to the bed and pulled her panties up over her knees, "if you would pay attention to what you're doing here."

He needed to think about something besides what a beautiful body she had, off-limits as it was. He needed to think about something other than taking her into his arms and holding her close and making love to her again and again until some of the happiness came back into her sad eyes.

But that wasn't going to happen, at least not for a couple of weeks. So he'd have to devise another way to try and keep her in his life. Have to find another way to get to know her as deeply and intimately as he wanted to know her.

"I'm *trying* to pay attention," Daisy countered in a slightly slurred voice as she struggled to line up her feet with the leg holes in her jeans. A task apparently not as easy as it would, on the surface, seem. "But this pain medication is making me woozy."

Jack could tell. His body reacting at the soft and sexy feel of her, he clasped the bare silky skin of one calf, fit it into the leg of her jeans, then did the other. Using both hands, he brought the denim carefully over her hips and the enticing curve of her buttocks.

"Oh, man." Daisy sighed as they both realized at once the futility of trying to zip up the jeans that had fit her so well only the night before. "I can't fasten these all the way."

Jack noted, even if she had been able to get past all the air Dr. Rametti had pumped into Daisy's stomach during the laparoscopy, to enable the surgeon to see what she was doing and make the needed repairs, the denim would not have covered the clear plastic bandage Daisy had over her navel. No, thanks to the shirt she had been wearing the night before, that would still be in plain view. Knowing that wouldn't do—Daisy felt self-conscious enough already—Jack tugged his short-sleeve blue polo shirt over his head and handed it to her. "You can wear this."

Daisy frowned even as her delicate hands curled around the fabric. "What about you?"

Jack shrugged. "I've still got a T-shirt on."

Daisy shot him a lopsided grin. "Yeah, well, without the polo shirt you look like a James Dean wanna-be. Or you would if you had a pack of cigarettes rolled up in the sleeve."

Jack slid the blue polo gently over her head. He knew his shirt smelled as if he had spent the night in it, but figured what the hell. It was something for her to wear home, and the sooner he got her back to the beach, the better.

Looking as if she wanted to get out of there as much as he wanted to get her out of there, Daisy grudgingly pulled her arms through. The sleeves of the polo, which landed just below the curve of his biceps, came down past her elbows, and the hem of it fell well past her lap. Nevertheless, she looked very feminine swallowed up that way in something of his. She looked up at him hesitantly. "You sure you don't mind? I feel bad about taking the shirt right off your back."

Or in other words, Jack thought, disappointed, she still resisted the idea of leaning on him, even for a few minutes. "It's okay," Jack said gruffly, telling himself that this wasn't the end of him and Daisy, despite the ever-retreating look in her eyes that said yes, it damn well was. That she had experienced as much of life—and loss—with him as she wanted to already. Wordlessly, he handed Daisy her red baseball cap and the coated elastic band that had been in her hair when she arrived, and watched as she fastened her hair in a ponytail, pulled the end through the half-moon-shaped back of her cap, then settled the brim down across her forehead. What she was thinking at that moment, as she finished dressing and held his eyes, Jack couldn't decipher and wasn't sure he wanted to know, anyway. Before either of them could say anything else, the discharge nurse came in.

She and Jack accompanied Daisy down together, and the nurse stayed with the wheelchair-bound Daisy while Jack dashed out to get his SUV. He parked beneath the portico and got out to help the nurse move Daisy into the passenger seat. As Jack helped Daisy out of the chair, not surprisingly she began to cry. Probably because she was thinking the same thing he was, Jack determined grimly. That this should have been a joyous occasion, she should have been leaving the hospital seven and a half months from now, with their happy healthy baby in her arms. But it hadn't happened that way, Jack told himself sternly as he wiped the tears from Daisy's face with his fingertips, gave her a comforting one-armed hug and pressed a kiss to her temple. And like it or not, he told himself as he swallowed hard against the tight knot of emotion in his own throat, they were just going to have to deal.

CHAPTER TWELVE

Tom walked into his son Mitch's Deveraux-Heyward Shipping office at 7:00 p.m. "Do you and Lauren have any plans for dinner this evening?" Tom asked.

As Tom feared his son would, Mitch hesitated, looking less than enthused. "Actually—"

"I thought we could go out together if you didn't have plans," Tom continued casually, not above being pushy if it resulted in him getting some time with family again. For the past five weeks they had all treated him like the pariah he supposed he deserved to be. Tom understood why they were angry and disappointed in him. Hell, he was disillusioned with his past behavior, too! His infidelity hadn't made sense at the time. It made even less now. But there was no point in wallowing in regret. That wouldn't change anything. And they all still had the rest of their lives ahead of them. Tom didn't want to spend his missing Grace and the kids, knowing he was the architect of their broken family. Not when he could still do something to fix things, even if it meant groveling a little, something else he never did.

Mitch buried his gaze in the papers on his desk and mumbled eventually, "Uh, sorry, Dad. It's not going to be possible. Maybe Gabe—"

Refusing to accept the brush-off yet again, Tom sat down in one of the chairs in front of his son's desk.

"Gabe's on call tonight." And Tom knew without even asking, the answer would be the same from his other two children. Amy and Chase would both cook up some excuse, real or imagined in order to continue keeping their distance from Tom. Not surprisingly, none of them had any trouble relating to Grace. In fact, from what Tom could see, they were spending more time than ever with his ex. According to Jack, all four of his children had even made an overture to Daisy the evening before. But Tom was persona non grata, and he was beginning to wonder dispiritedly if that would ever change.

"And anyway," Mitch continued, "I want to stop by to see Daisy."

The elephant in the living room. Feeling as if a cold draft had blown across his neck at the thought of the tragedy in his illegitimate daughter's life, Tom looked at Mitch. He wondered if his second-oldest son's information was more up-to-date than his own. "How's she doing?" Tom asked.

"I don't know." Mitch's eyebrows drew together in a worried frown as he rose and stuffed a stack of papers and his laptop computer into a leather carrying case. "I thought maybe you might know something."

Tom shook his head. "Jack hasn't called since nine this morning." Daisy had still been sleeping then, and hence, hadn't yet been told about the miscarriage. Jack had told Tom he planned to break the sad news to her himself. Tom hadn't envied him that. But he respected him for doing it.

Tom picked up the phone and telephoned the hospital to see if Daisy was allowed to have visitors.

"She okay?" Mitch asked as soon as the conversation was concluded.

Not bothering to hide his relief, Tom hung up. "Apparently so—she was released around noon today.'' He looked at Mitch, deciding it was time to stop shielding his legitimate children from his illegitimate one. "I think I'll drive out to the beach and check on her."

Mitch nodded as he got up from behind his desk. The resentful look on his face was back—the one that said he still couldn't believe Tom had cheated on Grace—the one that said he might not ever be able to forgive his father for the transgression. Then Mitch was gone. Computer case slung over his shoulder, already heading down the hall, for the elevators.

Tom closed up shop, too, then deciding not to call— he didn't want Daisy telling him she didn't want to see him, either—Tom looked up Jack's home address and headed down to his car. He drove out to the beach, stopped at a flower shop and bought a nice arrangement of pink roses then continued, paying careful attention to the street signs and house numbers. He had never been there before, never been to anyplace Jack lived, as it wasn't his practice to visit employees at their residences. Eventually, however, he found the small dark-gray beach cottage with the light-gray roof. He parked his Jaguar and got out.

JACK WAS IN HIS HOME office preparing a set of contracts that should have gone out earlier that day, when he heard the car door. He got up, looked out the window and saw Tom Deveraux getting out of his car. He had a large bouquet of flowers in his hand.

Not sure how Daisy would react to either the flowers or the father who had more or less abandoned her years ago, Jack stepped outside, quietly shutting the front door behind him.

"How is she?" Tom asked.

Jack didn't know how to answer that. She was heart-broken over the loss—so was he. "I think she's still a little stunned," Jack said finally, deciding not to try and sugarcoat things, even if Tom was his boss and probably would have preferred to hear that everything was just fine.

Tom raked his free hand through his hair, looking more uneasy than Jack had ever seen him. "Is she resting?"

"Yes." And Jack wanted to keep it that way. Daisy had been through hell the last twenty-four hours. If she could get a little sleep, all the better.

"Maybe the two of us could talk privately then," Tom suggested, handing the bouquet to Jack. "I don't want her to overhear."

Jack nodded his assent. "Let's go out back then, to the deck. We won't disturb her there." They walked around the house. When they reached the deck, Jack ducked inside momentarily, to put the flowers in the kitchen, to give to Daisy later. He came back out, two bottles of cold beer in hand and gave one to Tom.

Tom accepted his with a nod of thanks and twisted off the top. An awkward silence fell between them as they each took a drink. "I'm sorry about your loss," Tom said, sitting down in one of the Adirondack chairs overlooking the ocean.

Jack sat down beside him, knowing it was necessary for them to go through the motions of acknowledging their mutual grief over the loss, but wishing they didn't have to do it just the same. For him, the loss of their baby was just too painful to discuss. "Thank you," he said politely.

Tom stared at the waves rolling slowly in to shore. "Even though I wished you would have been up front with me from the start—'' Tom turned back to Jack soberly ''—you should have told me.''

''I know that,'' Jack said. He also knew it hadn't been easy for Tom to be civil to him since he'd found out that Jack and Daisy had slept together that night.

Looking as if he was beginning to swelter in the heat and humidity of the summer evening, Tom took off his suit coat, laid it beside him, then loosened his tie and the first two buttons on his shirt. ''I've had some time to think the past five weeks. I realize part of what happened is probably my fault. I never should have had you watching over her all these years,'' Tom confessed in a low, sorrowful tone. He fired a pointed look at Jack. ''It lent an element of intimate understanding to your relationship with her that would not have been there otherwise.''

In other words, Jack thought, Tom was saying that in the process of so closely keeping tabs on Daisy, Jack had become enamored of Daisy in some not necessarily healthy way. But Jack knew there was a difference between a fascination with someone and what had happened between him and Daisy. A lot of people fascinated him. No one else grabbed hold of his heart and soul the way Daisy had the night they'd come together. No one else left him unable to sleep, or think, or do much of anything. No one else conjured up such fiercely protective, genuinely tender or even highly exasperated feelings. ''I could have said no to your request,'' Jack replied. ''I didn't.''

''Could you?'' Tom regarded Jack skeptically. He took another sip of his beer. ''Looking back on it, I think it was more or less part of the job requirement at Deveraux-Heyward Shipping. Whatever I needed done, in a legal or even clandestine sense, you did.''

Jack ran his fingers over the condensation collecting on the outside of his beer. "I understood that you had your reasons."

"You just didn't know at the time what those reasons were," Tom said.

Jack shrugged, aware he wouldn't have trusted anyone else on a gut level the way he had trusted Tom Deveraux. He gave his mentor a man-to-man look as he replied, "I took your motivation to be honorable."

Tom picked at the curling edge of the label on his bottle, drawing it farther away from the glass. "Yes, it was, even if the initial transgression that got me into this predicament was not. The point is, Jack," Tom emphasized bluntly as his gaze clashed strongly with Jack's once again, "I vilified you for doing exactly what I had done—slept with someone on impulse."

Jack stared briefly at the weathered boards between his feet. "I don't think you know why I slept with Daisy that night." Jack paused, and leaned forward earnestly in his chair. "And I sure don't know why you—" Jack realized, from the sudden, annoyed look on Tom's face, he better tread carefully in what he alleged. He swallowed and ignored the uneasiness twisting in his gut. "Bottom line, I think our situations are as different as night and day."

Tom studied Jack skeptically. "You're telling me you love Daisy?" he stated sarcastically.

Jack threw up a hand in frustration. "I'm telling you I don't know what I feel," he said, being equally blunt. Then, thinking he owed it to Tom to be completely truthful, now that they were speaking man to man, added even more irritably, "I just know that they're complex and they don't seem likely to go away."

"You're sure about that," Tom said quietly, beginning to relax once again.

"Yes." Jack took a long swallow of beer.

Another silence fell, less tense this time. Tom looked at Jack with a mixture of respect and relief. "I want you to do right by her, Jack. She's had a reputation for being wild in the past. If you leave her now, after one week of marriage, simply because she is no longer carrying your child—"

Tom didn't need to tell Jack what the gossips would do—they'd have a field day. And Daisy didn't need that. "I have every intention of staying married to Daisy for the foreseeable future," Jack stated firmly. Maybe—hopefully—given the way the two of them were beginning to get on, forever.

Tom quirked an eyebrow. "What does she say?"

"We haven't talked about it yet," Jack admitted reluctantly. "Although, to be honest, I can see she has one foot out the door already. But I expected that. It's been her pattern in the past to run whenever the going got too tough. I don't intend to let her do that again."

Tom sighed and sat back in his chair as a cooling breeze blew across them both. "You can't keep Daisy married to you against her will," he pointed out.

Jack turned his glance briefly to the person flying a kite along the beach. "I can, however, convince her it would be in her best interest to stay married to me."

Tom's lips curved upward slightly. "You think so."

Jack turned back to Tom. "I know so, given a little time. Fortunately for me—" Jack shrugged "—she's under doctor's orders to rest as much as possible for the next week or so. And she's going to need someone to take care of her while she is recuperating. That person—" Jack angled a thumb at his chest "—is going to be me."

Tom nodded his approval as some of the old cama-raderie came back into their relationship. "I'm counting on you, Jack, to make this work for both of you. And it's not going to be easy," Tom warned. "Not with her recovering from this kind of loss. She may turn away from you. Hell, she'll probably push you away with both hands, but don't you do it." Tom paused and leaned forward, his voice dropping a confiding notch. "And there's one other thing. You seem to have some influence with Daisy. I want you to use it to convince her that I have her best interests at heart. And if she is my child, as we suspect, that I'll do right by her."

Jack believed Tom would. Tom might have made a mistake in siring Daisy, and letting the threats of others keep him away from her all these years. But now that the truth was out, Tom would find a way to make things right once again, in a way that eventually satisfied everyone. "Anything else?" Jack asked.

Tom nodded. "I want you to persuade Daisy to give me a chance to make it up to her, starting today."

"That's easier said than done," Jack warned. Daisy wasn't happy about the way she had been abandoned. Her resentment of everyone involved was not going to be an easy thing to overcome.

"I'm not asking you to work miracles, Jack. Just maybe open a door or two. I'll take it from there."

What could Jack say to that? He owed Tom every-thing. Without his boss's mentoring, Jack might still be working on the docks just the way everyone else in his family had done for generations. Tom had seen past the rough edges Jack had had in his youth, to the intelli-gence and scholarly bent Jack had tried to keep hidden from his tough-as-nails friends. Tom had encouraged Jack to stop running with such a disruptive crowd and concentrate on the grades and reputation that would determine his future. Without the steady encouragement and praise from Tom, Jack would not have worked nearly as hard on his schoolwork or studied so diligently for his college entrance exams. And certainly, minus the scholarships and private loans Deveraux-Heyward Shipping Company had awarded him, the costs of the private college and law school he had set his sights on would have been prohibitive.

Up to now, Tom had been the one doing all the giving in their relationship. Jack had worked for Tom. He had handled the Daisy situation the best it could be handled under the circumstances and not asked questions. But Jack hadn't begun to really pay his mentor back for the way Tom had changed the course of Jack's life. Now he had the opportunity to do that. He determined he would not fail.

"Consider it done," Jack said quietly, wondering even as he spoke just how he was going to manage this.

Before Tom could say anything else, the sliding glass door opened, and Daisy stepped outside to join them.

DAISY DIDN'T NEED to hear whatever it was the two men had been saying to know she had interrupted something important. The conspiratorial looks on their faces told her that. It was just too bad she hadn't been able to catch anything more than the low murmur of their voices.

"So what's going on?" she asked as casually as if she hadn't noticed anything amiss as the outside air hit her like a blast of heat. To her dismay, moving even slightly caused her pain that started in her abdomen and spread throughout her body, and she winced and swore and swayed a little on her feet. Jack and Tom both rushed for her, one on each side, helping her into one of the Adirondack chaises on the deck overlooking the beach.

"I just came by to bring you some flowers and see how you were doing," Tom said, settling into a chair opposite her.

Daisy wanted to believe Tom Deveraux was sincerely interested in her, that he could and would one day love her in the same way that he loved his other children. But the cynical side of her said it just wasn't so, that he was doing what he had to now to silence her and avert a scandal. She feared, in the final analysis, Tom would be no better than the Templeton family, that he would always find her lacking in both big and little ways. And because of that, would eventually turn his back on her and disavow her, too. "A little late to be playing the father act, isn't it?" Daisy said contentiously as she tried unsuccessfully to get comfortable. She tensed as the next thought hit. "Or did you come by to tell me the results of the DNA test?"

Tom shook his head. "They're not in yet."

"More's the pity," Daisy said, trying not to think of it as a reprieve, albeit a temporary one. She stretched out on the chaise until she finally found a position that didn't hurt quite so much.

"But I think I know the results," Tom continued firmly. "I think you're my child."

Daisy studied him, refusing to let him raise her hopes only to dash them again. "Like I said," she answered tiredly, wishing her head didn't feel so fuzzy from all the pain medicine, "it's a little late for all this, isn't it?"

Tom regarded her with enough kindness to make her cry. "It doesn't have to be."

Daisy felt tears pricking at the back of her eyelids again. Looking as if he didn't want to interfere, Jack stood awkwardly. "Maybe I should let you two talk this over alone," he said.

"No." Desperate not to be alone with the man who had abandoned her, Daisy caught Jack's hand before he could move away. She tugged him closer, and lifting her knees, motioned for Jack to sit beside her on the chaise so that Jack was between her and Tom. Reluctantly, Jack did.

"Mr. Deveraux and I," Daisy concluded coldly, "have said all there is to say."

Silence fell between the three of them, broken only by the sounds of children playing farther down the beach. As the moments wore on, Tom looked less like the successful executive and more like a person struggling with failure. Daisy didn't want to identify with the man who had ignored her her whole life, but she knew how he felt. Her heart was heavy, too, with all the opportunities lost, the hurts that would probably never heal.

"I'm sorry," she said eventually. "I know I opened this Pandora's box, but now I want to shut it." She angled her chin at him stubbornly, letting Tom know there was still a little kick-butt 'tude in her despite her fragile condition. "I don't want you acting like my father," she warned him stonily.

"Too bad." Tom finished what was left of his beer and put the bottle aside. "Because I've begun to feel like your father."

Daisy wrapped her hand around Jack's bicep and clung tight. "I want you to go away and leave me alone,'' she repeated. She knew she was hiding behind Jack; she couldn't help it.

Tom stood reluctantly. "All right, I will—for right now. But only until those tests come back and prove what you and I both already know in our hearts to be true.'' Tom regarded her sternly. "Then we have some making up to do, Daisy. And whether you like it or not, we're going to do just that.''

"THAT BASTARD,'' Daisy said as Tom walked around the deck and disappeared from sight. Unwelcome tears stung her eyes as they heard a car door open and close, then an engine start, his vehicle backing away. "How can he think he can just undo everything with an apology and a request to move on?'' she demanded, her voice quivering despite her attempt to appear cool, calm and collected.

Jack scooted back on the chaise and laced a comforting arm around her shoulders. "Maybe because that's the only way this situation is ever going to get any better,'' Jack said gently.

"Of course you would say that,'' Daisy fumed as she struggled to her feet. "You idolize the man. Oh, don't even bother to look surprised,'' she said, beginning to pace, as swiftly as her still-sore body would allow. She eased down on the weathered wooden bench that rimmed the edge of the deck. "It's clear every time you look at Tom Deveraux,'' Daisy said, rubbing a hand lightly across her aching middle. "You have this hero-worship thing going.''

Jack clamped his lips together, his resentment about what she had just alleged clear. He swung his legs over the side of the chaise. "Tom Deveraux is my boss, Daisy.''

"He's more than that." Daisy let her mouth run on ahead of her common sense. "He's a…"

"Mentor," Jack supplied calmly when Daisy's mental search failed to yield the right word.

"But you wish he was even more than that," Daisy accused.

Jack grew, if possible, even more exasperated, as he rested both his forearms on his thighs. "I admit I strive to earn his respect," he said after a moment.

Daisy tilted her head as she continued to study him. "Is it going to be possible to get it back—after what happened between you and me?"

Jack gestured in a way that let Daisy know he had his own lingering doubts about that. "I think the two of us have made a good start in mending fences." He looked at Daisy steadily. "I advise you to do the same with him."

Daisy felt her mood turn even more belligerent. "Why should I?" she demanded contentiously.

"Because you started this and that gives you a certain responsibility to see it through to the end," Jack lectured Daisy grimly. "You can't just stir things up the way you have and then walk away."

Daisy folded her arms in front of her defiantly. She hoped Jack would have realized by now he couldn't make her see her father through his eyes. Because their experiences with Tom just weren't the same. "I didn't know what I was getting into when I started my search for my biological parents." If she had…well, she would have backed off before she had gotten even more hurt than she had been by her abandonment years before.

Jack regarded her speculatively. "What did you think it would be like?"

Something wonderful and heartwarming enough to

appear in a family movie, Daisy thought. "I don't know." Daisy shrugged. "I always figured my father never knew about me."

"Tom didn't."

"But he guessed I was the result of his one-night stand with Iris! He certainly knew how nuts Richard and Charlotte were about the blue blood running through their veins and the exclusive ancestry of the Templeton family that they would never willingly just let one of their own go to be raised by persons of unacceptable lineage! He just didn't care enough to find out if I was his!"

"Tom told you why he didn't pursue it—the Templetons said it was all untrue and threatened to sue for defamation if he didn't back off immediately."

"I also know that if push came to shove, Charlotte and Richard would've avoided a scandal at all costs. Any blood or paternity tests required would have been done on the Q.T. If the results had indeed confirmed what Tom suspected, something would have been worked out so Tom could acknowledge me."

Jack sighed and shoved both his hands through his sandy-brown hair. "Grace and Tom probably would have divorced had that happened."

Daisy knew Grace wouldn't have wanted her around—Daisy would simply have reminded Grace of Tom's infidelity and betrayal. "They divorced anyway," Daisy said resentfully, taking a deep, bracing breath of sea air.

"A decade later."

"That wasn't my problem back then." And as far as Daisy was concerned, it wasn't a real excuse now.

"But it was Tom's," Jack pointed out with exaggerated patience. His eyes still on hers, he rolled to his feet and closed the distance between them. "He had four other children."

"Whom he would have walked through fire for, and probably still would. I, on the other hand, was expendable," Daisy said, unable to contain her bitterness over that devastating truth one second longer. Her heart aching with the rejection she had suffered, Daisy glared at Jack. "And now that I know all that, I have no interest in spending time with Tom, period. So don't think you can talk me into it," she warned, her voice shaking, "because you can't!"

Jack propped a foot on the bench beside her. Forearm on his knee, he leaned down. "I still think you should give Tom a chance to make it up to you," Jack insisted.

Daisy stubbornly ignored her husband's advice. It was clear Jack's feelings about Tom were muddled by all Tom had done for Jack over the years. And while she appreciated and understood Jack's affection and respect for the man, she simply did not share it, and probably never would. "Is that the only thing you talked about with Tom?" Daisy asked, wanting and needing to change the subject to something less painful to her.

Jack tensed in a way that let Daisy know she had inadvertently hit on something yet again. He put his foot back on the deck and moved away from her once more.

Not about to let him off the hook when he had gone to so much trouble to analyze her actions, she pressed on resolutely, stating what she had observed. "The two of you were out here an awfully long time." When she had finally gotten out of bed and made it to the patio door, it had looked—to her dismay—like one of those man-to-man or father-son talks. And Jack had been every bit as into whatever was being discussed as Tom had been. "So what else did you two talk about?"

"Business."

Sensing Jack was suddenly withholding every bit as much as he was telling her, Daisy regarded Jack skeptically. "Then why were you talking out here in this heat, when you could have been inside in the study or the living room in air-conditioned comfort?" she asked a great deal more pleasantly than she felt.

Jack sighed heavily and said, "Because we didn't want to disturb you."

Daisy lifted an eyebrow, moved to stand.

Jack put his hand on the middle of her back and led her back inside the house. "If you must know," he continued explaining, "I think your father came over here because he's concerned about the prospect of me taking care of you."

"Why would Tom be worried about that?" Daisy shot Jack a bemused look as he reluctantly let go of her and walked into the kitchen.

"Because he probably doesn't even know if I can cook," Jack retorted, checking out the contents of the refrigerator and freezer.

Daisy leaned against the counter, watching him. "Can you?" Thus far, all they had done was eat out or order in.

Jack nodded. "Learned when I was ten."

"You're kidding."

Jack shook his head, the expression in his eyes turning unexpectedly grim. "It was either that or eat bacon and eggs and sausage and biscuits every night for dinner. They were the only two things my grandfather knew how to cook. And the only two things he wanted to learn how to cook."

"Doesn't sound like much of a balanced diet," Daisy observed quietly.

"It wasn't, which is why he died of heart disease at age fifty-five. Anyway, if I wanted to eat anything else, I had to get on my bicycle, go to the corner market, buy it and fix it for us myself."

"So did you?"

Jack nodded as he pulled a package of boneless chicken breasts from the freezer and put it into the microwave to defrost. "At first it was just stuff like packaged macaroni and cheese, beans and hot dogs, and if I was really daring, a hamburger and oven French fries. But eventually I branched out, and by the time I was twelve I was doing all the cooking for both of us."

"What about your mother?" Daisy asked as Jack got out the makings for a salad.

"I know she left when you were three but…"

Daisy sank into one of the chairs in the breakfast nook. "You've never seen her since?"

"I've seen her."

A wealth of pain in those words. "She came back?"

Jack shook his head. "I tracked her down."

Daisy could see he didn't want to talk about it now anymore than he had before. Still, she had to know. "What happened?"

Jack shrugged, his broad shoulders pushing against the soft cotton of his sport shirt. "She still didn't want me around. And she didn't want anyone else to know about me, either." His gaze flicked back to her. "Apparently, she'd made this new life for herself in Cleveland—told everyone her family was dead. Her husband and three kids didn't know she'd had a baby out of wedlock years before, or that she had abandoned me.

She didn't think they would understand. So she asked me to leave and never come back or contact her again."

Daisy studied the sadness in his golden-brown eyes. "And you did."

"Yes," Jack replied calmly. "Because she was right. There was just no way we could fix what had been broken years ago. So we both went on with our lives."

Prior to the last five weeks of her life, Daisy would have encouraged Jack to keep trying, keep struggling to somehow make things work with his mother. Now Daisy wondered if he hadn't been the smart one, if they all wouldn't have been better off if she, too, had just been able to walk away after finding out the truth. Instead, she had needed to come back to confront everyone who had lied to her; she'd taunted Jack, seduced, and slept with him just to get even with Tom Deveraux, Iris, Charlotte and Richard. That hotheaded mistake had resulted in a forced marriage and a miscarriage, and a loss and a grief she would never fully recover from.

Now Jack wanted to believe they had married for all the right reasons. He wanted to take something that was all wrong and make it into something real, if not exactly wonderful.

Only, their life together wasn't that simple and never would be because she couldn't have the kind of life she had always wanted if she remained trapped in a marriage neither of them had planned on or wanted in the first place. So there was only one thing for her to do, Daisy realized with a mixture of sadness and defiance. And Jack wasn't going to like it.

THE LIMOUSINE PULLED UP in front of Richard and Charlotte Templeton's Charleston residence shortly after midnight. Charlotte waited until they were headed up the front steps, out of earshot of their driver, before speaking her mind. "I wish you wouldn't disappear in the middle of a party that way."

Richard sent her a scowling, sidelong glance as he opened the door and let them inside. "I didn't disappear."

"I couldn't find you," Charlotte repeated as they walked through the dimly lit foyer.

Richard shrugged uncaringly. "Then you must not have looked very hard."

On the contrary, Charlotte thought, her irritation growing by leaps and bounds with every second that passed, she had searched for her husband very thoroughly and discreetly. Richard had not been anywhere in the hotel ballroom where the gala had been held, the lobby of the hotel or even the courtyard just off the ballroom. And she sincerely doubted he had been in the men's room for the hour and a half he had been missing in action.

Not that it really mattered, she guessed, as the muscular dystrophy fund-raiser she had cochaired had been a rousing success, and everyone in attendance at the Roaring Twenties party had seemed to have a wonderful time.

Deliberately, Charlotte pushed her uneasiness aside as she ignored the aching in her feet and made her way up the stairs. She paused at the top of the landing. "Iris and I are going to see Daisy tomorrow. We'd like you to come with us."

Richard preceded her down the hall. "I don't think so."

"She could use our support, Richard."

Concern creased his forehead. "I thought she was fine."

"She is. At least she claims she is," Charlotte amended hastily.

Richard regarded her with barely checked irritation. "You obviously don't believe that."

"I don't see how she could be all right emotionally, having just lost a baby."

Richard's lips pressed together grimly, telling Charlotte that he cared less about Daisy's miscarriage than the pregnancy she had hidden from them. "I'm sure it was for the best," Richard said tightly as he shouldered his way past Charlotte and walked into his bedroom suite at the top of the stairs.

Charlotte followed her husband as far as the doorway of the bedroom he had occupied alone for the last twenty-four years. She watched as he took off his jacket and tossed it onto a chair. "I don't see how you can say that," she returned, wondering how he could be so unfeeling.

"I say it because it's true." Richard unbuttoned his shirt and removed his bow tie. "I don't want a Templeton heir who's descended from a family of dockworkers."

Too exhausted to stand any longer, Charlotte made her way to a wing chair next to the fireplace and sank into it. She ran a hand through her hair until she found the pin securing her twenties hat. She took off the delicate silk, net and rhinestone confection and laid it across her lap, then looked her husband square in the eye. "Daisy's husband isn't a dockworker."

"His grandfather was," Richard argued as he removed the gold and onyx cuff links from his shirt. "And his mother, from what I gather, was a common tramp."

Charlotte stiffened at Richard's rudeness. "Don't talk that way."

Richard looked at her as if she was an idiot. "Now you're defending a sixteen-year-old slut who got pregnant and left her baby with her widowed father to rear?"

Charlotte retained her ladylike demeanor. "We don't know the circumstances." It was wrong to judge.

He regarded her levelly. "We know enough to know that Jack Granger isn't good enough for Daisy. We know enough to realize that we don't want Granger and Templeton bloodlines mixing."

Charlotte privately admitted the marriage wasn't one she would have chosen for Daisy, but that was neither here nor there. "She's married to him now, Richard. We're going to have to make the best of it."

He sent her a contemptuous look. "You make the best of it. I'm tired. I want to go to bed."

Her cue to leave.

Charlotte rose with as much grace as she could muster. They hadn't made love in over a decade or more. Richard had been impotent and refused to seek help or even discuss his problem with her. And she didn't press him since she knew the condition was so difficult for him to face. It was why she'd tolerated his resentment all these years. If nothing else, she was a supportive wife.

Not that their love life had ever been all that exciting, Charlotte thought wistfully as her husband shut the door behind her and she made her way down the hall to her own bedroom suite. Their marriage had been arranged by their families. Both eighteen at the time when they said their vows, they'd had Iris that same year, Connor in the decade that followed, and they'd adopted Daisy the decade after that. And although Charlotte had loved and respected her husband from the very start, and been the best wife she could, even though it meant putting away her own romantic dreams, she had to wonder sometimes if Richard had ever loved or really respected her. All Charlotte knew for certain was that she felt responsible for the void in their marriage because she knew—even in the years before he became impotent—she had never been able to give Richard what he wanted or needed in the bedroom. Or, it sometimes seemed, anywhere else. And that, more than anything, Charlotte knew, was why he had turned away.

CHAPTER THIRTEEN

DAISY WAITED until Jack had gone to sleep, then got up and quietly got dressed and found her car keys. She was headed for the door when a sudden shaft of light overhead and a low masculine voice stopped her in her tracks.

"Dr. Rametti said you're not supposed to be driving yet."

Her insides quaking with dread at the thought of an emotional confrontation neither of them wanted or needed, Daisy turned to face him. Jack was standing at the other end of the foyer in low-slung pajama pants, arms crossed over his bare chest.

Daisy could tell by the indignant look on his face that he had never been asleep at all, but had simply been pretending, same as she. Ignoring the stiffness in her healing body, she propped a hand on her hip and resolutely stayed her ground. "I'll determine if I'm well enough. Besides, this time of night there's no traffic to be worried about." In fact, at 2:00 a.m., Daisy knew, she would be lucky if she saw a soul as she drove herself back out to Kristy Neumeyer's Paradise Resort.

Jack closed the distance between them with long, determined strides. "You could still encounter a drunk driver or an animal in the roadway." He paused just short of her. "*Both* would require some fancy maneuvers you might find you can't manage."

Okay, so she hadn't thought of that, Daisy thought as a shiver of pure sensual awareness swept through her. Determined not to get sidetracked by anything still medically forbidden to both of them, Daisy tilted her face up at his and quirked a cavalier eyebrow. "Would you prefer I call a cab?"

Jack shifted his weight and stood, legs braced for battle, arms folded against the bare, hair-whorled muscularity of his chest. "I would prefer you tell me what you're doing."

Their eyes locked. "Leaving."

He slowly lifted his hand and she felt the abrasion of his thumb as he gently rubbed the vulnerable spot beneath her ear. "I thought we had settled that," he murmured.

With effort, Daisy stepped away from the mesmerizing quality of his touch. "You gave your opinion."

"Obviously," Jack sighed, "you were withholding yours." He took her by the hand and led her into the adjacent living room and helped her ease down on the comfy sectional sofa. "So give it to me now."

Daisy watched as he sank down beside her. Knowing there was no helping it now—she would have to give it to him straight—she stated bluntly, "I'm tired of being other people's problem. And I sure don't want to be yours, not anymore." Bad enough she had grown up with an adoptive father who resented her, an adoptive mother who worried over her, not to mention two birth parents who would have done anything not to acknowledge her. Now, through no deliberate effort of her own, she had kept to the pattern and acquired a husband who had married her only because she was pregnant.

Now she wasn't.

It was just simple.

And even though she could see that the inherently gallant part of Jack did not want to admit that to himself, she knew it was true.

Once he was away from her, well, he'd see it, too.

But in the meantime, Jack only shrugged and looked all the more resolute. "So be something else to me," he said softly.

Daisy made no effort to hide her exasperation. "Like…?"

"My wife." Jack took her hand in his and lifted it to his lips.

Daisy shivered as he lightly kissed her knuckles. "You're telling me you actually want to be married now," she asked in a throaty whisper.

"I never knew it until you came into my life, but yeah—I like having someone to be with, and sleep with, and share dilemmas with."

Daisy had to admit she had enjoyed having a partner, too, if only for a few days. But this was not reality, she reminded herself firmly. It was fantasy, and fantasy faded under the demands of every day. She withdrew her hand from his, and wincing as she shifted positions, moved away from him. "You're forgetting one thing, Jack. We're not in love with each other."

Jack lounged back against the sofa, casually keeping his physical distance, and yet at the same time so clearly invading her emotional space. "Why do we need to be madly in love to be happily married?" he asked with a careless shrug. "Why does anyone?" He paused and looked into Daisy's eyes. "Maybe marriage would be better and simpler if people chose to become partners in life."

Needing to dispel the lingering romantic aura in the shadowy room, Daisy reached over and turned on a reading lamp. "I can see why you're an attorney," she told him practically. "You have an ability to argue any side of a case, no matter how inane."

Jack folded his arms behind his head and propped his ankle on his knee. "I'm not going to deny that. It's what I've been trained to do. However, in this particular case—" he gave her a sexy smile "—I happen to believe it."

Oh, how Daisy would have liked to let him seduce her. But that was what had gotten them into this fix. Although *she* had been the one doing the seducing back then. "We have no future," she stated firmly.

Jack grinned and persisted, "How about a present, then?"

His cavalier attitude pushed her over the edge. Suddenly it was all too much. This conversation. The future. And especially the present. Her hormones still running riot, tears blinding her eyes, Daisy struggled to her feet and told him in a low, choked voice, "I've spent my entire life to date living in a place where I was never supposed to be, with people who felt required to take care of me but who didn't really want to be doing that." She looked at Jack furiously. "It's *not* an experience I care to repeat."

Jack stood, and blocked her way to the door. "You are not and never will be an albatross to me, Daisy," he said compassionately.

"So you say now," Daisy retorted.

Jack wrapped his arms around her, enclosing her in warmth. "So I'll say forever."

Daisy buried her face in the solidness of his chest. "You can't possibly know that. We had to be together before," she said, forcing herself to be sensible. "Now we don't."

Briefly, hurt radiated in his eyes. "So you want to separate?"

Daisy swallowed hard. Hadn't they caused each other enough pain? Did they really want to risk any more? "Can we even call it that?" she countered lightly. "We were only married a week ago, Jack."

"Long enough to get me to like it," he countered, more than up to the middle-of-the-night showdown she had forced upon them. "And you did, too, Daisy."

Too much, Daisy thought. She drew a breath. She had to put her usual impulsiveness aside and be sensible here. She had to protect her heart before she fell apart.

Calling on her legendary stubbornness to give her the strength she needed to turn away from him, Daisy stared at the sinewy hardness of his chest and reiterated calmly, "I've got to stand on my own two feet, Jack." She had to be able to make herself happy before she could expect to do the same for anyone else. And God knew, a good man like Jack deserved a woman who could and would make his life wonderful.

She swallowed hard around the tight knot of emotion in her throat. "I want to go back to work and save enough money to get a place of my own." She wanted to start back where she had been, before Jack came into her life, and build a future no one else could take away from her.

"So do that," Jack advised, as supportive as always. "But do it here. We don't have to be husband and wife if you don't want to be, Daisy. We can be more like roommates."

Daisy regarded Jack skeptically. "And you'd be happy with that?" she challenged.

The sadness he'd felt at the loss of their baby was back in his expression. "I want to take care of you while you're recuperating," he stated simply. "If you still want to go after you've recovered, then so be it."

Daisy studied him with as much objectiveness as she could muster under the circumstances. "But you don't want that, do you?" Daisy whispered after a long moment. She wasn't sure how she felt about that. Thrilled. Scared. Perplexed. "You don't want me to go at all."

For a moment Jack looked just as lost and lonely as she felt deep inside, and just as determined to cover it up. A revealing silence stretched between them as he rested his hands on her shoulders. "If we hadn't lost our baby we'd still be living here together as lovers. I won't lie to you, Daisy," Jack confessed softly as he ran his palms down her arms to her wrists. "I'm not enthused about the prospect of giving up that part of our relationship."

Truthfully, Daisy thought as he linked hands with her, neither was she. "Meaning what?" Daisy said as her heart began to race at the sensuousness of his light, commanding touch. She lifted her chin at him belligerently and tried to pass off the entire conversation as a hypothetical joke. "That as soon as my body heals all the way, you're going to try and seduce me?"

Jack's lips curved upward—once again he was all indomitable male. "Let's just say if you're willing and the opportunity to be together presents itself, I won't pass it up," he promised. "And in the meantime," he told her as he tucked his thumbs beneath her chin, "even if we can't have sex, we can still kiss."

Daisy hitched in a breath. What they should be doing was getting to know each other, if they were serious about this, and she wasn't sure he was, beyond the physical, anyway. "Jack..." Daisy moaned as his lips touched hers. She told herself she shouldn't be doing

this—and longing swept through her. She told herself
she was definitely not going to let him tease her lips
apart—and she accepted his tongue into her mouth. She
told herself none of this meant anything—and yet, as
he continued to kiss her gently and reverently, the world
fell away. Until there was just the two of them, this
moment, this need for physical and emotional comfort
that only they could give. Her senses sharpening, she
went up on tiptoe, wreathing her arms around his neck,
deepening the kiss. The loss was still there, but now,
so was hope. And if not love, something that felt very
close.

Daisy clung to him, wanting this moment to never
end.

Looking as if he felt the same way, Jack scooped her
up in his arms and carried her back to the bedroom.
His expression tender, he lowered her to the bed,
stretched out beside her and traced the curve of her jaw
with his thumb. "Let me hold you, Daisy."

What could she say to that? It was what she wanted
and needed. What they both needed in the aftermath of
what had happened. "And then what...?"

Jack pressed a kiss into her hair and cuddled her all
the closer. "We'll take it one day at a time and things'll
work out. You'll see."

Daisy listened to the conviction in his voice and
wished she had Jack's confidence. But her feminine intuition was telling her things were going to get a lot
worse before they ever got better.

"I GATHER YOU'VE SEEN today's paper?" Iris asked her
parents as she joined them for breakfast in the formal
dining room of their Charleston home.

Their faces grim, Richard and Charlotte nodded.

GET 2

HOW TO GET YOUR
2 FREE BOOKS AND FREE GIFT!

1. Peel off the MIRA® sticker on the front cover. Place it in the space provided at right. This automatically entitles you to receive two free books and an exciting surprise gift.

2. Send back this card and you'll get 2 "The Best of the Best™" books. These books have a combined cover price of $11.98 or more in the U.S. and $13.98 or more in Canada, but they are yours to keep absolutely FREE!

3. There's <u>no</u> catch. You're under <u>no</u> obligation to buy anything. We charge nothing — ZERO — for your first shipment. And you don't have to make any minimum number of purchases — not even one!

4. We call this line "The Best of the Best" because each month you'll receive the best books by some of today's most popular authors. These authors show up time and time again on all the major bestseller lists and their books sell out as soon as they hit the stores. You'll like the convenience of getting them delivered to your home at our special discount prices . . . and you'll love your *Heart to Heart* subscriber newsletter featuring author news, horoscopes, recipes, book reviews and much more!

5. We hope that after receiving your free books you'll want to remain a subscriber. But the choice is yours — to continue or cancel, anytime at all! So why not take us up on our invitation, with no risk of any kind. You'll be glad you did!

6. And remember...we'll send you a surprise gift ABSOLUTELY FREE just for giving THE BEST OF THE BEST a try.

BOOKS FREE!

Hurry!

Return this card promptly to GET 2 FREE BOOKS & A FREE GIFT!

The Best of the Best™

```
Affix
peel-off
MIRA
sticker here
```

YES! Please send me the 2 FREE "The Best of the Best" books and FREE gift for which I qualify. I understand that I am under no obligation to purchase anything further, as explained on the back and on the opposite page.

385 MDL DRTA   185 MDL DR59

FIRST NAME   LAST NAME

ADDRESS

APT.#   CITY

STATE/PROV.   ZIP/POSTAL CODE

THE BEST OF THE BEST™ — Here's How it Works:

Accepting your 2 free books and gift places you under no obligation to buy anything. You may keep the books and gift and return the shipping statement marked "cancel." If you do not cancel, about a month later we will send you 4 additional books and bill you just $4.74 each in the U.S., or $5.24 each in Canada, plus 25¢ shipping & handling per book and applicable taxes if any.* That's the complete price and — compared to cover prices starting from $5.99 each in the U.S. and $6.99 each in Canada — it's quite a bargain! You may cancel at any time, but if you choose to continue, every month we'll send you 4 more books, which you may either purchase at the discount price or return to us and cancel your subscription.

*Terms and prices subject to change without notice. Sales tax applicable in N.Y. Canadian residents will be charged applicable provincial taxes and GST. Credit or Debit balances in a customer's account(s) may be offset by any other outstanding balance owed by or to the customer.

Charlotte tapped a perfectly manicured fingertip against the caption Newly Wedded Bliss Interrupted for Jack Granger and His Bride, Charleston Heiress Daisy Templeton-Granger. The article went on:

According to sources at Charleston General Hospital, the new Mrs. Jack Granger was admitted Wednesday evening for undisclosed reasons and released at noon the following day. We all wish Daisy and her new husband well.

"The mention itself isn't bad," Iris said. "Although it does open the family up to a lot of speculation and questions."

"Well, the photo is utterly appalling," Charlotte said in obvious distress, shaking her head. "What could Daisy have been *thinking* to leave the hospital dressed that way?"

Iris often lamented Daisy's wild-child way of dressing, but this time she found herself taking Daisy's side. "I doubt she expected a picture of her leaving the hospital with Jack to appear in the newspaper. Never mind as part of Bucky Jerome's gossip column on the society page."

"She still could have dressed more appropriately. Look at the rip in the knee of her jeans, the baseball cap and oversize man's shirt! And that husband of hers! What could Jack have been thinking, dressing in just a plain white T-shirt and old jeans. His hair doesn't look combed. And—" Charlotte regarded the photo closely and frowned "—given the scruffy look of his face, he obviously hasn't shaved, either. Heaven knows how many of our friends who volunteer at the hospital saw them that way!"

"I suspect that's Jack's shirt Daisy is wearing, Mother. She was probably cold or something."

"Then he should have brought her a sweater from home," Richard interjected grimly. "And taken care to look a little better himself. Doesn't that young man understand he has an image of class and refinement to uphold now that he is married to our Daisy?"

If he didn't yet, he would soon, Iris thought. And she pitied Jack in that regard—her father was a very rigid and unforgiving man. "I suspect they were both at the hospital all night," Iris said quietly.

Richard's eyes narrowed. "That's no excuse."

Iris had realized a long time ago that she never should have given Daisy over to her parents to raise. But at the time, she had been unwilling to give Daisy up entirely and desperate to keep her in her life, to know from the moment that she signed her over that Daisy really was all right.

But Daisy hadn't been all right, Iris concluded as she stirred artificial sweetener into her coffee. Instead, to Richard anyway, Daisy had been a living, breathing reminder of Iris's transgression with Tom Deveraux. Worse, Daisy had inherited all of Iris's faults and then some.

Whereas Iris had been occasionally prone to follow a whim, Daisy was impetuous to a fault. Although Iris was only occasionally ruled more by emotion than rational thought, Daisy seemed to be driven only by feelings. Plus, Daisy was as mule-headed as the day was long, Iris lamented, no matter what the forces marshaled against her.

Charlotte and Richard had struggled to rear Iris, with all her romantic dreams about love and passion and a white knight who would save her from an arranged marriage. They hadn't a clue what to do with a willful, outspoken, extremely temperamental child like Daisy.

Once the adoption was a fait accompli, Iris's marriage to Randolph Hayes IV a matter of record, Iris had tried to help smooth things over and be both a big sister and a surrogate mother figure to Daisy. But her parents had ignored Iris's advice on how to better handle Daisy as steadily as they had ignored Iris's wishes when they first arranged Iris's very advantageous marriage. Daisy had been similarly uncooperative—she hadn't wanted one mother hovering over her, she certainly didn't want two—and there was too much of an age difference between the two of them for them to be true sisters. The only Templeton with whom Daisy had ever gotten along was Connor. But that was no big accomplishment, Iris noted. The conflict-hating Connor got along with everyone. And like Charlotte, Iris thought wistfully, Connor somehow managed not to see or pick up on anything too troubling.

Whereas she—

Iris made herself stop. She wasn't going to let herself go there. What she had inadvertently witnessed years ago was in the past. So what if little had apparently changed since then? She wasn't going to revisit the trauma. Or let her father drag her into any more messes, either.

Oblivious to the dark and dangerous direction of his daughter's thoughts, Richard looked at Iris. "Did you destroy the evidence of Daisy's fact-gathering mission to Switzerland yet?"

Iris shook her head, forcing herself to regain her composure, and took a sip of her coffee. "I haven't had an opportunity. Maybe tomorrow, when Mother and I are at Daisy's, I can locate that red file of hers, that she seemed to be keeping everything in."

"See that you do," Richard said gruffly.

"Why do you need to take it from her?" Charlotte interrupted, looking distressed by what she obviously perceived as their scheming. "What good will that do? Daisy already knows the truth!"

Ignoring Iris's ever-present wish her father tone down his criticism of their mother, Richard looked at his wife as if she was hopelessly naive. "You know how impulsive Daisy can be, especially when she's angry or upset."

And there was no doubt, Iris thought anxiously, that right now Daisy felt very betrayed by all the Templetons. If she wanted to lash out, get even—what better way?

Charlotte stared at her husband, finally getting the gist of his fears. "You can't think Daisy would actually show those documents to anyone outside the family?" Charlotte looked as horrified as Iris felt at the mere suggestion of Iris's secret unwed pregnancy becoming public. "Aside from the Deveraux, I mean."

Richard shrugged. "It wouldn't be the first time that girl has dragged our family into scandal in some misguided immature quest for revenge."

Iris knew her father had a point. Daisy had been a staple in the Charleston gossip columns and grapevines for years. It had seemed, to Iris anyway, when Daisy was growing up, that Richard was always upbraiding Daisy about something—not being disciplined or tidy or ladylike enough—and Daisy was always responding in kind, by making sure she lived up to the criticism by forgetting important social commitments, or behaving like a total tomboy at her formal Charleston debut, or spilling grape juice and mustard or anything else that absolutely would not come out all over the Persian rugs.

Her high school years had been even more difficult, with Richard constantly after Daisy to live up to the family name and reputation and Daisy in and out of one scrape after another. She'd been arrested for trying to free animals slated for euthanasia, had demonstrated—unsuccessfully—for more legal rights for teenagers, been caught toilet-papering the house of the prep school bully, and photographed trespassing, singing and dancing on the prep school roof, the night before her high school graduation.

They'd all hoped Daisy would settle down once she reached university, but instead, because of another, much more serious family quarrel, her behavior had gotten even more embarrassing. Daisy had been kicked out of seven colleges in five years, then dropped out of school altogether, because she was angry with the family for not supporting her search for her birth parents. Worse, Daisy had told everyone in Charleston about her quest, further mortifying Richard and Charlotte, and unbeknownst to Daisy, really upsetting Iris. Who, in all of this, had the most to lose. Because Iris knew people were not going to understand why she and her parents had gone to such great lengths to conceal Daisy's birth, while still holding on to Daisy, and rearing her as one of their own. Anymore than Iris understood why Daisy had felt she had to dig around in the past in the first place. If she had only let things be... Just gone on with her life, the way Iris, and even Tom, had...

"I'll be damned," Richard swore, "if I let Daisy wreck havoc on our family's reputation."

Which was why, Iris thought nervously as her head

began to pound with the beginnings of a severe tension headache, her father was right—they had to find that paper trail and destroy it, before Daisy decided to use it as she acted out against the family.

CHAPTER FOURTEEN

"I'M GLAD TO SEE you're getting some sun," the scratchy male voice said.

Irritated to have her siesta on the private beach behind Jack's place interrupted, Daisy put her hand up to shade her face and opened her eyes. She couldn't believe her prep-school boyfriend had dared show his face to her. Then again, after what had been in the newspaper that morning, she could. Bucky Jerome probably wanted to see her reaction to what he had "reported" about her in his gossip column.

Pretending a lazy indifference she couldn't begin to really feel, Daisy settled more deeply into the beach chair. Glad for the sunglasses shading her red-puffy eyes, she said in a low voice, "Go away, Bucky."

"Or you'll what?" The five-foot-eight Bucky gave her a goading grin and took another deep drag on his cigarette before dropping down in the sand beside her. "Call your new husband out here to scare me away?"

Daisy regarded Bucky Jerome wordlessly. It was hard to believe she had once admired his never-say-die attitude. Now all his persistence did was annoy her. "What do you want?"

Bucky crushed the end of his cigarette in the sand. "The rest of the story."

Daisy turned her attention back to the novel in her lap. Although she had been reading on and off for over half an hour, she couldn't recall a word of the text. "There's no story to tell."

"Come on, Daisy." Bucky whipped his notepad and pen out of the deep front pocket of his loose-fitting cargo pants. "All of Charleston is wondering what landed you in the hospital day before last."

"Thanks to you they are," Daisy said, making no effort to hide her aggravation about that as she picked up the plastic bottle of orange juice she had brought out with her. It was slippery with condensation.

"So take this opportunity to set the record straight and give me something nice and juicy, or at least interesting, for my column."

Daisy sipped on her drink, which had turned unpleasantly warm in the morning sun, then wiped the excess moisture from her hand on the edge of the colorful beach towel that lined her chair. "It's private, Bucky." She gave him a look that told him if he were any kind of friend to her, or even an ex-friend, he would let it stay that way.

Bucky shoved a hand through his gelled black hair, pushing it off his face. For a second he looked conflicted. As if he were feeling guilty for pressuring her for the "inside story." "As private as your true lineage?"

Daisy stared at him, not sure what he knew but determined to give nothing away.

"I don't know about you," Bucky said conversationally, settling more comfortably in the sand beside her beach chair. He acted more like the friend he had once been to her, than the reporter he was now. "But me? I always found it kind of odd that Charlotte and Richard adopted an orphan from Norway. I mean, forget the fact, for a minute, that you were just about the cutest baby people in Charleston society had ever seen. Everyone knew about your family's obsession with blue blood. And there you were with, well, rather pedestrian roots. It just seems odd to me, in retrospect, that Richard and Charlotte would have brought home a child with uncertain or even peasant blood. On the other hand, if you were secretly royalty, or of some other highly desirable origins, then it all makes sense.''

Didn't it, though, Daisy thought with no small trace of irony. All these years, she had thought it was her lack of blue blood or aristocracy that had pushed Richard away and made Charlotte feel she had to constantly compensate for Daisy. Only to find out she was secretly born, albeit in shame, with fine southern blue blood, after all. And now, thanks to both the Templeton and Deveraux obsession with their good reputations, she had to continue to live in secrecy and shame—with a newshound like Bucky Jerome nipping relentlessly at her heels.

''I know you have a job to do, Bucky—'' Daisy said, just as candidly.

''Thanks for being so understanding.'' Bucky raked his thumbnail across his lower lip.

Daisy stared at Bucky through the black lenses of her sunglasses. ''But I'm not discussing that with you.''

Bucky shrugged, looking not the least surprised. ''Then let's talk about what happened over in Switzerland that upset you so much you ran away for a month.''

Without warning, Daisy felt prickles on the back of her neck. Pushing aside her uneasiness, that her scandalous beginning was about to become public knowledge, she asked Bucky warily, ''How do you know about that?''

"I get around." Bucky played with the end of his pen. "And believe it or not, I still care about you."

Daisy returned his assessing glance. Waited. Knowing full well there was more.

"Charlotte and Iris were both checking ever so discreetly with all their friends to see if anyone had seen or heard from you. And of course, no one had. There were even rumors that Harlan Decker had been hired to find you after you ran off to parts unknown, presumably in some sort of tiff, but Decker won't confirm that one way or another." Bucky lounged back on one elbow, uncaring of the sand that was coating his loose madras shirt. "If that was the case," Bucky continued, speculatively narrowing his eyes, "I'm surprised Decker couldn't find you. Unless of course his hands were tied and/or you were living off cash so you wouldn't leave a trail. Even more peculiarly, Jack Granger was driving your car around Charleston the entire month you were gone. Then, shazam!" Bucky snapped his fingers. "Ol' Jack takes off pretty suddenly, too. Only to return a couple of days later with you as his wife. Yep—" Bucky paused, shook his head "—this whole scenario sounds strange, if you ask me, and I can't help but think maybe, just maybe, all these events are somehow connected. The trip to Switzerland, your running off, your marriage to Jack."

Leave it to Bucky to know her well enough to be able to connect all the dots. Or almost connect them, Daisy thought. She damned herself for ever confiding in him when she was a kid.

"So—" Bucky sat up and picked up his pad and pen once again "—you want to tell me why you ran off and got married so suddenly, Daisy Waizy?"

So much for the gentle approach, Daisy thought. She

gave Bucky an exasperated look, irritated he would use his childhood endearment for her now. "We've been over that, too, Bucky."

Bucky grinned, undeterred. "You want to talk about something new?"

"I'd prefer not to talk at all," Daisy retorted as she heard a vehicle turn into the driveway on the other side of Jack's beach cottage. Hoping it was Jack, back from the quick errands he'd had to run, Daisy returned her glance to the shimmering blue-gray hue of the ocean.

"How about Rosewood then?" Bucky continued to prod Daisy with a smug smile as he shook another cigarette out of the pack.

Pushing aside her uneasiness, she asked Bucky warily, "What about it?"

"I was out there the other night at one of those private parties for the best customers." Bucky paused to light the end of his cigarette. "You know, an invitation-only type thing."

This time Daisy had no idea where Bucky was going. Somehow, that was even more nerve-racking. "So?" she asked.

"I saw your father."

Big whoop. A lot of people could make that claim. "What of it?" Daisy challenged right back.

"I thought he was retired, that your sister Iris was running the business now," Bucky persisted, taking a long drag on his cigarette.

Daisy took a deep, highly exasperated breath. "She's been running it for the past ten years. My father only works when he feels like it." Which wasn't all that often. And furthermore, Bucky and everyone else knew that.

"Selling antiques." Bucky blew a stream of smoke

away from them, but the wind caught it and threw it right back in their faces.

Daisy coughed and fanned the air in front of her. "I think he would describe it as matching the perfect piece with the perfect customer, but," she said, the semantics of the sale beyond her, "whatever."

Bucky gave her a look that reminded her there had been a time when she used to sneak a smoke with him behind the school, at the running track, wherever they thought they could get away with it without being hauled to the headmaster's office for a lecture and call to their parents. "Your family goes all out for their customers, provides them with whatever they want or need?" he questioned as he took another long, lung-expanding hit.

"I guess." Daisy shrugged. "I'm not involved in the business." *Never have been and never will be.*

"So, in other words," Bucky probed relentlessly, his lips curving into a speculative smile, "you don't know what goes on behind the scenes."

A shiver of dread went down Daisy's spine. "What are you implying?" she snapped before she could stop herself from reacting emotionally. It sounded as if he was hinting her family was involved in something illegal or unethical. Daisy couldn't imagine that. The business, and their reputations, meant too much to Iris, as well as Richard and Charlotte.

"Just asking a few questions," Bucky said lazily, stamping his cigarette out in the sand once again.

In the distance Daisy heard not one, but two, car doors. Relief flowed through her—at this point she would welcome any interruption at all—especially if it was Jack.

"Although I've got to say I'm surprised you don't

take photos out at Rosewood—sell them to the likes of *Town & Country*," Bucky remarked as he made a brief notation on the pad in front of him.

Daisy didn't like the innuendo in his tone or the presumption in his eyes, as though there was something shady going on. She didn't understand it, either. Templeton's Fine Antiques had an international reputation for quality and service. Iris ran it with painstaking precision and a great deal of pride. Yet Bucky was behaving as if there was some ugly secret behind what was, Daisy knew, a very legitimate business.

"Or maybe at some of the parties," Bucky continued to suggest with a raised eyebrow.

Daisy hoped whoever had arrived was on their way to the back of the house and the private beach beyond. "Those sell-fests are duller than a Hummingbird Society soiree in town."*Meant only to kiss up to invitation-only clients so they would purchase more at the auction barns.*

"Sure about that?" Bucky asked with a gleam in his eye.

Daisy knew a fishing expedition when she saw one. She wondered what kind of scandal Bucky was trying to cook up now. "What are you trying to say?" Daisy demanded as she saw Iris and Charlotte round the corner of the house and make their way through the sea oats, across the dunes. Not an easy task since both were wearing suits and high heels, which appeared to be sinking ankle deep into the sand. This was all she needed. Two Templetons. Ready to pounce. And make things that much worse with ace-reporter-in-the-making and newspaper heir Bucky Jerome.

"This absolutely does it." Charlotte glared at Bucky like the protective mother hen Daisy had always appreciated in her youth as she whipped her cell phone out of her Louis Vuitton bag. "I am calling Adlai Jerome right now and complaining to him about this gross invasion of privacy."

Bucky stood and, transferring pen and pad to one hand, pocketed his cigarettes with the other. "Daisy and I are old friends," he reminded Charlotte as he dusted sand off his clothes. "Or perhaps you've forgotten the two of us dated in prep school?" he said kindly.

Daisy only wished *she* could have forgotten that.

"I merely stopped by to see how she was feeling," Bucky continued with old-school cordiality.

"And doubtless interrogate her in the process," Iris said, looking not the least appeased by Bucky's too-polite manner.

Ignoring everyone, Charlotte continued punching in numbers, then pressed the cell phone to her ear. "This is *Mrs. Richard Templeton.* Adlai Jerome, please. If you don't want a lawsuit, you'll connect me immediately." Charlotte paused. "Yes. Adlai. Your son is here hounding my daughter Daisy. I want him away from her immediately and I want those shameless items in the gossip column to stop. There is such a thing as an invasion of privacy." Charlotte paused again, then smiled victoriously. "I knew you would see it my way, Adlai. Thank you." Charlotte cut the connection and glared at Bucky the same way she had glared at him every time he arrived to pick up Daisy for a date. "Your father would like to see you in the newspaper's editorial offices, Bucky. Right now."

Bucky turned to Daisy. "You think of anything you want to tell me? Anything you want to get off your chest or reveal? You know how to find me." Looking no less determined to get his story, he turned on his heel and walked off.

Suddenly feeling as if she needed to get out of the sun and the heat, Daisy stood and led the way toward the house. Her knees were shakier than she liked and she knew she had overdone it, that she would have been better off to simply stay in bed, the way the discharge nurse at the hospital had suggested. But she had gone outside thinking the ocean and sun would help her shake off the depressing thoughts. And for a few minutes, anyway, being outdoors, soaking in the beauty of her surroundings, had helped.

"What was that about?" Iris asked as Daisy opened the sliding glass door and preceded her guests inside.

Daisy got as far as the center island in the kitchen and sat down on one of the stools. She knew she should offer Charlotte and Iris something to drink or eat, but she felt too woozy to get it. "He wanted to know why I was in the hospital."

"You didn't tell him, did you?" Charlotte said anxiously, taking a seat beside Daisy.

"Of course not." Daisy leaned forward, so her weight was resting on the island. "I don't want my miscarriage in the newspaper."

Charlotte patted Daisy on the shoulder. "That's very wise of you, dear."

"Why are you here?" Daisy asked. She'd had Jack tell them specifically when he called them the previous day to inform them about her hospitalization that they didn't need to come over and see her, or do anything for her, she was fine.

"We wanted to tell you we're sorry," Iris said gently.

"And see what we could do to help," Charlotte continued.

Daisy felt tears welling in her eyes. "What could you do?" she asked around the ache in her throat.

"Lots of things, as it happens," Charlotte said lovingly, draping a maternal arm around Daisy's shoulders.

"For starters—" Iris picked up where Charlotte had left off "—I'd like to offer you a job at Templeton's Fine Antiques. You really should know more about the business, Daisy, since it's going to be yours someday."

Along with whatever nefarious activities Bucky felt was going on? "We've been over this," Daisy explained patiently to Iris and Charlotte. She did not want to get into it again. "I'm not interested in antiques."

Ignoring Iris's hurt expression, Charlotte smiled and said, "Daisy's right, Iris. We don't have to talk about that just yet, since Daisy won't be up to working for a while anyway. But there are some things she can do to get her life back the way it should be."

That, Daisy thought, had ominous tones.

Iris glanced at her watch, frowned and removed a datebook and cell phone from her purse. "Daisy, is there somewhere private I could make a call?" she asked crisply.

Relieved to get a break from the double-teaming, Daisy nodded and pointed in the direction she wanted Iris—who had never been there before—to go. "Jack's study, or the living room at the front of the house. The rooms are on either side of the foyer."

"Thanks." Iris rushed off, clasping her purse and datebook, already dialing.

Charlotte turned back to Daisy, her worry about Daisy evident. And as always when Charlotte was concerned, Charlotte took charge. "I'd like to take you shopping for a new wardrobe. Maybe help you and Jack look for a new residence.''

Something bigger and more prestigious, Daisy presumed.

''I've already talked to your father about letting you have access to some of the money in your trust fund and resuming your allowance.''

Daisy held up a hand to stop Charlotte's enthusiastic chatter. She knew Charlotte wanted to help, but upgrading Daisy and Jack's life was not the way. ''That's not necessary, Mother.'' Any money that came from her father would come with strings. Daisy wasn't interested in owing anyone anything at this point.

Except maybe Jack…

For reasons Daisy didn't quite understand, she didn't mind the thought of being beholden to Jack. Maybe because she knew he wouldn't take advantage or try and collect anything from Daisy that she did not want to give…

Ignoring Daisy's unbending attitude, Charlotte continued with brisk determination, ''I called Lauren Heyward—Mitch Deveraux's new wife—and asked her for a rundown on current listings in the Historic District, near our house.''

Daisy knew if anyone knew what was for sale in the most prestigious areas of Charleston, it would be Lauren. Unfortunately, Daisy wasn't interested in enhancing her lifestyle just to impress others. ''I *like* living at the beach.''

''And I want to get you involved in charity work.''

Daisy was sure she would.

Iris marched back into the kitchen, her datebook, gold pen and cell phone in hand. ''You're assuming Daisy wants to stay married to Jack Granger, Mother.

Without a baby in the picture, that may not be the case.''

"Of course she has to stay married!'' Charlotte countered, looking just as upset. "Marriage in our family is for life!''

Daisy knew they both meant well, but she didn't have the strength to battle them on this. Feeling the sting of tears behind her eyelids, she forced the words out in the gruff, confrontational tone she had perfected over the years when fending off a personal attack. "This is my life, and I don't want to discuss it with either of you.''

"Then what *do* you want?'' Charlotte demanded, taken aback.

"To live my life the way I see fit!'' Daisy raged back. "Without question or comment from anyone—especially family!'' Why couldn't they just accept the fact she was an adult now, free to make her own choices and live with the consequences, as she surely was?

For a moment, silence reigned in the kitchen, broken only by the sound of the central air conditioner. Then Iris stepped closer and wrapped a comforting arm around Daisy's waist. "Oh, Daisy,'' Iris said in a low compassionate voice. "All I'm saying is that you have a choice now—you can still take control of your life instead of letting circumstances control you.''

Daisy hunched her shoulders in an attempt to avoid melting into Iris's sympathetic hug. She didn't want their pity, she didn't want to be caught between them, she just wanted them to go away.

"No, she can't,'' Charlotte said staunchly, moving to stand on Daisy's other side. "Daisy has made her decision—now we all have to live with it.''

After a moment, Iris, giving up on connecting with

the stiff-as-a-board Daisy, looked hurt and moved away again. Daisy gritted her teeth as she met Charlotte's glance. "You make my marriage to Jack sound like a life sentence," Daisy muttered, determined she wasn't going to let her family make her cry. Not ever again. And especially not this time.

"Actually," Iris, ever the exceedingly practical one, countered, as she paced the adjacent family room, looking around casually as she moved, "it is, since being married to Jack will determine more about the quality and tone of your life than you could ever imagine. Which is why—" finding nothing of interest, Iris glanced up and continued with a stubbornness that nearly rivaled Daisy's "—you should have an annulment while you have a chance. I'm sure there must be grounds. We can call our attorney and have him do whatever is necessary to make this whole debacle go away. And in the meantime, Daisy, you can do what I did and go abroad to wait until the scandal dies down. I promise you that in six months or a year, no one will even recall your brief unfortunate liaison with Jack. And you'll still have your whole life—your future happiness—ahead of you."

Daisy found it ironic that Iris was suggesting the same remedy she had once used to try to get her life back on track after her love affair with Tom Deveraux. "That's your answer for everything, isn't it, Iris?" Daisy said resentfully as the blood rushed from her chest to her neck and into her face. "Just hide until all the trouble goes away."

Charlotte's features stiffened into the long-suffering mask Daisy recalled so well from her youth. "Daisy, please, let's not argue here or stir up any more unpleasantness."

Iris sighed loudly, appearing more upset than ever. "Mother—"

Charlotte turned to Iris, ignoring Iris's softly voiced warning to back off. "Daisy can handle this marriage. I know she can. Perhaps it isn't the one we all wanted for her, but with the help of her trust fund, it can be made to be advantageous all the same."

That was Charlotte all right, trying to make a silk purse out of a sow's ear. And Iris, trying just as hard to forget about passion and think about money and luxury and comfort. Daisy was gripping the center island now, wishing she hadn't brought her mother and sister inside. Had they stayed outside in the heat, the two would have been quicker to leave. And right now she desperately wanted both to go, before the situation turned really ugly, as it surely would if this conversation continued much longer. "I don't want an annulment," Daisy told both women stonily. "Or a divorce or anything of the kind. I want to stay married to Jack." He made her feel safe. More important, he accepted her for who she was, flaws and all. Daisy had never had that from anyone.

Charlotte looked both pleased and relieved at Daisy's decision, while Iris gaped at Daisy in stunned amazement. "You can't be serious. Daisy, we're talking about a lifetime commitment here."

Like Daisy didn't know what marriage was supposed to be? Even if no one close to her had ever had anything near the ideal? Feeling as if she would perish if she didn't have something cold to drink, and soon, Daisy moved to the refrigerator. "So?"

"So you barely know the man!" Iris protested in a vain attempt to reason with Daisy.

"How do you know how close Jack and I are?"

Daisy shot right back as she pulled out a big bottle of springwater from the refrigerator and got three glasses down from the cupboard. "You're as much in the dark about what is going on with me now as I was all those years when you were lying to me!" Daisy was so upset, she splashed water over the rims of the glasses.

"I did what I thought was best," Iris insisted.

"Iris is right," Charlotte continued with icy firmness. "We have to move on. What is past is over and done with."

"And how did I know you were going to say that?" Daisy asked sarcastically as she was hit with a blast of unbearable weariness.

In the foyer beyond, the front door opened, closed. Seconds later, Jack walked in carrying two bags of groceries, a pharmacy bag and a plastic bag containing half a dozen videos. He had arranged to work at home for a week, so he could take care of Daisy and help her recuperate, and was dressed accordingly, in tailored khaki shorts, a navy polo shirt and deck shoes—all were worn. His thick sandy-brown hair was brushed away from his forehead, and he had one stem of a pair of sunglasses looped through the first buttonhole of his shirt.

If he was surprised to see their guests he didn't show it as he nodded at Iris and Charlotte. "Hello, Mrs. Templeton. Iris." He set the bags down on the opposite counter.

Knowing a rescue about to happen when she saw one, Daisy put her glass aside and moved toward Jack, not stopping until the side of her body was aligned with the front of his and her head was against his shoulder. "I'm really tired," she moved up on tiptoe to murmur in his ear. "Can you help me back to bed?"

"Sure." Jack's arm closed protectively around her shoulders, his touch letting Daisy know in an instant that everything really was going to be all right. He turned to their guests, excusing them, "I'll just be a minute—"

"That's all right." Charlotte lifted a gentle hand. "We're going to be leaving. Daisy, you call me as soon as you're up to doing the things we spoke about."

"Or even if you just want to talk," Iris added awkwardly, gathering up her things.

Daisy acknowledged their offers with a nod but said nothing else.

As promised, the two showed themselves out. "I feel like I interrupted something," Jack said as soon as they were gone.

Daisy got as far as the closest sofa and collapsed. "Nothing I wanted to continue," she said, realizing too late that something other than the one-piece turquoise maillot she was wearing to sunbathe in would have been nice.

Jack went back to the kitchen, and unable to tell which water glass was hers, simply poured her a new one and brought it back to her. He sat down next to her on the sofa, the hem of his shorts and his hair-roughened thigh pressing against hers. "They were giving you a hard time?"

Daisy nodded and did her best to make light of it. "It was your basic lecture on the advisability of forgetting about all their lies and the deception and returning to the family fold ASAP."

Jack studied her implacably. "And?"

Daisy's shoulders stiffened rebelliously. "I said no, of course." Unable to take the soul-searching intensity of his gaze, she turned her glance away. "I can't be the socialite/philanthropist/dutiful wife Charlotte wants or the number-two person at Templeton's Fine Antiques, Iris wants me to be. I'm going to be a professional photographer," she finished in quiet determination. "And I'm staying married to you."

Jack took a moment to reflect on that. "What does your father—Richard—want?"

Daisy rubbed at her thigh unhappily. "Who knows?" *Besides wishing I'd just disappear so all the Templeton family's troubles could go away.*

Jack stretched his legs out in front of him. Daisy had been inside the house long enough for the warmth of sunbathing to leave her body. A glance downward showed the physical response of her body to the chill of air-conditioning, a fact Jack had noticed, too.

"How did they feel about your decision?" Jack asked as Daisy pulled a throw from the sofa over her shoulders and chest. He reached over to help her wrap herself in warmth, continuing, "I'm guessing they weren't happy."

Daisy snuggled against him, liking the warmth of his bare thigh pressed against her bent knee. "You're half-right." She rested her head on the solidness of Jack's shoulder and traced idle patterns on his chest. "Charlotte was happy—she believes marriage should be for life, and that your lack of blue blood and a bank account to match is something that can be worked around if she can convince Richard to tap into my fortune. Iris just—" Daisy drew a deep, stabilizing breath, straightened, moved away. "She doesn't want me repeating her mistakes. She saw her passionate one-night stand with Tom as a huge error in judgment, and senses my marriage to you is based on the same type of fleeting fling." Hearing how husky her voice sounded, Daisy took a sip of water to ease the parched tightness of her throat and continued her recitation matter-of-factly. "Richard probably thinks I'm just remaining married to you to annoy them and cause a scandal."

"Is that the only reason you're staying?" Jack asked gently. Getting up, he moved back into the adjacent kitchen and began methodically putting away the groceries. "To get back at your family—for all the lies?"

Thinking maybe she should give him a hand, since he was being so nice to her, Daisy got up and found her legs were steady again. "To be honest, up to now," she said, leaving the throw looped around her neck and shoulders like a beach towel, and walking over to join him, "it hadn't even occurred to me." She sat down on a stool and began taking things out of the bags for him and stacking them neatly on the center island between them. "But now that I think about it, I have to admit," she continued, tongue in cheek, "causing such a family ruckus is a bonus."

Ever the grown-up, Jack shook his head at her.

"Anything else happen while I was gone?" he asked casually.

She paused, letting the rebel in her go and turning serious once again. "Bucky Jerome was here."

Jack froze. "And...?" he prodded tensely when Daisy didn't immediately continue.

Daisy sorted through the videos he'd rented, which were, to her pleasure and surprise, all comedies. There wasn't a single downer in the mix. Which was good, because Daisy didn't need to be any more depressed. Aware Jack was still waiting for her summation of the encounter, Daisy said, "He's still asking me a lot of questions about our marriage and my hospital stay. And he was also asking me a lot of questions about Rosewood and the family business.'' Daisy frowned in consternation. ''It was like he was on to something—I don't know, nefarious or suspect in some way.''

Jack absorbed that as he put milk and juice in the refrigerator. ''What did you tell him about us?''

Daisy set her chin. ''To mind his own business.''

''Good.'' Jack braced his hands, palm down, on the center island between them. His gaze roved her face, lingering briefly on the faint tinge of sunburn across her nose. ''Is it possible there's something not on the up-and-up with the family business?''

''With Iris running things out there?'' Daisy restacked the videos and pushed them away from her. ''I hardly think so.'' The business was Iris's whole life.

''Then...?''

''I don't know.'' Daisy slid off the stool, aware she was beginning to feel tense and uneasy again. As though she couldn't quite trust the man who'd raised her as her father. There was no concrete reason for her to believe anything Bucky had hinted at, of course. And yet, on a gut level, she wasn't as sure of Richard's ethics as she was of Iris's. Why that would be, Daisy didn't know. It wasn't as if she had ever seen him do anything illegal or immoral. To the contrary, Richard had been so completely uptight in his behavior, he had made her and everyone else in the family miserable.

''Jerome upset you, didn't he?''

Yes, but not for the reasons you think.

Jack's mouth tightened dangerously. ''I'm going to talk to him and make sure he leaves you alone.''

''Don't.'' Daisy caught Jack's arm, her fingers curling around the swell of his bicep, before he could make good on his threat. ''It would just make matters worse. Bucky's a very nosy guy. The last thing we want to do is make him even more curious.'' And if Jack went to see him, that was exactly what would happen, Daisy knew.

Jack's muscles tensed. He pivoted toward Daisy and braced his hands on his waist. ''That's still no excuse for him coming here.''

Daisy brushed it off. ''He's just trying to figure out what happened, why we got married, why I was in the hospital, everything.''

Jack's golden-brown eyes narrowed all the more. ''It's none of his concern,'' Jack declared flatly.

''Agreed,'' Daisy said hastily, ''but that won't stop Bucky from trying to make a name for himself at my expense if you give him the impression we're hiding something. Besides, I imagine that practically everyone has figured out what happened with us, anyway. Now they're just waiting for us to split.''

Jack cupped her shoulders between his hands. ''Only we're not going to do that.''

Not yet anyway, Daisy thought. Given the way they were getting along, maybe not ever. Knowing she had to tell him the rest, she said, ''Bucky also knows I went to Switzerland.''

Jack gave her a long, searching look. ''Do you think he knows about Tom and Iris?''

Wondering idly who Jack's first allegiance was to— the Deveraux or her—Daisy shook her head and said confidently, ''There's no way he could know unless he figures out how Iris and my parents really brought me into the country.''

Jack accompanied Daisy back to the bedroom. ''How did they manage that?''

''By lying, and quite cleverly covering their trail, of course.'' Daisy headed to the bedroom to snatch a pair of drawstring shorts and a T-shirt out of the dresser, and disappeared into the bath. Leaving the door ajar, she stepped out of her swimsuit and into a pair of bikini panties. "The official story was that Iris, who was soon to take over the family business, had gone over to Europe to cultivate the international antiques dealers and learn the business from the masters in the trade. Charlotte and Richard went over to visit, and when Iris came back to Charleston, to run Templeton's Fine Antiques, Charlotte and Richard stayed on in Europe and took an extended tour of Scandinavia. In Norway, they came across a small orphanage that was closing and fell in love with one of the babies—they brought me home and adopted me."

"Only, none of that was true."

"No." Daisy slipped the T-shirt on and stuck her head around the edge of the door. His head propped on his arm, Jack was lounging crossways on the bed. "I wasn't born in Norway," Daisy explained as she stepped into her shorts and padded barefoot out into the room. "I was born in the convent in Switzerland, where I was named Edith Rose Wood at birth. Edith after my great-grandmother. Rose and Wood after the family's country estate. My parents had my passport issued in that name, and then took me to Upstate New York, where they had conveniently established a residence, and had my name legally changed to Daisy Templeton and another social security number assigned to me."

Jack watched as Daisy took her hair out of the scrunchy and began brushing it out. "That must have cost a pretty penny."

"I'm sure it did." Finished, Daisy put her hair up again in a loose but tidy knot on the back of her head. "But they wanted me brought up as a Templeton, and

I'm guessing they knew that in order to do that they had to keep Tom from finding a paper trail that would prove I was his child. Which is why I had such a hard time trying to track down my birth parents." Daisy went back into the bathroom and picked up a bottle of facial cleanser. She squirted a little on the flat of her palm and began smoothing it carefully over her face. "The orphanage in Norway I had supposedly come from had been closed for years, any records relating to me allegedly misplaced. And there was no record of me being adopted over there, or coming into this country under a passport in my name or my social security number now, as my parents claimed."

Jack watched while Daisy wet a washcloth with warm water. "You must've confronted Richard and Charlotte about this."

Daisy nodded as she removed the cleanser from her face. "They blamed the lack of a paper trail on bureaucratic mix-ups."

"But you didn't buy it," Jack guessed.

Daisy dried her face. "All I had to do was look into their eyes to see they were hiding something." She paused to pick up a tube of lip balm and applied it liberally. "I probably never would have found out the truth had Harlan Decker not thought to look through passports issued in other countries in the region, figured out I was Edith Rose Wood and sent me to the convent in the remote Swiss Alps."

"Harlan's good, all right." Jack scooted over, making room for her on the king-size bed.

Daisy dropped down beside him and, maneuvering through her lingering post-op stiffness, sat cross-legged on top of the neatly made bed. "Anyway, there's no way Bucky could figure out any of that on his own, unless he had copies of my papers.''

Jack's eyes narrowed. "Where are your papers, by the way?''

Daisy pointed to the closet. "In the red expanding file, in the outside zipper pocket of my luggage.''

"Given Bucky Jerome's curiosity, perhaps that's not the best place for them.''

"Agreed. I'll hide them until I can get to the bank and put them in a safe-deposit box.''

Jack stood, looking restless, uneasy again. "Hide them where?'' he demanded.

Daisy shrugged. "If I told you,'' she explained, "they wouldn't be hidden.''

DAISY AND JACK WENT OUT to rustle up a lunch of soup and sandwiches. Since he did most of the cooking, she insisted on doing the dishes then stretched out on the family-room sofa with the book she had been trying to read on the beach. Jack went off to his study to check in with his secretary at Deveraux-Heyward Shipping. She waited until Jack was busy returning calls before she went back into the bedroom. She knew Jack thought she was crazy, not to let him put her red expanding file in a safe-deposit box immediately, for safekeeping, or let him take her to the bank so she could do it on her own. While they were eating lunch, he had come right out and said he thought that Bucky Jerome was the kind of reporter who would or could cross the line in pursuit of a story. And Daisy knew that was true. But there was a reason she couldn't let the documents and photos in her red file out of her immediate possession just yet.

Touching the papers, looking at them, made it all real. When she saw her birth certificate that had been issued to her as Edith Rose Wood in Switzerland, or the legal papers that changed her name to Daisy Edith Templeton in Upstate New York, she felt at peace, and was able to say with confidence: This is who I am. This is where I was born. This is the whole of my life—my past, my present, my future. When she looked at the photo of the convent where she had spent the first six months of her life, or saw the picture she'd had taken of herself with the nun who had been with Iris when she gave birth to Daisy, she realized it was all true. It wasn't just a dream.

Sadly, the papers hadn't—just yet, anyway—made Daisy feel finally as if she belonged somewhere, to someone.

But she had realized finally that this might never happen. Even if all the Deveraux welcomed her with open arms, Daisy knew she might still feel, as she suspected Jack often did, as if she was allowed to come so close and no closer, as if she was, and always would be, on the outside looking in.

As for her "adoptive family," Daisy knew that Iris would be, in many ways, just her sister, that Charlotte and Richard would remain the parental figures in her life.

Initially, she had *not* been okay with that. She had wanted to replace them with loving, fantasy parents.

Now, of course, she knew that wouldn't happen. And maybe it shouldn't happen. Because the truth was, Tom and Iris hadn't brought her up. They might yet be a part of her future, Daisy acknowledged as she slid the photos and papers back in the red cover, and closed the Velcro clasp. But for now, Daisy was still in limbo. Struggling to figure out where—and with whom—she belonged.

RICHARD TEMPLETON WATCHED, from the back of his sleek black limousine as Ginger Zaring stepped away from the open-air marketplace and into his waiting car. The beautiful redhead was dressed just as he had requested, in a white silk halter dress with a pleated skirt and heels. It wasn't as easy, with his advancing age, to become aroused, but her lack of proper undergarments was definitely doing the trick. "Slide over there." He patted the seat opposite him. "And part your knees for me."

Ginger did as he asked, as he knew she would.

"I want to talk to you first." She regarded him steadily.

Richard smiled, reached into his jacket and withdrew a stack of one hundred dollar bills. Ginger leaned forward to get them and stuffed them into the zip lining of her purse.

"No thank-you?" Richard taunted.

Her showgirl legs spread dutifully apart. "I still need another twelve thousand by next week."

Richard slipped his foot out of his shoe and pushed it across her lap, lifting her skirt nearly to her waist. "Then we'll have to see what we can do about giving you the opportunity to earn it, won't we?"

Ginger grabbed her skirt, and was in the process of shoving it back down, when Richard quirked his eyebrow, letting her know, with a silent shake of his head, that just wouldn't do.

"Drop both your hands to your sides," he said quietly.

Swallowing hard, she did.

He toed her skirt back up until she was naked to the waist. Liking what he saw, he leaned back to admire the view.

Shaking with what he recognized as silent fury, Ginger said, "I've been sleeping with you for months, on the promise you would pay Alyssa's college expenses."

"Yes." Richard motioned, indicating he wanted her to part her legs more. "You have."

Reluctantly, Ginger moved her knees even farther apart. "You promised you would help me financially."

Richard watched as she nervously wet her lips. "And I shall."

Richard looked beyond her, to the lights on King Street. He waited until they were nearly even with Templeton's Fine Antiques, then rapped on the glass. "The back entrance."

Nigel, his chauffeur, turned the limo into the alley and pulled over. Ginger hastily pulled down the skirt of her dress, managing to make herself presentable mere seconds before Nigel opened the rear car door. Richard emerged from the limo and helped Ginger out, too. "We'll need an hour," he told his chauffeur.

Her head held high, Ginger allowed Richard to escort her into the building that had been in his family for generations. At 10:00 p.m., the shop was closed for the day and the shades were all pulled. It was eerily dark, quiet. He walked into the office and switched on the overhead light. Amused by the uneasy way the spirited Ginger was looking around, he took her by the arm, guided her inside and shut the door. "I don't know about this," she said, rubbing the goose bumps on her arms. Beneath the white silk of her dress, her nipples were pearling. "What if someone comes in?"

Richard let go of her, and slowly, methodically, took off his jacket. "What if they do?"

"Your daughter—"

"Won't say a word. Now..." Richard nodded at her

autocratically, enjoying the power he had over her, and said, "Let's see how you look without that dress."

Ginger's full breasts were heaving with each breath she took, but for a long stubborn moment, she did not move to obey him. Richard merely smiled, knowing full well who was going to win this battle of wills in the end. "Unless you'd prefer to go out in the alley and finish there," he said.

Ginger's exquisitely made-up eyes spit fire, but her hand went to the clasp behind her neck. Richard wasn't surprised to see the halter come down, the Marilyn Monroe look-alike dress land in a silky white circle at her feet. He'd found women would do anything when there was something to be gained. Enough money, especially the tax-free kind, and there was practically no limit on what was possible.

Of course, it helped if they had a cause bigger than themselves, say, a kid to put through college or a sick spouse. Although that could be a little risky, as he'd found out the hard, expensive way, since people in highly emotional situations could react quite nonsensically. But that wasn't a mistake he planned to make again.

Richard knew how to pick his lady friends these days. Knew how to court and cajole and convince and persuade. The higher the stakes, the more willing they were to do whatever turned him on. And these days, sad to say, it took more and more to arouse him. He needed risk. The thrill of discovery. A sense of the forbidden. He needed constant servicing in the age-old, time-honored, lord-of-the-manor way that he had been born to receive, he thought as Ginger fell to her knees, and slowly, patiently, gave him what he wished.

It wasn't easy finding intelligent, interesting women

who agreed with his demands. But where there was a will, there was a way. His biggest problem these days was boredom. The feeling that after years of philandering and wolfing around, he had seen and done it all.

Well, he thought quite wickedly as he tangled his fingers in Ginger's hair and forced her to stand, and then turn and bend over the surface of the desk. There were some bridges yet to be crossed…some places he'd always yearned to explore. Perhaps, he thought with a cynical smile, as he roughly parted his mistress's legs, thrust into her and heard her groan, not in pleasure but in pain, it was time he really put himself and his latest paramour to the test. And saw just how far it was possible to go. Without, of course, getting caught.

DECIDING HER DOCTOR had been right, she should take it easy and let her body heal, Daisy spent the next week in bed, getting up only to eat and shower and sit outside in the sunshine from time to time. She watched movies, she read, she slept.

At nights, Jack held her. During the days, he cooked for her and took care of her and worked on complicated Deveraux-Heyward Shipping Company business in his office at home. As Daisy listened to him doing business over the phone, she realized how much he loved his job, and how valuable he was to the firm. She didn't want to ever be the cause of him losing what he had worked so hard to attain.

Just as she knew she couldn't cocoon in Jack's lair forever.

Sooner or later she had to go back to the real world. She needed to build a life for herself, aside from this temporary-marriage or roommate situation or whatever the heck it actually was right now with Jack. And there was no time like the present to do that, so she brought up the subject Sunday evening while he was cooking dinner for both of them.

Bypassing the Cajun chicken sizzling aromatically in the skillet on the stove, Daisy headed for the dishwasher. Noting the wash cycle was done, she began putting the clean dishes away, and, aware this scene was too cozy, too domestic for comfort, quietly broached what she had been putting off for far too long. "I think you should go back to the office tomorrow."

Jack shot her a surprised look. "I can work at home as long as I need to."

"I know." Daisy ducked her head and concentrated on putting the silverware into the appropriate dividers. "But it's not necessary for you to be here any longer. Besides—" she looked up, able to feel his nonreceptiveness to the idea "—I've got to go back to work soon now, too. And this time I think I want something full-time."

"Like at a photography studio?"

"At Grace Deveraux's new television show."

Jack looked at her as if she had lost her mind. He put down the long-handled fork. "You can't seriously be thinking of applying for that job."

"Why not?" Daisy could feel herself getting defensive. "Amy said they want a set photographer to take pictures with a digital camera of the things Grace does during her show, so they can put them up on the Internet. I can do that. I work with a digital camera all the time."

Jack frowned. "You're also—"

"Her ex-husband's love child?" Daisy finished his sentence for him.

Jack released an exasperated breath. "I wasn't going

to put it so eloquently, but yes. That alone might disqualify you, Daisy."

Daisy squared her shoulders. "If it does, it does," she retorted, more than willing to do battle.

Jack extended a beseeching hand. "Daisy—"

She put up a hand to ward him off and stepped out of his reach. "*Don't* tell me not to do this, Jack. I've spent my whole life hearing what not to do. I don't need that kind of nonsupport from you, too."

"In this instance," he corrected just as short-temperedly, "I'd be right."

"Oh...go jump in the ocean." Daisy scowled and rushed out the door into the dusky light.

"Daisy—" Jack's voice trailed after her.

She refused to turn around. "I'm going for a walk." She tossed the words over her shoulder. Daisy had at least twenty minutes until it got completely dark and she intended to use every second of it.

She heard him swear as whatever it was he was cooking on the stove threw off a burned scent. Hands stuffed into the pockets of her shorts, head bent against the wind, Daisy headed across the dunes to the shoreline. The temperature had dropped into the low seventies— cool for that time of summer—the wind had picked up something fierce and the surf was rolling in. Barefoot, still steaming over her fight with Jack, she walked to the water's edge.

Seconds later, she heard someone come up behind her. Daisy turned, expecting to see Jack, wanting to continue their argument. Instead, she saw a striking woman in her late-thirties, with dark-red hair. She was looking at Daisy as if she wanted to say something. "Can I help you?" Daisy asked, aware the woman looked oddly familiar.

The woman smiled nervously and pivoted away before Daisy could figure out where she might have seen the striking redhead. "No," the woman said, and quickly headed back down the beach.

GINGER'S HEART was pounding. She didn't know what had gotten into her, thinking she could approach Daisy Templeton-Granger that way. After all, she had already talked to Richard's other daughter, to no avail. Iris had refused to get involved. Just because Daisy had sown a few wild oats and was fresh out of college herself, and bound to understand why it was so important Ginger's daughter get the same opportunity to test her wings, did not mean Daisy would help.

This was her father they were talking about, after all.

No, Ginger decided as the sun began to set, she was going to have to keep to the original plan. She had seven more days to earn the rest of the money, of doing whatever Richard pleased, no matter how sick, risky, perverted or degrading. Whenever, wherever he said. And then the rest of the money—all twelve thousand of it—would be hers.

And if he didn't give her the money?

Then, Ginger knew, she would have to sink to his level and hurt him and his family the way he had been hurting hers. Ginger could only hope, as she chanced another look back at Daisy, still standing on the shoreline gazing dispiritedly out at the ocean, that it wouldn't come to that.

CHAPTER FIFTEEN

"WHAT WAS THAT ABOUT?" Jack asked Daisy as he walked out to stand next to her on the beach.

"I'm not sure." Daisy bit her lip as they both turned and watched the curvy redhead disappear into the distance. "It seemed like that woman wanted to say something to me, but then, when I spoke to her, she seemed to chicken out or something, and just walked away." Daisy paused, doing her best, it seemed to Jack, to act as if they hadn't just had their very first fight, then looked back up at him, her expression still troubled. "I gather that means that you don't know who that woman is, either, then," Daisy said.

Jack shook his head. He just knew when he had looked out the window and saw her approaching Daisy so deliberately, he'd felt a flicker of alarm and worried she was up to no good. "She's not a neighbor," Jack said. "Not a close one, anyway, or I would know her."

Daisy frowned and shoved the hair from her eyes. "She looked kind of familiar to me. But I can't place her."

Jack fell into step beside Daisy as she headed off across the sand. "Maybe you've just seen her around—shopping or something."

"Maybe," Daisy agreed, but her words lacked confidence.

"Listen," Jack said, touching her elbow gently. "I'm sorry about what I said."

"That's okay." Daisy brushed past him, quickening her steps so they were no longer walking side by side. "You're entitled to your feelings. We both are."

Jack kept pace with her anyway. "I don't want to fight," he told her quietly.

"Then let's don't," Daisy said, breaking into a run and letting him know the subject was closed.

Once home, they ate dinner and then Daisy went to bed. Jack stayed up awhile, as had become their custom since he'd brought her home from the hospital. It wasn't the way he preferred to spend his evenings with Daisy, but it had been necessary, in the beginning anyway. After her surgery, she'd had trouble finding a comfortable position in which to sleep. And there were times when he knew she cried into her pillow for a good half hour or more before drifting off. But if he slipped into the bedroom to comfort her, she always pretended that wasn't the case at all. And then found some excuse to slip out of bed again as soon as he got in, and go watch a movie or read a book in the living room.

Realizing she needed her space to come to terms with the loss they had both suffered, he had tried to give Daisy the room she yearned for.

But his patience was wearing thin, Jack realized as he drank the last of the lemonade from his glass. He wanted to be able to do more than just hold her when she was slumbering. He wanted to be able to kiss her whenever, wherever, however he felt like it. And make love to her again and again. He even wanted, God help him, another baby with her. One they planned and made deliberately.

Not that they could start working on that right away,

however. For one thing, it would be another week before she got the all-clear from her doctor that would simply allow them to have sex. And although Jack didn't know a lot about such female matters, he guessed it would probably be a little bit after that before her doctor said they could try again.

In the meantime, he had to convince Daisy that they still had a future together. So what if it wasn't the romantic happily-ever-after version of love and marriage that every little girl dreamed about? It had been his experience very few relationships these days were put together that traditionally.

Couples either stayed together or they didn't. Same with families. Daisy might not realize it yet, but it was better to go into a relationship without stars in your eyes. Better to start with just a few promises and even fewer expectations and build something solid and lasting on that than dream of everything and lose it all, either one disillusioning moment at a time, or in one hideously traumatic event.

Sighing, Jack stood, carried his empty glass to the sink and began turning off the lights. He had just started through the darkened hallway that ran the width of the house, when he heard a commotion and a crash—like glass shattering—and then Daisy let out a bloodcurdling scream.

DAISY WAS TRAPPED and she couldn't get out, couldn't breathe, couldn't see who it was coming toward her, but she knew the person in the mask was obviously a would-be intruder, so she kept screaming until she felt warm strong capable hands clasping her shoulders and a firm reassuring voice in her ears.

"Daisy. Come on now. You're dreaming. Wake up, sweetheart, wake up!"

A strangled sob caught in Daisy's throat as she struggled to open her eyes. The hands shook her again, even more firmly. And then the darkness began to recede. The bedroom began to come into view. The bedside lamp was on and Jack was next to her on the bed. He looked as frightened and upset as she felt.

"You were dreaming," he repeated again.

And trembling and crying, Daisy realized. She tried to take a deep breath and only partially succeeded.

"You're okay," Jack said, climbing into bed with her. He sat back against the headboard and pulled her onto his lap. "You're all right, baby. You knocked your water glass off the nightstand, and it shattered. See?" Jack pointed to the mess on the floor.

Daisy nodded. She could see what had happened, she knew she'd been dreaming, but she couldn't get rid of the overwhelming fear or stop her shaking.

"What was your nightmare about?" Jack asked as he smoothed a hand through her hair.

Daisy shuddered as she buried her face against the warmth and solidity of his chest. "It's the s-s-same one I always have."

Jack's hand stilled. "A recurring dream?"

Daisy nodded, and clung all the tighter. "Since I was a kid."

"All the time?"

"No." She pressed the heels of her hands against her eyes to hold back the tears—they came anyway. "Just when I'm upset or under a lot of stress."

"Tell me about it," Jack encouraged in a low, unflappable tone.

She took a deep, stabilizing breath and waited for

some of the terror to ease. He was patient, waiting. Finally, she was able to speak. "I'm in this dark windowless room. It's small and it's kind of damp and close and awful. And I hate it there. And I'm scared, but I can't get out of there."

"There's no door?" Jack asked, gently rubbing her back, shoulders.

"There is." Daisy closed her eyes so she could visualize it better. "But there's something wrong with the door because whenever I try to open it, it won't budge."

Jack's hand stilled. "Is that why you screamed?"

Daisy shook her head. Fresh tears rolled down her cheeks. She dashed them away with the back of her hand. "No," she explained, wary of revealing too much to the person who had the power to hurt her more than life, but even more terrified of continuing to keep all the fear bottled up inside. "I screamed," Daisy explained in a hoarse voice, "because the person in the mask came in and shut the door, and then I'm trapped with the person in the mask."

"And then what happens?" Jack asked gently, even as his arms tightened protectively around her.

Daisy felt the hair on the back of her neck stand up. "And then the person hisses at me to be quiet and reaches for me, and I know the person is going to hurt me, and that's when I scream and that's always when the dream ends."

JACK'S CHILDHOOD had been no piece of cake. According to Jack's grandfather, until the day his mother had walked out for good when Jack was three, she had tried to abdicate her responsibilities to Jack and fought incessantly with her father when he wouldn't let her. And in turn according to all accounts, Jack's grandfather had called Jack's mother a no-good tramp every chance he got.

In retrospect, Jack could see both family members had a point. His mother reportedly had been a lousy parent, filled with angst and resentment and impatience, but given the fact she was only sixteen and unmarried when she had him, her attitude was, if not acceptable, at least understandable, in Jack's opinion. She had simply been too young and immature to have a baby and bring that child up responsibly. And her father should have known it and helped her take steps to either give her a lot more assistance in raising Jack in those early years, and still have something of a life for herself, or he should have helped her find a good home for her baby and give it up for adoption.

Instead, his grandfather had been of the opinion that Jack's mother had made her bed and should lie in it. Period. Age had not mellowed him one bit. To the day he died of a massive coronary, Jack's grandfather was a gruff, unsentimental, harsh man who had no time for any nonsense, nonsense being anything that didn't have to do with his work at the docks or the sports teams he followed.

But even given his miserable childhood, Jack had never had the kind of nightmare Daisy had just described. And he certainly had never had the same one over and over again. "What do you think triggered this one?" Jack asked, concerned.

Daisy sighed. "That woman on the beach. I guess the encounter with her unsettled me more than I realized."

"Any particular reason why?"

"I guess it was the way she was looking at me when

she first came up to me. Jack, it was like she knew who I was and had come there specifically to get something from me. And that just doesn't make any sense.''

No, it didn't, Jack thought.

Unless the woman had been sent there by someone like Bucky Jerome to try and strike up a conversation with Daisy and get information on her that way. Jack wouldn't put anything past Bucky at this point.

"Is that the only time you have the nightmare?" Jack asked. "When you're under stress?"

"Or when my life is particularly problematic," Daisy confessed on a shaky sigh, "and I feel like I just want to go somewhere and hide.''

Like the way she had been hiding at his place the past week, Jack thought.

Daisy sighed and brought her knees up to her chest and wrapped her arms around her legs. "I feel like my life has been out of control for a while now," she said. She buried her face in her knees. Then, resting her head on her upraised knees, turned to look at him. "That's why I want to get a regular job, a start on a real career as a photographer. I thought it might help.''

Jack worried Daisy was setting herself up for even more disappointment in applying for a job with Grace Deveraux, given that Grace still couldn't stand the sight of Daisy, due to the memories Daisy's mere presence conjured up, but this time he said nothing to discourage Daisy. He figured this was one lesson she was just going to have to learn the hard way. "Why photography as a career?" he asked, moving off the bed and bending down to pick up the broken shards of glass.

Daisy put shoes on her feet, grabbed the bedroom waste can and came around to help him. "Because," she replied, frankly meeting his gaze, "pictures don't lie.''

CHAPTER SIXTEEN

"ALL RIGHT, here's the setup for the next segment," Grace's son-in-law, Nick Everton, said as he led Grace and Amy Deveraux over to the living-room set on the soundstage for *At Home with Grace*.

Nick regarded Grace with a mixture of affection and respect. "Grace, we'll begin with the camera on you. You introduce Amy and talk about what an interior designer who specializes in redecorating actually does for a client, and then explain to her what you don't like about how everything is arranged in this room. Amy will further analyze the design problems for the audience and then we'll cut to commercial. Everybody got it?"

Grace, Amy and the crew nodded. Everyone took their places, the production assistant called, "Action!" and the tape began to roll. Feeling the purposeful, accomplished way she always did when she was working, Grace slipped into her role as show host as easily as a pair of old shoes. Not surprisingly, the segment went off without a hitch. So did the second—a cooking spot with a renowned Charleston, South Carolina, chef, and the third—a florist who demonstrated the proper arrangement of roses in a vase, as well as the final wrap-up of the day.

"Great job, everyone!" Nick smiled as he came up to give Grace and Amy congratulatory hugs. His handsome face filled with pride, Nick grabbed the conservatively tailored jacket of his Brooks Brothers suit off the back of a set chair and slipped it on. Nick's tall, fit form dwarfed both Amy and Grace. "Now we've got five shows in the can," Nick told them with satisfaction. Beside him, the pregnant Amy beamed. Joy filled Grace as she realized she had never seen her youngest child looking as happy and content as she had since she had met and married Nick.

"How long before we can begin signing up the stations to run the program?" Grace asked cheerfully as she took off her microphone and handed it to the soundman.

"We need at least ten—or a solid two weeks of shows—to sell the program," Nick said. "And then once we get twenty-five stations to air it, we'll set a debut and begin the publicity. In the meantime, we'll keep filming so we have as many shows ready to air as possible. I want to be able to go at least six months without repeating one segment. And even then, the repeated shows will be few and far between. The key to a program like this is staying current, giving the viewer something fresh and interesting every time they switch on the program."

"I agree." Grace smiled.

Beside Grace, Amy tensed.

"What is it?" Grace turned in time to see Daisy walk in. She had a portfolio under her arm, a camera bag slung around her neck, another looped over her shoulder and a determined look on her face.

"I didn't know you were interviewing for the show-photographer job today," Nick said in surprise.

Her stomach twisting the way it always did when she saw her ex-husband's love child, Grace did her best to maintain her outer serenity. "I didn't have anything set up," Grace told her daughter and son-in-law coolly. In fact, they hadn't yet even advertised the position.

"I told Daisy you were looking for someone, Mom," Amy said uneasily. "At the time, I thought maybe it would be a good idea for both of you...now that we know. Well, I'm sure you—" Amy cast a look over her shoulder and noticed that several crew members were within earshot "—know what I mean," Amy finished lamely, after a moment.

Grace did. And now that she'd had a second to absorb what was going on, she wasn't at all surprised. Amy was not just the baby of the family, she was the child who had always wanted most for Grace and Tom to put aside their differences and reconcile. To the point that during the fifteen years Grace and Tom had lived apart, the thirteen years they had actually been divorced, Amy never missed an opportunity to lobby for peace and reconciliation between her parents.

For years, of course, Amy hadn't known exactly what the problem was, nor had her three brothers, their new spouses or even Daisy herself. But now the secret was out, and it was clear how Daisy wanted Grace to handle the situation.

"I heard you're looking for a photographer," Daisy said, looking straight at Grace, as if there was no reason the two of them shouldn't work together. "I'm here to apply for the job."

"I think it would be best if we did this by appointment," Nick said in an effort to ward off any kind of personal confrontation between the two women in front of the show staff.

"Nonsense," Grace countered cordially, drawing on all her strength to remain every inch the true professional no matter what. Nevertheless, she could feel the blood moving from her chest up her neck. "I'll talk to Daisy right now. Let's go in my dressing room, dear, shall we?"

Aware her cheeks were unnaturally warm—and hence, probably pink—but unable to do anything about it, Grace led the way to her dressing room. She ushered Daisy inside then shut the door behind them and turned on some soothing classical music as background noise, to ensure nothing said between the two would carry into the hallway.

Daisy set down her portfolio and looked around admiringly. For once she was dressed somewhat conservatively, in a plain black tank-dress that fell to just above her ankles and thick wedged sandals. Her wavy blond hair was arranged in a loose French twist and held away from her face in a butterfly clip. She had discreet diamond studs in her ears and a hopeful look on her face. "Gosh, this is nice," Daisy said.

Feeling as if her entire body was stiff as a board, Grace nodded. She and Daisy were in agreement on Grace's dressing area. It was a large room, with makeup table and mirror, desk, sofa and Grace's stair machine, which she used every morning before makeup. It also had a private bathroom and a closet for Grace's own clothes. Her son-in-law had gone all out to make her as comfortable as possible, which was just one of the reasons that Grace had chosen to work with Nick rather than with the many other network and cable producers who were clamoring to have her star in one of their shows. The other reasons for choosing Nick had to do with the quality programs and level of success Nick was famous for. He knew when to cut corners and when not, and most of all, he was interested in the long, not the short, view.

Grace had suffered too much turmoil in her life thus far. She wanted something solid, that would last. She wanted this, her first solo TV show, to be something she could be proud of.

"I work with digital and traditional 35mm cameras," Daisy began as she sat down on the sofa and eagerly opened her portfolio. "I know how to upload photos onto the Internet and can perfect the digital photos on the computer. So if you want a picture larger or smaller, I can do that."

Grace held up a staying hand before Daisy could turn over her portfolio. Ignoring the crushed expression on Daisy's face, Grace said as gently as she could, "None of which is really relevant, Daisy." Deciding it was best to be as forthright as possible, Grace perched on the edge of her padded vanity stool and looked Daisy straight in the eye and continued, "I know you're very talented. That you've done work for Chase's magazine, that you've photographed properties for Mitch's wife, Lauren's, real estate business. You've helped Amy with her newspaper ads by photographing her redecorating jobs. And you recently had a cover shot on *Charleston Magazine*. But you also remind me, through no fault of your own, of something I'd like very much to forget."

It was Daisy's turn to flush. "That's not my fault," Daisy retorted quietly, looking younger than ever. "I didn't choose to come into the world the way I did."

Grace swallowed around the tight knot of emotion in her throat, aware she was doing as much to crush Daisy's innocence right now as Tom and Iris already had. Aware she had never felt so mean as she did at that very moment, Grace returned quietly, "It doesn't change the facts of your birth, Daisy, or what happened to precipitate it." *It doesn't change the way I feel. And right now, whether you or anyone else likes it or not, I have to be concerned about that.*

"So, in other words, you're going to blame me for what my birth parents have done," Daisy accused, getting to her feet.

Grace had been in Daisy's position once—full of talent, but ridiculously short of experience—and she hated dashing Daisy's hopes this way, but she felt she had to be scrupulously honest, for everyone's sake. "I'm sorry, Daisy. Seeing you upsets me." Grace lifted her hands helplessly, shrugged. "I wish that were different. I wish it could change, but I don't think it can."

JACK HAD ALWAYS HAD a problem leaving the office at seven or even eight in the evening. There was always so much more to be done, problems to be solved, contracts to be negotiated, new business to ensure, which was absolutely the way Tom and Mitch Deveraux wanted it. Now, with the merger between Deveraux Shipping Company and Heyward Shipping Company well under way, he had the additional responsibilities of enforcing the agreed-upon firewall that protected both companies during the interim period.

But, for the first time, he couldn't seem to think about his job more than the prescribed eight to ten hours a day. Instead, once the clock hit five his attention turned to Daisy.

He wondered what she was doing. How her day had gone. Was she feeling okay? Had she really gone over to see Grace Deveraux at the soundstage where she knew Grace was filming her new television show? And if so, what had Grace Deveraux's reaction been?

Jack tried calling Daisy at home, but there was no answer. So he packed up his briefcase and headed out into rush-hour traffic.

It was 6:00 p.m. when he reached the three-mile stretch of beach where he and Chase and Gabe Deveraux all owned homes. Daisy's car was in the driveway. Trying not to think how much it cheered him to see she was already home, he parked behind her car and headed inside.

The moment he was through the portal his happiness faded abruptly.

She was seated at his desk in the study, phone held between her shoulder and ear, using both hands to rifle through the drawers. His personal and business papers were spread out willy-nilly over his desk. As were paper clips, legal pads, several pens, scissors, a ruler, markers, a cut-out section of the city's social calendar of upcoming events from the *Charleston Herald,* as well as a homemade calendar for the rest of that month.

"No, that sounds great." She barely glanced up when she saw him. "Right. I'll be there. Promise. Okay. See you later." She hung up.

Jack didn't know whether to be glad she was so obviously back in the saddle, as far as her work was concerned, or peeved that she had gone through his stuff.

Daisy went back to scribbling on the notepad in front of her and paused to highlight something in the newspaper column in bright pink. "You're home early," she said as she wadded up the parts of the newspaper she didn't need and tossed them into the trash can in the corner.

Jack sauntered in and put his own briefcase down on the edge of his desk, any hopes he'd had of a kiss or hug or smile hello disappearing like the sun behind a cloud. He tried to read what she was writing, but her penmanship was so messy it was impossible to decipher upside down. "What are you doing?" he asked casually, trying not to feel irritated that she had commandeered his home office without asking.

"Working," she said in a crisp, businesslike tone that hinted he should simply go away and leave her alone.

"That's good." *I guess.* Jack didn't want her to overdo it, but he also recognized Daisy needed to do something to pull herself out of the funk she had been in since the miscarriage. And if her taking pictures again was the solution, Jack was all for it. Especially since he knew his work had helped him put the sadness over the loss of their baby aside, and move forward.

His gut tightening with the depth of his unease, he hazarded a glance behind her to see if she had gotten into the large file cabinets, the ones she shouldn't, under any conditions, see. And realized with mounting relief that she apparently hadn't. "How'd you get the desk drawers open?" he asked, as if he didn't mind her presumptuousness at all, when he absolutely did.

Daisy shrugged and glanced up. "I figured there had to be an extra set of keys around here somewhere." Daisy picked up her notes, folded them in half and slid them into a black leather day planner that looked brand new. She snapped the clasp shut and tucked the planner back into the fringed buckskin carryall she used as a purse. "I was right, of course, although it took me a while to find them." She gathered up her pens, the newspaper clippings and one of the legal pads. The other one she put back in his desk, in a different drawer than where it had come from, Jack noted, even more irked. "Why did you put them in your sock drawer?"

"Because it seemed logical." And he hadn't expected anyone else to go there to find them. Unable to help himself, Jack picked up his checkbook and file of monthly bills and stacked them neatly on one side of his desk.

"Say…" Daisy opened the bottom desk drawer and began flipping through the contents of that, too. "You don't by chance happen to have any of those little sheets of business cards that you can run off on your desktop computer, do you?"

Jack shook his head. "No. All my cards are printed at the supplier we use at work."

"Darn." Daisy lifted the legal pad and gathered up fifty or so loose business cards, with her brother Connor's street address and her cell phone number. "I guess I'll just have to use these tonight."

Although he could have used a lot warmer welcome for himself, Jack was pleased to see her looking so enthusiastic about something. "What's happening tonight?" he asked curiously.

Daisy stood. "I got a job at the Protect the Children charity fund-raiser."

Jack watched her stuff the rest of her belongings into a worn black canvas carryall. "That's the one for abused kids."

"Yep. A lot of people attend and the organizers have agreed to let me set up shop in an adjacent area to take pictures of some of the guests. It'll be about as challenging as taking prom photos, but at least I'll get paid for my time and have the opportunity to hand out business cards to anyone who might want them."

Jack admired her hustle. The determination to work and more than carry her own weight was something she shared with him. He looked at her homemade calendar for the rest of the month. "Are these all gigs? Or are you—we—planning to attend these fund-raisers?" She had something marked for every single evening of the following week.

"They're gigs." Daisy smiled at him proudly. "But don't worry," she reassured him quickly. "You don't have to go."

"I don't mind."

Daisy looked at him as if she could care less either way. "Suit yourself."

"What's the dress tonight?"

"A little more casual than that suit you've got on. Sport coat, shirt, khakis."

"Tie?"

"Up to you."

Jack followed her into the bedroom. He dispensed with his own suit jacket and slacks as Daisy stripped down to a transparent pink bra and matching thong, and went into the part of the closet she had commandeered for herself. She came out with a wispy pink and white tropical-print dress that had a high neck, no sleeves and almost no back. Noting there was no way she could wear the bra she had on with that dress, she slipped it off and put the dress over her head. The wispy material clung to her firm, high breasts and jutting nipples. As he watched her smooth the soft, feminine-looking fabric over her waist and hips, and straighten the drape around her knees and calves, Jack felt an instant reaction in his groin. No way, he thought as she turned to allow him to help her with the zipper that went from the small of her back, to just below her waist, she was going to this affair tonight without him.

Jack ripped off his tie and began unbuttoning his

shirt. "I take it this means you didn't apply for a job at Grace Deveraux's new TV show."

"Actually, I did," Daisy replied in a dispassionate voice. "She told me there was no way she could hire me."

Even though he at least had expected as much, he was sure that Grace's rejection must have hurt. "I'm sorry," he said quietly.

Daisy shrugged. "It's her loss. Although—" Daisy puckered her lips as she smoothed on soft pink gloss "—it would have been nice had Grace at least taken the time to glance at my portfolio."

Doing his best to comfort her, Jack said, "Well, maybe this is best."

Daisy shot him a look that seemed to say, "You wish."

CHAPTER SEVENTEEN

TOM FOUND GRACE just where Amy had said Grace would be—checking out the house-in-progress on Sullivan's Island. She looked beautiful, and surprisingly, given the end of her workday, not at all unhappy to see him there. Tom was shocked about that, to say the least. The last time they had seen each other five weeks ago, they had both been tense and angry. Maybe like him, she had mellowed now that she'd had time to cool down and reflect. Lord knew, he didn't want rancor defining their relationship. They'd come too far, shared too much of life, including their four kids, and the grandchildren on the way, to let that happen. "Scoping out the new house?" Tom asked casually as he walked across the planks that led up to the foundation.

"What brings you out here?" Grace asked with a winsome smile as she turned gentle eyes to his. The wind off the ocean ruffled the short, sexy layers of her golden hair. She put a slender hand up to push it out of her eyes.

She was in such a good mood Tom almost hated to bring it up. Tom walked farther into the shell of the sprawling two-story beach house. It was made of the new concrete and Styrofoam design, and would be, when finished, strong enough to withstand winds in excess of two hundred miles an hour. So, even if the worst were to happen and a hurricane hit the island, Grace's new home would be here for years to come. "Nick and Amy called me..." Tom walked onto the first floor, admiring the number of windows that had been cut out facing the ocean, giving Grace a spectacular view. "They told me about Daisy's visit to the television studio today to ask you for a job," he said as he walked over to the blocked-out kitchen, where Grace was standing. "They said you handled it well, at least on the surface, but Amy could tell you were both upset by the time Daisy left your dressing room."

Regret clouded Grace's pretty features. Wearing cotton sport pants that fell to just below her knee, a striped tunic and sneakers, Grace paced the spacious room. "Oh, Tom," she said in a weary voice. "I was awful to her."

Tom had feared as much. "What'd she say to you?"

Grace shrugged and walked through the open interior walls, to the dining room. "She just wanted to be considered for the job and I refused to do it." Grace glanced up, checking out the nine-foot-high ceilings before returning her steady gaze to Tom. "Not because she isn't talented," Grace continued with painful honesty. "She really is. But because I didn't want to look at her and be reminded every day of your infidelity. And I suppose my celebrity ego," she admitted.

Tom released an empathetic sigh. Who would have thought that one mistake could lead to so many years of hurt for so many people? "I'm sorry," he said quietly, matching her remorse. "I never meant to hurt either of you, but I did."

Grace headed for the back staircase and sat down on the second step from the bottom, sadness in her eyes. She scooted over so Tom could sit beside her on the bare wood tread. "Not as much as I've hurt myself," she acknowledged as he settled next to her. She clasped her hands between her bent knees and looked over at him. "I saw myself today, Tom, in Daisy's eyes, and I didn't like what I saw." Grace wrung her hands together and looked even more distressed. "I've become bitter, close-minded."

Tom laced a comforting arm around Grace's waist, aware what it was like to wake up one day and realize you had turned into what you never wanted to be. "You had good reason to feel resentful."

"Then," Grace agreed. "But it's been years. And we've both moved on." She shook her head self-effacingly, continued emotionally, "I should be past this."

"I used to think that, too," Tom interjected quietly as he let go of Grace and dropped his arm back to his side. "Until the day I saw you fresh out of bed with that young yoga instructor." Tom paused as the anger and jealousy hit him all over again. "I'm not a violent person." He forced himself to be as honest as Grace had been with him. "You know that. But I swear to God, I wanted to pummel him with my fists, and I've felt that way every time I've caught sight of Paulo since. It embarrasses me to admit it, but I can't picture that feeling ever going away."

"Paulo and I haven't seen each other since that morning you found us together," she told him firmly.

Tom shrugged and admitted in a tortured voice, "It doesn't make any difference, Grace. I close my eyes, and there it is. You in that robe and nothing else. Paulo in only a towel. Walking down the stairs like he owned the place. I can only imagine how horrible it was for you, finding me en flagrante in Iris's apartment when we were still married."

Grace's eyes glistened. She drew a breath and had to turn away for a second. "Pretty bad."

Tom reached over and took her hand in his, holding it tightly. "So we're even now."

"Except," Grace said sadly, covering their clasped hands with hers, "I don't have a child by someone else to deal with. You do. And for the sake of everyone—especially the children you and I share—I've got to do better, Tom." She gripped his hand tightly. "I've got to get to know Daisy and be able to look her in the eye and feel warmly toward her because she and our children are siblings. Which is why I've decided to give her the job on the show." Grace disengaged their hands and stood. She braced her slender shoulders accordingly. "I'm going to call her tomorrow and offer it to her myself," she declared.

Tom studied her face. "You'd do that?"

Grace pivoted to face him. "For all of us, yes, I would," she replied resolutely. Looking deep into his eyes, she continued softly, maternally, "I want you to be able to love Daisy the way she deserves to be loved by her biological father, Tom. I want her to feel a part of her Deveraux sister and brothers' lives, and to be a real integral part of all family gatherings. And most of all, I want us all to be a family again."

"I'd like that," Tom said. He stood, too, aware he had never felt so relieved or at peace as he was at that moment. He continued in a rusty-sounding voice, "You reaching out to Daisy this way—" *your forgiving me my transgressions* "—means the world to me, Grace."

Grace closed the distance between them. Abruptly, her eyes were shimmering with unshed tears. "But is it enough?" Grace countered softly, emotionally.

"What do you mean?" Tom asked, almost afraid to hope for more than what he had just been given.

Grace gripped his hands hard and searched his eyes. "Can the two of us start fresh, too?"

HERE IT WAS, Grace thought as Tom stared at her in silent apprehension. The fifty-thousand-dollar question. The one she had been thinking about for weeks and not had the courage to voice for fear she would be rejected. She swallowed hard, and knowing it was now or never, pressed on, "I want us to be friends, Tom. More than friends."

Because he didn't look opposed to the idea, she forced herself to continue in a low, quavering voice before she could lose her nerve. "My affair with Paulo was a mistake. I realize that now. Because I didn't love him. I was just using his interest in me to try and feel better about myself, about getting fired because I was suddenly too old to attract the right demographics for *Rise and Shine, America!* When the truth is—" Grace paused and hung her head "—the last thing I should have been doing was making a fool of myself over a much younger man."

Not surprisingly, Grace noted, Tom didn't argue that point.

Nor did he try to extricate himself from the tight grip she had on both his hands.

"I'm not cut out for casual sex or an affair," Grace continued. "I know that now."

This time Tom did pull away from her. "But it happened, Grace."

Grace's heart was pounding so hard she could hear it. "And…?"

"Like I told you," Tom said, raking a hand through

his hair, "I'm not sure I can forget. Especially after the way I misinterpreted things after you got fired, when you came back to Charleston, for good this time." Tom shook his head grimly, recalling. "I thought your asking me to pick you up at the airport, the fact you wanted us both to stay at the house, instead of one of us going to a hotel, meant that you wanted a reconciliation, Grace."

Grace released a quavering breath. "I did," she declared emotionally.

Tom looked at Grace and corrected her sternly, "Until Daisy came into the picture again with the news she was going to be looking for her real parents, and stirred the fires of your jealousy and resentment again. Then everything went all to hell." Tom looked completely defeated. "I can't keep going through that, Grace. And I don't think you can, either."

Grace rushed forward urgently, not aware until that very moment how very much she wanted Tom back in her life again—and not just as an ex or a friend. "Which is why I'm determined to befriend Daisy the way I would any family member through marriage. Look, I know my jealousy and resentment has been a problem in the past," she confessed guiltily.

His frustration with her apparent, Tom abruptly dropped his hands to his sides. "An understatement if I ever heard one."

"But that was before I knew firsthand how meaningless a tryst, with the wrong person, embarked upon for all the wrong reasons, could be. Now, having actually done it myself, I know how little value something like that has." She knew it had caused her nothing but grief. And all the mere dating she had done during her years in New York had not brought her any emotional satisfaction, either.

"Well, that much is true," Tom sighed, conceding reluctantly as he jerked loose the knot of his tie. "I have no romantic feelings for Iris."

If her years on her own and subsequent affair with Paulo had taught her anything, it was that she was never going to love any man the way she loved Tom. Maybe they would always have problems, Grace admitted practically. Maybe she would always disappoint him in bed and never be able to overcome her secret frigidity. But there was more to life than lovemaking. "So can't we move on?" Grace asked plaintively. "Try again, just one more time?" Grace was sure they could be happy again if Tom just gave them a chance to really move on this time and forgive each other their mistakes.

"I don't know," Tom returned seriously, looking every bit as hesitant as he was tempted. "There's a part of me, Grace, that wants that more than anything. And there's another part that says we've already hurt each other way too much."

TO SAVE MONEY and allow more of the proceeds of the five-hundred-dollar-a-plate picnic dinner to go to the charity, the Protect the Children annual fund-raiser was being held in a local elementary school in lieu of a hotel ballroom. The evening had a summer-camp theme. Gingham-covered picnic tables had been set up around the gymnasium. Bunches of wildflowers in galvanized buckets served as centerpieces. The waitstaff was dressed in camp counselor uniforms. And the fare being set up on the buffet tables included barbecued chicken, potato salad, corn on the cob, watermelon and cupcakes. Dozens of balloons clung to the gymnasium ceiling, and large murals, painted by the abused children the charity helped, decorated all the walls. A small group of musicians from the Charleston symphony were performing favorite childhood tunes onstage. At the far end of the gym, in the atrium just outside the doors that separated the gym from the principal's office, Daisy was setting up lights for the picture taking that would occur during the second half of the gala evening, while Jack put up the large background screen.

"Is this okay?" he asked.

"I think it should be pushed back a little farther against the wall," Daisy said. She waited while Jack made the adjustment. "Yeah. That's good." She measured the distance from the tripod to the screen. Turning, it was all Daisy could do to contain a beleaguered sigh as she came face-to-face with three members of the Templeton family—Richard, Charlotte and Iris—all of whom were dressed for a "picnic" à la *Martha Stewart Living*.

"You're embarrassing the family again," Richard said, looking as well put together as always. "I want you to come away from there right now, Daisy."

"I can't." Trying not to show her hurt at her father's lack of support for her efforts to establish herself in her chosen career, Daisy went back to setting up her camera. "I've been hired to take photos of all the guests tonight who want them, in exchange for supporting this very worthy cause. They'll make a nice party favor, so if you and Mother would like to be first," she offered as graciously as she was able.

Charlotte moved in closer, nervously fiddling with one of the pearl buttons on her tailored pastel-green sheath dress and matching jacket. Trying to smooth things over, she leaned forward and whispered helpfully, "Daisy, someone else could do this. You and Jack should be guests at this function not hired workers."

Iris sipped her mint julep and backed up Richard and Charlotte. "If you really want to begin a business like this, Daisy, you've got to do it in a top-drawer way. You can't lower yourself to take routine photos like this." Iris waved at the area disparagingly and regarded Daisy as if despairing over her lack of business sense. "You've got to be exclusive, sought after."

"And broke?" Daisy couldn't resist adding dryly. There was such a thing as letting your pride go before the fall. Not to mention drive you nuts with boredom.

"We could underwrite a studio for you in a prestigious location," Richard said, looking increasingly irritated.

Charlotte nodded vigorously, leaping to help. "I'll call my decorator in the morning."

"Thanks, but no thanks." Daisy held up a silencing hand. "I'd prefer to do this on my own."

"Isn't this like old times," Bucky Jerome drawled as he came up. He had a camera slung around his neck, a notepad and pen in his hand, and was obviously covering the event for the newspaper.

Bucky picked up one of Daisy's business cards, shoved it into the pocket of his shirt and gave her a sympathetic wink that spoke volumes about what he thought her family was doing to her with their lack of support. "Way cool, Daisy Waizy," he told her with a friendly smile that took Daisy back a few years to the time when the two of them had gotten along.

Daisy regarded Bucky, one up-and-coming professional to another. She didn't need Bucky Jerome's approval but she did appreciate the genuine nature of his respect. "Thanks, Bucky," Daisy said quietly.

He stepped back, a mischievous grin creasing his face. "Say cheese!" Bucky ordered, then took what had to be another very bad photo of Daisy, Jack and her family in front of the photo booth. Daisy rolled her eyes. She could imagine what that was going to look like if it made the society page.

"I'll make a mention you were working here tonight," Bucky told Daisy before he ambled off.

"I'd appreciate that," Daisy said.

"Well, the rest of the family wouldn't," Richard interjected unhappily. He looked at Jack for help. "Legally, can we stop Bucky from printing anything about this in the paper?"

"Right," Daisy said. "You wouldn't want anyone to see me caught *working*."

Richard, Charlotte and Iris glared at Daisy, unamused.

In response to Richard's question, Jack shook his head. "You don't need to sign a release for this sort of thing. Daisy is working here. Bucky's reporting that because he's covering the event. Period."

Charlotte put a hand to her forehead as if she felt one of her famous migraines coming on, the kind that in Daisy's youth had occasionally sent her to bed for days.

Richard glanced into the gymnasium, where Bucky was busy taking photos and chatting it up with other guests. "That boy is a nuisance," Richard grumbled.

"He's not a boy, Father." Daisy found herself in the odd position of defending her high-school boyfriend in front of her current husband. "And he's just doing his job." *Like I'm trying to do mine.*

Richard looked at Jack. "You're an attorney! Can't you do something about this to keep Bucky Jerome away from our family?"

Jack shrugged. "You could try to get a restraining order, but first you'd have to demonstrate how Bucky has harmed your family and remains a threat, and I don't see that as the case," Jack replied with an honesty neither Richard nor Charlotte appreciated.

"Well, we'll see about that." Richard walked off in a huff, Charlotte right behind him. That left Iris standing there with Daisy and Jack.

"Listen, Daisy, Father is right about this." Iris continued the campaign where their parents had left off. "Bucky is being a major pest. Can't you get him to back off?"

Daisy wrinkled her nose at Iris, perplexed. "What do you mean? I don't have any influence with Bucky."

"Yes, you do. He's still got a wild crush on you. If you asked him sweetly to back off and leave our family alone, he would." Iris glanced at Jack, who was looking disgruntled. "Sorry, Jack, but it's true. Feminine wiles work. And it's high time Daisy realized that."

"Listen, Iris, I know Bucky is a pest, but he has a right to be working this event, same as I do. Besides, experience has demonstrated that if I ignore him long enough he'll eventually go away and bother someone else." It was when Daisy let Bucky—or guys like him—know they were annoying the hell out of her that they kept coming back for more.

Looking all the more aggravated, Iris took Daisy by the arm and guided her down to the far end of the hall, well out of earshot of others. Ignoring Jack, who had tagged along and was standing sentry between the two Templeton women and anyone who might want to interrupt, Iris continued bluntly, "Don't you understand what Bucky is trying to do? He's trying to create scandal where there is none!"

Daisy studied the woman who had given birth to her and then denied it for twenty-three years. "You just don't want people digging around in your life for fear they'll uncover your affair with Tom that led to me."

Iris stiffened. "It's a lot more complicated than that."

"Is it?" Daisy wondered out loud. "Tom and Grace are pretty popular people in this town. Friends could feel they had to take sides in what still amounts to a pretty ugly situation. And Grace has a lot more star power than you do, especially with the new TV show she's taping here."

Iris sniffed. "Like it or not, Daisy, the prosperity of our family business depends on the respect and goodwill of our customers. I'm not going to be poor again."

Daisy lifted her eyes to the ceiling and scoffed. "You were never poor."

"The entire time I was growing up we were broke, Daisy. Leveraged to the hilt. If I hadn't married Randolph when I did and brought his money into our family, we would have been out on the streets in a matter of weeks. As it was, it took five years to pay off all the creditors, and another ten to put Templeton's Fine Antiques solidly in the black."

Daisy stared at Iris in shock. She had always suspected Iris had married the old goat for his money—what other reason could there have been, Randolph Hayes IV hadn't exactly been Prince Charming. But she hadn't known the straits had been that dire—the pressure on Iris so intense—she'd thought Richard and Charlotte had been the ones who had put Templeton's Fine Antiques back in the black! Yet, just talking about it, Iris looked and acted panicked. "So you sold your self-respect and solved all your problems," Daisy surmised grimly, sure about the decision she would have made in the same position—the opposite one!

Iris folded her arms in front of her. "It wasn't like that."

"Then how was it?" Daisy persisted angrily, really wanting to know.

"I did what I had to do for the sake of this family," Iris insisted.

Like Scarlett O'Hara after the Civil War, Daisy thought, her exasperation growing by leaps and bounds.

"And now I'm expecting *you* to do the same," Iris continued sternly.

Stepping closer to Jack, Daisy linked her arm through his. Smiling insolently to cover her hurt, Daisy quipped humorlessly, "Too late. I've got Jack here as my hubby. And although he's not rich, he's very kind. And very loving." Which was more than Daisy could remember about the old goat when he had been alive.

Iris's eyes flashed with anger. "Daisy, please, this once cooperate with me. I don't want Bucky Jerome to hurt you. I'm afraid he will, given the slightest opportunity."

"Don't worry." Daisy clung to her husband all the more. "Jack's a lawyer, in addition to being my husband. He and I have already talked about it," Daisy fibbed, "and he has promised me that he will help me with any and all legal problems that come up. Including those with Bucky or the family or anything potentially troubling in any way, so you don't need to worry, okay? Everything's going to be fine. I promise you. All you have to do, Iris, is chill."

"SHE SEEMED UPSET," Jack said as Iris walked off to mingle with the rest of the guests.

"Yeah, she was," Daisy agreed as she and Jack walked back to her camera. "They all are. They're so concerned about their precious reputations. And of course—" Daisy sighed her exasperation, trying not to notice how handsome Jack looked in the casual navy sport coat, creased khakis and light-blue shirt "—Bucky Jerome knows that, which makes it easier for him to get back at them."

Jack leaned against the wall, arms folded in front of him, while Daisy put out the pens and forms for people to fill out so she could match the photos with the proper names and addresses. "Why would Bucky want to get back at them?" he asked.

Daisy straightened the stack of her business cards, too. "Because they never approved of my relationship with him when we were dating back in high school."

"Because he was a troublemaker," Jack guessed, his eyes roving her upswept hair.

"I don't think that would have mattered had Bucky been rich enough, but he wasn't."

Jack's sandy eyebrow furrowed. "His family owns the newspaper."

"As well as several other small weeklies, in little towns scattered around the state, but that's it," Daisy countered, embarrassed to admit how incredibly snobbish and fortune-minded her adoptive parents née grandparents were. "Adlai Jerome is no Rupert Murdoch. And that's the kind of wealth they wanted to see me bring into the family. You know. Blue blood is one thing, but blue blood with millions or billions...well, now, that's a catch. They wanted me to make a fortuitous match, and they saw Bucky as standing in the way of that."

Jack's eyes hardened with the depth of his understanding. "What did you want back then?" he asked softly.

Funny, Daisy thought. Jack was the first person who had ever asked her that. "To be happy," she replied, looking deep into his eyes. "To be loved and accepted for who I am not who people wished I was." Daisy turned away, adding, "The usual things... The same thing I want now."

Her senses rioting at Jack's nearness, Daisy waved at the event organizer, who had come out into the atrium and was pointing impatiently at her watch. Daisy nodded back, signaling she was indeed ready to go. She pivoted to Jack, a ready smile on her face. "Come on. I've got to get people lining up for photos. Or I really will be in trouble."

Jack stroked her arm. "We can talk about this more later if you want."

Daisy shook her head. She didn't want to examine her past or Iris's, or the expectations placed upon them both by Richard and Charlotte as they were growing up. And she certainly didn't want to talk about how those same unreasonable familial demands had driven Iris into Tom Deveraux's arms. Because Daisy knew what she would find in the end. No matter what Tom's DNA tests proved, Iris and Tom Deveraux would never publicly acknowledge Daisy as their child. They would never make her feel better about having been given up. Instead, she was, and would remain, a source of family embarrassment and shame.

HALF AN HOUR LATER, figuring he'd gotten all the society news he could out of the charity event, Bucky was just about ready to leave the elementary school, when he saw Ginger Zaring getting out of the back of Richard Templeton's limousine. The voluptuous redhead was dressed in a short, ruffled sundress with a deep V neckline that did very little to cover her ample breasts, very high heels and way more makeup than he had ever seen her wear before.

Bucky snorted in disgust, aware that it very much looked like one of his original theories—that Ginger Zaring wasn't just shaking down the Templetons but playing the hooker for them at various events with the Templetons' society friends, too—just might be true. Not that this was in itself so surprising, Bucky thought as he ducked behind a tree so as not to be seen. Any number of high-expenditure businesses had been supplying high-class call girls to favorite clients as a perk of doing business with them for centuries. And working girls for the truly upper crust often also did something else as their day jobs. Their moonlighting was just for extra cash and/or kicks or entrée into a world they would never otherwise see.

In Ginger Zaring's case, Bucky was betting it was for cash. Because the voluptuous redhead hadn't looked to be particularly enjoying herself the night he had seen her biding her time at Rosewood, and she didn't look particularly happy to be there tonight, either.

Oblivious to Bucky's presence in the deserted schoolyard, Ginger looked around furtively, and a moment later headed for the side of the elementary school, away from the entrance to the gymnasium.

Bucky waited until the Templeton limousine drove off, then made his way around to that part of the school building, too. The fire door had been wedged open with a small wooden block. The wing of classrooms was dark and empty. At the end of the long corridor was another.

Bucky wandered down the hall, checking out each room in turn, finding nothing and no one until he reached the school library. His eyes widened in stunned amazement as he caught a glimpse of Ginger Zaring and the male she was there to service, and what they were doing was definitely X-rated.

BUCKY HUNG AROUND until the private party in the school library had ended and Richard Templeton had dismissed his girlfriend. He then returned to the *Charleston Herald* newspaper office. He still couldn't believe what he had seen, but there was no denying the sordid liaison. He was just glad Daisy hadn't seen it.

Not that he should care about Daisy at all after the way she had humiliated him years ago, dumping him the way she had, when everyone knew, or at least guessed the two of them had gone off to that hotel room to have sex for the very first time.

Okay. He'd probably always resent her for that—the fact she hadn't given him a chance to make it up to her, because he knew her first time had been astoundingly lousy. Over in about sixty seconds, once he had gotten her onto the bed. But she'd looked so sexy in her secretly altered parent-approved prom dress. He couldn't help himself.

Bucky didn't mean to get carried away, or push Daisy into something he knew—deep down—she wasn't really ready for. But he had done it, anyway, despite Daisy's last minute reservations. Hoping that once the deed was done, she would loosen up a little, relax, start to enjoy herself. Instead, she had only seemed to feel worse in the aftermath. And then she'd fled, the look on her face telling him she knew she had made a huge mistake, even going up to the hotel room with Bucky.

She'd never seen him after that night.

And after a few futile tries to talk to her on the phone he'd let it go. But now that they were both back in Charleston again, Bucky was surprised at how vulnerable Daisy seemed, how pale and drawn and sad beneath the surface bravura. Bucky didn't know what was going on with her and Jack. He didn't think it was love—he didn't think Daisy would ever let herself be emotionally accessible enough for that. But it was probably something—given the way those two looked at each other—that she should hang on to.

Meanwhile, Bucky thought, there was Daisy's father.

Bucky sighed and shook his head, thinking about how many lectures on responsibility and comporting-himself-with-dignity-so-as-not-to-sully-Daisy's-reputation he'd endured from that blue-blooded butt-wipe. Someone had to get that hypocrite back in line, Bucky thought as he ignored the paper's no-smoking policy and lit a cigarette. Bucky figured it might as well be him.

"THIS IS HORRIBLE," Charlotte Templeton said the next morning over breakfast. Furthermore, she couldn't believe Adlai Jerome was letting his son publish such rubbish!

Richard looked up over the top of the business section. He preferred she not speak during breakfast. When she did, he looked irritated. "What?" he demanded, clearly piqued.

"Bucky Jerome's column this morning!"

Furious, upset, Charlotte stared at the story Bucky
had written under the tag line Dangerous Love. Unable
to help herself, unable to wonder who Bucky was talking about—assuming, of course, it was true, and she
didn't for one second believe it was—Charlotte read it
again.

Dangerous Love

What prominent collector of very fine things is
stealing off to be with his flame-haired lady love?
Reportedly, there's a time and place for everything, for even this well-known and highly regarded "family" man. But the butler's pantry in
the middle of a very fancy party? A very public
library? Despite the rising temperatures, cooler
heads should prevail. Or a prominent member of
blue-blooded Charleston society could find himself
and his gorgeous mistress in the middle of a Cat-
egory 5 hurricane that has absolutely nothing to do
with the South Carolina weather.

"I mean," Charlotte continued heatedly, "Bucky
can't go around making assertions like that. People will
think it's true!"

"People will think what is true?" Richard grumbled,
reaching for the society section in his wife's hand. He
frowned disinterestedly as he read, then scoffed, shook
his head. He handed the paper back to Charlotte. "I
don't see why you're so upset. So someone in Charleston has a mistress. So what?" he asked in a low, bored
tone.

Charlotte's appetite vanished. She pushed her plate
of fruit away. "So maybe his wife would care!"

Richard forked up another bite of eggs Benedict. "I really don't see what the problem is."

Charlotte stared at her husband furiously. "It's not right for a husband to humiliate his wife and family that way. And furthermore, I would think you, of all people, Richard, would understand the need for decorum!"

"What I understand," Richard said, abruptly getting up from the table, "is the need for a little peace."

"Where are you going?" Charlotte watched him march away from the table.

Richard didn't answer. Didn't turn around. Simply walked out.

Charlotte sighed and went back to her newspaper. She still couldn't believe Bucky Jerome had written that article. Couldn't believe a truly prominent, cultured member of the Charleston elite and a "family man" would ever do such unwise, uncivilized things as what Bucky was suggesting.

For heaven's sake, what would happen if the philanderer's wife *did* find out? How could she possibly bear it? Especially if the worst happened and the affair became public knowledge.

"WE'VE HAD COMPLAINTS," Adlai told Bucky when he sauntered into the newspaper at noon.

"So what's new?" Bucky said with a disinterested shrug. He'd known he was going to get it for this, but he'd done it anyway, for Daisy's sake. It was past time Richard Templeton got a little payback for the way he had treated Daisy all these years.

Ignoring the very expensive cuckoo clock Bucky had given him for his birthday, Adlai continued his dressing-down with more than usual vigor. "I'm referring to the blind item entitled Dangerous Love." Adlai picked up the messages and began reading through the stack, top to bottom. " 'How many marriages do you think you've ruined—I'm here to tell you, quite a few.' And there's the other viewpoint. 'Come on, quit tantalizing us. Tell us who, when, where, how and why. Otherwise, we're going to think Bucky Jerome is making this stuff up.' "

Bucky gritted his teeth. Leave it to his father to seize on that. "I'm not making this stuff up," he said defiantly as he slung his backpack off his shoulder and slouched in a chair.

Adlai regarded Bucky with frank disbelief. "So you said."

"Hey—" Bucky unzipped the backpack, more than ready for this confrontation "—I've got proof."

Adlai swore, distressed. "Tell me you didn't take pictures," he said.

Bucky smiled and began getting out his proof. "I took pictures. The problem was, it was dark and you couldn't really make out their faces while they were in the act. So I went in after 'em and cleaned up—literally and figuratively."

Adlai froze. "What the hell are you talking about?" he grumbled.

Bucky pulled out a Ziploc bag, similar to the kind the police detectives used to transport evidence. "Lipstick-stained tissues. And tissues stained with, well, you can guess what that is." He waved the telltale tissues in front of his father's nose.

"Geez, Bucky." Adlai recoiled as if he'd actually touched the remainders of the illicit lovemaking. "What in blue blazes are you trying to do?" he demanded, even more upset.

Bucky handed over a stack of pictures only a porno magazine would print, then sat back in his chair and laid the plastic bag across his lap. "Report the hot and juicy society news, just like you told me to do."

Adlai frowned as he thumbed through the photo diary of the previous evening's occurrence. "You can't run these photos."

No surprise there, Bucky thought. He regarded his father, enjoying the stunned look on Adlai's face. "I didn't think I could. At least not in this newspaper."

Adlai handed back the stack of photos Bucky had printed out on his home computer. "Not in any, unless you want to get sued for defamation."

Bucky shoved the evidence and photos back in his bag then lifted his hands in self-defense. "Hey. Last night was a public event with newspaper coverage. Richard and his honey should've known better."

Adlai sank down in his chair. Now that Adlai knew about the sordid affair, he couldn't seem to let it go, either. "Richard Templeton? That stuffed shirt?" Adlai asked curiously. "Who's the woman?"

"Ginger Zaring, an airline reservations agent."

Adlai scowled as the talk turned to the *Herald* once again. "You're walking a fine line here, Bucky, you know that."

Bucky refused to let his father cow him out of doing his job. "I didn't say the names of the parties involved," Bucky defended himself. "And I'm serious about the potential for one hell of a stormy divorce. If Richard Templeton's wife finds out what he has been up to, there's no telling what could happen."

Adlai took a second to think about that. "You don't really think Charlotte would divorce Richard?"

Bucky shrugged, knowing if Charlotte Templeton

had seen what he had, she would. Then, Bucky thought, he would have the scoop on one of the biggest, most expensive, ignoble divorces Charleston had seen in years.

"Is that all?" Bucky started to get up. He wanted to get his DNA proof to a safe-deposit box, just in case Richard Templeton decided to come after him. One look at his proof of the night's activities, and Richard's lawyers were likely to tell Richard to leave Bucky the hell alone.

"No. Sit down," Adlai ordered grimly. He waited until Bucky complied before continuing. "No more blind items like that, Bucky. Got it? It's not what the people of Charleston are looking for. You want to write sordid, put it in a sexy screenplay. And while you're at it, lay off Daisy Templeton, too."

"Granger," Bucky corrected, glad for the change of subject to someone he would much rather think about. "Daisy's married now, you know."

Adlai huffed as the cuckoo bird slid out of the clock and let out an irritating screech. "Her family is complaining."

Of course, Bucky thought. It kept 'em from thinking about the real problem—Richard's disgraceful behavior. He regarded his father curiously. "What about Daisy?" Bucky asked, wondering if the two of them would ever be able to be friends again. "Has she called in?"

"No," Adlai replied sternly as he gave Bucky another chastising look, "but her parents have. And so has Tom Deveraux."

Bucky frowned. Jack he had expected. Not Tom. "That's unusual, isn't it?" he asked.

Adlai shrugged. "Well, Granger is counsel for Deveraux-Heyward Shipping. And Daisy is married to him. Bottom line, they are all upset about the way you have been hounding Daisy. Tom also mentioned he might not be running quite so many ads in the business section if we don't lay off."

Bucky refused to let pressure scare him. "He's bluffing."

"It doesn't matter," Adlai reiterated curtly. "You're upsetting important people, Bucky."

"So?" Bucky countered as he returned his father's narrow look. "The news does that. People don't always like the truth."

Adlai came around his desk to stand in front of Bucky, jaw clenched, face red with fury. "Obviously, I am not making myself clear, son. You want to keep writing that gossip column of yours? Then do it in a way that you don't offend so many people, especially those prone to take some sort of direct or indirect action against us. Otherwise, you're going to find yourself right back in classified ads."

Bucky left his father's office totally bummed. There was no pleasing that man. And no way in hell he was going to get famous writing about what tea cakes were eaten at which soiree. Not that he had wanted to be on this assignment anyway. What he wanted was the police beat. The EMS run.

Of course, there could be a crime involved in the goings-on between Richard Templeton and his mistress if he was paying her to have sex with him. Or if the sex were given in exchange for ludicrously expensive antiques. Which were, in Bucky's view, nothing more than old pieces of polished-up junk. But how to prove that? And who would care, even if he did? Except for the wife and maybe his daughters. Richard and his mistress were both consenting adults. Bucky had seen the woman—she had arrived voluntarily. She was certainly of age. If Ginger Zaring wanted to permanently mess up her life engaging in such reckless behavior with a prominent married man, that was her decision.

GINGER DREW A BREATH and put the newspaper aside.

Alyssa came in, her clothes for her movie-theater job on. She paused in the act of pinning her badge on her shirt. "Mom?" Alyssa looked at Ginger closely. "Are you okay?"

For someone who had permanently screwed up her life by trying to find the easy way out, Ginger thought. "Sure, honey." She smiled at her daughter, doing her best to act as if nothing was wrong.

"You look kind of funny."

Ginger's hands curled around the society section. *There was no way Alyssa would ever put two and two together.* "I'm fine," Ginger said even more firmly.

Alyssa got out the peanut butter and jelly and began making herself a low-cost meal to take to work. "How was your date last night?"

A mistake. Just like getting involved with Richard was a mistake. "It was fine, too," Ginger lied.

"Do you have to work today?" Alyssa added a small container of applesauce and a bag of chips to her lunch bag.

Ginger nodded as the telephone rang. "I've got the 4:00 p.m. to midnight shift." Relieved to have a reprieve from her only child's questions, Ginger picked up the phone and found Richard on the other end of the line.

"I have to see you," he said.

CHAPTER EIGHTEEN

DR. RAMETTI BREEZED INTO the exam room and greeted Daisy with a warm hello. She pulled up a stool next to the examining table where Daisy sat, wearing a pink paper gown and took a moment to study the notes her nurse had made on Daisy's chart before looking back up at Daisy. "You're looking good, like you've had some sun," she remarked as she pulled on a pair of surgical gloves. "How are you doing?"

Daisy shrugged as the nurse helped her lie back and scoot down to put her feet in the stirrups. "Okay."

Dr. Rametti patted Daisy's knee. "It'd be all right if you weren't, you know. It's only been two weeks since you lost the baby and a fallopian tube."

"I know." Daisy had never known time could go as slowly as it had the past couple of weeks. The only way she seemed able to get through each day was by staying as busy as possible, working every minute she could, and falling exhausted into bed at night.

"I read in Bucky Jerome's column that you got the staff photographer's job with Grace Deveraux's new television show."

Daisy didn't know how Bucky had known, and she wasn't about to call him to find out, but he had reported her career coup before Daisy had even shown up for work! Fortunately, for a change, there had been nothing salacious in the item, no lousy or embarrassing picture of her accompanying the article, just simple statement of fact.

Dr. Rametti adjusted the light so she could see what she was doing. "What's the show called again?"

Daisy closed her eyes and tried not to think about the pelvic exam she was undergoing. *"At Home with Grace."*

Dr. Rametti indicated Daisy should slide a little farther toward the end of the table. "Is it a talk show?"

"More like a home and garden, family and child type thing," Daisy said as she struggled to comply. "They do a lot of how-to segments, like Grace used to do on *Rise and Shine, America!* I photograph everything, and when the show is up and running, we'll put the photographs on the Web. And of course use a lot of the shots for advertising and publicity, too."

"Sounds challenging. Are you enjoying it?"

"Yes, very much so," Daisy was pleased to admit. Grace couldn't have been nicer to her once Daisy started working on the show. There were still moments from time to time when Daisy could tell that Grace was uncomfortable having Daisy around, but those moments were getting fewer and farther apart, and Daisy could imagine a day in the not so distant future when she would simply be Daisy to Grace, not her ex-husband's illegitimate child. And that was a relief. To both of them.

"It must have been a hard job to get," Dr. Rametti said conversationally as she stripped off her gloves and tossed them into the medical waste can.

Daisy nodded. She had been beyond stunned when Grace had called her just hours after Grace had flatly eliminated Daisy from the running, and said she wanted to let Daisy give the job a try after all. Daisy didn't flatter herself by thinking it was her talent that had gotten her in the door. She knew she was getting hired simply because Grace wanted to prove she could co-exist peacefully with Daisy, and saw that as a way to do it. That sort of reverse nepotism had almost been enough to make Daisy refuse the job, but in the end, her need for money of her own, and the freedom it would buy her, prevailed over her stubborn pride. Whether or not the job worked out in the long run, Daisy had reassured herself firmly, didn't matter nearly as much as the experience she would get from working on a television show.

Dr. Rametti picked up Daisy's chart. "You're not too tired?"

Daisy shrugged off the circles under her eyes as she sat up with the assistance of the nurse. "Tired can be a good thing right now."

Dr. Rametti made a notation, then looked up. "How are you doing emotionally?"

Daisy shrugged again, not really wanting to get into that—with anyone. "I'm fine."

Dr. Rametti lifted her eyebrow. Her nurse looked equally skeptical.

"There are times when it's tough, but each day it gets a little better," Daisy confessed after a moment.

"What about Jack?" Dr. Rametti gave her a brief, assessing glance, then continued empathetically, "This kind of thing can be tough on husbands, too, you know."

Another road Daisy didn't want to travel, she thought as she adjusted the paper gown across her waist. "Jack's been busy, too."

"I thought he might show up here with you."

Daisy was still trying to figure out what to say that

wouldn't disclose what she'd done—or more accurately failed to do—when a knock sounded on the exam-room door. Another nurse stuck her head in. "Mrs. Granger's husband is here. If it's okay, he'd like to come in."

Daisy swore inwardly. She had been hoping to avoid just this.

"Sure." Oblivious to the nature of Daisy's thoughts, Dr. Rametti turned back to her. "Well, I guess that answers my question," she said with a smile.

Looking capable and handsome in an olive-green business suit, Jack strode in and shook hands with Dr. Rametti. Briefly, Dr. Rametti brought him up to date. "Daisy's doing just fine. Recovering nicely. So you'll be happy to know you two have the green light to resume intercourse."

Easy for you to say, Daisy thought uncomfortably, doing her best to avoid Jack's eyes and not feel so exposed in her current position. *You're not trying to keep your heart intact.* It was dangerous for her to be feeling so dependent on him, given why and how they had entered into their marriage. Risky for him, too. She knew he was determined to be gallant about all this and do the right, the honorable thing. She also knew that he wasn't looking to get hurt any more than she was. Pretending they could make their marriage real via wishful thinking was a shaky supposition to make. People, Daisy knew from bitter experience, just didn't work that way. If they did, Charlotte would have been able to convince Richard to forget Daisy's origins and love her unreservedly. But that wasn't the case. And as far as Daisy's father was concerned, she was still just "Iris's mistake."

Dr. Rametti continued cheerfully counseling them

both, "I know you're probably both anxious to try again, but I'm going to advise you to be cautious and wait another few months, give Daisy's body a chance to recover fully from the trauma it suffered, before trying to have another baby. So, if you'd like to go on the Pill in the interim, Daisy...?"

"Sounds good." Daisy blushed despite herself and couldn't look at Jack as Dr. Rametti wrote out a prescription. No harm in being safe.

Dr. Rametti handed the prescription to Daisy. "It'll take a month before it's effective, so in the meantime, please use condoms and/or contraceptive foam. Okay?"

Daisy and Jack nodded their understanding. Jack thanked Dr. Rametti for all she had done. "Don't hesitate to call if anything comes up," the doctor cautioned. Then she and the nurse left so Daisy could get dressed.

"You could have told me about the appointment," Jack said the moment they were alone. "I would have been here with you for the entire time."

Daisy knew that, which was precisely why she hadn't told Jack about her medical appointment. "How'd you know I was here?" she asked as she scooted rather ungracefully toward the edge of the table and put her feet onto the step down.

Jack steadied her with a hand under her elbow, another at midspine. "I called you at the studio. They told me you'd left early because you had a doctor's appointment."

Daisy allowed him to help her down, then padded in her socks toward the tiny cubicle where her clothes were hanging. "Why did you call me?"

"Because Tom Deveraux asked me to," Jack said,

reminding Daisy once again just to whom Jack's first loyalty really lay.

Jack looked Daisy in the eye. "He needs to see you."

"DID YOU GET the papers from your sister?" Richard demanded as soon as Iris sat down in the country-club dining room.

Wishing she had made her excuses instead of showing up, Iris pretended to consult the lunch menu she already knew by heart. "Not yet."

Richard gave Iris a glare only she could see. "I told you I wanted them."

Heat crept into Iris's cheeks. "It's not that easy," she said, returning her eyes to that day's seafood specials. "After all the trouble Daisy went to get them, she's not just going to hand them over."

Richard closed his own menu and shifted it to the side of his plate. "So just take them and bring them to me."

Iris closed her menu, too. "I have to find them first."

"You were over there the week before last," Richard said with a smile as he sipped his sparkling water. "You had the perfect opportunity."

"I looked," Iris retorted irritably. At least she had tried to look while Daisy had been in the kitchen talking with Charlotte.

The waiter appeared, to bring Iris her usual unsweetened iced tea and take their orders.

"And?" Richard demanded impatiently as soon as the waiter had left again.

Iris shrugged. "Daisy's red file wasn't in the kitchen, family room, living room or the study at the front of the house."

Richard's forehead knit together. "You checked everywhere?"

"That I could." Iris studied the vase of fresh flowers

in the center of the table. "Jack's desk and the file cabinets in the study were all locked. And of course I couldn't rifle through every drawer with Daisy right there."

"That's no excuse."

"What do you want me to do?" Iris blotted her fingers on the starched linen napkin spread across her lap. "Break in?"

Richard's stony silence was Iris's answer to that. "What about the bedroom?" he asked after a moment.

Iris took a sip of her tea to soothe her parched throat. "I didn't have a chance to go back to that wing of the house because Jack came home and it was obviously time for us to go."

"We can't leave that paper trail in Daisy's hands. You know how impetuous she is when she's angry."

Iris broke open a paper packet of artificial sweetener and added a little to her glass. "I also know she's had plenty of opportunity to use it against us, and she hasn't." Iris paused to stir her tea. "If Daisy were going to tell anyone what she found out, she would already have done so."

Richard's eyes darkened. "I'm not just worried about her at the moment. I'm worried about Bucky Jerome and the way he keeps popping up wherever any of us are."

Resentment boiled up inside Iris. "If he's interested in the activities of our family, Father, it's only because—"

"What?" Richard leaned forward slightly, daring Iris to confront him.

For once, Iris refused to back down in the face of her father's considerable wrath. "You've gotten Bucky

interested with your flagrant extramarital activities,"
she hissed right back.

Richard slashed her a warning look. "You need to
be careful how you talk to me, dear."

"And you need to be careful where you are when
you indulge in such foolish and reckless activities," Iris
returned just as angrily. "I saw Ginger Zaring at the
elementary school last week. I read Bucky's column."

Once again, her father was all ice. "I don't know
what you're talking about," Richard said.

Yes, Iris thought, her father did. "If you don't care
about the business or the rest of us, you might at least
think about Mother," Iris said angrily.

The guilt Iris had hoped to see was simply not there.
"What does Charlotte have to do with this?" Richard
asked.

"Everything," Iris's low voice quavered emotionally. "She would be so hurt."

Richard regarded Iris evenly. "She does not ever
have to know."

"You can't keep—" Iris stopped, drew a deep
breath, tried again. "You can't do things like this right
under her nose and keep expecting to get away with it!
Sooner or later your luck is going to run out." And
then what would they all do? How would they survive
that? Talk about scandal!

But once again, her father seemed not to care about
his own sins, only those of his offspring.

"Don't tell me what to do," Richard said tightly.
"Now, back to what we were discussing. I want you to
take care of that file as soon as possible."

Iris gritted her teeth. "I won't do it."

"You're defying me?"

Looks like, Iris thought, but aloud she said nothing, simply stared at him.

Richard stared back at her while he pushed away from the table and stood. "I trust you will take care of the check." He walked off, leaving Iris alone with her black thoughts.

The knowledge of her father's fooling around was not news to her. She'd had her blinders taken off when she was ten and had accidentally walked in on him and the pretty blond landscape architect in the potting shed out at Rosewood. Iris hadn't understood a lot about lovemaking at the time, but she'd known not to tell her mother what she'd seen Richard and that woman doing, even before her father's sternly voiced warning.

After that, Richard had become a lot more careful. Iris had had no doubt he was still having affairs—her parents' separate bedrooms had told her that—but at least her father had had the good grace to keep it away from his family.

That had changed.

Now he no longer seemed to care, and in fact, appeared almost to want to get caught. And Iris had no idea what to do about that.

SEVERAL HOURS LATER, as Iris turned the Closed sign to the window of the shop and switched off the lights, she caught sight of Bucky Jerome once again. He was seated at a table against the window in the Starbucks across the street. He appeared to be working on something while enjoying a cup of coffee, but she knew he was really watching her. Watching all the Templetons. Too late, Iris realized she should have asked Tom Deveraux to meet her somewhere else, but when Tom had phoned her twenty minutes ago, needing to see her, she had suggested he simply come to the store. Tom had agreed. And since that moment, she had been able to think of nothing else.

How was it possible, Iris wondered, that she could still have feelings for a man who blamed her for the eventual breakup of his marriage?

Especially when Iris knew that Tom Deveraux had never loved any woman other than Grace. And probably never would.

Of course, that hadn't stopped her from trying to win him anyway, Iris recalled with no small amount of regret. Faced with the bankruptcy of her family and mounting pressure to marry an uninteresting man thirty years older than herself, she had thought, hoped, dreamed that Tom might rescue her. She had used her MBA to finagle her way into an internship in the executive offices of Deveraux Shipping Company, and then made herself indispensable to Tom. She had worked impossibly long hours on business matters she had no interest in. She had buoyed Tom's ego, been as supportive of him as his wife, Grace, should have been in the wake of his own father's death and the sudden handing of the company to him. Unlike Grace, who had been, in the days before her own meteoric career success, uncomfortable with the trappings of wealth and privilege, Iris had reveled in it. Appreciated it for the gift it was, and the responsibility and yes, duty, it demanded.

But that hadn't meant she had wanted to marry Randolph Hayes IV. Even if the future of her entire family depended on it. No, she had wanted Tom, with his own newly acquired wealth, to save her from that fate. So she had bided her time, waited until the time was right, and Tom had had both a major business reversal and a fight with the wife who had never once deserved him, never mind appreciated him, in the same day, and then she had sent out her own SOS. She had called Tom at home around midnight, crying almost incoherently, telling him something terrible had happened, that he had to come to her apartment immediately.

She'd made it sound as if there had been a death, and in a way, there had been—because unless Tom Deveraux saved her, her own life would be over. She'd been waiting for him in a beautiful negligee that revealed much, much more than it hid. She'd told him her father had just sold her to the highest bidder and sobbed in his arms. She'd told him she couldn't go through with it, couldn't marry someone who repulsed her. She was flesh and blood. A warm, willing woman. Too young to squander all that unused sexual energy. And to prove it, she made use of everything she had inherently known and given the performance of her life. She made him feel like the most desired man on earth. And it was then, when he had been collapsed on top of her, groaning and coming, in the middle of the living-room floor, that his wife had walked in.

MITCH DEVERAUX WAITED for the Deveraux-Heyward Shipping Company promotional tape to end, then hit the stop button on the VCR. "Mom did a great job on the voice-over, didn't she?" he said proudly.

Tom nodded. He, too, was pleased by the excellence of Grace's work. "The customers from both companies should feel reassured that the merger is going to benefit us all and result in even better, faster service."

"Mom refused payment for the half day she spent in the recording studio doing this. She said she couldn't accept money from family, but I think we should do something nice for her in exchange. Maybe make a donation to her favorite charity in her name and take her out to dinner. Or I could do the first and you could do the second.''

Tom glanced up from the calendar on his desk. He had a meeting with Iris Templeton in thirty minutes. And though her antique shop was only a few minutes away by car, he didn't want to be late. This discussion had been too long in coming as it was. ''Tell me you're not matchmaking,'' Tom said, giving his second-oldest son a stern, warning look. He'd had enough of that from Amy over the years. Now that she had finally stopped trying to force new life into Tom's relationship with Grace, he didn't want his three sons picking up the baton.

''You want me to stop beating around the bush and get straight to the point?''

''Please.''

''We four kids have talked. Now that we know what happened to cause such big problems with you and Mom, we understand why you couldn't be together and make things work back then.''

Tom was aware of that. After weeks of avoiding him like the plague, his four legitimate children were slowly but surely beginning to forgive him for what he had done, and coming back into his life once again. He knew they were still disillusioned and disappointed in him, and probably always would be. His involvement with Iris made him human, and they didn't want a father that flawed. But they were stuck with him, just as he could never separate himself from what he had done. And gradually, to Tom's relief, all four of them and their spouses were coming to realize that.

"But that's no reason you and Mom couldn't make things work now," Mitch continued hopefully.

Tom wished that were so. He gave his son a rueful half smile. "It's not that easy, Mitch." He and Grace had made reconciliation attempts before, only to have them fail. It was true they had both changed in the past few months. But had they changed enough?

"It could be," Mitch argued with the enthusiasm he usually reserved for two things, business and his new wife, Lauren, "if you and Mom forgave each other and agreed to move on, start fresh."

Tom paused, not sure what his son was referring to. "What would I need to forgive your mother for?"

Mitch shrugged. "There must have been something. I know you, Dad. You're not a dishonorable man. You wouldn't have turned to another woman and cheated on Mom without a darn good reason."

WAS THERE EVER A GOOD REASON for infidelity? Tom wondered as he cut short the conversation with his son and walked out to his car. At the moment it had happened, God knew he had felt justified, because he had believed his marriage to Grace was over in every way that counted. And for the life of him he hadn't been able to figure out why she had stopped loving him and started shutting him out the way she had.

The start to the relationship couldn't have been sweeter. Tom still recalled walking into that ice-cream shop near campus, the summer before his senior year of college, with a group of his friends. Grace had been working behind the counter. Her blond hair had been long back then, and it had been clasped in a bouncy ponytail. She'd had to wear a silly peppermint-striped uniform and matching hat, but she had looked adorable nevertheless.

Tom had been instantly smitten, and began flirting with her immediately. Grace flirted back, but declined a date. Tom didn't care that she was the only daughter of parents who ran a dry-cleaning store in a small South Carolina town, or that she'd had a very modest upbringing and was at that moment, working two part-time jobs to help pay for her college education. All he knew was that she was the sweetest, prettiest, kindest woman he had ever met. And that he wanted her to be his. And his alone.

He started going in for ice cream whenever she was working. He began studying there. Grace, who had agreed to be just friends with him, spent her breaks with him. But by the end of the summer, even that wasn't enough, and they started going out—platonically, of course—every single night she wasn't working and sometimes when she was.

By Christmas, they were stealing kisses in the library. And by spring, they both knew they wanted to be together in every way. But Grace couldn't—wouldn't—sleep with him without benefit of marriage. Her view was rather old-fashioned amidst the sexual revolution that had been going on at college campuses at the time, but Tom hadn't minded. He had loved her enough to wait.

They eloped the night after his college graduation, primarily because Grace didn't want any part of a big society wedding. And then moved to Charleston, where they purchased a house in the Historic District, close to the mansion they eventually inherited from his parents. Tom went to work. Grace stayed home and had babies, one right after another.

They'd had everything. Each other. Four kids they both adored. Money. Prestige. Social stature. But Grace still hadn't been happy. The closer he tried to get to her, the more she had pulled away. Until they were barely sleeping together even before she got pregnant again and miscarried shortly after Amy was born.

Tom still recalled how much that had hurt. Night after night, he had climbed into bed with her, only to have her coldly turn away. She hadn't wanted him, hadn't wanted to even kiss.

Looking back now, Tom could see Grace had been depressed, but he also knew it had been more. That there was something fundamentally wrong with their relationship for her not to want to make love to him, except to make another baby.

And that was when Iris had entered his life. Five years younger than he, she had made him feel young and virile, and yes—wanted, every second of every day. His ego had needed that in the wake of such constant rejection.

Still, he wondered if he would ever have strayed if he had been a little older and a lot wiser, or if Grace hadn't just turned him down for what had seemed like the thousandth time since their marriage, when Iris called that night and asked him to come over.

Not that it mattered now, Tom sighed as he parked his car and began walking down the street toward Templeton's Fine Antiques. He and Iris had gotten themselves and Daisy in this mess and now they had to deal with it.

Iris was waiting for him. She let him in the shop and led the way back to her private office. His own emotions in turmoil, Tom handed her the DNA test results. As expected, Iris perused them without a flicker of emotion on her perfectly made-up face. "Why didn't you tell me?" Tom asked quietly.

Iris handed him the medical report and retorted impassively, "Because it wouldn't have done any good. You wouldn't have given me what I wanted and needed to be able to keep Daisy. You wouldn't have married me."

Tom knew there had been more than one way to live up to his responsibility to Iris and Daisy, and he was filled with resentment at the opportunity denied him. "You didn't give me a chance to do what was necessary to take care of the both of you," he said angrily.

Iris sighed, abruptly looking unbearably weary. "I didn't need to," she told him sorrowfully. "I saw the expression on your face when Grace walked in on us that night. The regret and shame. I hadn't ever expected you to love me, Tom. Not in the way you obviously loved Grace. But I had hoped that we could forge an alliance that was built on our similar backgrounds and social responsibilities. It didn't take me long to realize that was simply wishful thinking on my part. The truth was, when I was your protégée you were all too happy to be my friend, but once we slept together, your guilt changed everything. You couldn't bear to be anywhere near me, couldn't look me in the eye. And I knew, even if I had been able to convince you to leave your family and make me your wife, that there was no way we could build a suitable home for Daisy. So we moved on. Both of us. And for that, Tom," she told him earnestly, "I still have no regret."

CHAPTER NINETEEN

"EVERYTHING IS READY, Mr. Deveraux," Theresa Owens said. "The table is set for three, the salad and dessert are already on the table, the hot foods are on the warmer on the table in the dining room, just as you asked." Theresa paused, pretending she didn't know something was up, otherwise Tom wouldn't be so secretive about the exact nature of his dinner and so tense. "So, if it's all right, I'll be leaving for the evening as soon as your guests arrive."

"Thank you, Theresa." Tom smiled at the woman who was as much family now as housekeeper. "I appreciate all you've done," he told her sincerely.

"No problem." Theresa headed back to the kitchen.

A half minute later, the doorbell rang. Tom heard voices, then Theresa showed Daisy and Jack into his study. She asked if anyone needed anything—they didn't—then excused herself. Her footsteps disappeared down the hall. In the distance, the back door opened and then shut. "So what is this about?" Daisy asked without preamble.

Tom had envisioned a more cordial meeting. "Why don't you two have a seat?" He gestured to the cherry leather sofa in front of the fireplace, and sat down in one of the two wing chairs that flanked either end of the coffee table.

Daisy crossed her arms in front of her and leaned against the mantel. "I'd prefer to stand."

So, Tom thought, sighing inwardly, it was going to be like this. Not that he should be surprised. Daisy always had been a rebel and a half, never more so when threatened or upset. "The DNA tests are back." He handed a manila file containing the information over to Daisy. "It's official. You are my daughter, Daisy."

For a second, Tom thought Daisy was going to burst into tears. Blinking furiously, she turned away from him and wordlessly perused the papers he had given her. "Fine." She handed them back to Tom as if she could have cared less. "If that's all—" She gave Tom another indifferent glance, then turned toward the door, looking ready to dash out.

Jack had been sitting on the sofa, but suddenly he was on his feet, too, moving subtly but deliberately to block Daisy's exit. Folding his arms across his chest, standing with his legs braced apart, Jack said, "I think your father probably has a lot more he'd like to say to you."

Daisy glared at Jack, looking as if she would like to deck him for taking Tom's side. "He's not my father," she stated icily. "Paternity tests do nothing to remedy that."

"You're right," Tom agreed, remaining in his seat with effort, when his every instinct was to go to Daisy and take her in his arms and welcome her to the family that way. Knowing, however, that was the last thing she wanted, or would accept at that point, he continued talking to her and Jack calmly, "Which is why I've asked the lawyers who handle the family trusts to create one in your name, Daisy. It's going to be equal to those of all my children."

"Which is…?"

"Twenty-five million dollars, to be used however, whenever you wish."

Jack looked impressed, but Daisy regarded Tom even more suspiciously. "How do the others feel about that?"

Tom shrugged. "I haven't told them."

Daisy walked toward the bay window that overlooked the formal garden. "Won't they resent my taking part of Deveraux-family funds?"

Tom met Daisy's glare head-on. He wasn't about to let Daisy make this about anything except what it was. "There's plenty to go around," he returned just as succinctly.

"So in other words, it costs you nothing," Daisy surmised sarcastically.

"Daisy," Jack scolded.

"Let's go into the dining room, shall we?" Tom suggested, rising from his chair and leading the way down the hall to the formally decorated room. Three places had been set at one end of the antique mahogany table that sat sixteen.

A mutinous look on her face, Daisy sat in the chair Jack pulled out for her. Tom took his place at the head of the table. Jack sat opposite his wife while Tom poured them all some Merlot. "I realize this isn't going to be easy," Tom said as the three of them unfolded their napkins and put them across their laps. "But I'm willing to try my hardest to make it up to you, Daisy. The question is—" he regarded her steadily "—are you prepared to meet me halfway?"

DAISY HAD EXPECTED Tom Deveraux to try and convince her that they should just forget the way he had abandoned her. She'd even figured he might give her a little money to ease his conscience—although not quite the millions he'd put in the trust fund. She hadn't expected him to go all fatherly on her the moment he had confirmation that she was indeed his offspring, but that was exactly what he was doing. And Daisy didn't know quite how to handle that. She had never been good with authority figures. Authority figures with guilty feelings they were trying to appease as quickly and easily as possible was something else indeed. "What do you mean, meet you halfway?" Daisy echoed as she dragged her fork through the artfully arranged spinach salads. Did Tom expect her to treat him with gratitude, respect, forgiveness, what?

"Are you willing to work on our relationship?"

Daisy had never been any good at making familial connections. Unlike the famously loving and loyal Deveraux clan, she simply had no talent for forging close and loving bonds with people. And the more intimate an attachment was supposed to be, the less able she was to further—or even maintain—it. She didn't know why that was. She just knew she got scared when people tried to be too touchy-feely with her. She liked casual relationships that didn't demand much in the way of personal confessions or familiarity. The kind that were low maintenance and always stayed the same. Easy and effortless. The kind that didn't let her get hurt when people kept secrets from her and looked at her as if there was something wrong with her that they didn't want her to know. Now, of course, she knew what that something was—it was her illegitimacy, the fact she was and always would be "Iris's mistake" to Richard, a source of shame and regret to Iris, someone who caused too much trouble within her family for her brother Connor's taste, and last but not least, the "Templeton heir" that Charlotte had never stopped worrying over.

"I don't see the need for that," Daisy said as she speared a mushroom. "Unless you're planning to declare to the entire world I'm your daughter."

"I want that..." Tom said.

Here it comes, Daisy thought. The crushing disappointment and further disillusionment she had been expecting from the get-go.

"Then I spoke with Iris."

Jack looked as curious as Daisy felt about that. "When?" Daisy asked.

"Earlier this evening," Tom confirmed. Sighing, he leaned back in his chair. "Iris pointed out to me that you are not only my biological daughter, but the half sister to my other four children, who happen to be the offspring of one of the most famous women in America." Tom's lips compressed as he continued quietly, "For years, people have speculated why Grace and I divorced—"

"And I'm the reason," Daisy cut in bitterly, realizing once more she had done nothing but made other people miserable just by existing.

"My infidelity was the reason," Tom corrected Daisy archly. "Grace couldn't get over it. And I didn't understand why at the time. Now I do." Tom paused to give Jack a man-to-man glance before zeroing in on Daisy once again. "We don't want this to end up in the tabloids, Daisy. And if I come right out and acknowledge you publicly, that is what will happen. Your face will be on scandal sheets, not just here in the United States, but in Britain and everywhere else."

"So you are proposing what?" Daisy demanded, her

appetite disappearing. She looked at Tom, suddenly feeling unbearably weary.

"That you and I and Jack spend time together. Because Jack is legal counsel for the Deveraux-Heyward Shipping Company, and we're in the midst of implementing a complicated merger with Heyward Shipping, we could do it without raising a lot of eyebrows. And then once we are seen together a lot publicly, people will assume we've become socially compatible, as well."

In other words, another cover-up, with me at the center, Daisy thought.

"So Jack and I will be known as close family friends of the Deveraux family," Daisy surmised, knowing this was what Jack had wanted for himself for a long time. Even if it wasn't what she wanted. And that had Jack not married her, it probably never would have happened. He would have remained Tom's loyal employee and nothing more.

"Except you and I and the rest of the family will know you are much, much more," Tom said quietly.

Daisy felt the pulse points pounding in her neck as she thought about all the lies this new ruse would entail. "And where does Iris figure into this?" she asked tightly.

Reluctantly, Tom admitted, "Iris thinks it would be best to simply leave things as is."

Daisy swallowed around the tightness in her throat. "So, in other words, she never plans to publicly acknowledge me as her daughter, either."

Tom hesitated before continuing gently, "She doesn't think it would help anyone to do so. And I have to say, after listening to her side of things, I agree. We both want to protect you, Daisy. You've been hurt enough already."

Daisy couldn't disagree with that. Nor could she deny she needed some sort of closure to all this, some way to put it behind her, and move on. What Tom was suggesting seemed likely to do just that. And given that she wasn't likely to ever get what she wanted—two parents who really loved her and were unashamed to call her their child—she figured she should just cut her losses. "What should I call you—in private?" Daisy asked finally, aware that although she was still sitting there calmly eating her salad, her heart felt as if it had just been torn in two.

Tom didn't even have to think about that. "How about Tom?" he suggested cordially.

Not Dad.

Not Father.

Just Tom.

Of course.

"I THOUGHT YOU'D BE happier," Jack said as they left Tom Deveraux's house.

Determined not to let anyone know just how devastated she was, Daisy breezed through the rosebushes that sat just inside the black wrought-iron fence that marked off the Deveraux property from others on the street.

"But you don't look anywhere near satisfied with the way things have turned out," Jack continued.

And why should she be? Daisy thought resentfully. "In case you didn't notice, Jack, I was just abandoned yet again," Daisy informed him as they walked to the end of the driveway.

Jack hit the unlock button on his remote. "Tom isn't doing that."

Ignoring Jack's frown, she climbed into the driver's side of the SUV and settled behind the wheel. "Sure he is," she said as Jack climbed reluctantly into the passenger side. "He's just doing it in a more morally acceptable way so he doesn't feel so guilty."

Jack sighed in obvious frustration and handed over the keys. Daisy started the vehicle and drove through the gates. "He's trying to protect you," Jack said, taking Tom's side for what seemed like the thousandth time.

Both hands circling the wheel, Daisy stomped on the accelerator with more than necessary force. "He's trying to protect himself and Grace and his kids and his company and everyone else who matters."

Jack glowered at her impatiently. "Including you."

Daisy shook her head and forced herself to drive more calmly. "I know you think he's been generous," she said.

"Given the size of that trust fund he laid on you, more than generous," Jack countered.

"But money doesn't buy happiness," Daisy asserted stubbornly.

"Maybe not, but at least you won't have to worry about finances." Jack messed with the stereo until he found a station he liked. "You can get rid of that junk heap you're driving and buy something else."

"I like my car," Daisy said stubbornly as they approached the highway that would take them to the beach. "It's fine. Although it was a little easier to spot in parking lots when it was two different colors instead of just one."

"He's not just giving you money. He's offering you time and attention and doing his best to make amends."

Daisy gripped the steering wheel. "You don't get it, do you?"

Jack shrugged. "Then explain it to me."

Daisy sighed, glad there wasn't that much traffic at 10:00 p.m. "My whole life I've felt like a source of shame to Charlotte and Richard. I didn't understand why. I knew, at least in the beginning, when I was younger, that I hadn't done anything to deserve it, but I knew just the same that there was something about me that embarrassed them and made them fearful and uncomfortable. It was as if they were always waiting for something to happen to bring them even more humiliation than they had already suffered due to what they considered my outrageous behavior. I didn't know what that was, of course, back then, I just felt like I was this bad seed they had adopted. And they were disappointed they couldn't break my unacceptable, non-blue-blood roots."

"Except you are blue-blooded," Jack pointed out as Daisy drove across the causeway that led to the beach.

Daisy frowned and put on the left-turn signal as she prepared to pass the slow-moving car in front of her. "A blue-blooded bastard born of an illicit, socially embarrassing love affair is not the same as being a full-fledged member of the family. *That* was made all too clear this evening when Tom explained how he was going to accept me as his daughter, but only out of public view, in the trusted circle of the Deveraux clan. So you see," Daisy continued as she checked her mirrors and steered the SUV into the left lane, "he may have laid out some money for me and told me what I wanted and needed to hear, and what he needed to say, but in the end, nothing has changed. I'm still, and always will be, a source of immense regret to all those closest to me.''

As much as Jack was loath to admit it, he knew Daisy had a point. She herself had done nothing to deserve the troubling circumstances of her birth, but she was still being punished, just as he had been punished all those many years by his grandfather for his own mother's behavior, and the fact that she, too, had given birth to a baby out of wedlock that in the end she had neither wanted nor been able to care for.

It was a hurt that never went away.

And what Tom had done, nobly intentioned as it was, had still been wrong. As long as the secrets continued, Daisy would feel rejected, that she wasn't good enough. But how, Jack wondered, as Daisy parked the SUV in the driveway at his house, could he possibly convince Tom Deveraux of that? Tom was his boss. And not likely to take his advice on any matter this sensitive, even if Jack was now Daisy's husband.

"I'll get the mail," Jack said as Daisy headed toward the house.

He walked back out to the mailbox, next to the street, while Daisy unlocked the door. She let herself in as he was closing the metal front of the box. He was only halfway up the walk when he heard her scream. And then scream again, even louder. Heart racing, Jack took off at a run, closing the distance in a matter of moments, and then he was inside the darkened foyer. "Daisy!"

She came out of the inky shadows at him, thrusting herself into his arms. "What happened?" he demanded, able to see the sliding glass door to the deck standing open, moonlight streaming into the rear of the house, partially illuminating the family room.

"There were two burglars here with flashlights. They were dressed in black, and they had watch caps pulled over their heads."

"Where?"

"I saw them slip out the back just as I came in."

Jack tried to put her aside, to go after them, but Daisy merely held on all the tighter, trembling so badly she could hardly stand. As much as Jack wanted to continue holding her, he had to make sure they were safe. Right now, he wasn't sure they were alone. He pushed Daisy into the living room and back into a corner of the darkened room. "Stay here," he ordered gruffly. "Don't move until I tell you." He let her go and headed back into the foyer and the hall that ran the length of the house.

At the opposite end of the first floor, the sliding glass doors to the deck still stood open. Jack could feel the breeze off the ocean and smell the tang of the salt air. There was broken glass on the floor from the multipaned window next to the doors, and that window was open, too. So this was how they had gotten in, he thought as he quickly made a tour of the rest of the house, hitting light switches as he went. There was no one there, nothing of value missing that Jack could see, but the place had been thoroughly ransacked, he noted dispiritedly. Every drawer opened and overturned, linens torn off the bed, the mattress askew.

He headed back to Daisy. The living-room lights were now on and she was, not surprisingly, not where he had left her. Instead, she was across the hall in the study. Staring grim-faced at the files strewn over the floor. Seeing what she was looking at, Jack let out a low oath. He had never wanted her to find any of this.

CHAPTER TWENTY

"HOW LONG HAVE you been keeping files on me?" Daisy asked in an accusing tone.

Jack knelt down to pick up some of the clippings spread out over the floor. Photos of Daisy at her cotillion, graduating from prep school, initial police reports written up about a vandalism perpetrated by her and some others students, until her involvement had been cleared up behind the scenes by former policeman turned private investigator Harlan Decker.

"And why do you have correspondence with the deans of the colleges where I was kicked out or flunked out?" Daisy demanded. "Why were these huge donations made?" She stood on shaking legs and advanced toward him. "Was this all your idea?"

Feeling guiltier than he knew he should, Jack began cleaning up the mess. Figuring he owed her an explanation, he admitted gruffly, "Tom's."

"Why?"

So much emotion in such a single word. Jack shrugged as he formed the loose papers into one big stack, aware the last thing he wanted to do right now was explain his actions. He paused to look Daisy in the eye. "Tom never said why. He just asked me to keep a discreet watch over you. If there was any sort of mention in the newspaper, he wanted me to clip it out."

Daisy stiffened, the expression on her face as annoyed as it was wary. "Why are the files here instead of at Deveraux-Heyward Shipping?"

Jack grimaced. "He keeps a firewall between the office and his personal life. He didn't want anything on you kept at Deveraux-Heyward Shipping. If I happened to see something in the newspaper while I was there, I made sure it came to his attention in some innocuous way, then brought it home and filed it here. If you got into a scrape, or in some way harmed your permanent record, I was to see what could be done to help."

"Hence the letters to the colleges," Daisy guessed, still struggling to put it all together.

Jack lifted the stack onto the desk. And figuring the hell with it—he could clean up later, Daisy's feelings were what was important now—he stepped toward her. "Tom's a generous man and quite the philanthropist in his own right." He paused, struggling to word what he had done in a way that wouldn't sound quite so much like a payoff. "I wrote letters on his behalf, pointing out that once you had left an institution of higher learning, there was no point in furthering the matter, when good could instead be done for the university, as reparation for any problems that had been caused."

Daisy's eyes turned as stormy as the ocean on a gloomy winter's day. "So in other words, you bribed them on my behalf, without my ever knowing about it?" Daisy summarized bitterly, glancing past Jack, toward the door.

Jack had the feeling if Daisy left, it wouldn't just be the room, and it wouldn't just be for that night. He moved subtly to block the exit. "Tom wanted you to be able to start fresh somewhere else. He knew you were having a hard time, and that you didn't have a lot of support from Richard and Charlotte.'' And for that, although they had never come right out and discussed it, Tom's and Jack's hearts had both gone out to Daisy.

Daisy studied Jack through narrowed eyes. "What else do you do for Tom on the sly?"

"That's it," Jack said evenly.

She propped a hand on her hip. "Just watch over me."

She didn't sound as if she believed him. Jack approached her, hands outstretched. "He wanted you to have a sort of guardian angel." At the disbelief in Daisy's eyes, Jack continued pragmatically, "It didn't begin that way. He didn't phrase it that way or think of it that way at first, but over the years that's how it evolved."

"And you were a willing participant."

Jack thought of the hours and days and nights he had spent worrying over, watching her. "Yes," he said simply.

"Why?"

Jack shrugged. That, he thought, was a lot harder to explain. "At first I was thrilled to be asked to do something so confidential for a man like Tom, to know he trusted me and had faith in me to that degree."

Daisy's blond eyebrow arched. "And then…?"

I became fascinated with you. I fell in love with you. But knowing how cheesy and completely unrealistic that would sound, Jack merely said instead, "I enjoyed being able to help someone, because I'd been in the same situation myself."

"Except you got something in return, Jack," Daisy pointed out sardonically. "You had your boss's undying gratitude."

"Okay, so there was a payoff for me, too," Jack

conceded, although he hadn't thought of it that way at the time, and he still didn't.

"And you're not ashamed?" Color flooding her cheeks, she studied him openly.

"I had a job to do," Jack retorted evenly. "I did it."

Daisy nodded her understanding, looking less than pleased. "For exactly how long?"

"About ten years." Jack admitted reluctantly. "Right after I graduated from law school and took a permanent job with Deveraux Shipping Company. You were about thirteen at the time and just starting to get into real trouble." And she had fascinated him, albeit on a completely different level, even then.

"How did he explain it to you?" Daisy asked curiously.

Jack watched her begin to pace. "That was just it—he didn't. It seemed like some sort of test."

"Which you passed with flying colors," she observed.

Heart in his throat, Jack watched Daisy sift through the stack on his desk. He felt like a defendant facing an unfavorable jury. "Look, as an attorney my job is to operate within the law but see to my clients' wishes. I regarded Tom as my client as well as my boss."

Contempt colored her low voice. "And you looked up to him."

Daisy spoke as if Jack's feelings of gratitude and respect toward his mentor were foolish and ill-placed. Jack struggled against the impatience rising in him. He had explained to Daisy how much he owed Tom Deveraux and always would. He'd thought, at the time anyway, that she understood how much Tom's attention and guidance had meant to him. Doing his best to contain his mounting frustration, he said, "I knew, whatever the reason, that Tom was deeply concerned about you, that he wanted to be able to watch over you directly but couldn't. So I did it for him.'' And for that, Jack had no regret.

Daisy had needed someone.

That guardian angel had turned out to be him.

DAISY SUPPOSED she shouldn't have been surprised to find that Jack had been deployed by Tom to keep tabs on her for more than the one night she'd returned from Switzerland, hurt and furious, and ready to confront all those who had lied to her.

Nevertheless, the notion that Jack had been secretly watching over her all those years was as unsettling as it was, in retrospect, utterly predictable. Tom Deveraux had obviously felt a lot of guilt for abandoning her the way he had. He'd been able to tell himself his actions were for the best when she was a baby, but as she got older, it had become apparent to everyone in Charleston what a mistake Richard and Charlotte had made in adopting her, Daisy thought. So Tom had dispensed Jack. And her husband, eager to please, had been all too happy to play her guardian angel for his boss.

''So now you know,'' Jack said quietly.

Daisy nodded, not sure when she had ever felt so betrayed. First by Iris and Tom and her parents, and now even Jack. The one person, the only person, in recent weeks, whom she had felt she could trust.

Which just went to show what *she* knew.

Nothing. Absolutely nothing.

Suddenly unable to discuss it anymore, to think what his past surveillance of her might mean to the two of them now, beyond the fact that once again Jack's loyalty had been first to Tom and then to Daisy, she looked at the mess surrounding them. Then asked with un-bearable weariness, "Do you want to call the police or shall I?"

Jack cut her off before she could reach for the phone. "I'm not going to report it," he said firmly.

Her heart knocked against her ribs as she noted the way he towered over her. She swallowed around the dryness of her throat. "Why not?"

"Because," Jack told her practically, once again all efficient male, "I want Harlan Decker to take a look first." Jack consulted the PalmPilot on his desk, picked up the phone and punched in a number.

Daisy knew if anyone could figure out who had done this, it was probably Harlan. The ex-cop had worked vice, robbery and homicide while a member of the Charleston police force, before retiring and opening his own detective agency.

"Harlan'll be over in about ten minutes," Jack said when he had hung up the phone. "He asked us not to touch anything else until he gets here."

Feeling frustrated, Daisy perched on the edge of Jack's desk while he prowled his study restlessly. She rubbed her arms against the chill that had come out of nowhere. She knew by the way he was acting, some-thing else was up. "You don't think this was just a random break-in, do you?"

Jack shook his head. "If they had just wanted to steal stuff for money, they would have taken the laptop, stereo, TV, but none of those things have been touched. Instead, they broke into my files, and from the looks of it—" Jack gestured at the information on Daisy littering the floor "—were very interested in everything on you."

"So I'm the target," Daisy guessed unhappily, al-

ready heading back to the master-bedroom closet,
where she kept her stuff.

The master bedroom, if possible, was in even worse
shape than Jack's study. Daisy's clothing had been
pulled out of the dresser drawers and dumped onto the
floor. The covers and the pillows had been ripped off
the bed, the mattress left askew. The drawers in the
bathroom had been opened and rummaged through.
Even the contents of the nightstand and Daisy's portfolio had been dispersed around the room.

Daisy swallowed, aware she had never felt so vio-
lated as she did at that second. "I know it may be
impossible to know for sure, but is there anything missing that you can tell?" Jack asked gently, coming up
behind her, and putting his arms around her.

Daisy shivered as the doorbell rang. It was so hard
to tell. There was nothing that couldn't be replaced easily, except...oh, no. Daisy looked behind the bureau,
next to the wall. And realized with a sinking heart that
the red expanding file containing her real birth records
was gone.

WHILE JACK WENT to let Harlan in and show him the
rest of the house, Daisy kept visually searching through
the bedroom mess. By the time Jack brought the cigar-
smoking Harlan back to see their bedroom, she knew
with certainty her file hadn't just been picked up and
rifled through, it was gone.

"Sorry about this," Harlan told Daisy sympathetically.

Daisy nodded at Harlan and looked at Jack before
telling both, "I think they stole everything I had from
my trip to Switzerland, the airline sleeve that had contained my tickets, the information from the embassy,

the adoption agency and the convent, copies of my passport as an infant, and the real record of my birth, as well as copies of the legal documents that pertained to my name change.'' Daisy scowled at the emptied-out nightstand drawer, ''They also got—if you can believe this—my post-op instructions from the hospital and the information booklet I received about dealing with a miscarriage.''

Harlan frowned. ''Who would want that, or even have known to come here looking for it?''

Daisy could think of only one person. ''Bucky Jerome?'' Daisy and Jack said in unison.

''Except...'' Daisy hedged.

Harlan and Jack looked at her. ''It just—it doesn't seem like Bucky's style. He's usually more in your face about his nosiness.''

Jack frowned. ''Bucky's the only one who's been asking about either of those things, Daisy. And the only one who would benefit from knowing.''

''But there were two people here, Jack,'' Daisy countered with a perplexed frown. ''Who would the second person have been?''

Jack shrugged. ''A friend of Bucky's? Someone else from the *Herald?*''

Daisy felt the color drain from her face as she sank onto a corner of the bed. ''Oh my God. If any of this shows up in the newspaper,'' Daisy said miserably. It would be like having her guts spread all over the streets for everyone to see.

Jack sat down next to Daisy and put his arm around her. And in that moment, Daisy didn't care what Jack had done for her biological father in the past, she needed and wanted Jack's protection more than ever.

Because Jack was the only one in this world who made her feel safe.

"I'll have a talk with Bucky Jerome," Jack said, jaw set. He gave her a reassuring hug then stood, his expression grim, and said, "I'll make sure he understands if any of this shows up in print we are going to sue him and the paper."

Harlan continued looking around. "I can't say whether Bucky Jerome did this or not. But I can tell you this, the break-in tonight was definitely the work of an amateur. A pro would have been able to pick those locks without any trouble at all."

Daisy took pictures of the carnage. Jack took a piece of the plywood he kept on hand for hurricane season and boarded up the broken window. There was nothing he or Harlan could do about the file cabinets behind Jack's desk, however. They were going to have to be replaced. The flimsy metal doors of the sleek black cabinets had been permanently bent out of shape with what they assumed was a crowbar.

It was past two by the time Harlan left, promising to help them get to the bottom of this. After three by the time Jack and Daisy had set the house to rights and remade the bed with clean sheets. Daisy still felt a little uneasy as she and Jack climbed into bed. But he put his arms around her, and exhausted, she fell into a deep sleep.

The next thing Daisy knew, she was back in that windowless room. It was black and awful and smelled slightly musty and mildewish. She was curled up on the corner of what felt like an uncomfortable iron cot—the kind she had slept on at summer camp—and she was crying so hard the tears were just streaming down her face.

The door opened, a shaft of light swept the room, and the person in the mask came in. "Be quiet now," the person breathed in a threatening whisper as goose bumps broke out all over her skin and she felt the unbearable urge to wet herself, "or I'm going to have to hurt you and I don't want to hurt you." Daisy still couldn't stop crying, so the person reached for her, fingers pinching into her bare skin. Daisy heard what sounded like a woman's voice, high-pitched, upset, in the foreground. And then the imprisoning hands closed all the harder around her upper arms, the voice telling her to shut up! Knowing this was her only chance for discovery, Daisy opened her mouth to scream.

JACK WAS SOUND ASLEEP when Daisy began thrashing next to him. She had slept fitfully nearly every night since the miscarriage. Sometimes crying, sometimes whimpering and curling into a fetal position. When necessary, he woke her up just enough to quiet her. She rarely remembered those times the next morning. Other times, all he had to do was put his arms around her and hold her close and she would lapse back into a deep sleep. But tonight was not one of those nights, he realized as Daisy suddenly sat bolt upright and let out a bloodcurdling scream that made the hair on his neck stand on end.

"No," she screamed again, even more loudly. "I won't be quiet! I want out of here! I want out right now! Mommy!"

Jack switched on the bedside lamp, sat up and grabbed her by the shoulders. "Daisy!" He shook her once, then again and again.

Daisy opened her eyes, still not seeing him, sobbing openly now. "I won't shut up!" she cried before letting out another bloodcurdling shriek of terror that set Jack's heart pounding. "Mommy!"

Desperate to stop her suffering, Jack shook Daisy all the more forcefully. "Daisy, wake up, sweetheart!" he instructed her loudly.

But instead of rousing, Daisy merely flailed out at him and tried to scramble from the bed. As Jack followed, she lashed out at him, and made it as far as the door before he caught up with her. Still trying to reach her, he clamped both his arms around her and held her close. "Daisy, it's Jack. Now come on. Look at me, honey. Look at me. It's Jack. It's Jack. Everything's okay. You're just dreaming. That's all. It's a bad, bad dream."

Slowly, Daisy's eyes cleared. She swallowed hard, still trembling from head to foot, and looked at him.

"You were dreaming," Jack repeated even more firmly. "You're awake now. You're safe," he reassured her gently as they leaned against the wall. And then Daisy broke down in the gut-wrenching sobs that just broke his heart.

DAISY DIDN'T KNOW what was the matter with her. She couldn't seem to stop crying. Couldn't get ahold of herself or stop the images of Rosewood flashing through her mind. Couldn't do anything but sag against the wall and hold on to Jack for dear life.

"Hush, hush," Jack whispered against her hair. He smoothed a hand down her spine. "You're all right now. You're safe. I promise you. Nothing and no one is going to hurt you now. You're safe."

Safe. Daisy had wanted to be this secure all her life, but not until she'd married Jack did she ever believe she could feel this way. And there was a part of her that still didn't trust the emotion she felt. At least not all the way. She lifted her head from the dampness of his shoulder and looked up into his face. Jack was looking down at her with such unbelievable tenderness, just the way he had looked at Rosewood, when he had rescued her weeks before and suddenly she knew what she wanted. To forget those horrible dreams and whatever had happened long ago to cause her to dread going out to Rosewood, to dread ever being locked in a small, windowless room. Or left crying, alone and afraid.

"Make love to me," Daisy whispered, already forging her lips with his. "Now, Jack. Please."

She didn't have to ask twice.

He threaded both his hands through her hair and lowered his mouth to hers, making her his and only his, for now, forever, and suddenly the past was just that. All that mattered to Daisy was the present. She locked her hands around the back of his neck and kissed him back passionately. She arched up against him, desperate with need and the yearning to have him buried deep inside her. Because when Jack made love to her he made her feel as if she was perfect. *They* were perfect. Together. And that was something she'd never felt before. Never even come close to feeling.

Aware his arousal was every bit as fierce as hers, she kicked off her shorts, opened up his pajama pants and took the hot, throbbing length of him in hand. Swearing, Jack broke the contact and lunged for the nightstand. Daisy blinked, not understanding, until she saw him reach for the box of condoms. And then belatedly, she remembered, too.

"Dr. Rametti," Jack muttered as he stripped off his pajama pants, covered his erection swiftly and came back to join her. She tugged her camisole top over her head and held out her arms. He came into them. Just that easily, they picked up where they had left off. They rubbed against each other intimately, teasing, tormenting, until control was all but gone and they were both moaning and shaking with need, and the time for waiting, for delaying was past.

Jack lifted her against the wall. She wrapped her legs around his waist. He slid into her in one powerful thrust. By the second, Daisy had begun to shatter. He followed soon after. Her fingertips dug into his back as they hung there together in ecstasy, and then came slowly back to reality. His breathing still coming as hard and fast as hers, Jack wrapped her in his arms, holding her close. "I think we just broke all land-speed records there," he murmured teasingly against her neck.

Daisy pressed a kiss in his hair and cuddled closer, knowing she had never felt as content—and wanted—and full of joy as she did at that very moment. It wasn't that Jack made all the bad things in her life go away—no one had that kind of power. He just made her think that the problems—and they still had plenty of them—weren't anywhere near as important as the joy and fulfillment the two of them felt whenever they were together like this, or just talking, being. Enjoying each other. Enjoying sex.

"I know."

He drew back to look at her. "Want to go again?"

Daisy grinned as he slowly, reluctantly, disengaged their bodies where they were still joined and ripped off the overflowing condom. "That's not possible." She creased her forehead, trying to recall what she had read on the subject, because what she had read was the sum total of her knowledge. She narrowed her eyes at him, and almost ashamed to admit how much she wanted him still, asked playfully, "Is it...?"

Jack slanted her a sexy smile, swept her into his arms and carried her over to the rumpled covers. "Maybe not this very second," he allowed with cheerful abandon, following her down onto the bed.

He reached over and turned down the bedside lamp to its lowest setting so the room was illuminated with a soft glow, then turned her gently onto her stomach and swung his body overtop hers so his knees were on either side of her and he was straddling her thighs. Keeping his weight off her, he flattened his palms against the bare skin of her back, and began a slow, heavenly massage that could have relaxed her no matter how tense she was. And she wasn't the least bit tense. Aware she had never been pampered like this, never even imagined it could happen, especially inside a marriage, Daisy groaned at the gentle kneading and caressing.

"Good?" Jack asked.

"Mmm," Daisy agreed. She had never felt anything so good in her entire life.

"Not too hard?"

"No."

"Too soft?" His fingers worked their magic on either side of her spine.

Daisy took a long, deep breath, wondering if anyone had ever climaxed from just this, because she was beginning to feel as if she would if he kept up his ministrations. "Perfect," she murmured.

"That's good. You keep right on enjoying yourself, you hear?"

"Mmm. I will." Daisy sank farther into the soft king-size mattress, her whole body feeling as if it was turning to the consistency of melting butter. And that was, of course, when the mood between them began to change once again. He left her shoulders to start on her calves. Worked slowly and patiently up to the backs of her knees. Then her thighs. Daisy's mixture of relaxation and pleasure faded completely, to be replaced by something else. Something distinctly sexual, and perhaps a little frustrating. "Jack," she moaned hungrily.

"You seem a little tense here," he noted as his fingertips worked the insides of her thighs.

"And you know why," Daisy murmured as he stroked the lower curves of her buttocks, tracing inward, until he reached the petal softness there.

"I think so." Strong hands turned her again.

He looked down at her with a sexy smile, ruggedly handsome in the soft light of the masculinely appointed bedroom. "You need a front massage, too."

"Somehow," Daisy drawled, loving the way he was still straddling her almost as much as the sight of his renewed arousal, "I had a feeling you were going to say that."

His hands started low, just above her knees. Relaxing, rubbing. Then moved higher, to the insides of her thighs again. A fierce burning started inside her, and by the time he reached the apex of her thighs, her every nerve ending was quivering, vibrating at the slightest contact. Looking as determined to make it last as he was to get her there, Jack moved past her feminine mound and gently massaged her waist. Rib cage. Shoulders.

Daisy arched as he kissed her breasts and sent a new round of pleasure ricocheting through her.

The next thing she knew, he was sliding downward and settling between her legs. She whimpered softly as he slid a finger deep between the tender folds, and then followed it with a series of light, butterfly kisses. She knew he wanted her to come, but if she did, it was going to be over too soon again and she had yet to enjoy his body the way he had just enjoyed her.

It took some doing, but she finally wiggled free of him. "My turn."

He looked at her, perplexed. "But you haven't—"

"My turn," Daisy reiterated even more deliberately. Enjoying the sight of him, naked, rumpled and aroused, she steered him onto his stomach. He chuckled, reluctantly complying, as she prepared to torture him the way he had just sensually tortured her.

Figuring he might as well give in—and pretend to let her call the shots in their relationship—for a few minutes anyway—Jack folded his arms beneath his head and let Daisy have her way with him. And what a way it was, he thought wistfully as her nimble fingers worked their way across his shoulders, down his spine, to the curve of his buttocks, and lower still, to the sensitive insides of his thighs. She knew just how to touch him, how to make him want her, and more important, give. And that was something. Jack had never wanted a woman in his life before Daisy, never imagined himself willingly sharing his bed, his home, his life. But now that Daisy was a part of his existence, he couldn't imagine a life—a night—without her. Not when she made him feel as if he knew how to love, and maybe even be loved, after all.

Daisy turned him onto his back. Stroked his shaft, bent her head and kissed the tip, then turned her attention to his chest once again, her sweet lips finding his pecs and the mat of hair and nipples. He groaned again and reached for the box on the nightstand. Daisy plucked the condom from his fingers. "Let me," she said.

She opened the packet with her teeth and pulled out the condom. After a moment's shy hesitation that was as sweet as it was comical, she was able to figure out how to open the latex sheath and roll it over his now-throbbing shaft. Figuring playtime was over, Jack wanted her beneath him. Wanted her to be his.

But once again, Daisy had her own ideas she was determined to implement. Looking beautiful and wild, vulnerable and possessive, with her wavy blond hair floating around her face and tumbling onto her shoulders, she straddled his body, took him in hand, and slowly, deliberately, lowered herself onto him. Jack moaned with a mixture of pleasure and frustration as she jerked in a shuddering breath and accepted him into her tight silky warmth a torturous half inch at a time. Able to see the depth of her arousal in her lidded eyes, he felt his need for her with every fiber of his being.

Hearts pounding in tandem, pulses racing, they moved together, slowly, awkwardly at first, then more and more expertly. Enjoying the sight of her riding him, as much as the physical act of their joining, Jack slid a hand between their bodies.

Daisy was trying to hide it, but he knew she was holding back, trying to keep some small part of her separate from him—and thought by not kissing him on the mouth she could manage it, but he wasn't going to allow the ruse. Smiling up at her with everything he felt for her in his heart, he continued watching her. Even as he found the tender nub, rubbing, stroking, making love to her by touch and physical possession until she was straining against him, whimpering with need. And still she rotated her body over his, taking the time to discover what she liked as she opened her body up to him in slow, inexorable, circular degrees, while beneath her he controlled each long, slow, deeply thrusting upward stroke. Until he was finding that spot inside her once again, the one guaranteed to send her over the edge with stunning intensity. The insides of her thighs were tightly nudging his hips, and she was arching back, gasping for breath, and she was coming exactly the way he wanted her to...so hard she was shaking and crying out... And he was following her, fast, hard, irrevocably. And this time there was no holding back, no pretending that something significant hadn't happened. Because it had, Jack thought in satisfaction. She had reached out to him in need, and he had answered her, and there was no turning back. No pretending that this marriage of theirs wasn't slowly and steadily becoming a real and viable one, after all.

CHAPTER TWENTY-ONE

"TOM, WHAT A NICE SURPRISE!" Grace said when Tom walked into the studio, where a gardening segment featuring houseplants was being set up.

Tom's son-in-law, Nick Everton, waved hello and went back to his producing duties. On the other side of the soundstage, Daisy caught sight of Tom, too, and deliberately went the other way. So much for the father-daughter unity he had tried to jump-start the previous evening, Tom thought.

"Did you come by to watch the taping?" Grace asked. To Tom's pleasure, his ex looked genuinely happy to see him. "Or," she continued, her voice dropping a notch, "has something come up I need to know about."

"The latter," Tom said, glad he could still come to Grace about family matters. "Is there somewhere we could talk?"

Grace cast a look over her shoulder and made a face. "My dressing room has been taken over by wardrobe people right now. How about we go over there?" Being careful where she walked—there seemed to be cables taped to the floor all over the place—she led the way to the dining-room set, where nothing much was happening at the moment. She leaned against the side of the table, folded her arms in front of her and crossed one ankle delicately over the other. "What's up?"

"Did Daisy tell you what happened last night?"

"No." Grace's smile was frozen on her face, but there was a new wariness in her eyes. "Why?" she asked just as softly, looking as if she, too, was braced for the worst.

Tom wished there were some way he could cushion the news, but there wasn't, so he just said it straight out. "She and Jack had dinner with me last night. The DNA results were in, and they were what we suspected."

Grace's expression remained serene as she hazarded a concerned look at Daisy. "How did she take it?"

Tom sighed, then motioned for Grace to sit. "With mixed emotions." He paused to help Grace into one of the chairs, and sat down opposite her. "Anyway, when she and Jack got home, they found their house had been broken into. Daisy caught sight of two intruders dressed in black, with ski masks pulled down over their faces. Beyond that, she couldn't give much of a description. Anyway, the only things missing pertained to Daisy's recent visit to Switzerland."

Abruptly, Grace's expression turned as somber as Tom's mood. She knew as well as he did what that could mean to both of them. If the tabloids caught wind of the real reason Tom and Grace's marriage had fallen apart years before, their divorce would become news again. Grace plucked at the crease on the knee of her buttercup-yellow tunic and slacks. "I gather no one was hurt."

"No. Thank God." Tom paused, glad Grace was taking what could be a devastating turn of events so well. "Jack called Harlan Decker in lieu of the police. Harlan thinks it was the work of amateurs who wanted only one thing. Information about Daisy."

Grace sat back in her chair, so her spine was touching

the ladder back. "Any idea who that might be?" she asked.

Shrugging, Tom did his best to appear that they were discussing something not so serious. "Jack thinks Bucky Jerome is the prime suspect. And apparently there was a woman who was hanging around the beach outside their place a few days ago, who seemed to want something from Daisy but took off before telling Daisy what. Anyway, I wanted to warn you. If it was Jerome, or some other ambitious journalist, or even the woman looking for something to blackmail Daisy with, for money, we could all have a problem on our hands. And if this leads to a leak of information, it could concern you."

"Thank you." Grace stood and straightened the hem of her tunic. "I appreciate your telling me," she said graciously.

Tom stood, too, and put the chairs back the way he'd found them. "I thought maybe the two of us should talk, come up with some strategy," he continued casually, wishing they had more time, but already Grace's producer, and their son-in-law, Nick Everton, was pointing at his watch.

"I think that's a wonderful idea, and I absolutely want to do it, but not here and not now." Grace gently grasped his arm just above the elbow, and steered him toward the soundstage exit. She leaned closer, still smiling up at him, and said, "Tell you what. I've got a full day of taping ahead of me, but I'm free this evening. Why don't you come by my place tonight around eight—" she rose on tiptoe and let her lips brush his cheek as they reached the double metal doors "—and we'll have some dinner and figure out what to do."

BUCKY HAD JUST SAT DOWN at his desk in the newsroom, when Jack Granger walked in. Steam was practically coming out the attorney's ears as he made his way toward Bucky's station. Which was odd, Bucky thought, since he hadn't written a thing about Jack's wife in oh…three days.

Jack stopped short of Bucky's desk. He looked as if he wanted to punch something. Namely, Bucky. "We need to talk." Jack pushed the words through his teeth.

No fool, Bucky kicked back in his task chair and folded his hands behind his head. "Okay. Shoot."

"Privately," Jack qualified.

Bucky preferred staying where there were lots of witnesses, until he noted his father rising from behind his desk and walking closer to the floor-to-ceiling windows that separated Adlai from the buzz in the newsroom.

Realizing if he didn't want Adlai involved he had to get Jack Granger out of the newsroom, Bucky swiftly grabbed his cell phone, pager and notepad, and led the way out of the newsroom, down the hall to the conference rooms where they interviewed people and brainstormed future articles. Finding an empty room, Bucky led the way in, switched on the overhead lights and shut the door behind them. "What's on your mind?"

"Were you at my house last night?"

Bucky tossed his stuff down on the table. "Why would I be there?"

Jack, who was half a foot taller than Bucky and outweighed him by some forty pounds, stood over Bucky. "Answer the question," he ordered him, like a bully shaking down a smaller kid for his lunch money.

Deciding sitting might be safer, Bucky pulled out a chair and sank into it. "No. I wasn't."

Jack still looked as if he wanted to throttle him. "You're sure."

"Positive. Why?" Deciding he better at least look unafraid, Bucky swiveled his chair around, leaned back and propped his feet on the edge of the table. "What happened?" he asked as he folded his hands across his lap.

Declining Bucky's pantomimed offer to take a chair, too, Jack instead folded his arms in front of him contentiously. "Someone broke in."

Now, this was news he was interested in. Bucky picked up his notepad and pen. "Any idea who it was?" Eager to get the details, he looked back up at Jack.

Jack sent Bucky a withering glare that under less compelling circumstances would have made Bucky quail. "You're at the top of the list of suspects, Jerome."

"Hey." Bucky spread his hands wide on either side of him, in exaggerated claim of his innocence. "I draw the line at breaking the law, Granger."

Jack lifted an eyebrow, not believing that for one minute.

"Okay," Bucky amended, "I draw the line at breaking the law in a way that could put me in jail. Breaking into your place would put me in jail."

Jack studied him a moment longer, then turned toward the closed conference-room door.

"What'd they take?" Bucky leaped up to keep Jack from leaving before Bucky got the necessary facts. "I'm assuming it wasn't a regular burglary or you wouldn't be here." Determined to keep him from running out on him, Bucky squinted at Jack and baited him into inadvertently revealing more. "You're not involved in anything nefarious, are you? You know, that would have one of your, uh…criminal friends enacting payback on you or something?''

Jack blinked in stunned amazement, shook his head. ''Where do you get this stuff?''

''I take it that's a no.''

''You only wish you had that story to write,'' Jack growled.

Bucky narrowed his eyes at Jack in speculation. ''So if you weren't the target, then Daisy was?''

''Why would you think Daisy was a target?'' he demanded, towering over Bucky.

''I don't know.'' Bucky shrugged and continued to watch Jack thoughtfully. ''Maybe it has something to do with the sleazy stuff Richard is involved in.''

Jack pushed Bucky back into the chair he had been sitting in and leaned over him, hands on the table. ''What sleazy stuff?''

Bucky scoffed. Jack Granger might be a corporate attorney, but he had the bad-cop routine down pat. ''You're telling me you don't know about his extracurricular activities,'' Bucky goaded.

Jack straightened slowly, looking perplexed. ''What are you talking about?''

''I gather that means Daisy doesn't know what Richard is up to, either,'' Bucky went on as if Jack hadn't spoken. ''I mean, it's not the kind of thing she would be able to keep her mouth shut about,'' Bucky speculated bluntly. ''I gotta figure, if Daisy knew, she would be complaining and carrying on about it herself. Telling her mother to take action.''

Jack had thought he was beyond the point in his life where he could be shocked—not true. Richard Templeton? Fooling around on Charlotte…and a reporter knew about it? Determined to keep the conversation on track, he passed on the opportunity to debate the truthfulness of what Bucky was claiming and instead simply demanded in the most reasonable voice he could manage, "What does any of that have to do with Daisy?"

"Maybe nothing." Bucky shrugged his shoulders. "Maybe something. All I know for sure is that Richard's paramour was at Templeton's Fine Antiques a few weeks ago, having what looked to me like a pretty tense and unpleasant conversation with Iris."

Jack clasped both hands around the back of his neck. "You think this woman is blackmailing the Templetons?"

"Maybe." Bucky tapped his pen against the notepad. "Or maybe she just wants to and is looking for something that would get her some hush money and that would be something on Daisy...."

Jack's glance narrowed. "Does this woman have a name?"

No way was Bucky giving that up. This was his story, however it unfolded. And he wasn't going to let Jack Granger ruin it. "Let's just say we have yet to be properly introduced."

Jack looked as if he didn't know whether or not to believe Bucky's avowed lack of knowledge. "What does she look like?" Jack bit out.

Bucky shrugged, figuring it wouldn't hurt to give a description that, while accurate and truthful, could also apply to thousands of women in the Greater Charleston Area. "Late thirties, early forties, auburn hair."

"And built," Jack guessed.

"Like a brick house," Bucky confirmed. Curious now because it looked as if Jack knew something, too, Bucky leaned forward eagerly. "You've seen her?"

"Maybe." His expression both stymied and concerned, Jack began to pace the conference room. He turned back to look at Bucky, watching Bucky's face carefully as he revealed matter-of-factly, "There was a woman hanging around our house a few days ago. She approached Daisy, but then took off."

Could it have been Ginger Zaring?

Bucky had to know.

"Hang on. I'll be right back." Bucky returned with a manila envelope full of black-and-white photos. "This the same woman?" he asked.

Jack swore virulently to himself as he thumbed through the lurid photographs that left no doubt Richard Templeton was cheating on his wife. "You shot these?"

"Yep," Bucky declared proudly, deciding to test Jack's knowledge by shocking the hell out of him.

"Where were they?"

"In the elementary-school library at the Protect the Children benefit."

Jack looked at Bucky as if he was sure he couldn't possibly have heard right. "The one Daisy and I were at?"

Bucky nodded affirmatively, adding, "Not to mention Charlotte and Iris."

Jack let out a stream of profanities that would have made his dockworker grandfather proud. "The SOB really likes to take risks, doesn't he?"

Bucky agreed there was no bigger horse's ass than Richard Templeton. He was glad to see Jack apparently loathed the man, too. It gave him and Bucky something in common. "Which would, of course," Bucky continued pragmatically, "make Richard Templeton a perfect target for blackmail."

Jack sighed, and handed the lewd photos back to Bucky. "Or a demand for marriage."

Bucky slid the photos back into the envelope. "You really think the woman would want to marry Richard Templeton?"

Jack shrugged. "Beats sneaking around like that, and he is rich."

Very rich, Bucky thought.

The two men were silent.

Which was probably why Ginger Zaring had approached Daisy on the beach that evening, Bucky thought. Ginger might have wanted to try and convince Daisy that Ginger and Richard were in love and should get married.

Initially, Bucky had figured Ginger was a high-class call girl, but a little sleuthing on his part had revealed that she was a devoted mother of a teenage daughter, about to head to a very expensive Ivy League school Ginger Zaring could not possibly afford on her own. And since Ginger's ex-husband had flipped out a few years before and gone to live in the wilderness or something, he couldn't be counted on to help, either, since he was willingly unemployed a great deal of the time.

One of Ginger's co-workers had told Bucky the divorce and resulting financial troubles had left Ginger bitter, and focused on only one thing—helping her beloved daughter, Alyssa, get ahead. Ginger might have figured wealthy Richard was the key.

One thing was certain. Richard was making a fool of himself with Ginger all over Charleston, to the point it was only a matter of time before Charlotte or Daisy or Iris discovered it, too, and the whole thing blew up in their faces. When that happened, Bucky still intended to be first with the scoop.

"Do you think Daisy is in danger?" Jack asked.

Bucky shrugged and did his best to look as baffled about what was going on—and why—as Daisy's husband apparently was. "You tell me—you're the lucky devil who's married to her. And while you're at it, maybe you can explain to me why your boss, Tom Deveraux, and Daisy's sister, Iris, were having a little tête-à-tête at Templeton's Fine Antiques right after closing last night. Iris looked upset during the meeting and Tom was definitely troubled when he left."

Jack blinked. "You were spying on them?"

"Observing those around me, the way any good reporter does."

Jack's expression became stony with resolve. "I don't know why Tom was talking to Iris."

"Sure about that?" Bucky was pretty certain Jack did know.

"Furthermore, it's none of my business or yours," Jack continued sternly.

Bucky tilted his head at Jack in silent speculation. "I'm sure that's what you'd like me to think, but the evidence here says otherwise. Bottom line, I've never known the Templetons and the Deveraux to be at all friendly. If they ever were, it was long before I was born. So why were Tom and Iris suddenly meeting clandestinely? What could they possibly have been talking about that was so important to both of them and upsetting, to boot? Thus far anyway, I can only come up with one explanation. You work for Tom and you're married to Iris's sister, Daisy. So the only connection between Tom and Iris is you and, by default, Daisy. So if Tom went to see Iris about something upsetting, it was likely about you and Daisy."

Jack flexed his shoulders, smoke all but coming out of his head.

"Then, of course, this tale of woe gets even stranger because if what you're telling me is accurate—" Bucky ignored the danger signs and continued theorizing bluntly "—on the heels of that meeting, your place is broken into last night."

"Which gives you more motive than anyone else, since you're the only one snooping around in our business, in hunt of a juicy story that just isn't there," Jack pointed out.

"Except," Bucky corrected, "I didn't *have* anything to do with said break-in. Because I was at three society parties and two benefits last night taking pictures and getting quotes for this morning's story. If you want to check it out, I'll give you the names and numbers of the hosts."

Jack seemed to be trying to decide if he could trust Bucky. Finally, he grimaced and said, "Look, I don't know what your plans are, Jerome, but I don't think either of us should say anything to Daisy about her father fooling around. She's had a rough time of it lately, being in the hospital and all."

Normally, Bucky would have said it was a mistake to keep anything from Daisy—she didn't like being kept in the dark. About anything. But in this case he couldn't help but agree with Jack Granger.

Whatever female problem Daisy had suffered had been rough on her. All Bucky had to do was look at her to know she was still getting over it.

"I agree," Bucky said quietly. News of the uptight Richard's debauchery would devastate Daisy and she'd already been hurt enough. So Daisy wouldn't hear it from him, Bucky promised silently. But if Richard did make that fatal misstep, got caught with his pants down and the sordid story got out, all bets were off.

JACK KNEW he had to keep Daisy away from Richard Templeton's mistress, and the first chance he got, he took steps to do just that. "You're sure it was the same woman?" Daisy asked after Jack had filled her in on the parts of his conversation with the nosy reporter that Jack thought Daisy should know. Finished with work for the day, she picked up her camera bags and headed out to the parking lot.

Jack shifted Daisy's load from her arms to his. "Bucky had a couple photos of her from a social event he was covering. There was no doubt it was the same woman."

Daisy paused as Jack opened up the back of the SUV. "And she went to see Iris at the shop."

Jack nodded, glad he had given Daisy a ride to work that morning on his way to the Deveraux-Heyward Shipping offices.

"What about?" Daisy persisted, seeming to sense something more was up than what he was currently telling her.

Jack shrugged, and revealed as much of the truth as he could while still sheltering his wife from any unnecessary ugliness. "Bucky didn't know," Jack reiterated calmly. "He just said the meeting between the two was tense. Anyway, if the woman comes near you again, I think you should stay away from her. Just let me handle her."

Daisy hopped up on the back so she was sitting in the cargo area beneath the raised hood. She looked pretty and sort of summery in a pair of cropped red slacks and a red-and-white bandanna print blouse that bared her shoulders and fell just above her navel. Her wavy blond hair had been caught up in a clasp on the back of her head to keep it out of her face while she worked. And her face and shoulders held the blush of sun because they had done part of the day's taping outdoors. Daisy clamped her hands on either side of her and swung her legs back and forth over the end of the SUV. "So what am I supposed to do if I see this mystery woman trying to approach me again, Jack—send out an SOS?"

"Yes." Jack parted her knees and stepped between her legs. He wrapped his arms around her hips and waist and tugged her closer, until the insides of her thighs were pressed against his sides, exactly the way they had been last night when they were making love. "That's exactly what you are supposed to do," Jack told her firmly but lovingly. He paused to give her a long, thorough kiss designed to make up for all the hours they had spent apart. Drawing back only because of where they were, he gently touched her face. "Because like it or not, you are now connected to Grace and the breakup of her marriage, and she's celebrity enough to be fodder for the tabloids. Information like that, along with the proof that was stolen from our place last night, could fetch a lot of money on the open market."

Jack didn't want to see any of the parties involved exposed to such devastating hurt.

"Did you tell Harlan Decker any of this?" Daisy asked.

Jack nodded calmly, even as he pushed his guilt—for keeping anything from Daisy—away. "I told him everything." Including the parts Jack had kept from Daisy. "He's going to see what he can do to figure out who this woman is.'' And he was going to do so by tailing Richard Templeton. ''But it may take a few days before we know anything.''

Hopefully, once they did get an identity on the woman, Jack would be able to take steps, legal or otherwise, to prevent this entire situation from blowing up in their faces. And protect his wife in the bargain. Because this was something Jack never wanted Daisy to know.

DAISY KNEW that although Jack was trying to play it cool, deep inside he was still edgy about the previous night's break-in. She was, too. Especially since it looked as if Bucky Jerome was not responsible for the theft of Daisy's private information.

Which was why, like it or not, she was going to have to involve her family. Connor was out of the country on business—he was in Aruba with a group of big-time investors, vacationing and trying to put together some big consortium for a new ultraluxurious resort on the Atlantic. Details of which were top secret. She didn't want to go to her father—she was not up to a lecture from him. She didn't want to upset her mother—Charlotte would worry too much if she knew Daisy and Jack had walked in on a burglary in progress. So that left Iris, who, as it turned out, was involved in this mess anyway.

''I'm going to have to tell Iris so she'll be forewarned, too,'' Daisy told Jack as she climbed into the passenger seat beside him. Daisy pulled her cell phone out of her bag and punched in a number. ''Hopefully, she hasn't already gone to a dinner party or something.''

Iris's maid, Consuela, answered on the second ring. "This is Daisy. I'm looking for my sister," Daisy said.

"She's out at Rosewood doing inventory, Daisy. She said she would be late getting home."

"How late?"

"Ten or 11:00 p.m."

"Thanks." Daisy hung up and told Jack.

"You want to go out there?" he said.

Daisy noted he didn't look particularly eager. In truth, neither was she. "I think we'd better," she said reluctantly. If the family was about to be blackmailed about Daisy's birth and Iris's pregnancy, Iris needed to be warned as soon as possible. And Daisy sensed it was a conversation best had in person. Besides, she wanted to see the look in Iris's eyes when they talked about the mysterious woman. This time Daisy wanted to know for sure that her birth mother wasn't keeping anything vital from her.

Not surprisingly, Daisy and Jack were quiet on the ride to Rosewood. As always, Daisy was loathing any foray onto the property where the single most traumatic experience of her life had occurred. But maybe it was good she was going there again, Daisy told herself firmly. Maybe if she went there enough—with Jack at her side—she would be able to desensitize herself to the sprawling estate. And finally put those nightmares about the dark and dank cellar, which Daisy knew had long since been remodeled, behind her. It was worth a try anyway, since Daisy imagined Jack was as tired of losing sleep over her bad dreams as she was.

"I'm looking for my sister, Iris," Daisy told the security guard at the gate when she arrived.

The uniformed guard gave them a welcoming smile. "Ms. Templeton-Hayes is in the main house. A wine shipment was delivered earlier today and she's doing an inventory in the wine cellar.''

Daisy was disappointed to learn that the inventory taking place was in the main house instead of the auction barns. "Great," Daisy grumbled dispiritedly after the guard waved them through.

Jack slanted her a curious look as he parked in front of the house.

"I just hate that cellar," Daisy explained. "I got locked in one of the rooms down there during a Halloween party when I was six."

Daisy drew a deep, bolstering breath. "I know it's foolish, but I'm always afraid I'm going to get locked in one of the rooms downstairs again. They supposedly completely redid the cellar a few years ago, but when I dream about it I always remember the way it was when I was a kid," Daisy said as she used her key to let them into the mansion. "It was really creepy. Kind of dark and musty and cold and it had this old mildew smell." Doing her best to shake off the unpleasant memories Daisy led the way back to the kitchen and into the huge butler's pantry. At the rear of the large room, filled with stainless-steel racks and shelves, was the door to the cellar. As Daisy neared it, a wave of nausea hit her, followed swiftly by an answering unsteadiness in her knees. Here they went again.

"You don't have to go down there if you don't want to," Jack said.

"No, I want to go." Daisy swallowed hard. She was being ridiculous. With Jack next to her, and Iris already down there, there wasn't a possibility in the world she was going to get trapped in one of the rooms. She was not going to be a baby about this. Deliberately, Daisy shook off her unease. Trembling slightly, she forced herself to go through the open door and into the brightly lit basement.

The warped splintering staircase Daisy recalled had been replaced, the concrete walls covered in the same elegant rose brick that was on the exterior of the mansion. It looked as if the concrete floor had been redone, too, and painted a pretty, dark gray, she noted as she descended the stairs. There were rows of canned goods, cleaning supplies, fresh linens on neatly arranged shelves. Beyond that, a long hall and another series of doors. As Daisy started in the direction she guessed the wine cellar was located, she felt sick again. Almost dizzy with a combination of panic and—revulsion. This time, Jack caught her arm and brought her close. Wrapping his arm around her waist, he asked again, "Are you remembering anything else?"

"No." But it was right there, playing on the edges of her memory.

Daisy gulped as footsteps came around the corner. Iris was dressed in business clothes and had a Palm-Pilot in her hand. It was clear from the look on her face she had overheard what they were saying. "What's going on?" she asked, warily.

"Daisy's been having nightmares about the time she got locked in a room down here."

Knowing she needed to sit down, Daisy groped her way to a low bench that ran along one wall and sank onto it.

Iris looked at Jack as if they were the only two grown-ups in the room, then turned back to Daisy. "Why would you be having nightmares about that now? It happened years ago."

"I don't know." Daisy was getting tired of explaining her weird behavior when it came to this place, and her fuzzy, unpleasant memories of it. She shuddered and rubbed her arms to ward off the chill that had descended upon her. "I guess getting trapped down here really scared me. And that fear is still there, buried in my psyche, or something." Because it keeps resurfacing.

"In Daisy's dream, there's a faceless, nameless person in a costume or a mask or something." Jack looked to Iris for an explanation.

Iris looked at Daisy, really concerned now. "Who is it?" she asked.

Had there been some sort of abuse, or attempted abuse? Did Iris know about it?

"I don't know," Daisy shrugged and explained how the person in her dreams kept telling her to be quiet or he'd have to hurt her. Daisy rubbed at the tension building in her temples. "It's all sort of vague and weird and scary." Although, since she had been married to Jack, the dreams had become more distinct. It was almost as if it was safe to remember now that she was married.

"Well, nothing like that happened," Iris said, looking piqued at all the talk about something that had happened so very long ago. "I was with Mother when we found you. You were absolutely hysterical, but you were also quite alone and unharmed. Mother did scold you, of course. We had a vermin problem here that October and we didn't want any of you children playing down here during the Halloween party, period. And you and the other children knew the basement was off-limits, which is why I think you probably came down here to hide, because you knew you wouldn't be found by any of the other children. And hence, would win the game."

That sounded about right, Daisy thought. She had always liked to win. Although after that episode she had never played hide-and-seek again. And never liked closed, locked, dark, cold, musty spaces, either.

"How long was Daisy down here?" Jack asked.

"I don't know." Iris shrugged. "Maybe fifteen or twenty minutes. A group of kids were playing hide-and-seek and it took that long for us to determine you were missing."

"Were any of the grown-ups in costume that evening?" Jack continued his interrogation on Daisy's behalf.

"No. Just the children. And none of them had scary masks, either. Mother forbade it. Children of that age sometimes get easily spooked, even when they know it's Halloween and everyone is wearing costumes."

No joke, Daisy thought. Feeling better, she stood and found her legs would hold her after all.

"What brought you two out here?" Iris asked.

Jack explained about the break-in, what had been taken, as the color slowly left Iris's face.

"Did Bucky Jerome have anything to do with that?" Iris asked, immediately jumping to the same initial conclusion Daisy and Jack had.

"He says not," Jack replied.

"Well, that's a relief," Iris said, sitting down on the bench Daisy had just vacated.

"Not really," Daisy put in as she paced to the wine room and back, looking around thoughtfully as she went, "since we don't know who's in possession of the information that was stolen from me. Bucky thinks the break-in may have something to do with an auburn-haired woman he saw at the shop giving you a hard time a couple of weeks ago. He thinks she might have it in for the Templetons. And Jack and I agree because the same woman was loitering outside our beach house, one evening, earlier this week.''

''She bothered you?''

''No. She left before she said anything. But the encounter gave me a weird feeling…'' Daisy paused. ''So I wondered—Jack and I both did—if you might know the woman's name, or anything about what might be ticking her off about us.''

For a second, Iris froze, then, still looking a little pale, she slowly shook her head. ''No. Although it could be a disgruntled customer, but I usually do what needs to be done to make things right if someone is unhappy, so I don't think that would be it, but I'll check my records anyway.''

''Thanks,'' Daisy said. ''We'd really like a name because then Jack and I could go talk to her.''

Iris nodded, her expression deadly serious. ''In the meantime, I'll talk to Father and ask him if he knows who might have broken into your home and stolen those documents, and then I'll alert our family attorneys to the situation—they'll know what to do. Theft and blackmail are against the law. Once people understand we're not going to be taken advantage of that way, and will in fact happily put them in jail for extortion, they'll hand over the damaging information rather than try and use it. In the meantime—'' Iris looked at Jack and Daisy steadily ''—it sounds like the two of you are really going to have to be careful.''

''Your home hasn't been broken into, then?'' Daisy asked Iris. Was it only she who attracted so much trouble?

''No. And neither has Mother and Father's,'' Iris retorted, standing once again. "But then we both have state-of-the-art security systems." Iris looked at the two of them sternly. "Really, Daisy, you and Jack should consider investing in the same."

CHAPTER TWENTY-TWO

TOM WASN'T SURE what to expect when he stopped to pick up a bottle of wine and headed over to his ex-wife's rented town house for dinner. To his relief, Grace looked serenely happy when she opened the door and ushered him into the historic home. Built with only two rooms downstairs, located right behind each other, hence the name single house, and two rooms up, the abode was luxuriously appointed and cozy, and perfect for Grace.

Instead of her signature tunic-and-slacks set, she was wearing a long hyacinth-colored skirt and matching sleeveless top in a whisper-soft fabric that clung gently to her slender, womanly curves, and made her look both very feminine and very beautiful. He inhaled the familiar scent of her Chanel N°5 as he stepped inside and handed her the bottle of wine. "We're going to be in the sitting room upstairs. I hope that's all right with you," Grace said, bypassing the more formal rooms downstairs for the coziness of the upstairs room.

"You didn't have to go to all this trouble, Grace," Tom said when he walked in and saw the table set with flowers, fine china and a sumptuous dinner for two. On an antique marble-topped buffet, there were several warmers and a salad ready to toss.

"Don't worry," Grace teased him, alluding to her

notorious lack of cooking skills. "I had our meal catered."

Tom grinned. "I wouldn't have minded if you had cooked." He would eat her burnt offerings anytime.

Grace indicated Tom should sit down on the sofa opposite the table. "Thank you, but I'm going to need a lot more practice before I subject anyone to my poor attempts again. Although, I must say," Grace continued with a smile, "the daily lessons I'm getting on my new television show are helping me understand a lot more about the culinary arts." She picked up the bottle of his favorite Pinot Noir she had already opened. "Care for a glass of wine?"

Tom nodded, touched she would have remembered that and helped himself to one of the appetizers on the coffee table in front of him. "Please."

"So, tell me about what's going on with you and Daisy now." Grace slipped off her sandals and sank down beside him on the sofa, curling her legs up under her and smoothing out her skirt. Grace's eyes were serious. "I noticed she avoided you today."

Tom sighed, knowing that was an understatement and then some. He also knew he needed to talk to someone, and there was no one who had ever understood him better than Grace. Tom helped himself to a stuffed mushroom, another of his absolute favorites. "That's probably because of the conversation we had last night. I let her know that now the DNA tests are in, and we know she's definitely my child, I am setting up a trust for her equal to that of our children. And that I want a relationship with her. Albeit one conducted under certain public and private parameters, to avoid creating a scandal."

Grace's eyes were as filled with sympathy as he had

hoped they would be. "I'm guessing Daisy wasn't happy with that arrangement?"

"No." Tom grimaced in frustration.

"She wants to be equal to our children in all respects," Grace surmised. Looking, Tom thought, surprisingly empathetic toward Daisy's feelings.

Tom sipped his wine, aware Grace needed to be apprised of the situation, even if it upset her again, as talk like this usually eventually did. He looked at Grace earnestly. "I think Daisy wants all the family secrets out in the open, but I told her that just isn't going to happen. It's going to be hard enough for her and me to repair the damage that has been done without being in the public eye at the same time. We have a lot of fence-mending to do. That won't be possible if the tabloids get involved."

To Tom's relief, Grace seemed to understand. "That must be a comfort, to finally know for certain that Daisy is your child and be able to deal with it."

It would have been a lot better had Grace been with him, Tom thought. She had so much love to give. She was such a good mother. She always knew the right thing to say and do, whereas he... He, too often, simply relied on Grace to speak for both of them, and tell their children what was in both their hearts. Aware Grace was still waiting for his reaction, Tom nodded, "It is a relief, you're right, to finally be able to deal."

Grace covered his hand with hers. "For me, too, Tom. We skirted that issue for too many years, thinking all the while we were doing what was best, but all we did was rob you of your chance to be a father to Daisy and put an unbearable strain on our marriage, trying to keep that secret. The irony, of course—" Grace let go of his hand, sat back and sipped her wine "—was that our marriage ended anyway. Probably because of the lies, as much as the actual infidelity.''

Tom regarded his ex-wife with respect. ''You seem to have come to terms with it.''

Grace's lips curved in a rueful smile. ''And I have Daisy to thank for that. Working with her, having to be around her, has been a revelation. One I wish I'd had much sooner. She's a wonderful young woman, Tom. Smart and talented. Not afraid to speak her mind or face her demons. I admire her for that.''

''So do I.'' Tom looked into his glass, his sense of personal failure increasing exponentially with every second that passed. ''I just wish I had been able to give her what she needs.''

Grace helped herself to a stuffed mushroom and handed him one, too. ''Why don't you tell everyone you're her father?''

Tom set his wineglass down on the coffee table in front of them. ''Because if I did that, it wouldn't be fair to you, Grace. Because it would unleash the hounds of hell on your tail as every tabloid reporter in the Western Hemisphere try to figure out who her mother is.'' Because then they would know who Tom's lover had been, and wouldn't that be a scandal.

Grace frowned, and looked at Tom as if her heart went out to him for the predicament he was in. ''Iris still won't claim her?'' Grace ascertained.

''No.'' Tom finished one appetizer and helped himself to another. ''She's firm on that. And I know that hurts Daisy, too.''

Grace sipped her wine, then pointed out thoughtfully, ''You and Iris may not have a choice if those documents that were stolen from Daisy are made public.''

''I know.'' Guilt filled Tom anew.

Grace shot him an imploring look. "So why not take control of the situation and tell everyone that you're Daisy's father, and she's your daughter, and you couldn't be prouder?"

Tom stared at Grace in amazement as the sentiment behind her words slowly sank in. "You'd really stand up with me and do that?"

"I'll go you one better." Grace smiled, all warm, willing woman. "I'll help *throw* the party where we announce it, although we'll have to have it at your house. My place here isn't nearly big enough. I just think we should do it soon before it's done for us."

Tom liked the way his ex thought. "What about Iris?" he asked, knowing there could still be troubled seas ahead.

Grace lifted her slender shoulders in an elegant shrug. "I suggest you tell Iris what you and I are going to do and let Iris make her own decision. It will probably eventually come out anyway. Hopefully Iris will make the right decision, but even if she doesn't, the truth will one day be known. And won't that be a relief?" Grace asked him seriously but happily. "To end all these secrets and lies? To be able to tell people what went wrong with our marriage, as well as how we plan to make it right."

"In regard to Daisy," Tom ascertained, wary of reading too much into Grace's long hoped-for change of heart. He didn't want to fool himself into thinking resolving the Daisy situation might mean a reconciliation between him and Grace, because experience had shown him time and time again that it was never that simple or easy between the two of them.

"In regard to a lot of things," Grace corrected, looking him straight in the eye, seeming, for one long moment, to be promising Tom a lot more than simple friendship.

"Now, about this party we're going to have." Oblivious to the thundering of Tom's heart and the rush of blood in his loins, Grace smiled. "It's going to take me a few days to pull everything together in terms of caterers and invitations and music and everything. So what do you say we work on the plans as soon as we finish dinner?"

CHARLOTTE WALKED into the political fund-raiser at the Mills House Hotel in downtown Charleston. The president was slated to attend in support of his party's candidate for the U.S. Senate, and everyone who was anyone in Charleston was there for the ten-thousand-dollar-a-plate predinner cocktail hour and private reception—except her husband.

No sooner had Charlotte pinned on her name tag and accepted a glass of champagne than their old friend, Peyton Heyward, approached her. Peyton had recently agreed to merge family shipping companies with Tom Deveraux. Charlotte had heard it was because Peyton had been looking to cut back his hours somewhat, as well as pass the company on to his daughter, Lauren, a real estate broker who specialized in historic properties, and had no interest in the shipping business, and Peyton's new son-in-law, Mitch Deveraux, who did.

"Charlotte, you look wonderful this evening!" Peyton kissed her cheek.

"Thank you, Peyton." Charlotte was glad someone appreciated her new sapphire-blue silk dress. Richard hadn't.

"So do you." At fifty-eight, the successful executive was in fine shape for a man his age. His blond hair was streaked with silver, his brown eyes warm and kind behind his wire-rimmed glasses.

"Where's Richard?" Peyton stepped up to the bar and bypassed champagne in favor of seltzer water with lime.

Charlotte sipped her champagne, wishing all the while her husband could be half as attentive as the widowed Peyton. "Richard stayed home this evening," she confessed regretfully. "He wasn't feeling well."

"Really?" Peyton, an avid golfer and sportsman himself, did a double take. "I saw him on the links this afternoon, and at the club afterward. He seemed fine."

Richard had looked perfectly well to Charlotte, too, when she'd gone down to his bedroom to see if he was ready to go and found him in a silk dressing gown, propped up in bed, reading. "You know how it is when you're coming down with something." Charlotte hated herself for telling the white lie, but saw no way around it. "One minute you're fine, the next you're not."

Peyton smiled at her sincerely. "Well, tell him I hope he's better soon."

"I will, Peyton. Thank you," Charlotte said as Bucky Jerome entered the dining room. Excusing herself politely, she headed over to talk to him. "Bucky, may I have a word with you?" she asked as soon as he had finished taking photos of the candidate and several party VIPs.

"Sure." Bucky, who prior to Daisy's miscarriage, anyway, had never had trouble getting along with Charlotte—only Richard—followed Charlotte willingly over to stand in a corner, next to a potted plant. "What's up, Mrs. T.?" Bucky asked casually.

Charlotte kept her eye on the crowd coming in and her voice low. She did not want their conversation to be overheard. "That blind article you wrote in your column. The prominent collector of very fine things involved in a reckless affair." Charlotte paused, aware Daisy's ex prep-school boyfriend had no reason to tell her what could be for some unlucky Charleston wife a life-altering thing. Charlotte looked Bucky straight in the eye. "Who were you talking about?"

Bucky floated a hand over his gelled black hair before narrowing his eyes at her. "Why do you need to know?"

Charlotte edged closer, aware that at five foot eight, Bucky did not tower over her intimidatingly, the way a lot of young men did these days. "I'm just curious."

Bucky regarded her with regret. "I can't tell you."

Like heck you can't, Charlotte thought, knowing Bucky well enough, and for long enough, to be able to see when he was lying. "Is it anyone I know?" Charlotte persisted.

Appearing increasingly uncomfortable, Bucky looked over his shoulder. The Secret Service were coming in, as well as several prominent members of the president's staff, which meant the president would soon follow. "Like I said, Mrs. T., it's nothing you should waste your time thinking about. You just take care of yourself, okay?" Bucky rushed off to take photos of the dignitaries, camera in hand.

Charlotte stared after him, vainly attempting to reassure herself all was well, even though her feminine instinct was telling her that was not the case.

Richard was married, a resident of Charleston and a collector of very fine things, but he would not do anything so outrageous as what Bucky had alluded to in his column. Richard would not cheat on her. As for those silver lamé thong panties she'd found in Richard's jacket—they were probably a prankish memento of a bachelor party. Just like his bowing out of the benefit tonight was of no consequence. He was simply ill.

And if he was ill, Charlotte decided, she should be home with him. Instead of here at this gala. "You're not staying for dinner?" One of the co-organizers asked as Charlotte bypassed the rest of the dignitaries still filing into the ballroom.

"No." Charlotte had only the tiniest regret she would not be there to personally greet the president during his first foray to Charleston that calendar year. "I've really got to get home to Richard. He's not feeling well."

"Give him our best."

"Thanks. I will."

It was eight-thirty when the limo pulled up in front of their home. Their driver started to get out. Charlotte held up her hand. "Thank you, Nigel," she said firmly. "I'll see myself in."

Nigel hesitated, a peculiar look on his face. "Ma'am…"

"Yes, Nigel?" Charlotte waited for any sign of duplicity on their longtime driver's part.

"Nothing," Nigel replied.

And in that instant, Charlotte knew her suspicions were very likely true. "I'm a grown woman, Nigel, and no fool. And if you wish to remain in my employ, you won't even consider picking up that phone when I step out of this car. Is that understood?"

Nigel didn't have to think long about to whom he wanted his allegiance sworn. He nodded grimly. "Yes, ma'am."

Her legs trembling slightly with the fear of what she might find, Charlotte quietly let herself inside and made her way stealthily up the back staircase. She heard the sounds first, throaty moans and Richard's crudely uttered instructions.

Heart pounding, more furious than she had ever been in her life, Charlotte walked back down the stairs and into the library. Ever so quickly and efficiently, she opened the wall safe.

Bypassing the jewels, cash and important family documents, she picked up two things. A red expanding file that had no business being there. And a small pearl-handled gun.

Walking over to the desk, she picked up the phone, punched in number one on her speed dial. When Iris answered, she said simply, "I'd like you to come here right now and meet me upstairs in your father's bedroom."

Giving Iris no chance to answer, she terminated the connection. Then punched in number two on her speed dial, called Daisy, told her the same thing, then added, "And bring your camera—and Jack."

Regretting that she could not call their son, Connor, too, to witness this momentous event in all their lives, as he was still out of the country on business, Charlotte straightened her shoulders. Her heart set on what she had to do, for all their sakes, especially Iris's and Daisy's, she headed back upstairs.

"CHARLOTTE SOUNDED really funny, Jack," Daisy said as she and Jack hurried toward his SUV.

"Did she say what was wrong?" Jack asked as he paused to open the passenger door for Daisy.

Trying hard to contain her building sense of foreboding, Daisy threw her camera bag onto the floor of the front seat and replied nervously, "No. Just that we were to meet her in Richard's bedroom at home."

It wasn't like Charlotte to be secretive in her requests, Daisy thought. She was always the first one with an explanation or rationale when she wanted one of her children to do something. But this time she had offered neither, just made a terse, implacable demand that was, upon reflection, very unlike Charlotte.

"But you're sure she's upset," Jack said.

"Oh yes," Daisy said. Very upset, as it happened.

Jack reached over to squeeze Daisy's hand. "Well, we'll find out in a few minutes what's going on," he said.

Daisy nodded. Whatever was happening, she was glad Jack was there with her. He was so strong and confident. He always seemed to know exactly what to do. And unlike her never-take-sides older brother, Connor, or her incessantly disapproving father, Jack didn't seem to mind if she leaned on him for support. Instead, Jack welcomed the chances to nurture and protect her.

Iris was just pulling up when they arrived. Unlike Daisy and Jack, who had just returned from an evening run on the beach when the call came, and were dressed in shorts and T-shirts, Iris was wearing a shimmering evening gown with a name tag still affixed to one shoulder. Her expression as perplexed and worried as theirs, Iris immediately demanded, "Do you two know what's going on here? I was supposed to meet Mother at the fund-raiser but she apparently left early—something about Father being ill."

Daisy and Jack shook their heads. That would explain why her mother was upset. But it didn't explain Charlotte's wanting Daisy to bring her camera.

More curious than ever, the trio let themselves in and

hurried up the stairs. Iris was first into Richard's bedroom. She had barely cleared the portal when she gasped loudly and said, "Oh my! *Mother, what are you doing?*"

Jack and Daisy crowded in after Iris. When Daisy and Jack saw what had Iris so upset, they both drew in quick, urgent breaths, too.

Richard was in bed with a naked woman. It was the same auburn-haired woman Daisy had seen on the beach, and she was ashen-faced, silently crying. Richard, on the other hand, merely looked peeved as all get-out to be caught with his pants down, so to speak. Charlotte was seated in a wing chair next to the fireplace, a gun clasped in her hands and pointed at the two occupants in the bed.

"Mother, you don't want to do this!" Iris said desperately.

"Everyone, stay right where you are!" Charlotte demanded shrilly. Without taking her eyes off her husband or the woman, she said very steadily, "Daisy, I want some pictures of this. I'm going to need them for the divorce."

"Charlotte, for pity's sake. You don't mean that," Richard said, looking even more annoyed as the woman beside him clung to the sheet, holding it up to her voluptuous breasts.

Charlotte smiled, looking stronger and more defiant than Daisy had ever seen her. "The hell I don't. You've humiliated me for the last time, Richard Templeton. Impotent, indeed! There was nothing nonfunctioning about what I saw when I walked in here, you lousy, cheating philanderer!"

Daisy decided her mother was right. Charlotte *did* need some pictures of this for verification. Otherwise, no one would ever believe it. With trembling hands, Daisy pulled her digital camera out of the case and began snapping away, glad the sheet covered what she had no wish to see. But the fact they were in bed together, distressed, told it all. How did the saying go? Daisy thought. One picture was worth a thousand words. And these photos said her father was one of the biggest hypocrites of all time.

Charlotte spoke to them. "Jack, Iris, Daisy, you are all witnesses to what was going on here tonight in my absence."

"They're all witnesses to the fact you are holding a gun on me!" Richard grumbled as Daisy, figuring she had enough now, checked her photos for accuracy, and finding them readable, put her camera away.

"Perfectly understandable, if you thought you had intruders," Jack said. "Still, you don't want to fire that or accidentally discharge it, and I'd feel a lot better if you handed that weapon over to me," Jack said calmly. Holding out his hand, he took one step near her.

In answer, Charlotte took the safety off. "Stay right where you are, Jack. I don't want to have to hurt you. As for the gun, I'll hand it over when I'm good and ready, and not one second before," she said.

Good for you, Mother, Daisy thought. *Good for you.*

"First, I have a few things to say and do," Charlotte continued with a stubbornness that rivaled Daisy's.

"We're listening, Mother," Daisy said quietly.

"First—" Charlotte picked up a stack of papers on her lap "—I believe these belong to you, Daisy."

Daisy stared at her birth records and beneath those the red expanding file. "Where did you get this, Mother?" she asked, amazed.

"In the library safe downstairs."

Iris glared at the woman in the bed. "You helped him break into Jack and Daisy's cottage, didn't you?"

"I didn't want to, but it was the only way I could get him to pay me the money he promised me." With a trembling lip, the woman explained about her daughter, Alyssa, and the college tuition that was due.

"I'll see you get the rest of the money you are owed for all four years," Charlotte said. "In return, I want you to tell the truth—and I mean the whole truth—about what happened between the two of you in any legal venue that I choose."

The woman looked stunned, but more than willing to agree to Charlotte's terms. "Agreed," she said emphatically.

"And," Charlotte continued, "I want you to swear to me that you will never get yourself in such a degrading and demeaning situation again."

"Believe me, I won't ever make a mistake like this again." The woman turned and glared at Richard.

"Then I suggest you get your clothes and leave," Charlotte continued coldly.

The woman slipped, naked, from the bed, grabbed her clothes and ran sobbing out the door and down the hall.

"Fool," Richard spat, sending a disgusted look at his wife. "You should have had her sign a confidentiality agreement first. Otherwise, what assurance do we have that she'll keep quiet?"

"None," Charlotte said.

"Be quiet!" the person in the mask hissed.

Daisy froze, startled at the unexpected memory.

"At the very least," Richard continued furiously, oblivious to the mystery unfolding in Daisy's head, "you should have threatened to hurt her or her daughter if she told what she saw or heard here tonight!"

"You tell anyone what you've seen and I'll be forced to come back and hurt you!"

"Oh my God," Daisy gasped out loud. She stared at her father, no longer seeing him—here—beneath the sheets, but with a mask on, his pants down around his ankles, a woman, one of the caterers, kneeling before him, his...

"Oh my God," Daisy repeated again, even more horrified, a hand to her mouth. "All those years ago! At Rosewood!" She pointed an accusing finger at her father. "It was you who locked me in the cellar. You who threatened me! You who was wearing that hideous Halloween mask!"

"Why would he have done that?" Charlotte asked, confused.

Iris looked at Daisy. And Daisy knew from the pained expression on Iris's face that Iris had experienced the same. Shock turned to dismay, grief to revulsion. "You walked in on him, too, didn't you?" Daisy asked Iris hoarsely.

Iris nodded, looking every bit as sick and miserable as Daisy felt. Tears filled Iris's eyes. "I was ten when I saw Father with a woman in the potting shed out at Rosewood."

Charlotte looked horrified. So did Jack. "You exposed our daughters to that?" Charlotte's anger became all the more lethal.

"They wouldn't have seen anything had they not been where they shouldn't have been," Richard countered coldly, not the least bit apologetic for getting caught in flagrante delicto. "Furthermore, a gentleman is entitled to his pleasure wherever, whenever, however he wants it.''

"In other words, there are whores and then there are wives. Is that what you're saying?" Charlotte asked, each word a chip of ice.

"Exactly. Although…" Richard shot dagger-filled looks at both Daisy and Iris. "From the licentious behavior of our two daughters, you'd never know the difference here.''

Charlotte's jaw tightened. Fury unlike anything Daisy had ever seen shimmered in her kind eyes.

"Mother, please, don't shoot!" Daisy rushed forward, heedless of her own safety. Jack was right behind her, pushing Daisy aside, shielding her with his body. "I don't want anything to happen to you!" Daisy cried.

"It won't," Charlotte said calmly. She sent an apologetic look at Jack, Iris and Daisy, sorry she had frightened them. "There are no bullets in this gun, Daisy," Charlotte said gently. Demonstrating the truth of her words, she put the safety back on, opened the chamber, showed them all this was so and then handed the weapon to Jack.

Aware he had been cowed by a humiliating trick, Richard swore virulently. Letting the sheet drop to his waist, he folded his arms in front of him angrily. "You're going to pay for this, Charlotte.''

Charlotte scoffed, stood. She moved to stand next to Daisy and Jack. "No, Richard, you are the one who is going to pay. Jack here is going to help me find a killer divorce attorney who'll make sure I end up with everything—the house, the business, the jewels.''

Richard chuckled nastily. "You don't believe in divorce.''

"Once upon a time, I didn't." Charlotte let Daisy

wrap a comforting arm around her waist. "But that was just one of many mistakes. For instance, I should never have allowed you to talk me into separating Iris and Daisy. I knew how important the mother-child bond was. I should have championed that above all else." Charlotte sent an apologetic look at Iris, too. "But instead, I let him convince me that we couldn't live without money. That Iris's marriage to Randolph Hayes IV was our only hope for survival. And I helped push you, Iris, to a life of marital servitude that was in many ways worse than the one I've endured all these years."

"Mother, I agreed to it," Iris interjected compassionately, coming forward to put an arm around Charlotte, too. "You didn't force me into anything."

"I didn't help you, either." Charlotte's eyes blurred with tears as she reached out and hugged both her daughters. "And I should have," she said in a low, choked tone. "I should have helped you both."

"I JUST DON'T UNDERSTAND how Father could do something like that," Daisy said as she and Jack got ready for bed a few hours later.

Jack layered toothpaste onto his brush. "A lot of people have affairs, Daisy."

Daisy sat down on the rim of the tub and smoothed lotion onto her legs. "Would you?"

"Cheat on you?" Jack's eyes followed the caressing motions of her hands as she worked the soothing cream from ankle to upper thigh. "No. Never." His glance returned to her face. "What about you?"

"No." In fact, Daisy couldn't imagine ever making love with anyone but Jack, now that they'd been together. And it had as much to do with how she felt about him, as it did that they were married, and hence, had promised each other to be physically intimate with only each other as long as that lasted. Because she not only cared about him, she felt connected to him in some fundamental way. It wasn't a tie she wanted to end. To the point, she had begun to think about asking him if maybe, just maybe, he might want to try and have another baby together.

But that was neither here nor there now, she thought, given the rather messy and difficult family circumstances they found themselves in. Because like it or not, Daisy thought, Jack was now—by virtue of his marriage to her—going to be embroiled in a lot of nasty talk about the Templetons, and their sudden and surprising divorce, too.

Silence fell between them as Jack brushed his teeth, rinsed, spit.

Once again, Daisy's thoughts turned to the traumatic revelations of the evening, and her father's part in it. For the life of her, she could not understand how Richard could have behaved the way he had. "I still can't get over it, Jack," she said as she recapped the lotion. "How could my father have taken that woman home, to his bed, while Mother was out?"

Jack blotted his lips on the towel. "I agree it was lousy."

But, Daisy thought, it had given her mother—indeed all of them—the wakeup call they needed to finally see the light about Richard and his selfishness. She understood now why she had never liked or trusted or respected him, why she had been unable to earn his love. Because the simple truth was, her father was not capable of love. The only person he loved or cared about was himself. Knowing that freed and relieved Daisy in some fundamental way. Because she knew now, bottom line, it wasn't her, it was him. Richard was the one who was flawed and unlovable. Not her.

"What I don't understand," Jack said, a protective note coming into his voice as the two of them walked into the bedroom together, "is how Richard could have locked you in that room and frightened you so."

Daisy shrugged as she slipped off the short pink and white–striped kimono robe, and climbed into bed, clad in just a white camisole and coordinating pink tap pants. She sat up against the pillows, drew her knees up to her chest and clasped her arms around them. "He wanted to finish what he'd started with that caterer," Daisy said, resting her chin on her upraised knees. Now that her memory of that awful evening was finally coming back, she couldn't seem to shut out the torrid sounds and pictures. She closed her eyes against the onslaught of awful memories. "I heard them, Jack," she told him miserably. "He was moaning." She'd thought he was in awful pain. And she had never understood. Never gotten over the shock of her first sight of the male anatomy.

Jack climbed into bed beside her and sat up against the pillows, propped against the headboard, too. "And you never realized it was him until tonight?"

Daisy was quiet, thinking as she curled her bare toes into the coverlet. "I think maybe deep down I always knew, but I was so young—six—and he had frightened me terribly and it just seemed safer to think it was all a figment of my hysterical imagination, especially since that's what Mother and Iris thought." Daisy paused as she turned to look at Jack. "I know I wouldn't have wanted Mother to be hurt. Because despite the cold, disapproving way my father always treated me, my mother always loved me and did her best to try and protect me.''

"As did Iris," Jack interjected, reaching over to rub her back.

Daisy moved into Jack's arms. She wrapped her arms around his waist and laid her head against his chest. "I've found out in the past few months that Iris's life was harder, more lacking in love, than I had ever imagined.''

Jack continued rubbing her back with soothing motions. "Iris seems to have landed on her feet.''

Daisy acknowledged that was so with a rueful smile. "Probably better than I would have.''

Jack slid a hand beneath her chin and lifted her face to his. "Don't sell yourself short, Daisy. You're every bit the strong woman your mother and sister are, in your own right.''

Daisy warmed at his praise even as she struggled to come to grips with all that had been revealed. "Then why do I feel so disillusioned, in despair?'' she asked him softly.

Jack shrugged his bare shoulders ineffectually and told her matter-of-factly, "People surprise you. And disappoint you. It's just the way life is. A lot happened tonight,'' he soothed her gently when he saw she was still troubled. "It's going to take you a few days to absorb it all, but then you'll be okay, as will your mother and your sister, and even your father.''

Daisy rubbed her hand across the satiny-smooth muscles of his chest. She loved the way he felt, so strong and warm. She loved the way he conducted himself, so tough and tender and capable. "You can really be that pragmatic about it?'' She searched his face.

Jack tangled his hands in her hair and tenderly

stroked the length of it. "I lost my naiveté a long time ago, Daisy," he admitted honestly, looking deep into her eyes. "I'm not sure, given the way I grew up, that there ever was a time when I was able to be innocent and hopeful and pure of heart as you probably were at one point. But in certain ways, my cynicism about the murkiness of life has served me well, because it's enabled me to appreciate the good things that do come along."

Daisy smiled, able to see where this was heading. "Good things like what?" she teased.

"Like you," Jack whispered, and lowered his lips to hers. He kissed her sweetly, evocatively. "You're the best thing that ever happened to me, Daisy. And don't you ever forget it."

A whisper of longing threaded through her. Followed swiftly by a wave of lingering disillusionment and disappointment. She so did not want to follow in Charlotte's and Iris's footsteps and make a fool of herself over a man by believing and seeing what she wanted and needed to believe rather than what was really true. "You're just saying that because you want to make me feel better after everything that happened," she baited, only half teasing, as she waited to see what his reaction would be.

Jack's eyes darkened to pure liquid gold. "I'm saying it because I'm in love with you, Daisy."

Daisy caught her breath at the raw emotion in his low tone. "Don't say that unless you mean it, Jack," she warned, tears suddenly blurring her eyes as myriad feelings welled up inside her. To date, everyone close to her had betrayed her in some way or another. She couldn't bear it if Jack deceived her, too. Or worse, was just saying and doing this to fulfill what he saw as his duty after the devastating evening she'd had.

"I mean it," Jack reiterated gruffly, his arms tightening around her. "And one of these days, Daisy Granger, you're going to say it and mean it, too."

The next thing Daisy knew, she was lying beneath him, sideways on the bed, on top of the covers instead of beneath.

He kissed her temple, her cheek, the slope of her neck. "I'm so sorry for everything you've been through," he whispered in a voice thick with emotion. "If I could, I'd erase it all and give you the happy childhood you deserved."

But he couldn't do that for her, any more than Daisy could erase the unhappiness of his youth, so they concentrated on the present instead, loving each other slowly and patiently. Passionately. And without reservation. Until Daisy accepted Jack, not just as her husband, but as the love of her life, until she realized just how lost she had been without him.

Afterward, Jack held her close. "I love you, Daisy," he whispered in her ear.

Her heart filling with tenderness, Daisy snuggled closer. She knew he wanted her to say it back. And she wanted to be able to, but she couldn't. Not yet. Not until she knew for certain that this—like the baby they'd made together and loved for just five short weeks—wasn't going to be taken away from her, too.

WHEN THE PLANS for the party, announcing Daisy as his daughter, were complete, Tom stood. "It's late, Grace," he told his ex-wife with obvious reluctance. "I should be going."

"I know." And yet, even though it was past midnight and she had a long day of taping ahead of her, Grace made no move to show him out.

Tom gave her a slow smile, reminiscent of their first, heady days together. "I don't want to leave, either," he said with a commiserating smile.

Grace knew that, too. She felt the same way. This evening had been like going back in time, to everything good they had ever had in their lives. It had made her realize all over again how very much she cared about Tom. How much she loved him, and always would. And it had made her question whether she really wanted to go on without him, and the answer was a resounding no.

He was the only man she had ever wanted. The only man who had ever made her want to share her life with him. And she knew, more than ever before, that her ex-husband felt the same way, too. It was in his eyes every time he looked at her, in every fleeting touch, every avoided touch.

Which left only one solution to their problem, Grace knew.

Grace took a deep breath. "So don't go," she told Tom softly, seriously. "Stay."

CHAPTER TWENTY-THREE

GRACE AND TOM STOOD for a long moment, not speaking, just looking into each other's eyes. "If I stay here any longer tonight, Grace," Tom said finally, taking both her hands in his, "I'm going to make love to you."

A tremor of anticipation swept through Grace, along with the familiar uncertainty. As she gazed up into his eyes, she was struck by the intensity of his expression. He seemed to want to join not just their bodies this time, but their hearts and souls and lives in a way they hadn't when they had been married. Grace swallowed, even as she melted into the tenderness of his touch, knowing she had to be honest with him about her fears as well as her desire. "That's what scares me," she said, looking deep into his eyes, "because that's where our problems started." And she didn't want to fail him again.

Tom's expression remained concerned.

In the past, Grace had readily accepted defeat when it came to sex. In the beginning, of course, she had tried to enjoy herself in the marriage bed, but when she had been unable to get past the mixed messages in her head, that her mother had repeated often to her in her youth—that told her sex for pleasure was wrong versus the ones that said it was her wifely duty to please her husband—Grace had given up trying to be something she wasn't and had simply faked it. She'd thought, at the time, she was doing her husband a favor. In retrospect, she realized she had done them both a grave disservice in keeping her hang-ups secret from him. Because he had sensed something was wrong anyway, and ended up suffering, too.

Now, having spent so many years alone, having wasted so many years away from Tom, the only man she had or would ever love, Grace was not willing to continue on the same path. She looked up at him shyly, knowing this was going to be one of the most challenging things she ever had to do. "But maybe it doesn't have to be that way," Grace continued hopefully, willing to make herself truly vulnerable to her husband at long last.

The regret on her ex-husband's face faded. "Maybe if we just start fresh?" Tom suggested huskily. "See what happens?"

Grace nodded, knowing if they were patient with each other, if they were honest about what they were feeling or not feeling, this was something that likely could be overcome. "That's what I want more than anything," she told him softly.

Tom smiled, all the tenderness he had ever felt for her in his eyes. He leaned forward and brushed his lips against her temple. "Sounds good to me, too."

Grace's heart raced as she thought of the momentous occasion ahead. In many ways, this was even more nerve-racking than her wedding night had been. "Can you give me a few minutes to change?" she said.

"Sure." Tom smiled. "Want me to fix you a drink?"

Grace nodded. They'd finished a bottle of wine much earlier, but the coffee and hours of working on the party had long since dissipated any of the relaxing effects.

And right now she needed to relax just a little bit. "There's some champagne downstairs in the fridge."

He laced his arm around her shoulders and kissed her temple. "I'll take it from here. And Grace—" he paused to kiss her again, slowly and lingeringly "—take all the time you need. We've got all night."

Grace glided across the hall to the bedroom, her heart racing, while Tom headed downstairs to the kitchen. She could hardly believe she was doing this. Hardly believe that the reconciliation she had wanted deep in her heart, but never expected to have, was finally happening.

What do you wear, Grace wondered as she riffled through the clothes, *when you finally realize what you want more than anything in this world is to please your man?* Grace knew what Tom needed, what he had always needed—someone sexy and appealing and sophisticated and smart and at ease in his monied world. Grace had, in the course of her network television job, become sophisticated and at ease in the world of privilege and money. She had always been smart. She had never ever been sexy. She was the mom next door. That was how the network execs and marketing gurus had always described her. That's why women liked and trusted her, and men could be persuaded to listen to her, even when she had been interviewing heads of state, economists and politicians.

But no one had ever turned to Grace for advice on how to catch or keep a man. Because the truth was she had no clue. Which left her in a quandary. Because she wanted Tom back. And not just for tonight. She wanted to remarry him. She didn't know how or when exactly she had come to that decision, she only knew it was true.

Getting fired had been the worst thing that had ever happened to her, and it had been the best. Because it had made her stop and reassess her life and decide what was important to her, and what wasn't, and in what order. She knew now her priority was home and family. Work played a part, of course, it would always play a part. She liked being connected to the outside world, doing good, bringing information to people in a pleasing down-home sort of way. But most important to her was the love of her children, and Tom. Which was why she had to get him back.

But how did she do that? How did she make him want to do more than simply sleep with her again? Grace wondered as she debated the merits of wearing a brand-new black lace negligée or the cotton pajamas she had favored when she had been his wife. How did she get and keep Tom's attention in that strictly man-woman way?

TOM HAD JUST BROUGHT the ice bucket of champagne and two crystal flutes up to the second-floor sitting room, when Grace emerged from the bedroom across the hall. She was wearing a lacy black negligée and matching robe and a pair of satin mules, and she had never looked lovelier in her life.

The blood rushed to Tom's groin and he wondered how he was going to be able to keep a lid on his desire long enough for Grace, who had never been at ease in the bedroom, to feel comfortable climbing into bed with him again. Deciding to take his seduction of her as slow as possible, Tom poured them each a flute of champagne. "To us." They touched glasses and sipped. And Tom wanted her all over again. Wanted her desperately.

But Grace was already trembling, and not, he noticed in frustration, from desire.

"What's wrong?" he asked quietly, worried now that they were at the moment of truth, that things were going to go bust all over again.

Grace gulped as all the color left her face, and she looked as if she might faint if she didn't get ahold of herself soon. "I'm afraid I can't do this."

Tom's heart hammered in his chest as he braced himself for the rejection he was sure was coming. "Sleep with me?"

Grace's lower lip trembled as she replied in a low, hoarse voice, "Please you."

Tom blinked as the meaning of her words slowly sank in. "Why would you ever think that?" he asked, stunned. No woman had ever turned him on the way Grace did, or ever would. He loved everything about her, from her soft, slender curves, to her pretty woman-next-door looks.

"Because I never…really liked…" Grace flushed as she attempted to get the words out of her throat.

"Making love with me?" Tom guessed.

Grace drew a trembling breath, nodding. "Making love, period." Reluctantly but deliberately, she lifted her eyes to his. "And that wasn't right, but…I couldn't…Tom…every time we… I kept hearing my mother's voice, saying that lovemaking was for one reason and one reason only…for making babies. And when we were doing that, when we were trying to have another baby, well, it was okay."

"But not really pleasurable," Tom guessed, thinking of all the times she had faked it with what he was just now realizing had obviously been—for her—an Academy Award–winning performance. And later still, all the times when, unable to perpetuate the lie anymore, she had simply turned away from him. He had thought it had been disinterest on her part, but instead, she was telling him, it had been shame that had made her resist his bedroom overtures. "Oh, Grace," Tom said softly, understanding at long last what the problem really was. "You should have told me."

Tom could tell by the way she was looking at him that Grace hadn't wanted to hurt him—and she still didn't. But she also knew, as did he, that they would never get back together unless they were brave enough to be completely honest with each other about their needs, wants and expectations. "The problem wasn't you, it was me." Grace stumbled through the rest of her confession, tears glimmering in her eyes. "And it still is because I've never once climaxed in my whole life. I have to face it, Tom, as much as it pains me to admit it—I'm frigid."

Tom set his glass down. At last, he thought, something they could fix. "How do you know?" he asked patiently, more than willing to put this at the very top of his To Do list.

It was Grace's turn to blink and look completely flummoxed. "What?"

"How do you know if you don't try?" Tom asked, smiling, as he realized truth was what had been missing in their marriage bed, not love. And with love, anything and everything was possible. He took Grace in his arms and cuddled her close to him. "I meant what I said earlier, Grace," he murmured, running his fingers through her hair, kissing her temple, her cheek, before returning with unhurried pleasure to her lips. "We have all the time in the world. And tonight we're going to take it."

"MY RULES TONIGHT," Tom said as he led her into the bedroom beyond, and up onto the four-poster bed.

Grace had never seen Tom looking so sexy or determined as he did at that minute, not even on their wedding night. It was also the first time in a long time that he had approached their coupling without the expectation of mutual disappointment and a less than stellar ending. The combination of his confidence and patience were like a balm to her wounded soul. She felt as if an albatross had been lifted from her, a very necessary permission granted, and she smiled at him willingly. "And those are?" she responded in the same gently teasing manner.

Tom removed his tie and dropped it over the back of the chaise lounge. "For every sip of champagne we take, we have to spend five minutes kissing. And we don't stop until we empty the bottle."

Grace eyed the magnum, already anticipating more of Tom's delectable kisses. "That really is going to take all night."

"Exactly," Tom quipped happily as he unbuttoned his light-blue oxford-cloth shirt and stripped it off, "my point."

Mouth dry, Grace watched as Tom's slacks, socks and shorts went the way of his suit. At ease in his nakedness as she had always wanted to be, he turned down the covers and slipped beneath the sheets.

"What if I decide I want to do more than kiss?" Grace challenged playfully as she, too, slipped beneath the sheets, beginning to relax now that the secret was out, and Tom had taken the truth in stride and decided to help her rather than turn away from her permanently.

"Then we'll have to see," Tom determined with a lazy shrug of his broad, muscular shoulders.

"See what?" Grace asked, her nipples beading beneath the lace of her negligée. She had never had trouble responding to Tom's initial kisses or becoming aroused—she just had never been able to get beyond the tingling state. Never known anything in the aftermath of lovemaking but frustration, contempt for herself and her own inability to respond completely.

Tom traced his fingertip along the plunging vee of her bodice, lightly caressing the swell of her breasts and the hollow in between. "Just how patient you can be."

Her heart thudded against her ribs as he cupped her shoulders and came closer still. His lips tugged at her earlobe and played at the corner of her mouth as he turned her, ever so gently, onto her side. Then adjusted the pillows so their faces were aligned with maximum comfort. "You've got to help me out here," he murmured as he fit his lips over hers, lightly tracing her lips with just the tip of his tongue. Aware she wanted, needed more, Grace slid closer and wreathed her arms around his neck. His lips were soft and warm, and accepting his invitation, she plunged her tongue into his mouth, too. Their tongues swirled together in a dance that was more erotic and emotionally satisfying than anything Grace had ever experienced. And she kissed him back, her body burning with everything that had been missing for her, everything she had always wanted but never felt was within her reach. And still he kissed her, gently tantalizing, taking full possession of everything she offered him, slanting his mouth across her, deepening the kiss, until her heart pounded in her chest. And she wanted...she wanted...

"Tom?"

"Hmm?"

"I want you to touch me."

He pushed the flimsy bodice of her negligée aside and traced her nipple with his thumb. Ribbons of heat swept through her, accompanied by a new restlessness unlike anything she had ever felt. She kissed him again, abandoning herself to the taste of champagne and man and the unique flavor that was him, until she was gripping his shoulders and surging against the hand on her breasts. Chuckling softly, he bent to take her in his mouth. "I think you're getting the hang of this." The gentle suction of his lips and tongue made her simultaneously want to ask him to stop and beg him to continue loving her like this forever.

"Tom?" She stroked the width of his shoulders, the hardness of his chest muscles.

"Hmm?" He kissed his way up the slope of her neck and recaptured her lips again. Slowly, sensually.

When she could breathe again, Grace kissed the back of his knuckles, looked into his eyes. "I want you to touch me there, too."

Tom smiled as he lifted the hem of her negligée and rubbed his palm across the gentle slope of her abdomen. "Like this?" He inched toward the nest of curls.

Grace hesitated.

He covered his fingers with hers, looked deep into her eyes. "Show me, sweetheart, show me what feels good."

Emboldened by the love and tenderness in his eyes, Grace did. Until warmth flowed through every inch of her body, a peculiar weakness stole through her limbs, and deep inside, a strange urgency built. She moved against his hands restlessly as the dampness flowed between her thighs. Without warning, she was tingling all over in a way she had never tingled before.

"I'm ready," she said, unable to keep her hips from moving.

"I don't think so." Tom chuckled again and slid lower still.

Grace gasped as he kissed the inside of first one knee, then the other. They had never indulged in this kind of love play. She had never permitted it. "Tom—"

Tom rested his face against her thigh, lifted her hips and spread her legs to allow him better access. "Let me love you, Grace. Let me love you the way I've always wanted to love you."

Aware they were really headed toward uncharted territory, Grace shut her eyes, trembling all the harder. More from nerves now than desire. And then Tom's lips were on her skin once again, caressing. Frantic at the out-of-control way she was beginning to feel, she gripped his shoulders, intending to push him away, but he caught her wrists and anchored them against the mattress on either side of her, increasing her vulnerability tenfold. Grace tensed, not knowing what to expect, and then his tongue flicked over her, every caress of his lips exciting her all the more. "Oh, Tom," she whispered, no longer knowing if she wanted him to stop or go on, only knowing that the pressure inside her was building, heating, and she was moving beneath him as she opened herself up to him. Needing, wanting, pleading.

To her dismay, he refused to be hurried. The hardness of his shaft pressing against the inside of her leg, he aroused her body by slow inexorable degrees, until both their bodies were slick with sweat, and she was rocking against him uncontrollably, feeling as if she would die if he didn't complete their lovemaking. "Please, Tom," Grace whispered. "Please don't make me wait." She wanted to feel him deep inside her. She wanted them joined together in the most intimate way possible.

"I don't want you to wait," he whispered back, slipping his finger deep inside her as he stroked the pearl hidden in the tender petals with his tongue, making her twist and writhe beneath him. Grace's heart filled with love as she met his passion unreservedly for the first time in her life. Barriers came down. Pleasure built, and then she was rocketing past the edge of control, into sweet, sweet oblivion. The impact of her release rocking her to her soul. As if from a great distance, Grace heard Tom's low mutter of satisfaction mingle with her whimpered incoherent cries, and then he was loosening his hold on her wrists, and sliding up the length of her body. Lifting her hips, and surging, hard and hot and commanding, inside. Taking her, pleasuring her, once again, until the world fell away, and it was just the two of them, this moment, this place, and the love they could no longer, would never again, deny. Loving and wanting Tom more than she had ever loved anyone in her life, Grace lifted herself high to receive him, and then he, too, was flying, taking her with him, sweetly, securely. And for the first time in years, Grace knew everything really was going to be all right.

BUCKY JEROME WALKED INTO his father's office, wondering what Adlai was summoning him about this time. As far as he knew, he hadn't done anything objectionable. Yesterday or today, anyway.

Adlai frowned at Bucky and motioned him to a seat. "I just got off the phone with Tom Deveraux."

Bucky dropped into a chair and let his hips slide all the way to the end of it. He frowned back at his father, wondering when these dressing-down sessions were ever going to end. "I didn't *do* anything," Bucky said.

"I know that," Adlai interrupted in exasperation. "This time I called you in here for a good reason."

Bucky let his rebellious scowl fade. "Oh."

"Tom and Grace Deveraux are throwing a black-tie party at Tom's house this evening. They are planning to make a big announcement and they specifically asked that you be there, covering it for the newspaper. They'd like whatever it is to be mentioned in your column tomorrow, along with a picture, if possible."

So now he was a puppet on a string. Or a reporter getting handed a scoop. Bucky decided to think of it as the latter. "Did they say what they're announcing?" he asked his father curiously.

"No." Adlai continued sifting through a pink stack of messages. "But I have the feeling it's important. Tom sounded both happy and serious."

Bucky rubbed his jaw speculatively, wishing he'd thought to delay his shave until tonight. Now he'd have to do it twice. And wear a tux. "You think those two are getting married again?" Bucky asked his father, trying to see if Adlai was holding out on him or really had no clue. "They've been seen around the city, holding hands and kissing, the past couple of days."

"He didn't say." Adlai shrugged, not that interested. "You got any problem being there tonight?" He looked at Bucky speculatively.

"No. None at all." Bucky started to exit the office.

"Bucky—"

Bucky turned.

"The item about the Templetons this morning, about Charlotte Templeton filing for divorce from her husband, Richard? That was a pretty big scoop."

Bucky shoved his hands in his pockets and tried to act nonchalant about it. Inside, however, he was beaming. Praise from his father was rare. Bucky looked his father in the eye. "Everyone knows about it. Charlotte kicked Richard out of their home day before yesterday. She brought in movers to clear out everything from his personal suite of rooms."

Adlai took a second to think about that. "You didn't say why they're divorcing."

"Mrs. T. caught Mr. T. with his pants down, so to speak, on the property. Apparently, there are pictures." Bucky removed a hand from his pocket and gestured offhandedly. "At least that's what the rumor mill is saying."

"None of that is in your column."

Bucky knew what his father was thinking by the look on Adlai's face. Here was the paternal criticism he had expected. "I'm not going soft," he declared.

"Then why didn't you allude to Richard Templeton's indiscretion in your 'Around the City' column?"

Because it would have hurt Daisy, Bucky thought, and he didn't want to inflict any pain on Daisy. He figured her parents' divorce and humiliation had to be bad enough. But not about to tell his own father that, he merely shrugged. "Just trying to shield the newspaper from any defamation claims."

"Right," Adlai retorted dryly, clearly not believing that for one second.

"Besides, Richard Templeton isn't even in the area anymore. Apparently, he was barred from their country estate, Rosewood, too—so he's gone off to Europe to lick his wounds. And you know what they say, out of sight, out of mind."

Adlai set the messages on his desk. "You wouldn't happen to still be sweet on Daisy, would you?"

Bucky put both his hands over the back of the chair and braced his weight on it. "There'd be no point in that, either, since Daisy has already found her man."

"Her husband, Jack," Adlai guessed thoughtfully.

Bucky nodded.

Briefly, compassion showed in Adlai's eyes. "When that marriage was announced, I wouldn't have given a plug nickel for it," Adlai remarked.

Bucky wouldn't have, either. Which just went to show how much he knew.

"IS IT MY IMAGINATION, or are Grace and Tom glowing?" Daisy asked as she and Jack arrived at Tom Deveraux's mansion for the party in her honor.

Jack hazarded a glance at Grace and Tom, who were busy consulting with Theresa and the catering company. Grace was in a pretty sea-foam-green evening gown and Tom was wearing a black Armani tux. They were standing side by side, and although they weren't holding hands, they might as well have been, for all the intimacy flowing between them. "They're definitely glowing," Jack said. In fact, he had never seen his boss looking so happy in all the years he had known him.

"You think they're in love again?" Daisy asked hopefully.

Jack grinned. "I know I am." Unable to keep his hands off his woman a moment longer, he steered Daisy into the closest room—which happened to be Tom's study. He took the purse from her hand, tossed it onto the sofa, then tugged Daisy toward him, positioned her intimately against him and delivered a heart-stealing kiss that left them both breathless.

"Much more of that and we'll never make it through the party," Daisy whispered emotionally.

"And we can't have that, not given the announcement Tom and Grace are going to make tonight," Jack murmured, wrapping his arms around her all the tighter. He held Daisy against him, loving her softness and her warmth. He still couldn't believe she was all his.

"I keep wanting to pinch myself, to prove this is really happening," Daisy murmured as she rested her cheek on his chest. When Tom and Grace had called to tell Daisy of their plans, she had been first flabbergasted, and then moved to tears, by the ex-spouses' bravery.

"Believe it," Jack said, glad Grace had finally seen Daisy for the wonderful person she was, and that Tom was finally doing the right thing by Daisy in claiming her publicly as his child. Figuring both things were worth celebrating, Jack slipped a hand beneath Daisy's chin, lifted her face to his and bent his head to kiss her once again.

The sound of a masculine throat clearing had them moving apart. "Sorry to interrupt," Tom said, smiling warmly at them both, "but Daisy, you're needed in the sunroom. Nick and Grace want to talk to you. Something about a change in the show's taping schedule."

"Okay."

Daisy gave Jack's hand a squeeze, then, leaving Tom and Jack alone in Tom's study, she went off to find Grace and Nick.

Tom waited until Daisy had left before turning to Jack. "I'd like to have a word alone with you, too." He gestured for Jack to sit down in a chair in front of his desk. "First, I want to tell you how pleased I am by everything you've done for Daisy," Tom said quietly.

Happy to have Tom treating him like a member of the family instead of a simple employee and trusted friend, Jack replied sincerely, "I care about her."

"I can see that." Tom gave Jack a satisfied glance and leaned back in his chair. He rubbed the back of his neck, looking sheepish. "Which makes me feel all the worse about what I did."

Jack frowned. "I don't know what you mean."

Tom shook his head, sighed his regret, then continued candidly, "I should never have sent you after Daisy the night she got back from Switzerland, when she left here all upset."

Jack hadn't minded that, and in fact would have gone after Daisy in any case, to make sure she was all right, even if Tom hadn't instructed him to do just that.

"And I certainly shouldn't have pressured you to make things right after the two of you spent the night together," Tom continued even more regretfully.

"I would have done that anyway," Jack said firmly.

"Because of her pregnancy," Tom guessed, looking at Jack with new respect.

"And because I take responsibility for my actions," Jack confirmed, still feeling damn guilty about that. "I never should have slept with Daisy that night. I knew it then. I know it now." As her father, Tom had had every right to punch Jack out for that.

"But the point is, you two did become intimate that night, Jack, and then Daisy got pregnant and lost the baby. That could have been the end of your relationship with her. My point is that I had no right getting you involved in my personal problems regarding Daisy, or later, getting involved in your private life by asking you to remain married to Daisy after the miscarriage, Jack. And for that, I'm very sorry.''

"Things have turned out all right." He didn't like the new defensive note in his voice.

"It seems so," Tom said happily, then paused a long, telling moment. He leaned forward across his desk and continued meaningfully, "I just want you to know I'm grateful for all you've done, Jack. And from here on out," Tom continued firmly, "whatever you need, you just name it."

"HAVE YOU SEEN DAISY?" Jack asked Mitch. Almost an hour had passed since she had left him and Tom and gone off to talk with Grace and Nick. The Deveraux mansion, formerly quiet, was now filled to overflowing with guests. And Tom and Grace were getting ready to make their big announcement.

"She's around. She's been flitting from room to room talking to guests as they arrive," Mitch said. He looked at Jack closely. "Did you two have a fight or something?"

"No," Jack said uneasily, wondering if Tom and Grace's second-oldest son knew something he didn't. "Why?"

Mitch shrugged, and ever the tactful business executive, said, "She seemed kind of—I don't know—agitated when Lauren and I came in. Maybe she's just worried about the announcement, you know, how it will be received, how Bucky Jerome will write it up."

"I think Bucky will do right by her," Jack predicted, spying Daisy, who looked more beautiful than ever in a pale-tangerine halter dress, gliding in through the doors from the garden, as white-coated waiters brought around trays of champagne, and Tom and Grace headed for the staircase at the front of the house.

"Bucky didn't at first," Amy pointed out, joining her brother Mitch.

"Things have changed," Jack murmured. Thanks in no small part to his dealings with Daisy, Bucky had found he had a heart in there, after all. And so had Jack.

Tom nodded at Jack, then Daisy, signaling Jack he wanted the two of them together when Tom and Grace made their announcement. Charlotte and Iris Templeton, looking as confident as only old money Charlestonians could, joined Grace and Tom on the sweeping front staircase. Jack took Daisy's hand and led her to the stairs, too, as the people gathered there with them circled around down below.

Tom lifted a palm, asking for silence, and then waited until he had everyone's attention. "Grace and I have asked you here tonight because we have something we would like you all to know."

Jack was relieved to see Grace reach over and squeeze his hand, demonstrating her support of her ex-husband and current love.

"There's no easy way to stay this, so I'm going to say it straight out," Tom continued soberly. "Years ago I made a mistake that eventually cost me my marriage to Grace. But there's a saying that out of everything bad comes something good. And that has never been more true than in this case. I want you all to know that I have a daughter with Iris Templeton-Hayes. And that daughter is Daisy Templeton."

A gasp of surprise went through the crowd as Bucky Jerome stood in the foreground taking photos for the *Charleston Herald*.

Iris stepped up in a way that Jack never thought she

would. "I kept this news a secret from everyone except my mother and father for years, thinking that it was the best way to shield Daisy from the pain of my foolish indiscretion. But of course it wasn't, because Daisy deserves to know her father, just as Tom deserves to know his daughter."

Iris looked at Daisy, her eyes shining with love and thanks for the forgiveness that had since been afforded her. "I want that to happen as much as they do," Iris continued gently, "so I would ask that you all lift your glasses and join us in a toast acknowledging our beloved daughter, Daisy."

"Hear, hear," the stunned crowd murmured in unison as they sipped champagne in Daisy's honor.

"And I have an important announcement, too," Daisy said with a brittle smile, removing her hand from Jack's and stepping away from him.

She turned to Jack, a mixture of hurt and betrayal flashing in her Deveraux-blue eyes. "It seems tonight is a night for surprises," Daisy continued in that excessively cordial voice Jack had learned long ago to distrust. It was the voice that usually signaled Daisy about to do some major acting out.

"For instance, I just found out that my husband, Jack, here, only married me because my birth father, Tom Deveraux, pressured him to do so," Daisy stated in a crisp, deeply apologetic voice. "And Jack, being an employee of Deveraux-Heyward Shipping, could hardly say no to his boss's outrageously antiquated demands. Not if he wanted to be a member of this family, anyway. So," Daisy concluded, her face a polite, blank mask as she turned to face Jack once again, "I am here tonight to tell all of you that Jack and I are getting a divorce."

CHAPTER TWENTY-FOUR

JACK CAUGHT UP with Daisy as she reached the rear of the house. He clamped an iron hand on her wrist, another arm about her waist. Smiling tightly at the caterers bustling around the kitchen, he led her through the back hall and up the rear stairs. In all the time he had worked for Tom, he had never been on the second floor of Tom Deveraux's mansion. He didn't care. He just wanted Daisy somewhere quiet and private. Somewhere they could make sense of what happened. Taking her down the hall, he ducked into the first available guest bedroom and shut the door behind them. "What the hell was that?" he demanded angrily.

Daisy whirled away from him. "What do you think it was? I was breaking up with you!"

Jack's heart pounded in his chest. He couldn't believe everything was going so wrong, so fast. Worse, he didn't have a clue what Daisy's fury was about! Noting she looked as if she might run again, he positioned himself between Daisy and the door. "Why?"

Daisy clenched her fists at her sides. She glared at him, the betrayal she felt evident. "Because I heard you and my father," she stated in a low, embittered voice. "I know why you married me. Because he forced you to do so."

Jack couldn't believe Daisy thought he was that shallow and unfeeling. Not after all they had come to mean to each other. His fury fueled by the depth of her insult, he glared right back at her. "No one forces me to do anything, Daisy," he said coldly, resenting the implication he was a bought man. "Least of all your father." If he hadn't wanted to marry Daisy or stay with her, he wouldn't have done it, period.

Daisy tossed her head and began to pace. "You work for him. You would have lost your job."

Jack sighed and shoved both his hands through his hair. "That had nothing to do with it."

"Right," Daisy agreed with a provoking sarcasm that hit him where he lived. "It was your innate gallantry. Your desire to protect and defend and go to bat for all things Deveraux, including and especially me, Tom's illegitimate daughter. Face it—" her voice rose in anguish "—I was your entrée into this much-desired family and your plan almost worked! You almost became what you always wanted to be—a bona fide member of this family through me!"

Jack stared at her, barely able to comprehend her accusations, they were so far off the mark. "If you think that's all I'm about, then you don't know me at all."

"No, that's the problem, Jack!" Daisy stormed toward him as hot, angry tears brimmed over and slid down her cheeks. "I do know you!" She jammed a finger at his chest, angrily punctuating every sentence. "I know how long you watched over me, getting me out of one scrape after another. I know how fascinated you were with me. And how much, from that very first night we were alone, you wanted to make love to me!"

He caught her hand and forced it down between them, before she could jab his sternum again. His fingers closed over hers. "I told you that was a mistake, that it should never have happened that way."

Abruptly, Daisy went very still. She tilted her head up to his. "But if it had been up to you, it would have happened."

Jack wasn't going to lie about that. "Eventually, yes," he admitted with reluctant honesty, "if I'd had my way it would have happened."

Daisy shrugged off his grip, stepped back. She studied him, vibrant color sweeping into her cheeks, and continued her prediction. "In a nice tidy socially acceptable way."

Jack swallowed, knowing the more he revealed, the deeper his trouble. He also knew now was not the time to lie to her, or withhold anything, since that was what had gotten them in this mess in the first place. He regarded her steadily. "I think that would have been the proper way to go about it, yes. I think the chances of you being hurt by what we did, when we did it, would have been a lot less if we had done things the normal way. But it still wouldn't have changed the outcome, Daisy." He still would have fallen in love with her, and unless he was dead wrong, she would have fallen in love with him.

"Right." Daisy tossed him a bright and breezy smile that in no way matched up with the pain reflected in her eyes.

"I still would have lost the baby. Because—" she gave an offhand shrug reminiscent of years of hurt "—that's just the way my luck seems to run."

Jack swallowed and went toward her. "It wouldn't have kept us apart, because we were destined to be together, Daisy. That wasn't clear to me then, but I sure as hell know it now."

"Well, I don't." Daisy spun away before he could wrap her in his arms.

Jack braced his hands on his waist. Not sure when he had ever felt more frustrated, or more afraid, he scowled at her reproachfully. "You can't just dump me after a misunderstanding."

Daisy scoffed, every wall she'd ever had around her, every wall he'd ever torn down, right back up. She was the hellion he had first started chasing, all over again. "Haven't you learned anything at all about me by now, Jack? I can and will do whatever I damn well please, no matter who disapproves! And that includes you!"

A cold sweat broke out on the back of his neck as Daisy assumed her haughtiest society-girl posture and swept around him. "I'm warning you," he told her grimly. "You walk out that door, Daisy, you give up on us now, after all this, and it's over." He wasn't going to let her hurt him the way the rest of his family had.

Daisy turned, more sadness than he had ever thought to see in her eyes. "That's the thing you still refuse to let yourself face, Jack," she said, the tears she had been defiantly holding back spilling over her lashes once again. "It's *been* over ever since I lost our baby. Because that baby was the only reason we were ever together for more than a few hours in the first place. Somewhere deep down, you know it, too—you just haven't let yourself accept it."

THE DOOR CLOSED QUIETLY behind Daisy. Fighting the impulse to go after her—the impulse he supposed he would always have, no matter what, Jack sank onto the bed and put his head in his hands. Upon reflection, he didn't know why he was surprised by any of this.

Daisy had never once said she loved him. Even in their most intimate, tender times together, she'd always held herself back, let herself get just so close to Jack and no closer. Like a fool, Jack had kept telling himself that time, and his steady presence, would remedy even that. One day, he had supposed, Daisy would let the rest of her own fears of abandonment go and tell him that she loved him, too. Not lightly or in passing, but with her whole heart and soul.

But it hadn't happened, and tonight, with the truth slapping him in the face, he was forced to admit, finally, that it never would. Daisy had been forsaken as a kid, and then left out on a limb even after the truth about her true parentage was known. It didn't matter to her that all that was changing, that her family was finally doing what they should have done for her from the very beginning—tell the truth and claim her proudly. She was still expecting disaster, and he just couldn't do it anymore. Couldn't keep going after a wife who ultimately did not want him in her life.

He was tired of being with people who kept themselves apart from him. Tom Deveraux had put up an emotional firewall between the two of them from the very first that was just now beginning to come down, and that had happened only, Jack knew, because Tom had felt that Jack was making Daisy happy. His grandfather hadn't known how to love, his mother had been afraid to. And Daisy—Daisy who wasn't afraid of anything else in this life, simply wouldn't let herself open up her heart and take the risk.

Jack had learned early on not to ask for anything for himself. As a kid, he had known he had to watch out for himself because no one else was going to do it for him, no one was going to just be there for him, seeing that he got what he needed, never mind wanted. So with the exception of the encouragement and the mentoring he had received from Tom, which again was something that'd had its limits, he'd had to do for himself.

As long as Jack had lived by that credo, he had been okay. Maybe not really happy, and a little too lonely, but his life had hummed along on an even, acceptable keel. It figured the one time he had let himself hope for something more, something important and wonderful and emotionally fulfilling, he'd get shot down so hard and fast and cruelly he still found it difficult to believe.

Well, no more, Jack thought resentfully as he swallowed around the tight knot of bitterness rising in his throat. He stood, jerking off his tie and the designer-label suit jacket that had never suited his blue-collar upbringing. He wasn't going after Daisy, wasn't staying here a moment longer. This time he was through.

CHARLOTTE APPEARED in the doorway to Daisy's old room. Despite the fact her life had been turned upside down, too, earlier in the week, the woman Daisy had known all her life as her mother, looked calmer and more in control than she had in years. It was Daisy who was confined to her big old canopy bed, several stuffed animals from her childhood tucked under the covers with her.

Charlotte gave Daisy a pitying glance. It was clear, Daisy thought, that her mother did not know what to say. "Honey, you can't stay in there all day."

"I don't see why not," Daisy mumbled, pressing her face deeper into the down pillow with the soft-as-silk pink cotton-cover. After the horrible scene she had created last night, on the very eve that Tom and Iris finally claimed her as their own, she didn't see how she could ever show her face in Charleston again. That being the case, she felt the best place she could be was deep beneath the covers of her childhood bed.

Looking pretty and in control in a red suit and Italianleather pumps, Charlotte folded her arms in front of her. "You're really not getting up?"

"No," Daisy said stubbornly, aware she had never needed mothering as much as she did today and that Charlotte was giving her just that.

"Okay then. I'll just send your visitor up." Charlotte smiled at Daisy mysteriously, then floated off before Daisy could guess who her visitor might be.

Daisy took two seconds to consider. Was it possible? Was it Jack? Oh, Lord! Daisy put a hand to her hair, which was a rumpled mess, and leaped out of the bed. She dashed across to her old-fashioned dressing table, caught sight of her red, swollen eyes in the oval mirror attached to the back of it, groaned and sprinted back to the bed just as footsteps came back down the hall. But they weren't heavy masculine footsteps, Daisy noted, frowning. They were light, feminine ones that sounded as if they were made by high heels.

Seconds later, as Daisy was dragging a brush dispiritedly through her hair, Grace Deveraux rounded the corner. To Daisy's increasing despair, and, Daisy told herself firmly, relief, Grace Deveraux was alone.

"I figured you might be having a hard time," Grace said sympathetically. Looking every bit as pretty and together as Charlotte, albeit in a gold silk shantung pantsuit, Grace came closer and sat on the edge of Daisy's bed, much as Charlotte had earlier that same morning.

Daisy didn't have that much experience dealing with Grace, but she knew when she was being double-teamed by a pair of experienced mothers, and Grace and Charlotte were now working on her in tandem.

Which really ticked Daisy off.

All her life she had been told to either ignore or forget her feelings, no matter how devastating or infuriating the event that had her upset, and act genteely—that is, as if nothing had ever happened. This was one time when she damn well was not going to do it, Daisy decided furiously. She wasn't going to pretend that what she had overheard last night between her husband and her birth father hadn't been the very last straw in a long line of last straws, because it had.

Daisy tossed her hairbrush on top of the covers and glared at Grace. "If you're here to get me to apologize to Tom—"

Grace shook her head and perched a little more comfortably on the end of the big four-poster canopy bed. "I'm here to see to you, dear."

Daisy didn't like the expression in those deep-blue eyes. Grace was looking as if she could wait Daisy out all day. "There's nothing you can do to help," she stated plainly.

Grace's eyes turned even kinder, more reflective. "That's what I said, too, after I lost *my* baby."

Daisy blinked. Now they were headed into uncharted territory. "What are you talking about?" she asked warily.

Sorrow clouded Grace's face and crept into her low, deeply commiserating tone. "I had a miscarriage, Daisy, the year after Amy was born. And I'll be honest with you—the experience damn near ripped my heart out."

Daisy knew, because that was how she had felt, too. She swallowed hard, glad to finally be able to talk to someone who had been through the same. "People think it shouldn't matter because the pregnancy wasn't very far along."

"Well, then they're wrong! From the moment you start carrying that baby inside you, that life is real to you, and your every instinct, as a mother and a woman, is to protect that infant."

Daisy nodded, tears welling in her eyes.

"I know I wasn't even showing, but our baby was real to me."

"And to Jack," Grace countered.

"And to Jack." Because Jack had grieved, too, every bit as deeply as she had, Daisy knew. That was one thing they'd had in common.

"Of course," Grace continued discussing their dual situations pragmatically, "my situation was a little better because I already had four children with Tom. And a little worse because complications of that miscarriage left me unable to bear any more children, ever."

That wasn't the case for Daisy. And she was very glad.

"I'm sorry," Daisy replied softly. She reached across the covers to touch Grace's arm in silent sympathy. "I didn't know."

"And there's more, Daisy." The sorrow was back in Grace's eyes. Along with the firsthand compassion and understanding Daisy needed. "I became depressed after I lost the baby," Grace admitted reluctantly. "But I wouldn't admit it to myself, or anyone else. I withdrew. I held people at arm's length, especially Tom. And that wasn't fair."

Daisy understood why Grace had reacted that way, because that was how she had felt in the days and weeks that followed her miscarriage, too. But there was a huge difference in their situations. And Grace needed to know that. "Jack and I married for the sake of the baby," she stated firmly.

Grace lifted her exquisitely plucked eyebrow. "But you love him."

Daisy settled deeper into the covers. "He was just with me to please Tom."

Grace slowly shook her head and regarded Daisy with an unending supply of patience. "Daisy, Jack is a grown man, and one of the most disciplined, goal-minded individuals I have ever been privileged to know. He made himself what he is today. I know he *thinks* Tom is to credit for that, because Tom encouraged Jack when Jack was at a real crossroads in his life. But the truth of the matter is that Jack would have figured out he was meant to go to college and law school and live a different kind of life than the one in which he had been raised, whether Tom was there to mentor him or not. It might have taken a little longer, but I have no doubt that Jack would have made something of himself no matter what."

Daisy felt that, too. "So what's your point?" she demanded, unable to keep the belligerence from her tone.

Grace looked Daisy straight in the eye. "Jack risked everything he held dear to go after you, to love and protect and care for you. And he did it at great cost to himself and his career."

Daisy shrugged, and kept the ice intact around her heart. "He seems to have landed on his feet."

"Really."

"I'm sure Tom will forgive him eventually for what I did last night," Daisy continued defiantly.

Grace moved delicately to her feet. Glancing down,

she smoothed the nonexistent wrinkles from her pantsuit. "That's a moot point now."

Something in Daisy unthawed just a tad. "What do you mean?"

Grace sent Daisy a sad, reflective smile. "While you're cowering here, feeling sorry for yourself, like the whole world is against you, Jack is taking action."

No surprise there, Daisy thought. Jack had always been a man of action. She sat up straighter against the pillows propped against the headboard. "What kind of action?"

Grace turned at the doorway. "The kind Tom and I never ever wanted to see. Jack handed in his resignation to Tom this morning. He's at his beach cottage packing up his stuff as we speak."

Daisy stared at Grace. That couldn't be true. But apparently, it was. Reminding herself of what Jack had done to her, Daisy folded her arms across her chest. "Maybe that's for the best," she said stubbornly.

Grace turned her hands, palm up, and gestured ineffectually. "Perhaps it is, if you can't find it in your heart to forgive him," she agreed.

Warmth started in Daisy's chest and moved swiftly to her face. Before she knew it, she was scrambling out from beneath the covers, standing on her knees on the middle of the bed. "He lied to me! He deceived me! He made a deal with Tom behind my back, to stay on after I lost the baby."

"I know Jack made mistakes," Grace said quietly. "I also know the entire time, he was trying to protect you."

"Well, I don't need that kind of protection," Daisy grumbled even more obstinately as she sat back on her heels. She didn't need to feel as if she was living life on the edge, always waiting for the love just within her reach to slip away again.

"You're right," Grace agreed sweetly, coming nearer once again. "You don't. What you need, Daisy," Grace continued, her voice breaking emotionally, "is what I've found with Tom—a partner who loves you enough and cares about you enough to risk being honest, even when it hurts." Grace paused, blinking back empathetic tears. "I'm the first to agree with you, Daisy, that there should be no more secrets between you and Jack, and the entire Deveraux-Templeton families."

Daisy drew a deep, bolstering breath, aware that the inner vulnerability she had thought she had shelved for good the night before was back full-force. "But you also think I should forgive Jack, don't you?" Daisy asked huskily, tears of regret and longing clouding her eyes and clogging her throat.

Grace nodded and reached out to embrace Daisy in a warm, maternal hug—the kind every stepmother should give a hurting stepchild. "I also think you should go and see him. And when you do, bear this in mind. The bigger the mistake, the bigger your heart has to be."

DAISY STAYED IN BED another ten minutes after Grace left. She half expected Charlotte to come up to check on her. Charlotte didn't. Which left Daisy to fend for, and think for, herself. And the first thing she wanted to do was take a shower, wash her hair, find something not quite so outrageous to wear. Because serious conversations deserved serious clothes. And Grace was right, Daisy realized as she brushed her hair into a dignified upsweep on the back of her head and put on a plain white sheath and matching sandals, if for nothing else but closure, she had to seek out Jack one more time. One last time, she amended fiercely. Because there was still no way she was forgiving him or Tom Deveraux for what they had done.

An hour later, she was driving along the causeway that connected the city with the beach where Jack lived. Fifteen minutes after that, she was parking in his driveway, right behind his black SUV. Relieved he was still here, she got out, walked to the door. Used her key and let herself in.

She didn't have far to look. Jack was in his study, emptying out the banged-up file cabinets that still hadn't been replaced. He was wearing khaki shorts and a worn university T-shirt. He hadn't shaved, and the golden-brown beard lining his face gave him a faintly dangerous look. Standing there, Daisy realized all over again just how appealing she found him in every way, regardless of his appearance. But the feeling wasn't mutual, she noted as he looked up when she entered the room, then went wordlessly back to his work.

Daisy's heart sank. Closing the door on their time together was going to be harder than she realized. Too late, she realized he had been afraid of being abandoned, too.

Heart pounding, she dropped her purse and keys on the chair closest to the door and sauntered over to the file cabinet where he was working. "Hi," she said softly.

And just that quickly it became clear to her exactly what she was about to throw away. Not just a marriage that had been made for all the wrong reasons, but turned out to be more right than anything she had ever felt before in her life. But also friendship with the only person in the world who had ever understood her and accepted her for who she was. Jack had watched out for her when no one else had. He had made love to her as if she was the only woman on earth and he was the only man. He had opened up his heart and soul to her, and encouraged her to do the same. And, she saw now, he hadn't done any of those things because he cared about pleasing Tom. He had done them because he was drawn to her in the same undeniable way she was drawn to him. Because they were right for each other in a way only two people who were destined to love each other for the rest of the lives could be. And she had been about to throw it all away.

Why? Because he'd made a secret deal with her birth father behind her back? She'd already forgiven him once for doing Tom's bidding—the night of the break-in when she had discovered how long he had been acting as her unofficial guardian angel. So there was technically no reason she couldn't forgive him for promising Tom he would stay with her after the miscarriage and make sure she was all right. That, she knew in retrospect, had been the only decent thing for Jack to do at the time. And he was, above all, a very decent, loving, caring man.

No. The reason she had walked out on Jack was because he scared her. Because opening up her heart to him meant doing the unthinkable for her—it meant walking on the wild side and making and keeping a commitment to him that would last a lifetime. It meant opening up the possibility of being hurt again more than she had ever been hurt in her life. And Daisy had thought—erroneously, it now seemed—that it would be safer to go on alone than risk being disappointed or disillusioned again.

But she saw now, after only a mere twenty hours or so, what a lonely and foolish way that would be to spend the rest of her life. When everything she had ever wanted was standing right here in front of her.

The question was how to make Jack see she'd had a change of heart. And planned to change her way of life. Starting here. Starting now. If—and she was beginning to see it was a very big if—he would let her.

Daisy swallowed hard around the building apprehension in her throat. "I thought maybe we should talk."

His expression was completely devoid of hope as he continued stacking files in cardboard storage boxes. "We said everything there was to say last night."

Daisy swallowed hard and recalled what Grace had told her. *The bigger the mistake, the bigger your heart has to be.* "Not everything." She edged closer and put a staying hand on his forearm before he could pull out another file. "I was wrong to ask you for a divorce the way I did."

Jack straightened slowly. "You didn't ask. You stated. And as for methods—" he plucked her hand from his forearm like an unwelcome mosquito, and smiled at her sardonically "—it got the point across."

Don't give up. "Bucky Jerome didn't print a word of what I said last night in his column today," Daisy pointed out with all the cheerfulness she could muster.

"No reason to," Jack retorted even more dryly. He gave her a long, telling look. "The news is already all over town."

Daisy gulped. This was definitely not going the way she wanted. What had happened to the Jack who had chased her halfway across the country, and insisted, no matter what, on staying in her life? As her lawfully wedded husband?

Aware her knees were beginning to feel as shaky as the rest of her, Daisy backed up until her hips touched the edge of Jack's desk. Adopting what she hoped was a breezy posture, she braced herself against it. "Along with the true facts of my parentage, which was in the newspaper." And, because of the connection to Grace, would soon be picked up by the wire services, if it hadn't been already.

Jack leaned back against the dented file cabinet. He folded his arms implacably in front of him. "So you finally got what you wanted," he said, looking neither happy nor sad about that.

Daisy braced her hands on the edge of the desk on either side of her. "Not quite." She tilted her head up to look into his face. Took a deep breath and tried again. "I want you, Jack."

His sensual lip curved into a cruelly disbelieving smile. "So you say today." His glance narrowed as he took in the length of her before returning slowly, deliberately to her face. "Who are you trying to tick off this time?" he asked in a soft, sarcastic voice that sent her spirits tumbling all the more. "Can't be Tom, he's given us his blessing. Ditto Charlotte and Iris."

It was Daisy's turn to pause. Neither woman had said anything of the kind to her. All Charlotte had wanted was for Daisy to get up, out of bed, and start dealing with the problems Daisy faced instead of hiding her head in the sand the way Charlotte had for so many years. "Since when?" Daisy demanded, irritated Jack was once again one step ahead of her when it came to family matters that concerned Daisy.

"Both telephoned me this morning, telling me they hoped we would work things out."

Daisy curled her toes and dug them into the flat, padded sole of her sandal. "What did you tell them?" she asked hopefully.

"That it wasn't going to happen."

Okay, don't give up just yet. "Why not?" Daisy asked, doing her best to emulate Jack's calm but determined behavior when she had been the one turning away from their marriage.

"Because," Jack retorted gruffly, his golden-brown eyes suddenly filled with hurt, "I don't have any interest in trying to make someone who doesn't love me love me."

"But I do. Love you."

The room went so silent Daisy could hear their watches ticking.

Jack's eyes glimmered wetly. "That's not funny, Daisy," he said in a low, choked voice.

"It's not meant to be," she said as emotion boiled over and the tears she'd been holding back flooded her eyes and spilled down her cheeks, too. She pushed away from the desk, wreathed her arms around him and aligned herself against him, letting the soft warmth of her body penetrate the hard steel of his. Tilting her head back, she looked deep into his eyes, no longer caring that her heart was on her sleeve. "Because I do love you, Jack," she said purposefully as even more tears flowed. "I just didn't want to admit it." Daisy gulped. "I didn't want to take a chance that you would walk away from me, too."

Something in her words must have gotten to him, because suddenly he was smiling and his arms were around her. "Don't you know I would never ever do that?" he asked her huskily, pressing kisses in her hair, on her temple, down her cheek.

Daisy cuddled closer, aware she had never felt so

wanted or happy or so safe as she did at that very moment. Still, for the sake of clarity, she felt she had to point out, "You left me last night."

"Only," Jack replied sternly, "after you told me it was over, that you would never under any circumstances forgive me."

Once again, their gazes clashed. "I was a fool," Daisy admitted soberly, knowing all the love she felt for him was reflected in her eyes. "But I'm not that reckless anymore," she promised seriously. *Not enough to give you up.*

A smile slowly curved the edges of his lips as Jack threaded his hands through her hair. "You're not."

"I can be as conservative, as normal and down to earth as you need. See?" Daisy stepped back and held her arms akimbo. "Look at the way I'm dressed." Even Charlotte would have been proud, her white sheath was so classic and discreet.

"I noticed." Jack let his glance drift over her lazily before returning to her eyes. "And for the record, Daisy, you don't have to do that," he said as the pads of his thumbs delicately stroked her cheeks. "I like you reckless. I like you just the way you are, so you don't have to change a thing."

Daisy breathed a sigh of relief and looked up at him, admitting softly and shyly, "I'm glad, Jack, because I like you just the way you are, too."

He studied her eyes, sensing there was still something amiss. "But?"

Daisy figured while they were at it, they might as well put all their cards on the table. "We need love, too—the real, enduring enough-to-last-a-lifetime kind."

"Oh, Daisy, don't you know?" Jack kissed her sweetly, passionately, and then tenderly once again.

"Given the way I love you, and the way you love me, the way we feel about each other is never going to go away."

"SO, YOU'RE REALLY hanging up your own shingle?" Tom asked several days later as Jack and Daisy worked together to clear out Jack's office at Deveraux-Heyward Shipping Company.

Jack nodded as he removed his diplomas from the wall. "I'll be available to help during the transition, with whomever you hire to replace me as company counsel, but from now on my office is going to be at the beach."

Daisy took Jack's law books from the shelves and put them into moving boxes. She turned to look at Tom, knowing they had a ways to go before they would ever feel like father and daughter, but also that with time it was going to happen. And that Tom would accept her the way her adoptive father slash grandfather, Richard Templeton, never had. With that knowledge had come an inner peace and happiness Daisy was still marveling over. "My brother, Connor, helped Jack and I find space in a commercial building on the Isle of Palms," she told Tom. "We've rented suites that are side by side."

"Does that mean you're going to leave Grace's show, too?" Tom asked curiously.

"No," Daisy said. "I'll be there for a while longer, but eventually I want to go out on my own, too."

"Good for you." Tom gave Daisy the same kind of approval Jack had, then paused as he looked at both her and Jack. "I know I've let you both down—" Tom began with difficulty.

"It's all right," Daisy interjected quietly as she

linked hands with Jack and held on tight. "We forgive you."

Jack nodded, letting Tom know this was so, that he and Daisy were in unison.

"And we ask that you forgive us for all our mistakes, too," Daisy continued. Because she and Jack had certainly made a lot of them on their way to falling and staying in love, and making a real commitment that would last not just for however long it was convenient, but for a lifetime.

"Done, then," Tom said. A contented silence fell between them.

"I read in Bucky Jerome's column this morning that you and Grace are getting married again," Daisy remarked.

Tom clapped a hand to the back of his neck and massaged the tense muscles there. "I don't know how he found out about that. Grace and I hadn't told any of the kids. Heck, we hadn't told anyone."

That was something, Daisy thought, that Bucky Jerome could have guessed. One look at Tom's and Grace's faces, not to mention the way they couldn't seem to stop touching each other whenever they were together, was clue enough. The older couple was in love again, and in fact, Daisy realized, had probably never truly been out of love with each other, despite their difficulties. "Then it's true?" Jack asked happily.

Grace entered Jack's office. Like Daisy, she had come over straight from work at the television studio. "Yes." Grace smiled as she stepped into Tom's waiting arms. "It really is."

"When and where?" Daisy asked.

"On the yacht, at sunset tomorrow night," Tom said.

"We want you two to be there," Grace added. "You're family now, you know. Both of you."

Daisy and Jack knew. And nothing had ever felt better.

Hidden Treasures
by Judith Arnold

Erica Leitner's lifelong dream is to live in a small rural town, teach school and become an earth mother. The quiet rustic life she's fabricated for herself suddenly becomes a lot more exciting when she discovers a box of hidden treasures as she plants her first garden—and hunk Jed Willitz, rebel with a cause, who's back in town on business, claims the box is his!

Look for other Superromance books by Judith Arnold in the months to come! And be sure to watch for her MIRA novel *Heart on the Line*, to be released in August 2003.

Heartwarming stories with a sense of humor, genuine charm and emotion and lots of family!

On sale starting March 2003. Available wherever Harlequin books are sold.

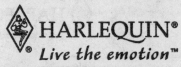

HARLEQUIN®
Live the emotion™

Visit us at www.eHarlequin.com

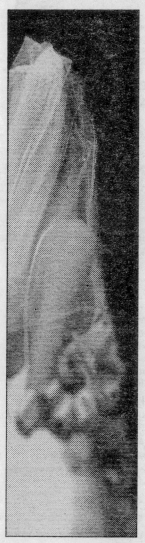